Revelations

Tor Teen Books by J. A. Souders

Renegade
Revelations

Revelations

J. A. Souders

TOR®
TEEN

A Tom Doherty Associates Book
New York

REVELATIONS

Copyright © 2013 by Jessica Souders

A Tor Teen Book
Published by Tom Doherty Associates, LLC
175 Fifth Avenue
New York, NY 10010

www.tor-forge.com

Tor® is a registered trademark of Tom Doherty Associates, LLC.

Library of Congress Cataloging-in-Publication Data

Souders, J. A.
    Revelations / J.A. Souders. — First edition.
        p. cm.
    "A Tom Doherty Associates book."
    ISBN 978-0-7653-3246-2 (hardcover)
    ISBN 978-1-4668-0096-0 (e-book)
    1. Undersea colonies—Fiction.   2. Secrets—Fiction.
3. Memory—Fiction.   4. Genetics—Fiction.   5. Science fiction.
I. Title.
    PZ7.S7246Rev 2013
    [Fic]—dc23

                                                    2013023853

Tor Teen books may be purchased for educational, business, or promotional use. For information on bulk purchases, please contact Macmillan Corporate and Premium Sales Department at 1-800-221-7945, extension 5442, or write specialmarkets@macmillan.com.

First Edition: November 2013

Printed in the United States of America

0 9 8 7 6 5 4 3 2 1

Dedicated to the loving memory of my grandma
Dolores Heiland,
who was instrumental in making me who I am today
and taught me that anything worth having
is worth fighting for, and that being a lady
isn't synonymous with being weak.

Revelations

CHAPTER ONE

PATIENT EVELYN WINTERS: *Female. Approximately
16 years of age.*

Patient still displays signs of amnesia. Evaluation shows worsening fevers, syncope, failure to heal from multiple wounds and infection of said wounds. Patient has failed to respond to standard treatment. Recommended course of action has met with refusal by patient's significant other. No next of kin available. Unsure of patient's ability to consent for herself due to diminished mental faculties.

—MEDICAL RECORD LOG, DR. DANIEL GILLIAN, MD

Evie

My life is just about perfect.

At least I think it is. It's hard to be sure since I can't remember anything from the last sixteen years. My hopes. My dreams. Everything. Gone. As if they never existed. And I will probably never get them back.

It hurts just thinking about it, so I try not to, but the thought festers in my mind as I sit on the beach by the water's edge and push my bare feet into the surf. The waves lap at my ankles as I dig my toes into the sand. It feels good— the chilly water against my heated flesh.

I just *know* I'm running another fever. I'm never not, lately. I scratch at my healing shoulder before remembering myself and shoving my hands into the cool sand. It's only been a few days since my release from the confines of the local medical facility—I'd been there just a few weeks, but it'd felt like forever. Dr. Gillian said, despite the failure of the wound on my shoulder to heal completely, I was healthy enough to leave. I'm not convinced he actually thinks that's true, but he's done so much for me since I got here, he almost feels like family. Or I think so anyway. I don't really remember what family feels like. But, anyway, he's done so much for me, Dr. Gillian, that I could hardly refuse, and even though I wasn't at all sure I was ready to leave the hospital, Gavin was impatient to get me home.

Home. Another pang of something I can't really describe hits me, and tears well in my eyes. I trace my fingers over the etched lines of the silver rose pendant lying between my breasts. I really, really want to go home, I know that. I just don't know exactly where "home" is.

Gavin's dog, Lucy, bumps my shoulder with her head, whining softly. I dig my fingers into her soft fur, staring into the water until the tears that sting my eyes are from the sun sparkling on the surface. Even at sunset, the solar rays are still intense to my eyes, but a bit of my bad mood slips away. It's beautiful today, as it always is, the sky flickering now with the oranges, reds, and pinks of the setting sun.

This is my favorite time of day. When the sun is setting and the last of its fiery fingers caress the water line before relinquishing their hold to the darkness of night. And I can watch as the stars pop out, one by one, to pinprick the sky with their silvery light. The breakers crash against the shore in a steady rhythm. It's lovely. Peaceful. Calming. Like somewhere else I used to know.

Home, I think again, holding the pendant tightly in my fist. Gavin tells me I came from beneath those waves. But I don't know if home is really there. At the bottom of the sea in a place I can't remember and I'm not sure if I want to. Or if it's with Gavin and his wonderful family: His brother, Tristan, and all his chattering and curiosity. His sister, Ann Marie, with her easy happiness, and his mom, whose quiet strength—the same strength Gavin has in spades—resonates from her in waves.

I'll admit, when they're around, it's easy to forget that I haven't always been here. That I haven't always been a part of their family. But still, I know I don't really belong. I'm not sure I belong anywhere.

That thought making my heart squeeze, I push up from the sand, click my tongue so Lucy will follow, and go back into the house I'm supposed to consider my home.

Gavin

The bucket of tallow oil weighs heavy in my hand as I drag it up the two hundred and thirteen steps to the lantern room. I don't suppose we really have to light the lamp anymore, but it's become a custom. My family has kept the lighthouse going since the War. Using the light not to guide ships, but people.

It was one of the few buildings left standing after everything, but our cove was still in better shape than a lot of places. More importantly, it was safe—from raiders and starving animals—due to the coast on three sides and the wall they'd built around the town. My ancestors had hoped to guide those lost in what is now known as the Outlands to the safety of our town. I don't know if my family always lived here or if we took it over when we came across it, but we've been here ever since. No one new has come in ages, not since the mayor was sent from the city to keep an eye on us, but we still make the tallow and light the lantern every night. Just in case.

It's technically Tristan's job—ever since I started spending all my time hunting and providing food for the family—but he has a hard time dragging the bucket all the way to the top, and anyway I don't mind doing it. The mindless repetition of dragging the oil to the top, pouring it into the lamp, winding the clockwork, and lighting it usually gives me some much needed thinking time.

Today, though, I'm just going to enjoy the view. I can see Evie down on the beach, and now that she's with me after being in the hospital for way too long, I just want to bask a little. Even though I've been back on the surface for a little over a month, I can't get over how grateful I am to be home. My mind still reels thinking of what I—we—went through. Genetic mutations. Brainwashing. A beautiful princess needing rescuing. Okay, that part's not true. She rescued me. I just decided I couldn't leave without her.

A smile curves my lips as I glance down over the rail. Far below, the light from behind me shines on her blond head, then continues on its way. She was the only shining light from that hell.

But it's hard to be happy looking at her now. I can tell from how she's holding on to Lucy that she's unhappy, and considering the way she's staring out into the water, I can't pretend I don't know the reason. She's homesick. Even if "home" is the last word I'd use to describe Elysium.

Hell. Living nightmare. Bottomless pit of everlasting tortures. Those descriptions would fit it a lot better, but it's not like she remembers what *really* happened. She didn't even want to leave until she was forced to. By me. No, scratch that. *Because* of me. Because she'd risked her life to rescue me. And it had cost her much more than either of us had anticipated.

I watch, leaning over the rail, as she gets up and walks into the house, Lucy prancing by her side. She never once looks up at me, though I'm sure she knows I'm up here. Not sure if I should feel stung or just let her be; after all, I should know better than anyone how difficult it is to feel lost in a world that's not yours with no one you know or trust. And while I know she cares for me, ever since she left the hospital there's been this awkwardness between us. Like neither of us quite knows what to do with the other now that it's safe for us to touch.

Huffing a sigh, I turn to pick up the now empty bucket, then make my way down the stairs. It's much easier with gravity and an empty bucket on my side.

Taking my time, I put the supplies back into the fuel room, then clean up the already meticulous space. When I finally admit to myself that I can't get it any cleaner than it already is, I wander into the house.

It's quiet, as it usually is after supper, except for the sounds of Tristan playing in his room, making sound effects from whatever toys he's deemed worthy of his time. Mom must have nixed unplugging the water heater for him to play video games for today. Good, because I'm filthy. I glance down at my sooty hands and arms. I need a shower. Besides, I have to pass Evie's room along the way to the bathroom. It'll give me the perfect excuse to check on her.

The floorboards creak and groan as I walk. I used to try and learn which floorboards to use or how to step to avoid them making noises, but it's useless. They're old and they all creak. In fact, I see a loose one poking up near Evie's doorway. I'll have to run to the general store for nails to fix that so she doesn't trip on it. And while I'm at it, I should probably see if I can trade something for some paint. The walls are peeling and Mom's been making noises since Evie came about wanting to fix up the house.

I'm careful to avoid the loose board as I stop at her doorway. But when I peek my head into the room, she's back to staring out her window to the black sea. One hand rests on Lucy's head, which rests in Evie's lap. The other rests on the glass, palm pressing to it, fingers curled slightly, as if she's reaching for something. In the reflection, I can see tears sliding down her cheek. I back away from the door, so she can't see that I saw her, swallow the lump in my throat, and continue on into the bathroom. With a flick of the wrist, I turn on the water. At first it only drizzles out and I glare at the pipe.

"Work, damn you," I mutter. I don't want to have to fumble around in the pump house in the dark. Then it pulses and shoots a stream from the rusty faucet, pouring blackish water into the tub. God, I hate well water. After another half a minute, the water turns clear and steam starts rising from the bottom of the tub. I quickly adjust the temperature and step into the spray.

While I'm scrubbing my skin, I contemplate how to help Evie. I hate seeing her so sad, missing a home she doesn't remember, but going back isn't an option. So the question is, what can I do? I stay in the shower a while longer than I normally would, staring at a crack in the tile, but still no answers come.

Even after I'm finished with my shower and dressed in clean clothes and staring at the ceiling in my room, I don't know. She needs her memories back; that's obvious. But how do we get them back, when we don't know what caused her to lose them in the first place?

Lucy's growl and a movement out of the corner of my eye makes my blood run cold and I jump up, grabbing the bat that is lying next to the bed. My mind flashes back to being in Sector Three, and for a second, silly as I know it is, I'm sure one of those *things* followed us back. Something is creeping around my house—and all I've got to defend myself is a baseball bat.

I grip the bat tightly and tiptoe to the doorway. But what's standing there makes me stop in my tracks. *Not again.*

It's Evie, and she's staring at me with the blankest expression on her face. Her eyes are completely empty. Dead, almost. I've seen those eyes before. In Elysium. On the Enforcers. And, unfortunately, on her.

"Evie? Are you all right?"

She tips her head to the side and I fight back another shudder. *"My life is just about perfect."* Then she slowly turns and walks down the hallway, her white nightgown fluttering behind her.

I'm so in shock, it takes me a minute to realize she's already at the end of the hall and around the corner.

Shit! She must be sleepwalking. I chase after her, but she's already back down to the beach when I catch up to her. She's only walking. How is she moving so fast?

"Evie!" I reach for her hand, pulling it toward me and hoping it'll make her stop. It does. But when she turns, I can only stare at her, while she seems to stare *through* me. She shakes me off and walks forward again. If she keeps going the way she is, she'll end up in the ocean.

I rush forward and make another grab for her hand. She tries shaking me off again, but I ignore it and say, "Where are you going?"

She turns to face me. Blinks once, and says, "Home."

A chill slides over me. "Home?" I ask dumbly.

"Home." She twists back around and yanks away from me, splashing her way into the water.

I lunge forward and pull her back. She spins around and this time, when she looks at me, my instincts yell at me to let her go. I don't.

A wave crashes over us, pulling us apart and knocking me to my knees. Freezing salty water collapses over my head, burning my eyes and nose. I shove up, coughing, and push my hair out of my eyes. She's out of reach already. I don't even think the wave bothered her.

Her nightgown is soaked and her skin glows through it in the moonlight. In normal circumstances, I'd appreciate the view, but I barely give it a passing thought as I wade deeper, trying to reach her before she gets to the drop-off.

"Evie! Stop. Please," I try again, knowing it's useless. Even though the air around me is hot, I'm shaking.

When I'm close enough, I grab for her arm, but we're both slippery from the water and she pulls easily from my hand. The moonlight pours over her and while her eyes are red, they're as empty as they ever were.

I've heard that if you slap someone in shock, it wakes them up from whatever it is that they're doing. I dismiss the thought as soon as I've had it. I can't hit Evie. But another wave crashes on top of her, knocking her over, and when she just stands up and keeps going, I realize I don't have a choice. I don't want to hurt her, but I want her alive. So I grasp her again with one hand and bring the other one up to slap her just hard enough that I hope it'll wake her up . . . but before I can even make contact, she's got my wrist and she's squeezing it, pushing my arm back.

She twists around so she's staring me down. Her eyes are inky bottomless wells. Empty and dangerous. Before I can react, her other arm swings around and I catch a glimpse of her fist as it connects to my jaw. The impact shoves me back and then water is surrounding me and my head spins so much with my ringing ears that I can't figure out which way is up. I panic at first, flopping around, trying to get to the surface so I can breathe. But instinct forces through my panic and reminds me to relax and let my body float. My feet touch bottom and I shove to a standing position. Above the surface, I gasp for breath, shoving my hair from my eyes and searching for Evie, but she's gone. I can't see her.

I turn around in a circle as quickly as I can, but the water slows me down. It doesn't matter, though. *I can't see her.*

"Evie!" I shout, my voice hoarse from seawater and coughing. I push forward toward the drop-off. "Evie! . . . *Evie!*" Nothing. No answer, except the waves as they push toward shore.

My eyes are blurry from the salt water and the panic tears burning them. "Evie. Please! Answer me."

Then, by some miracle, the moonlight reflects off of something white and I know it's her. "Evie!" I shout again, pushing toward her, forgetting about the drop-off in my hurry to get to her.

I go under mid-yell, swallowing seawater, but push up and spit out what I can. I just keep saying her name as I swim closer, because I can't seem to say anything else. She's not moving and her hair is all over. I can't even tell which way she's facing.

My heart stops when I get to her and see she's facedown. I roll her over and drag her out as fast I can, using the waves to my advantage, but when I get her onto the beach and kneel over her, she's not breathing.

"Oh God. Oh God," I whisper, shoving her hair from her face. I breathe into her mouth, but her chest doesn't even rise. There must be water in her lungs. I have to get it out.

"Come on, Evie." I push on her chest, shoving on it harder and harder, screaming her name. "Evie. Please. Come on. Please." I kneel closer to her mouth and push more air into her lungs, hoping to displace some of the water. Nothing happens. I shakily feel for a pulse, moaning when I don't feel one.

"Wake up, damn it," I say, pumping even harder on her chest. I refuse to give up. I'm not going to let her die. Not now. Not like this.

CHAPTER TWO

Notice: You are now entering the Outlands. Safety cannot be guaranteed past this point. Proceed at your own risk.
—Sign posted at exit gates to the Outlands

Gavin

I pace the hallway in front of Evie's room. The old worn hardwood floors creak with each footstep and I feel exactly how I felt six weeks ago when I carried her into the hospital. Except at least she was breathing then.

My legs shake as I remember how pale she was this time. Her lips turning blue no matter how often I tried pushing air into her lungs. Her body was as limp as the sacks of flour I used to cart around for Mr. McGreely, and just as hard to run with. I tripped twice in that short run and cut a long deep gash into my arm trying to protect her when I fell. If Asher hadn't heard my yells and come running, then rushed to get Dr. Gillian . . . I don't even want to think about that.

I stop pacing and glance over, scowling at the dark-haired

boy leaning against the wall by the corner, talking quietly with my mother. Asher. Former best friend, current asshole. But there's no doubt that I owe him a huge debt after tonight.

The door I've been pacing in front of squeaks open. Dr. Gillian looks exhausted and I know I don't want to hear what he's going to tell me, but still, I have to ask.

"Is she all right?"

"She'll be fine."

I don't really hear what else he says—something about a dry drowning and her being extremely lucky—because my whole body sags in relief. She'll be fine. That's all I hear. Over and over in my head. *She'll be fine.*

"Gavin," he asks, pulling my attention back to him. "Did you hear me?"

I nod quickly. "Yes. Of course. Whatever you want."

It's obvious from the look he gives me that he knows I hadn't heard a word. With a sigh, he takes off his glasses and polishes them on his shirt. "I'm concerned, Gavin."

I don't say anything. I don't want to hear what he has to say.

"This . . ." He pauses. "This episode she had, where she walked into the ocean, she says she doesn't remember any of what you said happened."

I nod. I expected that. She didn't remember anything the other times, either.

"She also told me this is the third time she's blacked out in almost as many days."

"Um . . . well, technically it's only twice. The first time

I'm pretty sure she only freaked out because Lucy was running straight at her."

He lifts an eyebrow. "Gavin, we need to be serious here. You have to realize how grave this is. What she's having, these blackouts—they're what's called a "fugue state." It's concerning because I'm not sure if this is a psychiatric issue or a physical one. I can't even run any of the basic tests like a CT scan to make sure there isn't some sort of brain damage. I simply don't have the equipment." He screws his face up in frustration, before straightening his features. "She needs to go to Rushlake. This is just . . . beyond what I can do here." He spreads his hands out in front of him in a helpless gesture.

"You know I can't go to the city. Not after . . ." I trail off, my gaze drifting over to Asher. I allow myself a second to glare at him before focusing on the doctor again.

He pats my shoulder. "This *will* happen again. Will you be around next time? More importantly, can you afford to watch her every hour of every day to make sure that when it does, she won't walk back into that ocean?"

I open my mouth, but no words come out. He's right. There is absolutely no way I can be around her 24/7. Even if I could give up hunting and everything else to be around her, I have to sleep sometime.

He nods at me, then at someone behind me before turning back around and disappearing through the door.

"I'll take her."

I slowly turn to face Asher. "Absolutely not. *If* she goes,

I'll take her. This is none of your business and we don't need your help." It burns that I already owe him for helping with Evie. I'll be damned if I'll owe him another favor.

He touches my arm. "Gavin, come on. Let me help."

"No." I cross my arms over my chest. "The last time I let you 'help,' I ended up losing everything. I'm not letting you do that to me again."

My former best friend's face pales and then reddens almost instantly. "Oh, come off it, Gavin. They're never going to let you into the city." He glances at my clothes. "Even if you do manage to clean up enough."

"We'll get a visa from the mayor."

"My father?" Asher barks out a laugh. "Good luck with that. He won't give you one."

"He'll have to," I say.

Asher laughs again, but this time there's no humor in it. "That's where you're wrong. He doesn't have to do anything he doesn't want to." Then he shrugs. "Go ahead and ask him though. Good luck." He starts to walk away. "You know where to find me when you change your mind."

Evie

The air is heavy with heat and humidity. Between that and the exhaustion from almost drowning, my whole body feels leaden. So I just lie here and stare at the spiderwebs of cracks spreading across the ceiling and walls. I imagine them as thin fingers reaching for me, coming to steal me away from this world where I don't belong. I almost wish they would, so I'll stop endangering Gavin and his family.

This makes three. Three incidents since I left the medical facility. Three times I've hurt Gavin or almost hurt someone dear to him. The first was the day they brought me to live with them. The dog, Lucy, came out to greet me—well, everyone really, but she ran straight for me with her tongue lolling out and her teeth showing. The next thing I know she's on the ground underneath me and Gavin is prying my hands from around her neck.

Luckily, everyone agreed that they'd have reacted the same way, given the fact that I'd never seen a dog before and it did (kind of, sort of, probably not but maybe) look like she might be attacking. No one, including the dog, seems to resent me for it. Now Lucy follows me everywhere, like a little yellow dog-shaped shadow.

The second time, I don't even know what started it. I was sleeping. When I woke up, I had broken into the room where Gavin stores all of his hunting gear. I was standing in the middle with an assortment of weapons around me, and one in each hand. When Gavin had called my name, I'd spun around with both weapons drawn, my head screaming at me to *kill the Surface Dweller.*

Now I've almost drowned myself—and Gavin—trying to get "home." I don't even know where that is!

I can't stay here. I can't stay where I'm going to harm someone because my brain decides to shut off and my body just does whatever the hell it pleases.

With a sigh, I lie back against the pillows and close my eyes against the hominess of the room. I don't want to see how they've made this room nice for me, with soft, sweet-smelling bed linens and the beautiful furniture. They're a little scratched and damaged, but it's easy to tell they're the best in the house. And so is this room. With the beautiful flowers which are changed every few days—by Gavin's mother no doubt—and the white lacy curtains at the windows that look like they're almost brand new. Ann Marie's wedding stuff filling up her side of the room. I don't want to see any of it, because I've done nothing but cause them problems and they've done nothing but try and make me feel comfortable and at home.

For a while there'd been the soft murmur of voices and I'd hoped Gavin would come to visit me, but the murmur died down a while ago and Gavin never came. Maybe that's for the best. I don't know what to do. It's happened three times. It's sure to happen again. And next time we may not be so lucky.

Eventually the door creaks open and Gavin pokes his head in. My heart soars when I see him. I open my mouth to say his name, but he places his finger over his mouth and scoots in, shutting the door quietly behind him. He strides across the room, his long legs eating up the floor in two steps, and when he pulls me gently into his arms, my heart skips a beat.

He lifts my chin with his finger so I'm looking into his beautiful silvery gray eyes, and for what feels like forever and no time at all we stare at each other. Then, finally, his mouth is on mine. My eyes close and my stomach flutters as my head spins. For a moment, as our lips touch, I feel right. Like maybe I *am* home.

Then he pulls away and reality crashes in again, like the waves crashing against the shore. This isn't my home, and I'm going to end up killing someone if I stay here. I have to talk to him.

But before I can, he says, "We have to be quiet. I snuck in. The good doctor thought it would be better if you rested without me bothering you." He rolls his eyes. "Mom's got the door guarded, but she had to use the bathroom, and everyone else is asleep, so I took advantage." He smiles, then kisses my nose before nudging me over with his hip and lying down beside me.

"And when she comes in to check on me?"

He shrugs and crosses his arms behind his head.

With a shake of my head, I pull the arm he has closest to me down and then wiggle around until I find a comfortable spot, and lean my head against his shoulder. It feels so nice to have him next to me like this. I don't want to ruin it by talking about how broken I am.

When I wake he's still there, standing next to the one window in the room and gazing out through the salt-stained glass and leaning against the peeling windowsill. Hearing me shift, he turns. He looks exhausted and I can tell he didn't get a smidgen of sleep last night. Guilt licks at me. I know it's because of me. Once again I'm causing problems just by existing.

I run my fingers over the grooves of my necklace. His eyes follow the movement of my fingers before moving back up to meet my own. We stare at each other, and I'm sure we're both doing our own survey of the other. The tension in the air is palpable, but then, as if someone flicked on a light switch, the tension disappears. Gavin's lips quirk into a small smile and he moves toward me. Before either of us can say anything, the door to my room squeaks open and we both turn toward it as the doctor bustles in. He lifts an eyebrow when he sees Gavin, but doesn't say anything to him. He just asks how I'm feeling.

The words slip out without conscious thought. "*I'm just about perfect.*"

Gavin's head whips around and he blanches. He exchanges a look with the doctor, who says, "Well, let's just take a look and make sure of that, shall we?" After a series of noises I can't interpret, Dr. Gillian finally says, "Everything seems fine. And I don't believe there's anything else I can do here." He stares at Gavin when he says it and I have a feeling he's saying more than what I hear.

Gavin won't meet my eyes, proving my suspicions. I don't like it. What aren't they telling me?

I open my mouth to ask, but Dr. Gillian continues quickly. "I'm going to release you, but you're to take it as easy as you can in the next few days. If you feel something out of the ordinary, you need to let me know immediately."

I want to know how I'm supposed to tell what's not normal when everything is strange, but I don't ask. He's not going to know either.

Chapter Three

Memory is a fickle creature. As easy as it is to lock something into your memory, it is as simple to unlock it. For a memory system to function properly it is essential not only to activate the relevant information, but also to inhibit irrelevant information. There are many memory phenomena that seem to involve inhibition, although there is often debate about the distinction between interference and inhibition.

—Excerpt from Dr. Friar's essay on manual manipulation of memory recall

Gavin

I walk Doc out of the house. He takes a moment to reiterate, "She really should go to Rushlake."

I know!, I want to shout. Instead, I hand him the package of cookies my mom baked last night, the fresh fish I caught this morning while Evie was sleeping, and some of the venison jerky he loves so much. "Thanks for everything, Doc."

He stares for a moment, then sighs. "It might be a good idea to focus on discovering what the trigger is. Sometimes it's just a matter of preventing it." Then he says, "My favorite part of making house calls to you all is still the payment. And calls in the winter are always the best. Ginger cookies are my favorite." He lifts the package of cookies and winks before turning around and making his way down the path that leads to the rest of the village.

I swipe my hands over my face. How the hell am I supposed to find her trigger? There doesn't seem to be one. The first time she attacked my dog. The second, she was sleeping. The third? Who the hell knows? Where's the correlation?

A hand lands gently on my shoulder and I can tell by the way my nerves tingle that it's Evie. Fixing a smile on my face, I turn to face her and give her a once-over. She doesn't look near as tired as she did this morning. Not even close to how tired I feel.

She gives me a small, puzzled smile. "Why did you give him fish?"

"Payment for making a house call."

"Payment? Fish are money?" She looks even more confused, and I bark out a laugh.

"No. We don't really have a lot of money, but I fish and hunt, so generally we trade him for his services. He needs food and we need medical care." I shrug. "It works well for both of us."

She frowns. "So you gave away your food because I needed medical care?"

I have a bad feeling about this conversation. "We pay for

all medical services with food or Mom's sewing—even people from the city love the clothes she makes. That's how it works here. Mr. Steris trades his services—he's a metalsmith. And Mr. Pok barters his best ale."

"But you gave up *your* food for *me*."

I kick at the dirt with the toe of my shoe and shove my hands in my pockets. "Yes, but that's how we always pay for things. Not just medical care. We buy grains from the farmers, or from Mr. Pok, or Mr. Steris, or anyone in this town really, by trading meat or whatever Mom makes. Some pay us, like the mayor's wife. But mostly the barter system works well for us."

"That's not what I mean!" she yells, startling me. "You gave your food up for me! Food that could be used for feeding your family or trading for things that are much more important than me."

Her eyes are all bright and shiny, and panic makes my nerves tingle. I hate when girls cry. I never know what to say, how to help. Unsure what to do, I pull her to my chest and hug her tightly.

"It's not a big deal, okay? It's just some fish and cookies. And my mom loves to bake."

"But I'm causing you problems by just being here." She plays with the necklace at her throat.

Finally I get it. I lift her chin up with my finger so I can look at her face. "Look, Evie, it's not a hardship to have you. I love having you here. And I *like* that I'm able to do something to help you. I've felt so useless lately. You saved my life, Evie. And all I could do was wait for the doctor to help you when you needed me. So, if all I can do is give a few hours of my time catching some fish and giving them to Doc, then that's what I'm going to do."

"Still, I can't impose on you like this. It's not right. I need to do something to ease the burden on you."

"No, you don't." Her immune system is just barely beginning to tolerate the surface. What does she think she's capable of doing to help?

She purses her lips, and a determined look comes into her eyes. "You have to lock me into my room at night. Starting tonight. At least I won't walk into the ocean."

I almost want to laugh, but then I realize how serious she is. "No, Evie, that's crazy. I'm not going to lock you up like a criminal."

Her gaze is hard like a diamond. "You will. I refuse to endanger you and cost you any more fish."

I can't help the laughter that bubbles up in my throat. She's serious. Dead serious, but the way she said fish was just so ridiculous. I have to press my lips together to keep from laughing out loud.

"Gavin, please . . ." The hard edge is gone from her voice. Now she sounds desperate. It tears at me. But so does the thought of locking her up.

"What if you have to go to the bathroom?"

"I'll hold it. I'm not a child. Now promise me, or I'm not going another step with you." She crosses her arms.

Maybe it would be for the best, I tell myself. It's to protect *her*, not me, after all. I sigh. "All right. We'll try it."

She blinks, then sighs and hugs me tightly. "Thank you."

"Anything for you." I kiss the top of her head and hold her for a few minutes, enjoying the feeling that she's all mine.

After a long time, she pushes away. "What was Doc talking about? About having to go to a city. And something about a trigger?"

Damn it. She heard. I clear my throat to give me time to come up with something. I can't take her to the city. They'll chew her up and spit her out. I can't let her go through that. Not after everything she's already been through. "He thinks you should go into the village. Meet some more people so you're not always cooped up here and wallowing." I grin at her even as my stomach turns from the lie. "Who knows? Maybe something there will trigger some of your memories."

The way she watches me, I know she doesn't believe me. She's going to call me out on it. I know she is . . . but then she nods. "Well, I do feel a little shut in." She smiles and slides her hand into mine. "I'd love to see your village and meet some of these people you've talked about."

She looks so happy with the idea, guilt weighs on me like an anchor. For a minute I want to tell her the truth, but then she pulls me in the direction Doc took.

"It's this way, right?" Her voice is light and bubbly. I don't think I've heard that sound from her. Ever.

I let her pull me down the path.

Evie

Nerves threaten to strangle me, but I'm excited. My heart is beating so fast I'm out of breath after only a few steps. I've heard and seen it from a distance, but I've never been to the town proper. I should have. Maybe I don't feel like I belong because I've never tried to be a part of life here.

I lick my lips. The town's buildings loom in front of me, and even though my nerves make me queasy, my curiosity is overwhelming. I try to imagine what these people will be like. Gavin has shared some stories about them. And I met a few of the women when they came to visit me in the medical center. I hope the others will be like them.

I take a few hesitant steps toward the town, passing the hospital—a run-down building that looks a lot like Gavin's house, inside and out—and take it all in. One pristine white building towers above all the rest, with a tall spire that juts up into the sky, and it has a large clock on the side of it.

Gavin follows my gaze. "That's the mayor's house. They built it right after I was born, when the city sent the mayor to . . . uh . . . help us."

I glance over at him only to see him scowling at the ground, but then he points to another building slightly closer to us. "And that's where Ann Marie and Josh are going to move. It's the newest building. My mom and Ann Marie say it's beautiful inside. And they say the building is strong enough to withstand the hurricanes even though it's so tall."

I frown. "Hurricane?"

Gavin's younger brother, Tristan, jumps in front of me, startling me. I almost scream before gaining control of myself. I had no idea he was even following us.

"Oh, it's a really bad storm and it's so cool!" he says. "The winds are so strong they can rip trees right from the ground and toss them miles away. Once, a few years ago, one totally tore our neighbor's house apart while they were in it! And another time . . ."

"Tristan! That's enough," Gavin says, giving him a look.

"Sorry," he mutters, looking anything but. If I wasn't horrified about the hurricane, I'd laugh at his expression.

I turn back to Gavin, my heart in my throat. "What's a storm?"

He glares at Tristan. "It's just something where there's a lot of wind and rain. No big deal, usually."

That sounds terrible. "When is the next . . . hurricane?"

"Don't worry about it. They only come during the summer and it's been years. We'll be fine." He shoots Tristan another look.

I nod, but swallow, my stomach feeling hollow.

Gavin clears his throat. "Er . . . as I was saying, the mayor's house is the largest, and they've been adding new buildings around it since then with the help from the city. We should go so you can meet some more people." He sees my expression and adds, "Everyone is really friendly. Don't worry. They're going to love you."

Tristan grabs my hand and starts pulling me farther into town. It doesn't escape my notice how Gavin doesn't so much as protest Tristan tagging along. He must do it a lot. It makes my heart flutter a little knowing how much Gavin cares for his family. How close they are. How close they *want* to be. It's odd how the village changes the farther inland we go. The buildings closest to the shoreline—the two or three of them that aren't completely fallen down—are small, squat, wood structures that have seen their fair share of wind, rain, and sunshine. They were probably pretty once, but now they sit in various stages of disrepair. The windows are coated in thick scales of salt water, and the wood is grayed and cracked in places.

The buildings on the other side of those are sort of strange. Gavin tells me people live in them, so they must be housing of some sort, but they don't look anything like Gavin's three-story house with its red bricks, faded black shutters, and wraparound porch. They're barely taller than me. All four walls and the roof are made with ridged metal sheets that are stained red with rust. There are so many holes in the metal, the walls are practically none existent. A strong wind could probably blow them all right over. As we pass, I glance in the open doorway of one and see a chair and table that look like they've seen better days. From my position, it's hard to see if there's anything else in there, but as I'm looking, a woman steps out, wiping her hands on her jeans.

When she sees Gavin, she lifts a hand in an absent wave. Her gaze moves to me and although she looks curious now, she extends the wave in my direction. I flutter my fingers back and she smiles in return before walking around the side of the house. I follow her movements with my eyes and watch as she climbs into a knee-high fenced-in area. I recognize a group of chickens. Gavin has some behind his house and every morning Tristan goes out and gathers eggs for breakfast. I wrinkle my nose when I think about how dirty and gross-looking they are before he washes them. I don't even want to *think* about where Gavin told me they come from. I shudder and Gavin glances over.

"Are you all right?"

"Yes. Of course." My stomach still tumbles like driftwood in a wave, but I press my hands to it.

He gives me a strange look, then shrugs and continues forward. We pass some more of those strange little metal houses, which are placed randomly on the sand until we get to a set of buildings that seem to be laid out with more thought. They're all an equal distance apart and the same distance from the dirt path. While they're in various stages of completion, it's easy to see they're all going to look exactly the same as the one finished one. Two floors high, if the windows are any indication, with white walls and light blue roofs. It strikes me then, how dirty everything is here. Even the new buildings and the ones that are still skeletons of what they will be have a thick layer of dirt and grime. I don't know why, but it bothers me. *Dirt leads to disease. And disease to death.*

We follow a large path, passing another row of those apartment-type buildings before getting to other buildings in various states of repair. Some look brand new, like the general store. Tristan disappears into the building without saying a word and Gavin only shakes his head.

Next to that is something called Sheriff's Office and it, too, looks new, but not quite as . . . shiny as the general store, whose windows glisten in the bright sun and blind me even through the dark sunglasses I'm forced to wear to protect my eyes.

Across the street, other buildings look old and worn out. Tired, almost. Like the building called Bar. There are even metal poles on the dusty windows. Next to that is a dusty building housing the Metal Smith, with a hole in its brick wall. The roaring and banging sounds coming from the large opening make me nervous, and, for some reason, it's hotter standing outside of it than it is anywhere else. The air is all wavy in front of me.

A man—at least I think it's a man—wearing a striped shirt and jeans with some kind of black apron pokes his hat-covered head out the opening. When he sees Gavin, he waves. "Gavin! Do ya have a minute? I finished the repairs on the shotgun. Thought you'd want a peek."

Gavin grins and pulls me over to the opening while the man disappears inside again. When he returns, he's holding a gun. He hands it to Gavin, then does the funniest thing. His eyes move over to me. He blinks. Then blinks again. Then his eyes grow round and he whisks his hat from his head and balls it in his hands. "Pardon me, miss. Didn't see ya there." His dirt-streaked face turns bright red.

Gavin glances over, but quickly goes back to studying the gun. "Oh, Frank, this is my girlfriend, Evie. Evie, this is Frank. He's the metalsmith. He's a genius. If it's made from metal he can work magic."

Magic?

Frank blushes even more, wringing his poor cap in his hands so tightly I'm afraid he's going to tear it.

I do a little curtsy. "It's a pleasure to meet you."

Frank looks slightly confused, but nods. Then he turns his attention back to Gavin. "What'cha think?"

Gavin looks up and nods. "Another great job, Frank. Thanks!" He holds his hand out and I watch with interest as Frank takes it and shakes it. I've seen Gavin do that with Dr. Gillian, too. "I'll have Tristan drop by with the rest of that boar I owe you later. Okay?"

Frank nods. "Or whenever." He focuses back on me. "He's good folk." He jerks his head toward Gavin. "You won't find a better person than Gavin, miss. He oughtta be mayor, instead of that yahoo they got in the mansion now." He spits on the ground as if just saying "mayor" leaves a bad taste in his mouth. I jump away and try not to show how disgusted I am by it, but I must not hide it well, because he says, "I beg pardon, miss."

I force a smile and try not to look at the ground where he spat. "Think nothing of it."

He gives me that strange look again, but smiles back before winking. "I charge the mayor up front and double."

Gavin laughs. "Next time charge him triple." He pulls the shotgun's strap over his shoulder and takes my hand, waving with the other as we leave.

When we get back to the street, I turn back around in time to see Frank shove his hat back on his head and disappear behind the wall again.

Gavin takes me on a tour of the town, stopping at almost every building to introduce me to the people inside. There are so many people, considering how small the township really is, that I can't keep them straight. Only two stick in my head. Mr. Pok, who runs the feed and grain store, and Mrs. Little, who runs the general store with her three adorable daughters.

After asking about his mother, Mrs. Little hands Gavin a bolt of fabric. "Here's the rest of the payment for that pheasant your ma brought me the other day. Sure was a pretty thing. Tasty, too." She winks at him. Then she hugs me. My whole body tenses. Gavin's mom and sister are big on hugs, too, and it always makes me feel peculiar. But, as I do with them, I force myself to relax and then, unsure what else to do, decide to hug her back.

"Welcome!" she tells me. "I'm so glad to see you're well enough that you can visit!" While she's talking, another customer comes in behind her. A boy that looks to be about Gavin's age.

Everyone in the town has been a bit strange to me, but this one is the most bizarre one yet. His dark hair has a blue streak in the front, and his button-down shirt is loose over his slacks. Instantly there's tension in the air. I glance over at Gavin, who is scowling again. The new boy, on the other hand, stops in his tracks when he sees us. They watch each other carefully, reminding me of the way Lucy behaved when a different dog came over and wanted me to pet it. They circled and growled at each other for a long time, while I sat petrified—I still don't know if I was scared of them or of myself—until Gavin's mother came out and chased the other one off with a broom.

Mrs. Little clears her throat and we all turn to her. "It was wonderful finally meeting you, Evie. You come back here anytime, ya hear? Gavin, you get on back to your mom now. She'll be waiting for that fabric and I don't have time to be cleaning up after the two of you."

Gavin looks like he's going to argue, but Mrs. Little places her hands on her hips and Gavin ducks his head. "Yes, ma'am." He walks past the boy, who nods his head and smiles at me as we pass. I smile cautiously back and the boy's grin grows.

As soon as we slip out the door, I grab Gavin's arm. "Who was that?" I ask.

He shrugs and keeps going. "No one."

"Didn't seem like no one." I have to rush to keep up with him. He seems in a hurry to get away from the store.

"Just an old friend."

I stop and turn, calling over my shoulder, "Well, if he's an old friend, then I should meet him. Maybe we should be friends, too." I only take one step before Gavin's in front of me, his hands on my shoulders.

"He's *not* your friend. He's not *anyone's* friend. You can't trust him. Ever." His eyes are cold and hard. It's scary, but kind of sexy too. Heat spreads from my stomach outward. I've never seen him like this. I glance over his shoulder and see the boy walk out of the store. He pauses when he sees Gavin, then turns and walks in the opposite direction.

"Why not?" I ask, moving my eyes back to Gavin's.

He's quiet for so long, I think he's not going to answer, but finally he says, "He— His father is the mayor. And the mayor is sent from Rushlake City. People from Rushlake *never* do anything without expecting payment in return, and you *do not* want to owe what they want to be paid." His eyes are haunted, and though I know he's not telling me the entire truth, I can't push him. It's obvious the real reason isn't something he wants to talk about.

Instead, I peer over at the building next to us. It's brick, like the rest of the buildings, but like the general store almost the entire front is a shiny glass window. The words "Butcher" are painted across in black and gold paint. "So . . . what's this place? Are you friends with the owner, too?"

He glances over. "Sal works here. I generally bring my game here after I field dress it. They turn it into steaks or sausages or whatever it is we want. It's also where we bring the chickens when they stop laying. The farmers bring their cows and pigs." He grins at me. "So, yeah, he's a friend of mine."

"Great." I push through the door. "Then introduce me."

Like at the general store, a bell tinkles whenever the door moves. "Be out in a sec!" a man calls out from a door behind a counter filled with various meat products. My stomach twists seeing them all laid out behind the glass, glistening red in their icy beds.

Swallowing hard, I turn away from the counter, which runs almost the entire length of the wall farthest from the door, leaving only a small space behind it for whoever runs the shop. Above that space are large pieces of meat—as large as me at least—hanging from giant hooks on the ceiling. The rest of the shop is empty, all the way to its clean white walls. That's where I keep my eyes.

Just then a man's voice booms through the room. "Gavin! I was hoping you'd stop by soon. Doc stopped by with those blue gill you'd caught . . ."

I turn as he talks, but what he's saying is lost when I see him. He's a large man, barely fitting behind his counter in either height or girth. His hair—what's left of it—is dark. His skin tone is somewhere between Gavin's golden hue and Doc's dark color. But it's his apron that I'm staring at. That I can't tear my eyes from. It was probably white, once upon a time, but now it's completely covered in blood.

The rusty scent of blood is thick in the air, getting thicker the longer I stand here. It makes me nauseated and not a little scared. A horrible chill enters my bones and I shudder.

As if from a distance, Gavin asks, "Evie, are you okay?"

I nod, digging my fingernails into my palm and trying to force a smile. I will not be an inconvenience. Not again. It's just a little blood. From the animals. It's part of life.

My head spins, and I glance around trying to find something, anything to look at besides the blood on this man's apron. I see the counter with all the meat in it, but instead of steaks and chops, it's littered in body parts.

Human body parts.

Arms with their hands pressing against the glass as if trying to break out. Legs split open with their bones showing. Even severed fingers.

It's not real. It's not real. It's not real. But when I turn away from the counter, looking at the butcher again, he smiles at me and I fight back a scream. His face is streaked with blood, his teeth painted in it and bits of gore. His whole body is blanketed in blood. From head to foot. Gleaming, shining brightly in the sun. Blood.

When we get to the end of the trail, there's a body lying on the floor, surrounded by the light of my flashlight, just as I expected. But what's there is far worse than anything I was anticipating.

There's a man leaning over the body of a woman, who is most certainly dead. Or at least I hope so, because the man is ripping her apart . . .

. . . He slowly turns, so he's facing us, then tilts his head to the side, watching us.

A shiver runs down my spine, and Gavin's breath catches. I tighten the grip on the pistol, preparing to raise and fire if need be.

"It is my privilege to follow Mother's orders. We don't question Mother." *Then he leaps toward us. . . .*

I run. I don't stop to think. I couldn't if I tried. I don't know where I'm running to. I don't care. As long as it's far away from the butcher and his display of severed body parts.

The world spins uncontrollably. Black spots swim in front of my eyes. I can't catch my breath and my heart is pounding as if trying to escape the confines of my chest. I hear Gavin calling my name, but it's as if he's kilometers away. I'm vaguely aware of falling before I completely succumb to darkness.

Chapter Four

Attention Outlanders: Only preapproved individuals are allowed entrance into Rushlake City. To obtain approval, please visit your local mayor for a visa.*

*Approval is not guaranteed. All outlanders approved for entrance are subject to the Rushlake City Community Standards. Any violation of these standards may result in the forfeiture of the visa and formal ban from readmittance.

—Notice on village bulletin board

Evie

When I wake, I just stay where I am—from the softness under me I assume it's my bed—while visions of what happened flit in and out of my memory. My body is stiff and sore. My arms feel like lead and it hurts to breathe—like I'm inhaling glass slivers. When I open my eyes, I find myself staring directly into Gavin's silver-gray eyes.

"Gavin!" I exclaim, my voice hoarse, forgetting everything that happened to grab him in a hug. I don't know why, but absolutely every time I see him, it doesn't matter what I've been through. He makes me feel better.

He clings to me, his arms shaking a little. He just holds me like that for the longest time, and I enjoy every second of it, even though the pressure he exerts on my still-healing shoulder makes my chest ache.

He pulls back and looks into my eyes. "It happened again."

I don't know what to say to that. It's not like I can deny it. It did happen again. Obviously.

I nod anyway.

"Damn it!" He pushes away from me to pace the small room.

Shivering from the sudden coolness that fills the space his warmth vacated, I hug myself and follow him with my eyes. There isn't much room for him to pace, though. Not with all of the paraphernalia for his sister's wedding packed onto her side of the room. He curses when his foot becomes entangled in something white and lacy.

"Gavin," I whisper, my throat raw and burning and guilt eating a hole in my heart.

He spins back around and crushes me to his body again, causing me to squeak when I try to breathe. He buries his face in my neck.

"You scared me," he whispers into my skin.

"I'm sorry." I smooth his hair. "I didn't mean to upset you."

Before he can say anything, there's a knock at the door.

The boy from the general store, the one with the blue hair, pushes his head through the opening.

Gavin jumps up and blocks his way. "What the fuck are you doing here, Asher?"

"Nice way to talk around a lady, *Mr.* Hunter." Asher lifts a brow and crosses his arms over his chest. "You kiss your girl with that mouth?"

"Kiss my ass."

"Nah. You're not my type. I prefer them slightly less hairy." He grins at Gavin and I see the corners of Gavin's mouth twitch before he firms them back into a straight line. Asher sighs. "Just thought you'd like to know my dad is on his way here."

Gavin blanches. "What the hell did you do?" Then, before Asher can respond, anger flushes his face. "What is wrong with you? Destroying my life wasn't enough the first time?"

Asher glares at him. "*I* had nothing to do with this. He heard his newest resident went tearing through town screaming her head off, then passed out twenty feet from the ocean. He thought he'd 'check in on her and offer assistance if it's needed.' I, on the other hand, thought I'd actually be helpful and give you a heads-up. Especially since this might be a good way to get her the help Doc thinks she needs."

Gavin pauses his glowering long enough to shoot me a worried look.

Just then there's another knock on the door, and Gavin's

mother peeks around the corner. She focuses on me, but I have the distinct feeling she's talking to Gavin. "Evie has another guest. And he brought flowers!" Her smile is forced when she says it. Her eyes flicker to Gavin and Asher and then back to me. "Are you up to seeing him, dear?"

"Uh . . ." I look at Gavin for help.

"Of course she's up to seeing me," a male voice says from behind Gavin's mother. "I won't stay long." He pushes past her and stands just inside the door while I stare. His hair is blond streaked with silver, but otherwise he is an almost exact duplicate of Asher, only older. Wait. No. I look briefly at Asher, then back to his father. The mayor's eyes are completely different. They're a sea-foam green, and cold. Hard. They remind me of someone else's, but, of course, I can't pull up the memory. As always, my mind keeps the pieces of my former life just out of reach.

His eyes flick over Gavin and his nose crinkles—only for a second, as if something smells bad—before he studies me. His eyebrows raise a fraction, and there's something in his expression I don't quite understand. But the way his eyes roam over my body makes me want to pull the blankets up further. I grip tighter to Gavin's hand.

Gavin squeezes back, but steps forward, holding out his other hand to the mayor, who ignores it. Gavin clears his throat and lets his hand drop.

The mayor smiles, but it's neither kind nor happy. "So, Evelyn, is it?" He looks to Asher for confirmation, but Asher doesn't so much as nod. The mayor narrows his eyes at his son and turns back to me.

"Yes . . . sir," Gavin answers, and although it's only an instant, I hear the hesitance before the "sir."

"I'm Kristofer St. James. I'm the mayor of this fair town. I see you've met my son."

I nod and take the flowers he offers me. I don't like him. I don't need Gavin's warning not to trust him. Everything in me is warning me away from him.

"How are you feeling, young lady?"

"Fine," Gavin interjects quickly before I can. "She's just fine. She doesn't need anything. *We* don't need anything."

"Gavin," Asher says under his breath.

Gavin glances over to him, then me, then seems to make up his mind about something. The mayor watches us all with this knowing look on his face. For some reason this makes me angry. What is he so smug about?

"I'd like to request a visa to get into the city," Gavin says, completely confusing me. The city is where Doc wanted me to go, but Gavin had said that going into the town proper *was* the city. So why he'd need permission from the mayor, I have no idea.

The mayor's eyebrows lift and he looks to me as if asking if he misunderstood before turning back to Gavin. "Why?"

Gavin tells him, but only of how I don't remember anything from before I came and that Doc is at a loss to what it could be. I'm grateful he doesn't mention the blackouts and freakouts, but then he goes on to explain that Doc had suggested that someone from the city with more training and experience would be able to help me, and I realize he lied to me. The city isn't the town. It's somewhere else altogether. And Doc thinks they can help! I can't understand why Gavin would keep this from me.

My blood boiling, I skewer him with a look, promising myself we *will* talk about this when the mayor leaves.

The mayor taps his finger against his lips. "So . . . you want to take Evelyn to Rushlake in the hopes of finding a doctor who will overlook your Outlander status and treat her. Do I have that right?"

"Yes . . . sir."

"And how do you propose to pay for her care? Do you have any money?"

Gavin looks at me, then at the mayor. "Um . . . no."

"I see." The mayor moves to look out the window. Gavin and I glance at each other, then look back at the mayor when he says, "You do realize that is out of the question, don't you, Gavin?"

"Sir?"

"There is no reason for me to allow you to travel to the city so you can beg for help. Which is essentially what you'd be doing: begging for someone to help you. Do you have any idea how badly that would reflect on me?"

Gavin only shakes his head, but his frustration is practically palpable.

"Besides, where would you stay?" the mayor continues.

"No one needs your wild game there. They have stores full of anything *money* can buy. Would you sit on the street with an empty cup? Or, maybe play some kind of instrument and let people throw coins at you? Find some kind of tent city where the other beggers live?"

Gavin doesn't say anything, but his teeth clench. I'm not sure why, but this is the final straw that sets me off. This is Asher's *father*?

I shove myself to my feet and the room spins for a second, but my voice is cold and calm when I say, "Mr. Mayor, I can't imagine anything Gavin Hunter would do that would reflect as badly on you as your own behavior. I consider our business complete. Good day, sir."

"I beg your pardon?"

The silence in the room is thick with tension and fear, though I can't remember feeling less afraid since I woke up in the hospital.

I focus my gaze directly into his eyes, unblinking, as an invisible string seems to pull my posture straighter than my injured shoulder has allowed in weeks. "I will not be treated like a commoner."

"Evie . . ." Gavin whispers, but I silence him with a flick of my wrist.

At first, the mayor meets my stare with red spots of anger on his cheeks, but after a moment he pales and looks away. A wave of dizziness threatens to overwhelm me as the adrenaline of my anger fades, and I turn. Gavin gets to his feet, his eyes wide with concern, and reaches hesitantly toward me. I shake my head slightly. I will not let the mayor see even a moment of weakness.

The mayor clears his throat, and says, "Perhaps you misunderstood me. I didn't say I wouldn't help *you*, Evelyn."

I glance at the mayor over my shoulder. He smiles and watches me for a minute before gesturing for us to sit again.

I wait for him to take a seat first before lowering myself to the edge of the bed.

He continues, "I said *his* going would be out of the question. Not yours."

I look to Gavin, only to see a tic in his jaw. The mayor goes on, either unaware of Gavin's increasing annoyance, or not caring. "Gavin is an Outlander; he would never make it in Rushlake. But you, Evelyn . . . you're different. You were obviously raised with a certain . . . quality, shall we say, that is lacking in the average Outlander. Even if you can't remember any of it."

"Say what you mean, Mr. Mayor."

He smiles and nods graciously, like he's indulging me. Obviously trying to take the power back. It sets my teeth on edge, but I let him speak. "I would be willing to sponsor your treatment. Set you up with the best doctors and the best places to stay while you're there. You wouldn't have to beg, or borrow. Steal." He glances at Gavin. "To get the help you need. You'd only get the *best* care."

Remembering what Gavin said about people from the city, I say, "And what do you suppose I would I owe you in return?"

The mayor waves a hand in front of his face, the diamond on his pinky ring sparkling. "There's no need to worry about that now. We're both reasonable people. We can come up with something at a later date. But Gavin stays here. You'll have to go alone."

I look down at Gavin and he shakes his head. "No," he says softly.

The mayor smiles, as if confused. "Beg pardon?"

Gavin stands, drawing himself to his considerable full height as he sets his shoulders. "I said, no. She's not going alone." His voice is strong, but I can tell from the way his throat is working that he's not comfortable standing up to this man.

The mayor only continues to smile and looks at me. The ultimate decision is in my hands. If we don't go, it'll be my choice. My choice to continue putting myself, and Gavin's family, in danger. I can't let that happen.

Still, I shake my head. "That's unacceptable. I won't go without Gavin."

The mayor shrugs. "Suit yourself. Request denied, then."

"Mr. Mayor, I have been led to understand that you're unable to guarantee the safety of your citizens outside the gates. Do you honestly expect me to go unescorted into a territory you yourself cannot control?"

"I have offered you my terms." For whatever reason, he's decided he's back in control.

"Very well. I can see there's no point in any further discussion. When you are prepared to grant my very reasonable

request, we can continue. Until then, I'll ask you to leave."
I stand, walk straight past the mayor, and open the door,
waiting for him to go.

The angry red spots are back in his cheeks. I've pushed
him too far, I can see that, but something in me won't back
down. I don't even know where these words are coming from.

"Will you let them both go, if I go?" a voice says from
behind me. I whirl around to see Asher staring at his father.

I turn just enough so I can see both the mayor and Asher.
The mayor purses his lips and this time I can't control the
shudder. It's so familiar; it makes the blood in my veins freeze.
I just wish I could place where I've seen it before.

"You want to go to the city?" the mayor asks him.

Asher shakes his head. "No. Not really. But Evelyn needs
to go and the only way that's going to happen is if they get
visas."

"Why are you offering?" his father asks with narrowed
eyes. Then he pauses. "Who is this girl to you?" Gavin lifts
a brow as if he is wondering the same thing.

Asher only smiles. "You've been wanting me to go to the
city for months now and I've refused." He shrugs. "So, *Pops,*
what's it going to be? I'll go to the city like *you* want, only I
take Evie and Gavin, like I want. We'll call it a gentleman's
agreement."

The mayor narrows his eyes and it's so quiet I can hear the
splash of each wave as they pummel the shore even through
the closed window.

Finally the mayor nods. His eyes sparkle and I'm reminded

of a cat I saw the other day toying with a mouse it had caught. I have to wonder what he's got up his sleeve. "Fine. But there are things I need you to do in the city when you get there. Do you understand?"

Asher makes a face, but nods. "Fine."

"I'll have Greta draw up the papers." The mayor walks away, his dismissal obvious, but his easy approval unnerves me. He was so set on denying Gavin passage. Why would he be comfortable sending his son with us—an Outlander he obviously detests and the crazy newcomer? It doesn't make any sense.

I keep these thoughts to myself. I'll talk with Gavin about them later when Asher isn't around to be offended.

But Gavin is obviously less concerned than I am about offending Asher. He turns to him and says, "We don't need your help. We can figure out how to get into the city on our own."

Asher steps right into Gavin's face. "You don't understand. The city is *not* going to let you in, even with your visa. No matter what you think. You're an Outlander and without a sponsor you don't get in. *So get over it.* You *need* me."

To his credit, Gavin doesn't even flinch, let alone back down. "I don't want you doing me any favors." His voice is infused with anger. He's practically vibrating with it. I can feel the hum of his emotions from here.

Asher takes a step back, but I don't think it's because Gavin intimidates him. "I'm not doing it for you." His eyes meet mine and I tilt my head in confusion. "I'm doing it for her. And it's not a favor." With that he turns around and starts to walk away. "We should leave first thing in the morning. Meet me outside the village gates at sunrise."

Gavin's soft snores beside me are oddly soothing. At least he's sleeping. I have to admit, I'm a little jealous, but he didn't sleep the night before, so I doubt he'd have been able to pull off another night without somehow figuring out a way to secure his eyes open.

But I'm restless. The more I lay awake staring at the ceiling, the more I want to jump up and pace the room like Gavin does. My heart feels like it's going to pound out of my chest and even though I'm breathing, I feel like I'm suffocating. I keep wringing my hands to relieve the ache that isn't there. My body needs to move, and move now. Or I'll explode. I'm sure of it.

Carefully, so I don't wake Gavin, I slide out from underneath the sheets and out of bed. He stirs and instantly I freeze. He only rubs a hand across his nose and rolls over so his back is to me. The T-shirt he fell asleep in pulls tight across his back, showcasing the muscles in his back and shoulders.

I stare. Who wouldn't? But even though my whole body protests, I turn away and make my way to the door instead of crawling back in beside him and making him help me forget all my worries about tomorrow. He deserves to sleep.

Even so, I'm disappointed when the cool doorknob turns easily in my hand and the door opens without so much as a whisper. And not just because Gavin promised to keep me locked in, but because it means nothing is stopping me from continuing on my path to get out of the ever-shrinking room and get some fresh air down by the shoreline.

With the floor cool and smooth under my bare feet, I shuffle as quietly as I can down the hallway and out the back door, which I've learned doesn't squeak like the front.

The sand is still warm from the day, but is soft, crunching softly as I walk. The water laps at the shore, making soft whooshing sounds. The instant I hear it, the tension in my body starts to ease. And when I see the ocean, the rest of it fades away.

Pulling my skirt tight against my body, I sit close enough to the waterline to let the water lap at my feet, but not enough to soak me if an errant wave decides to go a little further than normal. I lay down, crossing my arms underneath my head and staring at the stars. They're almost the best part here. They're just so beautiful and free. I feel wistful just looking at them.

My mind wanders as I lay there, and before long I feel myself drowsing. I know I should get up and walk back into the house before I do manage to fall asleep—Gavin could wake up and if I'm not there, who knows what he'd do?—but I can't summon the energy.

Without warning the hair on the back of my neck tingles and I know I'm not alone. But I don't get up. I know who it is. There's only one person who can make my nerves jangle like a whole fistful of bells.

Gavin.

When I feel him stare down at me, I open my eyes, finding myself peering into the most gorgeous gray ones. They're worried at the moment, as they are most of the time, but I give him a shy smile and the relief in his eyes is almost instantaneous.

"Hey," he says.

"Hi."

"Scared me. I didn't know where you'd gone. Why didn't you wake me up?"

I reach up and press a hand to his cheek, enjoying the scratchy feeling of his stubble against the sensitive part of my wrist. I stare into his eyes. The beautiful gray shines in the moonlight like polished silver. A delicious thrill courses through me as his gaze travels down my face to my throat and comes to rest on the little v-shaped patch of skin on my chest. It's almost like he's taken his fingers along that path instead of just his eyes.

And when those same eyes flash up to meet mine again, my heart skips a beat, then pounds so fast it's like it's in a race against itself. The want—no, need—is burning so brightly in his eyes I can feel its echo within me.

I move my fingers to the back of his head, tangling my fingers lightly in his hair, then pull him down so his lips are a hair's breadth from mine. He continues to stare down into my eyes as if they're not the only things that he's seeing. It's like he's seeing into my soul and seeing me, really seeing me. As terrifying as it is, it's also thrilling.

"I love you," I whisper, unable to stop myself. But instead of the sad look that's come into his eyes every other time I've said it, his lips slowly curve into a smile. One that swells my still racing heart to the point it almost hurts.

"I love you, too. Always," he whispers back, and I have only a moment to think how much I've wanted to hear those words without his usual hesitancy, before his lips breach the short distance between us and I can't think anymore at all.

His lips are soft and hard at the same time, like he's holding back. I pull him closer, savoring his taste. He pulls back almost instantly, his eyes roaming over my face, that familiar worry gleaming in them for only a second before it disappears and he kisses me again. This time he's not holding back. I kiss him back, desperately craving his taste. His scent. His feel. Him.

His hands are rough over my body, but I don't care. He's making me feel more alive than I've felt in a long time with each touch of his fingers on my skin. The stubble on his chin is scratching my skin and I crave every delicious scratch.

He only pulls away for air, but every time, I feel like I'm drowning and hyperventilating all at the same time. It's too much, yet not enough, and I never want it to stop.

CHAPTER FIVE

During the War it seemed that even Mother Nature was taking sides. While massive rains of almost biblical proportions were only one of her weapons, flooding destroyed many cities and left others cut off completely from the "mainland." The rains were followed by drought, which left many previously inhabited lands barren.

—EXCERPT FROM *A BRIEF HISTORY OF THE 21ST CENTURY*

Evie

Gavin and I stand outside the gates, our packs resting on the ground by our feet. The moon has set and the sun hasn't risen yet, so it's practically pitch dark. I shiver in the chilly air. While I love the cold, I'm not used to it.

I wonder, though, if it's really the weather that's making me shiver or if it's my nerves. One of the first things Gavin taught me when I was released from the hospital was that I should never leave the gates of the village when it's dark. There are too many hungry animals that hunt at night. He wasn't very specific about *what* animals, but I didn't really expect I'd stray too far from him and never asked.

Even Gavin appears nervous as we wait. I know he is thinking of all the things that could, and probably will, go wrong. He's already got his shotgun in one hand and his body is tight as he surveys his surroundings. After a minute, though, he relaxes and picks up his pack with his free hand. He slings it over his shoulder and stares out over the coast.

That nervous energy of his is still humming, and he looks so sad looking out over the water that my heart clenches.

I want to tell him it doesn't matter. That I'm okay not remembering anything of my past. But I can't. It wouldn't be true and he'd know it. Besides, it's not the only reason we're going. It's not even the reason he's going with me. It's just *my* most important reason, so I keep my mouth shut and reach for my bag instead.

The movement causes Gavin to turn toward me. "You ready?"

His voice is still thick with sleep and his drawl even more pronounced than usual. He stifles a yawn and crosses to me. The dark circles under his eyes, barely visible in the pre-dawn light, make me remember he hasn't been sleeping again. And it's my fault. We'd done nothing more than kiss, even after I'd let him pull me back to bed, but I'm sure he stayed up all night to watch me, even after I'd fallen asleep. He's going to make himself sick if he doesn't get some sleep soon.

I nod in answer to his question, but keep a stranglehold

on my pack, twisting the strap in my fingers. Gavin glances down and eyes my bone white fingers, made even whiter by the pressure I'm exerting on the strap. He places one of his bronzed hands over mine. The contrast is striking, but that's not what causes me to shiver. It's the warmth of his hand on mine.

He doesn't say anything, and I look up from our hands to see him watching me carefully. It's not the look he gives me when he's trying to see if I'm all right. It's different this time, and it makes my breath catch.

The sun is just rising behind him and while the sky is slowly starting to lighten, his gray eyes are still in shadow. A lock of his hair has fallen over one of his eyes. I reach up to brush it away, but he grabs my hand and just presses it to his cheek.

My stomach flutters and my heart trips in my chest. I can't tear my eyes from his, not that I want to, even when the sun comes up behind his head and threatens to blind me. I could stare into them forever and never have another care in the world.

But before anything can happen, Asher tosses his bag at our feet and says, "Mornin'! A great day to destroy our lives, don't you think? The birds are singing, the sun is shining . . ."

Immediately I step back, the pack dropping from my loose fingers, while Gavin makes a disgusted sound. He roots around in his bag and says, "If you didn't want to go, why'd you volunteer to take us?"

Asher shrugs. "Well, it certainly wasn't for you."

Gavin gives him a tight smile. "Anything you do for Evie, you're doing for me. Or did you forget that?"

Asher's mouth thins into a line.

Gavin shrugs. "But if you want to stay here, stay. I'm sure I can figure out some way to get into the city on my own."

Asher snorts. "They wouldn't let you within a hundred feet of the gates without me and *my* paper." He pulls a paper from his bag and waves it back and forth.

Gavin tries to grab for it, but Asher only folds it up and shoves it into his pocket, then smiles at me, nodding his head. "And a fine morning to you, Princess." He wiggles his eyebrows at me and I have to fight a chuckle. It's obvious he's only doing it to upset Gavin, and from the way Gavin is fuming, I would say it's working.

Shaking my head, I say, "Good morning, Asher."

Gavin glares at him. "'Swear, if I didn't need you—"

"Well, you do. Get over it." Asher reaches down for my bag at the same time I do and our hands bump. He gives me another of his cocky grins. "A gentleman always assists a lady with her luggage. Hunter can handle the rest."

Gavin makes a grab for the bag, but I say, "I can take it," and lift it before he can. It's heavy for me, but there's no need for the two of them to start a quarrel now, especially over something so petty. I refuse to be a bone they fight over. And if they've started this stuff now, it's going to be a *long* trip.

Asher, however, keeps his hand on the bag so I'm not able to flip it onto my back. His tone changes, losing that air he had before. "Are you sure? It's at least a week's walk from here. You'll need all the strength you have to get there. And after yesterday . . ."

"I'm sure. I feel just fine today," I lie, giving him my most winning smile. I'm freezing and I ache everywhere, not to mention the bag feels like it weighs a hundred kilos. My arms threaten to shake as I struggle to keep the bag in front of me.

It's obvious neither of them believe me. Asher continues to frown and even Gavin is watching me with a strange expression. Guess I'm not as convincing as I hoped. After a minute, Asher turns on his heel, dropping my bag, and runs back into the village.

"*Now* where is he going?" Gavin tosses his hands into the air.

I let the bag drop back to the ground and try to decide whether I should sit while Gavin starts his pacing. I've just about made up my mind to when I hear the strangest thumping sound. It even vibrates the ground. Nervous, I look to Gavin, who frowns in the direction Asher went. He doesn't seem scared, only confused.

When I turn back around, I see Asher riding what looks like a cloud of dust, but is actually a giant animal with long legs and an even longer neck. Clamping down on the squeal that wants to erupt from my mouth, I step back into Gavin, who rubs a hand up and down my arm.

Asher drops down off the leather seat and stands next to me. The beast lifts its head and shakes it back and forth, causing the straps on its head to jingle.

Pure panic makes my heart race and I gasp and jump away, bumping into Asher, who chuckles. The beast blows out a breath and I have to fight the urge to flee. The beast is tall, looming above me. Maybe even taller than Asher. It's silvery, but glows pink in the sunrise. Its eyes watch me with every move and, if I didn't know better, I'd say they were laughing at me.

"Relax. She's a good horse. She won't hurt you," Asher says, his tone soft and gentle.

I don't relax, but I do stop trying to run away from it. "A horse?" I've heard of horses. I think. The term is familiar to me, at least. I glance at its sides. I thought they had wings, though. There don't appear to be any. That's disappointing. I've been wondering what it would be like to fly.

"There are no cars outside Rushlake. You want transportation—it's the horse or nothing."

"Transportation?"

He gives me a smile. "You really are a princess, aren't you? Trans-por-ta-tion?" He pronounces each syllable slowly.

I know the word, but it doesn't fit. I don't see how this animal could be used for travel. How would you control it?

Gavin fills me in. He always seems to know exactly what I'm thinking. "We ride her." He pats the large thing sitting on its back. "And she'll carry us to where we need to go. The city's a long way from here, you'll want her to do the walking for you. Trust me."

He's always matter-of-fact when he has to explain the

obvious to me, but I can't help feeling stupid every time. It's always worse in front of other people.

"Plus the best part is she works for hay and sugar cubes." Asher chuckles to himself and gives the animal a pat on the neck. It makes a soft sound and I catch a glimpse of large teeth under its loose lips.

I swallow hard.

Asher pats something on the back of the animal. "See that seat? That's how we ride her. She's also used by the farmers to do . . . whatever it is they do." Gavin snorts, but Asher ignores him and continues, "She's a good girl. Aren't you, Starshine?" She raises and lowers her head in what I can only call a nod. He pats her neck again and she leans her large head down and nibbles on his hair.

Afraid she's going to eat him, I gasp, but she pulls away and huffs out a breath as if to tell me to stop being ridiculous.

Curiosity outweighs terror, and I reach out a hand to touch her neck . . . but curl my fingers into a fist and drop my arm at the last second.

Asher takes my hand. "It's okay. She won't hurt you." He smiles down at me, then turns to the horse. "Evie, this is Starshine. Starshine, this is Evie."

He places my fist on her neck and my heart pounds. After a minute, though, when the beast does nothing more than stand there, my heart settles and I uncurl my fingers to rub my hand down her neck.

It feels different from anything I've ever felt before. The skin is warm, and firm. The hair is soft and thick, coarse. I have to admit I like the feeling. And that she's very pretty. Tentatively, I step closer. Starshine moves her head and stares at me, the straps over her head jingling.

I'm startled, but I don't move. Her eyes are the prettiest blue I've ever seen. I swear I can see kindness in them. And intelligence.

"See? She's a good girl. So?" Asher's eyes sparkle with mischief. "May I offer the lady assistance in mounting her noble steed?"

Before I can say no, Asher bends and nudges my foot into his hand. He murmurs a few instructions to me, but it's all I can do to hear him, much less understand before I find myself in the seat on the horse's back, one leg on either side of her wide chest. My skirt hikes up my thighs and I fight the urge to tug it back down. It won't do any good anyway.

He winks at me. "Probably should have worn jeans instead of that skirt, Princess."

I ignore that, although Gavin said the same thing to me this morning. But the hand-me-down pants from Ann Marie make me uncomfortable. I can't really explain why, but I feel out of place in them. Not to mention, they're a bit large in the hip area, making me jealous of Ann Marie and her figure. Even though my skirt is just as borrowed, it's somehow more familiar.

"Uh, Asher, I . . . I don't know how to ride a horse." I try to not look as terrified as I feel. It's a long way back down to the ground and I clutch tightly to the saddle in hopes of keeping myself firmly in place.

He only grins and swings into the saddle behind me, causing me to grab wildly for purchase and shriek when the whole thing tips slightly.

"Not a problem. I'll be right behind you. I promise I won't let you fall."

Before I can even think of what to say, Gavin grabs Asher's arm and tugs—sending Asher crashing to the ground with a thump—before taking the leather straps attached to the horse's head and walking forward with her. The horse starts walking and I cling to the knobby thing again, trying not to scream when the saddle shifts with each step.

Gavin looks up at me from where he walks next to the horse's neck. "You're doing great, Evie. Just keep holding on to the horn"—he taps the thing sticking up from the seat—"and holler if you want me to stop." Then he leans back and kisses my leg just below the knee.

My stomach flutters and I smile down at him, wanting to run my fingers through his hair. Actually, I want to do much more than that. But I'm too afraid to let go of the horn.

Instead, I glance behind me to where Asher is just now pulling himself into a sitting position. He glares at Gavin for a second before pushing himself to his feet and limp/running to join us again. This time he stays on the ground.

No one really talks. We're all probably just too nervous, but as the tortuous sun drags itself across the sky and nothing happens, I begin to relax. The horse's steady gait rocks me until, between that and the heat of the sun, I start to drift.

I try to fight it, but after a while I give up and let myself float, staying awake only enough to not fall off the horse. It's not like it matters if I'm alert. There's nothing worth paying attention to anyway. Nothing to see, except kilometers and kilometers of sand and pale blue sky. There aren't even any clouds to stare at. Which makes me a little sad. Gavin had taught me, when I was first allowed to go outside, how to pick out shapes in the clouds. We'd spent hours that first day, nuzzled up next to each other, pointing out different shapes between kissing. The kissing was my favorite part. Even now my stomach flips thinking about his lips against mine. Or on the side of my neck. How he held my face between his palms. Or ran his fingers through my hair, just staring at me, my heart beating so hard in my chest, I was breathless just from looking at him.

And now, the last few days. Nothing. Like we're just really good friends.

A sigh escapes my lips and I blink back to the present to find I'm staring at him. He turns around with a frown.

"All right up there?"

I smile at him. "Perfect."

He grins at me and the sun shines on him, highlighting his golden hair and making his bronze skin glow. My heart starts hammering as fast as it had in the memory and, for a second, I feel dizzy as we beam at each other.

Then Asher clears his throat and I realize with a start we've stopped walking.

"Are we going to stand here all day and stare at each other

or are we going to try to get to the city sometime before the next war?" Asher grins at both of us.

For the very first time I can remember, Gavin actually blushes. He quickly turns around, makes a clicking sound, and starts forward again. Starshine continues on while I drift back into hazy, sleepy boredom.

It isn't until the sun is high in the sky that Asher forces my attention back on the trip. "Forest dead ahead!"

Gavin scowls. "Can we not say 'dead' in conjunction with forest? I've had quite enough of dead forests, thank you very much."

This confuses me, but I'm completely focused on the forest. It doesn't look at all how I pictured. "Forest" may be a bit of an overstatement, actually. It's just a collection of sad-looking trees.

Asher taps my knee and I glance down at him. "Not much of a forest, huh? It's really just a bunch of scrub oak clumped together and some pine trees with palmettos tossed in for good measure." He rubs a hand over the back of his neck. "But it'll feel great to get out of the sun for a while. And the shade will cut some of this awful heat."

He's right. It feels about twenty degrees cooler the minute we step into the shade. Shortly after entering, we find a clearing and stop for a rest and some lunch. Which, to my dismay, consists of jerky. And even though my nose wrinkles at the sight of the shriveled meat, I eat it anyway.

I just want a solid hour or two to nap, but entirely too soon, Gavin is telling us we need to start going again. And I find myself back on the horse and traveling down that worn path again, trying to ignore how bored and sore I am. Asher is mumbling to me about something, but I'm so hot and tired, his voice is more a droning sound than anything else. I'm finding it harder and harder to stay awake. Suddenly, the entire saddle jerks to the side and I let out a short scream when I feel myself tilting sideways as someone jumps up behind me.

Before I can fall, a strong arm snakes around my waist and pulls me close to a toned chest and stomach. I relax almost instantly. I know who it is even before I look behind to smile at Gavin.

"It's okay," he says in my ear. "I won't let you fall."

His voice is husky and I shiver, relishing the feel of him being so close. "Okay."

Asher heaves a world-heavy sigh beside us and we turn to frown down at him. "I see how it is. Completely ignore me. I'll be just fine being the only one on foot."

Gavin smirks at him. "It'll get some muscles in those skinny little bird legs of yours." He leans against me again and gently pushes my shoulder until I'm facing front, then traces his fingers down my arms, whisper light, until his hands are over mine.

"Grab the reins," he whispers. And I do, because when he talks like that, it's hard to resist anything he asks me to do.

His hands tighten around mine, causing my hands to tighten around the reins. For the next little while I amuse myself by letting Gavin teach me how to control Starshine. It's fascinating, how just a slight pressure from my fingers or my heel tells her exactly what to do. I have to admit I'm quite enjoying myself, but I'm enjoying the feel of Gavin's body against mine more. Wicked thoughts—thoughts I have no business thinking ever, let alone with Asher less than an arm's length away—fill my head and I bite my lip, hard, to try and force them away.

Unfortunately, or maybe it's fortunately, Gavin seems to be thinking the same thoughts. He kisses down my neck, starting just below my ear and moving toward my collarbone. My breath catches in my throat and I let my eyes drift closed.

Now this is more like it, I think.

His hands move from mine to rest on my hips, his fingers trailing along the edge of my waistband, inciting little fires along every single one of my nerve endings. My fingers slip from the reins and I start to twist around to face Gavin, but he only breathes, "Don't," in his gloriously husky voice, then goes back to brushing his lips along my neck. The stubble on his jaw prickles my skin.

A throat clears and I blink heavy lids. I try to focus on Asher, who's grinning up at us. He hands me the reins. "You might want to hang on to these, Princess. Horses have a way of knowing when their riders aren't paying attention."

Blushing, I take them from him. "Thank you."

Gavin only continues his onslaught to my nerves and hormones by nuzzling my neck and running his rough fingers across my stomach. I have to force myself to concentrate on breathing and paying attention to the path ahead of us.

"Stop!" My voice is hoarse and I have to clear my throat. "Stop."

Gavin chuckles but does as I ask. He crosses his arms across my waist and rests his forehead against the back of my head. It isn't long before his breathing evens out and his body sags against me. I'm fairly certain he's fallen asleep. It's slightly uncomfortable, but I don't dare wake him up. He needs the rest.

By the time we finally stop to make camp for the night, my back hurts from leaning over the horse. When Gavin helps me down, my legs are stiff and patches of my skin feel raw from the leather saddle, so it's hard to walk at first. I stumble my way over to where Asher is setting up camp.

"All right, Evie?" Gavin asks. He sounds more rested than I've heard in days, especially considering he'd been sleeping on a moving horse in what had to be the most uncomfortable position ever.

"Just tired . . . and sore." I rub at the tightness in my arms.

Asher smiles over, knowingly. "You'll get used to that. Couple more days riding and you won't be sore at all."

"Wonderful." Just what I wanted, more pain.

To take my mind off all that, I help Asher set up the tents—one for each of us. But still my back aches to the point that when we're finished, I'm grateful the only thing left to do is wait for Gavin to come back from hunting for some fresh meat.

I settle myself next to the campfire Asher is setting up. Asher keeps sneaking glances at me, and when he sits next to me, he asks, "How are you feeling?"

"Still a little sore." My stomach growls and I press a hand to it in an attempt to make it stop. "And hungry, I guess."

Asher laughs and scoots closer. "Me, too. Wonder what our famous hunter will bring back."

"Famous?" I give him a sidelong glance.

"He's the best in the village, Princess. Why do you think they always send him to go?"

"I'd never thought of it before." I trace patterns into the dirt. It's true. Gavin *is* always off hunting.

"That boy can catch anything." Asher shakes his head. "But it's not a job I'd want. Never being home . . . Only getting to see my family between trips . . ." He glances over at me as if he's going to say more, but then turns back to look at the crackling fire.

I can't pretend that I don't understand what he's telling me. That life with Gavin is going to be difficult. When I'm not having issues anymore, Gavin is going to have to go back to a normal hunting regimen. Which means he could be gone for days at a time, and I'm going to spend a lot of time alone. And worried.

But he's the only thing I've got in this world. Or any world, really. I can't remember what life is like without him.

I miss being able to remember.

Gavin's given up so much of his life for me, and it doesn't seem like that's going to end any time soon. I know he can't afford to sit around babysitting me forever, but I'm lost without him. It's like I've lost *myself* somewhere along the way, and I don't know what's important to me, or what I want out of my life.

Asher and I stare into the fire in silence while worry twists my stomach into knots.

When Gavin finally comes back, he's got some kind of fluffy, bloody thing in his hands, and he's wearing a huge smile.

"Caught a rabbit!" he says so excitedly that even though my stomach turns, I give him a smile back. Then bite my lip against the burning in my stomach and force myself to look away until Gavin's got it cleaned and strung up on the spit he placed over the fire.

He comes to sit next to me, the rabbit skin in his hands. "I'll save this and take it back to Mom. She'll have this whipped into a hat for you in no time." He looks so proud of himself that I have to smile back at him and try to look as excited as he is about it.

However, I don't miss the look of amusement Asher gives Gavin. He catches my eye and shakes his head, then goes back to poking the fire with a stick.

Before too long Gavin is dishing out the meat, and despite the fact that I really don't want to eat it, I dig in. Gavin sits next to me, his hip pressed tightly against mine. No one talks during our meal. It isn't uncomfortable like before, but I'm not stupid—I can still feel the tension between the two boys. Although I'm curious, I don't ask. Gavin will talk to me about it when he's ready.

When we finish eating, Gavin gathers all the bones. Without saying a word to either Asher or myself, he walks into the woods. He's gone for so long, I begin to get worried and start wondering if maybe I should go look for him. Just when I've made my mind up, he reappears.

"I want to show you something," he says, ignoring Asher. "Come on." He smiles at me and holds out his hand. Without hesitation, I take it and let him lead me to the tree line.

"Hey!" Asher calls. "Where are you two off to?"

Gavin gives him a look. "If it was any of your business, I'd be taking you too."

Asher glares at him. "You better not be ditching me."

Gavin scowls. "Don't tempt me." Then he tugs on my hand and pulls me into the darkness of the woods.

Even though it's pitch dark in the trees now, Gavin navigates expertly through them. The woods are filled with strange sounds—a kind of chirping. The rustling of leaves in the trees. Closer to us on the ground, a strange sound that sounds like someone asking, "Who?"

I'm sure I feel something slither over my shoe, but when I tell Gavin and ask him what it might be he just says, "Don't worry about it. You don't want to know." Taking him at his word, I cling to his hand and follow, trying my best not to think of what could be around us.

Eventually, we reach a break in the trees. He steps out into it, but I'm more hesitant. There's something about this place. It's solemn. Peaceful. I'm not sure I should disturb it.

But Gavin pulls me out of the trees. Moonlight streams over him, giving him a ghostly appearance, and I shudder.

"Come on. You don't want to miss this." He tugs me into the center of the circle, then drops down in the grass to lie on his back and look up into the sky, like we're going to look at clouds again. Unsure, I lower to the ground next to him and look up. In this circle, for as far as the eye can see, there's nothing but the blue-black of the sky and the silver of the stars.

"Oh . . . wow," I finally say when I can get my breath back. "That's even prettier than the stars over the water."

"That's because the light from the village mutes them. Here, there's nothing to dim the sparkle. And each of them has a story," he says. He points to some stars. "Like there, that's Orion. He—"

"Was a hunter. He was turned into a constellation when he died," I finish for him, excitedly, almost giddy with the awareness that I actually know something.

"Yep." He sounds a little disappointed.

I give him a sidelong glance and point up. "What's that one?"

Gavin

I don't know how long we lie there, staring at stars, me pointing out constellations I'm sure she already knows, but too soon, I push to my feet, then lean over and help Evie to hers.

"Time to head back to camp. Asher is probably freaking

out." Under my breath, I mutter, "If we're lucky, maybe a coyote ate him."

"Gavin," Evie says, but there's laughter in her voice.

Sighing, I push through the underbrush, following the path we made earlier. Halfway there, I see a really pretty flower. It actually looks like two flowers attached to one another. The bottom part has orange, spiky petals and the top part is white and looks almost like a rose. It seems to almost glow in the moonlight. Remembering back to the gardens Evie had in Elysium, I don't think she's ever seen one like this.

I glance behind me, but she's not paying attention to me. She's watching the ground with a nervous expression. I'm sure she's hoping to avoid whatever slithered across her foot earlier. Probably just a snake looking for his burrow. But her distraction is enough, and I pluck the flower from the ground and carefully keep it from her sight.

It doesn't take long before the sounds of a crackling fire and Asher's grumbling find us and I push through into the little clearing with our tents.

Asher jumps up quickly, panic on his face. When he sees it's just us, the panic turns to relief, then anger. "Where the hell have you been? I was worried you got eaten by a bear or something."

I wave him away. "Bears haven't been seen here in years."

While Asher glowers at me, Evie slips past and weaves her way sleepily toward her tent. I stop her by placing my hand on my shoulder. "Wait. Evie. I found this for you."

She turns back around, confusion written on her face. I shove my hand forward, opening it, and show her the flower sitting in the palm of my hand.

She smiles and reaches out to take it, but I ignore her hand, pushing her hair aside, then sliding the flower in behind her ear to hold her hair back. She touches the flower and beams up at me, and for a second I see the girl I met in Elysium instead of the shadow of her she's become. Then the smile slides off her face and it's almost like a veil lowers over her eyes. They go from sparkling with joy to dull and lifeless.

She tilts her head, still looking at the flower, then plucks it from behind her ear. She pegs me with her eyes and I fight a shudder. "My flowers are *not* to be removed without my permission. Mother *will* be informed of this."

She skirts around me while all the hair on my body stands on end.

Not again.

She walks straight toward the woods, and I have to force my shaky legs to move forward. Just hearing her say "Mother" with that expression has made my muscles weak. But I have to stop her from wandering into the woods. Bears may not be an actual problem, but coyotes are. Along with snakes, bobcats, and panthers.

As if to prove my point, the telltale scream of the panther punctuates the air. It sets my teeth on edge how eerily it sounds like a woman.

"Uh . . . Evie?" Asher says, following me, following her.

To my—albeit short-lived— relief, she drops to her knees

just on this side of the woods. She's muttering to herself, but it's so quiet, I can't make out more than a few words.

". . . Unbelievable . . . poor thing . . . never have I . . ."

The entire time she's mumbling, her hands are moving—she's clenching one of her hands. Her other hand travels from in front of her, to beside her.

"Sara," she says without looking up. "These need to go to the Science Sector. Macie is expecting them."

Macie? My stomach sinks when she turns to look at us. What makes my chest even heavier is that I know when she looks at me, she isn't seeing me. Her eyes are still dead and dull.

She tilts her head to the side, looking around. "Where's that foolish girl now?" she mutters. She focuses on me and for a second I think she actually sees me, but she only says, "Locate Sara Penderson. Tell her she is to report to me right away. These herbs need immediate transportation." Then she turns back to the ground.

It hits me then, what she's doing, and it breaks my heart because I'm powerless to help her understand it's not real.

Asher meets my eyes over her head. "What is she doing?"

"She's tending her garden," I say, my voice cracking.

CHAPTER SIX

Of all the creatures found in the Outlands, the vulture-hawks are the most dangerous. Created by scientists during the War to help clean up the massive quantities of carcasses left behind by war and natural disaster, their hawk-like traits quickly proved to be useful as an almost perfect weapon.

—Excerpt from *Hunter's Field Guide to the Dangerous Animals of the Outlands*

Gavin

I don't know what to do. I feel as lost and terrified as I did when she ran into the ocean. She's just sitting there, thinking she's cutting flowers. I'm afraid to touch her. Afraid that'll be the thing that breaks her completely.

Asher kneels next to me. "What should we do?"

"I don't know," I whisper.

For almost ten minutes we sit next to her, both of us unsure what to do. The more we sit here, the more I'm worried she's never going to come out of it.

But all of a sudden she blinks, her eyes focusing on mine.

"Gavin? Where . . . ?" She looks around, confusion written plainly on her face. She peers down at her hands, covered in dirt, then back up at me. Her chin trembles and she lets out a long, low sigh and closes her eyes. "It happened again?"

I touch her shoulder, but she jerks away, so I drop my hands and say, "Yes."

Her hands curl into the dirt. "I see." She swallows. "I, uh, I don't feel so well. I think I shall try to sleep now." Her voice is hollow as she slowly pushes herself up from the ground, dirt and dead leaves clinging to her skin. I jump up to help her, but she pushes me away. I'm sure I see tears sparkling on her lashes. I watch, helpless, as she walks toward her tent and into it.

She's always reminded me of the dolls Ann Marie used to play with when we were younger. But now, like this, Evie reminds me more of my grandmother's china dolls—the ones for show, not play. Fragile. Delicate. Where one wrong move—or a rogue baseball—would shatter them into a million pieces. I want to cradle her in my arms and hold her as close to me as I can. But I know better than to think she'll let me.

When I turn, Asher is staring at her with wide eyes and he's almost as pale as she is.

"Is she okay?" There's a slight tremor to his voice and when he looks at me, I see fear that mirrors mine. I don't want to see it. It only reminds me how powerless I am.

The answer is obviously no, and I want to shout that at him, but I bite down on the anger. Instead, I shake my head.

"I don't know. I just don't know," I say, letting fear turn into anger. "Why don't you go do something useful and get more wood for the fire?" I probably shouldn't be angry with him right now. He really has done us a favor by convincing his father to let us go. Except now I owe him a favor. Again. And I'd promised myself I'd never owe him for anything again.

Asher glares at me for a minute and I stare right back. Then he takes off into the trees. It isn't hard to hear him crashing around. It's a good thing we've already eaten; any game that was nearby is definitely gone now.

After a few minutes, I go in to check on Evie. She's asleep, so I sit on the ground by her head. When she calls my name out in her sleep, I lean down and whisper, "I'm here, Evie. I'm never going to leave you." I touch a hand to her freezing cheek. "We're going to find a solution to this. I promise."

I'm not sure if she hears me, but she seems soothed. My hand shakes when I pull it away. I don't know what to do. We're still days away from the city and I'm afraid she's not going to make it that long. That she'll have another episode and there'll be nothing I can do to stop it.

What started this, this time? I slip back out of the tent to sit next to the fire, thinking. She seemed like she was fine, a little tired, obviously, but she'd been laughing and joking with Asher while she helped him set up camp. She'd been just fine when we'd watched the stars. It could have been anything.

Asher startles me when he tosses an armful of wood in a

pile next to the fire. He doesn't say anything to me, only glances at Evie's tent, then heads back into the trees for more wood. After one more trip, he hunkers across from me. Silent, he pokes the fire with a stick, every once in a while tossing more wood onto it.

Afraid to fall asleep, I sit and fight to stay awake, but my eyes start to droop as I watch the dance of flames.

"How long has she been like this?" Asher asks, startling me. He, too, is staring into the fire.

I don't know how much I should say, so I don't say anything.

He looks up and meets my eyes over the flames. "Come on, Gavin. What do you think I'm going to do to her? What do you think that information is going to do?"

"I don't know, but I'm not taking any chances. You've hurt the ones I love enough."

Asher throws his hands in the air. "Christ! You still haven't let that go? That was years ago. We were kids! I didn't even know what I was doing!"

I look away from him. "It's not about that."

"The hell it isn't. Don't think I don't know why you didn't want me to help you get to the city. Don't think I don't know you warned Evie away from me."

My head jerks back in his direction. "What did you expect, Asher? You betrayed me! My family! To please your daddy you betrayed mine. And for what? To prove that you weren't one of us. Weren't an Outlander like me."

"I didn't know that was going to happen!" Asher shoves

the stick into the fire. A log falls and splits in two with a loud *crack*, sending a shower of sparks flying into the air.

Suddenly, Evie screams. It sounds like a name, but I can't make it out. Asher and I run to her tent, and I crawl into it with her. There's barely enough room for us; my head brushes the ceiling of the tent even sitting. Her eyes are open, but they're glazed, and it's obvious she isn't awake. She claws at the bag, trying to force herself out.

It's gut-wrenching seeing her like this. I lean down and whisper in her ear like I've done so many nights before. "It's okay. You're fine, Evie. I'm right here and Mother's long gone. Just rest now." I pet her arm, trying to soothe her. After a few more minutes of coaxing, she finally sinks into another fitful sleep. The only comfort I have is she won't remember anything in the morning.

I look up again and see Asher watching me with horrified eyes. "What *happened* down there, Gavin? And don't you *dare* bullshit me. I don't care what you think of me. I just want to help."

Glancing back down at Evie, I brush a strand of hair from her face and then sigh when she murmurs something about Timothy. "More than you could ever believe," I say. "Much more than you could ever believe."

Even though I wasn't going to tell Asher the whole messy story, when I sit back down by the fire it all slips out. I don't know why, but once I start I can't stop. It's like reliving it all over again, but seeing it from someone else's perspective.

My whole body feels separated from itself. I don't feel any of the terror I experienced the first time. I tell him about finding the tunnel in the cave, and the long trip down that ended with my hunting partner and I stumbling into Elysium, and the turret, which detected unregistered DNA, that claimed his life. Evie finding me, protecting me from Mother's wrath, and how she gave up everything to help me escape. How, because of me, she found out she'd been brainwashed to be an assassin for Mother, then later turned into breeding stock because of Mother's whims. The whole story of her being an Enforcer, and what it does to her.

When I finish, Asher is just staring at me, his eyes wide. He glances down at Evie and shakes his head. "Maybe it's better that she doesn't remember any of it."

"I thought that at first, too, but now she's got these damn nightmares every night. And flashes of memories when she least expects it. Sometimes, I barely recognize her anymore. Not to mention these strange episodes. I'm not sure if that's any better."

Asher goes back to staring into the fire. After a minute, he looks up at me again. "Why didn't you ever tell anyone?"

I frown. "Tell anyone what?"

"About me? You're so set that I ruined your life. Yet you know something about me that could destroy me, yet you haven't ever told anyone."

I blink. It takes me a minute to realize what he's talking about. I shake my head and roll my eyes. "One, because it's not any of my business, or anyone else's for that matter. And two, I'm not like you. When someone tells me something in secret, I don't share it with anyone for *any* reason."

He narrows his eyes at the fire, as if he's trying to puzzle that out. I decide that I'd rather be lying next to Evie than sitting out here with him. To make sure she can't sneak out of the tent without me knowing, I slide into the sleeping bag with her. Before long I find myself falling in and out of sleep, waking several times throughout the night to soothe Evie back to sleep when she has another of her fits.

When she wakes me for what feels like the thousandth time with a sharp kick in the shin and screaming incoherently again, I know I'll need to talk to Asher first thing in the morning and go over the map with him to come up with a better, faster route to the city. Evie needs help and she needs it quickly.

The birds singing in the trees wake me. I groan as I sit up. The little bit of sleep I've been getting is only a giant tease that makes my muscles sore. My joints pop when I stand and stretch.

To my surprise, Asher is already awake and poring over the map.

Trying to rub the sleep away, I run a hand over my face. "What'cha doin'?"

He startles, but moves over so I can sit next to him. "Trying to come up with a faster route."

I don't know why it annoys me that he had the same thought as me. I would have had to ask for his help anyway, since he's gone back and forth from the city much more than I have. At least this way it isn't a favor. So I nod and glance down at the map. "What do you think?"

"The fastest route is this way, through this town." He slides his finger over a black dot. "If we go that way, it will shave off at least three days from our trip. With any luck we could be in that town tonight and then another day, maybe two, and we'd be in Rushlake."

"Why didn't we go this way in the first place?"

"No one does." He won't look at me.

"Why?"

He hesitates, before finally saying, "I don't know. But my father was adamant that we never go that way."

Well, that's ominous. I think about it, weighing the risks. It's not smart to ignore that kind of warning in the Outlands. But with Evie getting worse and worse . . .

"Let's do it," I say.

We don't waste any more time; we both head back to camp and start tearing it down.

"We'd move faster if we don't carry anything that isn't necessary." Asher folds up his tent.

I lift an eyebrow. "You want to dump it?"

He shakes his head. "Starshine can carry it. This will be nothing for her. And then we'll have both hands free if we need them."

I nod. "Yeah, okay, let's get it all together."

We spend the next few minutes packing everything up and only when I have to, do I wake Evie. She's groggy and her eyes are still glazed with sleep, but she's lucid and able to walk and talk.

It worries me how flushed her skin is, but I can't think about it right now. There's nothing I can do about it. The only way to help her is to hurry our asses up and get her to the city.

Asher helps Evie onto the horse, while I break down our tent and then start securing our supplies to Starshine. I've just about tied the last supply, when I realize it's gotten really quiet. Too quiet. I look around, trying to figure out what has my instincts humming. The only sounds are Asher and Evie talking quietly. He's got her laughing again, with that stupid fake Southern gentleman charm he likes to use. Reluctantly, I have to admit I'm grateful. He's taking her mind off what happened last night. And considering how far it is to the city, and my increasing fears she won't make it all the way there without having another issue, making her happy needs to be a priority. Even though she's smiling and laughing, I can't help but hear how tired she sounds.

I glance around again, reassured that Evie is safe.

All of a sudden a scream tears through the silence. The three of us share a startled look and fear makes my nerves vibrate. I don't know what's screaming, but whatever it is, that's a sound of terror and pain. I've heard it before in the Outlands and it never leads to good things. The worst part is, it doesn't sound very far, and it's growing closer.

"What is that?" Evie's voice is shaky, and she's watching me with equal parts fear and trust and that scares me to death because I have no idea what to tell her. But I know we have to get out of here.

"You don't want to know," I finally say. "But we have to move. Now!" I fumble trying to tie the last item to Starshine, because the screaming is now so close I know whatever it is, is going to break into the clearing any second. My heart is beating so fast, it practically hurts and I can feel it pound in my head.

Then my worst fears come true: the animal—a deer, I think—bursts into the clearing. It's hard to tell exactly what it is because chunks of its skin are shredded off, claw marks mar the parts that aren't torn off, and blood covers the rest of it. One ear is completely gone and its mouth is open in its scream. And surrounding it, trailing behind it, is a whole flock of birds.

They're huge. At least three times larger than any bird I've ever seen. I curse under my breath. I've never heard of them being this close to the village. And I've never personally seen one, even considering I've been hunting in these woods since I was a kid. It makes me nervous that they're here. Not just for us, but for what it means for the village.

I can only stare in shocked horror as two of the birds grab the deer on each end of its body, lifting it into the air. I want to close my eyes. I know what's going to happen. I want to run to Evie and block her from seeing this, but I can't move. I'm petrified, stuck exactly as I am, forced to watch the deer's grizzly end as the rest of the flock latches on to it.

Horrible ripping and shredding sounds mix with the flapping racket. The deer's screams get louder and tear into my heart for only a second before it's abruptly cut off. And in just another second I see why. The flock breaks into three, flying into the trees with three different parts of the deer.

My stomach lurches as I glance at Evie and Asher. If it were just me, I probably wouldn't even be worried. I can protect myself, but I can't protect all of them and Evie has to be my top priority. I have to get out of here. I have to get Evie out of here.

"What are those things?" Evie asks. She doesn't look as nervous as I know she should be.

"Vulture-hawks," I say, trying to keep the fear from my voice. "They usually don't bother humans, but they're mean."

"I can see that," Asher says, staring up into the trees.

"We should get out of here. Now." I glance around for my gun so we can get going and my heart sinks when I see it. Oh God. It's still lying where I left it when I went to help load up Starshine. Just a few feet from where the birds disappeared into the trees.

I'm not willing to leave it behind. We'll need it. I'm sure of it.

I race toward it, hoping the birds will ignore me for their kill.

Something heavy falls to the ground just inches from my outstretched fingers. I'm certain it's the deer, but it's hard to tell after the work of the birds.

I don't want to, but it's like I have to. I look up into the branches and see them staring down at the deer—at me—with their red beady eyes. One of the birds makes its telltale caw, which sounds more like the screech of a hawk than a vulture, but has a way of making your skin crawl. Suddenly they're all making the same screeching sound. I slam my hands against my ears in an attempt to block out the sound. They start dropping from the tree to resume their attack on the dropped carcass. Their movements would be fascinating if they weren't so violent. I can hear the crunch of bones between their beaks.

We have to get out of here.

Then, without warning, one of the birds swoops down off its branch and flies straight toward me.

I duck and it misses, but there's an unmistakable look in its red eyes. It's out for blood.

"What the hell?" Asher yells at me. "I thought you said they don't bother humans!"

"I said they *usually* don't bother humans." Without sparing Asher a glance, I grab the shotgun.

Before he can react to that, the rest of the birds descend. Evie screams out when one claws at her wounded shoulder. Her eyes turn dark blue, the haze fading from them as if someone flipped a switch. I recognize that look. That's the one she got in Elysium whenever her "Conditioning" kicked in.

In a lightning-fast move, she snatches one of the birds from the air in front of her, but it pecks at her face, going for her eyes, and only misses because she tosses it aside. It squawks when it lands on the ground and struggles to get back up.

She immediately grabs another, but this time grabs its head and the muscles in her skinny arms bulge. A second later, the bird's head is no longer attached to its body.

Blood sprays into her face, but she only bares her teeth in a snarl and lunges for another.

Holy hell.

I grab Asher, who's trying his best to beat away the birds attacking her, but only getting his clothes and skin shredded in the process. There's already a long gash across his left eyebrow.

"Get on the horse!" I yell, hissing when a claw pierces the skin on my shoulder.

"What?" he yells back. The air around us is a frenzy of beating wings and piercing screeches.

I swing the gun like a bat at another bird. "I said, get on the horse. Get Evie out of here! I'll catch up." It gets around my swing, but I swing again and manage to knock it away.

If he doesn't hurry, I don't know how much longer I can keep them back. Starshine whinnies and starts to rear, but startles back to her feet when Evie plants a foot on her neck.

She's trying to stand, I realize, despite the horse's restless movements.

"What about you?" Asher swings his arms around again, causing the birds to scatter for a minute.

I force a smile. "I've got this. No big deal." He doesn't

look convinced and I raise my voice. "Get her the hell out of here. If you want to make up for what you did to me years ago, you'll get on the fucking horse and get her out of here."

He glances over at Evie, who is batting away more birds. One is tugging on her hair and she's screaming as it threatens to pull her off the horse. Another keeps swooping at her, but missing. She can't seem to get ahold of them anymore, and as I watch, her foot slips off Starshine's neck, dropping her hard onto the saddle. Asher takes a step closer to her.

"Don't you dare let anything happen to her," I yell to Asher, dodging another bird, and rearranging my grip on the shotgun. It's time to put this thing to use as more than a club. "Get her to the city. No matter what."

At first he doesn't say anything, but then he nods.

"Thank you," I say.

"I'm not doing this for you." He vaults onto the horse, taking the reins. A bird screeches as he knocks it away with a closed fist. The rest scatter when Starshine shakes her head violently.

Good enough. I nod and he nods back.

"She'll be safe. I promise," he yells back.

That gets Evie's attention and she looks over, her eyes clearing as they meet mine. The Enforcer is gone. For now.

She shakes her head, and struggles to get down, but I only smile at her.

"I love you, Evie." I press my fingers to my lips, then hold them out for a second, before I slap the horse on her back flank. She rears, then takes off away from the camp with a thunder of hooves.

Although I'm worried as hell to leave her in Asher's hands, I'm also relieved that I know she's getting away and safe. For now, at least.

That leaves me standing in the thick of all the birds, as they dive bomb and swirl around me, trying to grab pieces of flesh.

I pump my shotgun. "Bring it on!" I yell, and shoot.

CHAPTER SEVEN

Danger! Nuclear Materials. High Levels of Radiation Present.
—Rusted sign attached to one lone section of
chain-link fence in the Outlands

Evie

No!" I yell. "Gavin!" I struggle to get away from Asher, but it's no use. My muscles are weak and I don't even so much as budge him. "Gavin!" But he's gone now. I can't see him. The birds have completely covered him.

My heart is in my throat, my stomach on the ground. I want to scream. I want to cry. I want to kick something until my toes are bloody. But none of those are going to do Gavin any good.

And as much as I want to get away from Asher and run back to Gavin, there are two birds who did not stay with Gavin. One tears at me, while the other tries to rip chunks from Asher. I bat at them with my arms, but my coordination is off and I miss every time.

My arms are more like limp noodles than muscle and bone. I don't understand where all the strength I had just seconds ago went.

One of the birds reaches out with its claws and grabs a hunk of hair, trying to lift me from the seat. Screaming, I flail around trying to dislodge it. If it weren't for Asher still holding me tightly around the waist, I would already be up in the air.

Holding me has left him open to the second bird, which slashes at him repeatedly. With each swipe of its talons it opens up another gash on Asher's body. He winces every time, but doesn't let go of me, or the reins. He just continues to press Starshine to run faster. I'm still no use. I'm just too slow. My arms don't want to cooperate. It's as if I'm trying to swing out underwater.

But then the bird slices across Asher's neck with its talon and, when I see the blood run down Asher's throat, there's this click inside of me. Just like before.

Everything seems to disappear except that gash. My blurry vision clears. My hearing is better, and even though I can still hear the slash of wings against air, the thunder of the horse's hoofbeats, and the birds' screeching caws, I'm able to differentiate one from the other. They're no longer just a mess of noises. But the most important change is the strength I feel in my arms and legs. I don't feel ill anymore and my muscles are no longer spaghetti.

As if on instinct, I grab the horn in front of me and push myself up on my arms. Asher removes his arm from around my waist and I kick my legs around so I'm completely turned around in the saddle and facing Asher, who stares at me wide-eyed for the shortest of seconds before turning his attention back to the trail in front of us and hooking his arm around my waist again.

I reach out to snatch the bird that's yanking on my hair. It wrenches out a good amount of hair and my vision swims for a minute as each strand disconnects from my head, but I don't let go. Instead, I adjust my grip on it like I had with the bird earlier, so I'm holding it with one hand on its head and the other around its body. Then I twist and yank.

There's a loud cracking, snapping sound and soon the bird is in two pieces. Without so much as a wince, I toss it to the ground and go for the second bird. Unfortunately, it saw what I did to the first and won't be as easy to grab. The good part is, it's got its full attention on me now. It dives at me instead of Asher this time.

I miss, but not because I couldn't get my body to cooperate—it flies just close enough to strike out at me, but never close enough for me to grab it. Then, after the fifth dive, I see my opening. Right before it tries to claw at me again, I twist my body to the side and lunge forward, practically falling onto the ground, but I've got the bird and Asher has me.

Again I rip its head off and toss the halves over Asher's head. Even through the horse's hoofbeats, I can hear the parts thump onto the ground.

Satisfied, I search the air to make sure there's no other, but it doesn't appear that any more have followed us. That only relieves me for a minute as I glance at Asher. For an instant I have the strongest, strangest urge to . . . kill him. To take his head between my hands and twist so I can watch his lifeless body hit the ground with a thud.

Just as quickly as I think it, I force the thought away, shaking off the shock. That's disgusting. Why would I possibly want to hurt Asher, let alone kill him? The hate and anger I feel toward him completely fades as I glance at his neck and the slashes over the rest of his body, then mine. We're both entirely lucky that we survived that. And if two were this hard to beat, I can't imagine what Gavin was—*is* going through.

There's so much adrenaline pouring through my veins, but my whole body is tense with anger. Is this something normal for me? Am I usually this angry? If . . . *when* I get my memories back, will I even like myself?

It's no use, though. As clear as my mind feels right now, I still can't recall anything. And the worst part is I don't know who I'm most angry with: Gavin for forcing me to leave, me for not fighting harder to stay, or Asher for taking me away.

However, anger is as useful as tears, which is to say not at all. So, I force my mind away from Gavin and focus instead on what I did to the birds. I have no idea how I was able to do what I did, but it didn't feel wrong. It felt right. Like that was how I was supposed to be, and I've just been living in a fog all this time. It's the first time I've felt right since I got here. I sneak glances at Asher trying to determine how he feels about what I did.

Asher only looks at me a few times, but I don't see disgust or any of the other things I imagined would be in his eyes after what I just did. Things *I* feel about what I just did. In fact, he seems impressed—the wonderment in his eyes speaks volumes—and not at all surprised that I did it. Or even that I *could* do it. It's as if he knew, which is odd, since *I* didn't even know I could do that.

Without warning, because I can't see where we're going, we burst out past the trees and into the full sunlight—and heat—of morning. I wince and shadow my eyes with my hand, but even then we don't stop. In fact, Asher pushes Starshine to run even faster.

I glare at Asher, but he won't look at me. Won't even let me turn around to sit properly. Instead, I'm stuck facing him, facing where Gavin got left behind.

"We have to go back!" I yell.

"No."

"But Gavin needs us!" Needs me. I can't leave him.

"He's smart. He'll figure out how to get out of that and find us. If we go back, we'll just get hurt." His eyes meet mine for a moment before focusing back on the path. "*You'll* get hurt. I'm not taking that chance."

"But look what I did to those birds! I could help him!" Even though what I did to the birds disgusts me, I wouldn't hesitate to do it again to save Gavin.

He shakes his head. "That was only two birds, Evie. Not a whole flock."

"But—"

"I'm not going back, Evie!"

His jaw is tight as he clenches his teeth and I know beyond a doubt that no matter what I say or do at this point, I'm not going to get him to change his mind. He thinks Gavin is dead. That much is obvious, but *I* refuse to believe it.

Gavin's not gone. He can't be.

If he doesn't want to go back to find Gavin, I'll force him. I sit up as straight as I can, and then in one quick movement I bring my arms and legs up to my chest and wedge them between Asher and me. Then, as hard and as quick as I can, I push. Asher's mouth forms a little "o" of surprise as he flips over the back of Starshine to land on his butt on the ground.

Starshine starts to slow, but before Asher can get back up, I spin around so I'm facing forward, grip the reins as I settle my feet into the stirrups, and tug on the reins as Gavin taught me. Starshine circles around, stomping her hooves, so we're both facing Asher. He's back on his feet now, brushing at the dirt on his pants and wincing.

I dig my heels into Starshine's sides and she bolts forward again, this time back in the direction we came from. Asher jumps out of the way just in time as we thunder past, but before we get more than a few meters—just inside the tree line—I hear a shrill whistle.

Starshine stops so quickly that she ends up standing straight up on her back legs and I find myself dangling from my fingertips. She leans a little to the left and I'm horrified to see she's going to fall directly onto me. I let go of the reins and fall to the ground with a thump. Somehow, Starshine manages to stay upright before dropping her hooves to the ground again with a thud that shakes the ground.

I scramble to my feet and climb onto her back again, but before I can kick her into action, Asher jumps onto her back behind me. He grabs hold of me, pressing my arms tightly against my sides. Even though I'm struggling, I can't seem to call up the strength I had earlier. He manages to twist me around, so I'm facing him again, somehow keeping my arms by my side and wrapping his own tightly around me, so I can't manage to get even a finger between us. But I continue to fight, struggling as much as I can.

"Stop it! Just stop. This is ridiculous. Don't make me hogtie you, then hitch you to the horse like a blanket." He lifts an eyebrow. "I'll do it. Gavin asked me to protect you. And that's what I'm going to do. You're not going back that way. *Now stop trying to fight me!*" He shouts the last part, startling me, but that's not what makes me stop. It's what he said about Gavin.

I open and shut my mouth a few times, before I finally force out in a whisper, "Gavin put you up to this?"

He rubs a hand over the back of his neck. "Er . . . yes. But he'll catch up with us. Now come *on* before more of those things follow us." He glances around at the trees as if expecting the flock to appear at any minute, which I've no doubt is completely possible.

With no choice left, I try and get more comfortable. It's not an easy task. My thighs ache, not only from straddling the horse, but because of the way I'm turned and pressed tightly against Asher.

After wiggling and shimmying for a few moments, I finally let go of embarrassment and propriety and just hitch closer to Asher. I wrap one leg around his hip, letting the other lie over his thigh.

The adrenaline I had just moments ago rushes out of my veins as fast as it poured in. The horrid heat feels like I've ridden straight into a volcano. My head spins and my thoughts are all fuzzy and mushy.

I curse myself for it. I'm so sick of being sick. My eyes slowly close, and I fight to keep them open, but I'm losing the battle. I don't want to fall asleep now. I want to go back for Gavin. But my body doesn't care what I want and, despite all the sticky blood on his shirt, I slump over into Asher's chest.

His arm tightens around me, pulling me even closer. "It's okay. I've got you," he says.

I can't fight it anymore, so I stop trying, letting the exhaustion and sleep take over.

The slowing of the horse wakes me and I blink my eyes against the bright sun. I'm still tucked up tight against Asher, which makes me feel guilty and uncomfortable. I push away gently and clear my throat when we stop.

As if someone throws a switch, everything floods back and rage wells up inside me. My hands curl into fists, my nails biting into the flesh of my palm. I open my mouth again to demand we go back for Gavin. I don't care that Gavin told

Asher to leave, or that he'll meet us. We need to go back. But Asher looks down at me and the rage rushes out of me just as quickly as it came. He looks as miserable as I feel. Exhaustion is pouring off of him in waves.

Unsure of what to say, I close my mouth. Instead, I look down and notice the bleeding from the wound on his neck has slowed. And while it's still trickling blood, he's already lost a lot. His throat and shirt collar are covered in it. And so am I.

When he slides down off the horse, he stumbles a few steps before falling to his knees. I quickly slide down, ignoring the deep ache in my own joints and limp over to him, but he pushes me away.

"I'm fine," he says, his voice rusty. "Just tired."

I reach out to his bloody gash. "This needs attention. It's bad."

"It's fine. I'm fine," he says again, but when I go to get some water from the canteens and some cloth to clean his wounds anyway, he doesn't stop me.

Trying to locate Gavin's pack, I search through the supplies quickly. I'm sure he has some kind of first-aid kit. He's a hunter. Accidents happen. He'd need something to handle them. Of course, that makes me think about how he's all alone out there with *nothing* to help him.

If he made it out at all. My breath hitches at the thought, and I press a hand to my mouth before I quickly push the thought away, refusing to even think about it. If I do, then I'll fall apart, and I don't have time for that right now.

I find the little white box with the red cross on it and open it. There are only a few packets of sterile bandages and some gauze left. Since it's better than nothing, I sit next to Asher and pull out a few of the packets, pouring water on the gauze. I gently dab it on his neck, trying to get enough of the dirt and blood from the wound to see how bad it is.

He hisses, but doesn't stop me. The wound is deep. Thank Mother it missed any major blood vessels or muscles, although it still has to hurt like crazy.

"I'm sorry I kicked you," I say, not looking at him.

Asher rubs a hand over his chest. "Not gonna lie. It hurt like hell. But I get it. Let's just forget it. Consider it water under the bridge."

I nod. Using some gauze and the smaller adhesive bandages as a tape, I carefully bandage it. It's not pretty, but it's functional. Finished, I start to pour some more water onto the spare gauze to clean his throat, but he stops me.

"We may need those in the future. Here." Asher takes off his shirt and hands it to me. "Use this."

I wash the rest of his neck, trying to get the remainder of the dirt and blood off him. Probably not strictly necessary, but it gives me something to do and makes me feel useful.

After not being able to go back and help Gavin, I feel I need to do this one thing. My chest feels heavy when I think about him. Did he make it? Is he coming for us? Was he hurt? Does he need us? Does he need *me*?

Even though it's completely clean, I continue to scrub at Asher's neck. He grabs my wrist and stops me.

"Evie." His voice is soft. He waits for me to look up and, when I do, I see something in his eyes. But I refuse to acknowledge it. Not now. Not ever.

His eyes search my face, but I tug my hand from his grasp and turn away, meticulously placing each bandage into the box one by one and making sure they're placed perfectly before I stand and put the box back in the packs.

"You should rest," I say. "You've lost a lot of blood. And we should wait for Gavin to catch up." He doesn't say anything, and I can't stop myself from continuing. "It shouldn't be too much longer before he does, but I'll pull the stuff off Starshine. She should be able to rest, too."

At first he doesn't do anything, but I don't turn around. I just continue to uselessly pull at the ropes. When I can't get my fingers to cooperate enough to undo the knots, I move to the saddle straps and unbuckle them. I'm just about to try and lift the saddle when Asher's hands fall on top of mine.

He doesn't say anything. We just stand there, my hands on each side of the saddle, his over the top of mine. It's almost suffocating, him being that close, but I need it. I want to lean against him and soak up the comfort I know he'd offer. And Mother knows I need all the comfort I can get right now.

But then he sighs, and the moment passes. "I've got this," he says. "You shouldn't be lifting anything this heavy."

More exhausted than I care to admit, I nod, slipping my hands out from under his before ducking underneath his arms. I sit back down on the sandy ground a few meters away, as just those simple tasks have already exhausted me. With my whole achy body elated at being able to sit, I begin tracing designs with my finger in the dust.

I'm working so hard to keep from thinking of Gavin that I don't notice anything until I feel a burning in my shoulder. I hiss and yank away, twisting to see what's trying to take a chunk out of me now.

Asher sits behind me, holding a wet cloth in his hand. "You got clawed, too," he says quietly.

Moving my gaze to my shoulder, I see long gash marks next to the old ragged, infected wound that never seems to get better. I nod, gesturing for him to continue before turning away again.

He carefully cleans all the gashes on my upper chest and arms, and even tries to tend to the wound in my shoulder. Then he washes the blood from my face. When he finishes, I hug my legs to my chest and rest my cheek on my knees, closing my eyes against the bright sunlight. My head pounds from the intensity of its glare.

Asher sits next to me, and then taps my leg. I glance over to see he has a pair of sunglasses in his hand. *His* glasses. I take them with a grateful smile. "Thank you."

He shrugs. "You looked like you needed them."

For the next several hours we wait, Asher occasionally getting up to rustle through the pack or check on Starshine before sitting down a distance away from me. We stay lost in our own thoughts until the sun starts to disappear behind the horizon.

A strange sound comes from the direction of the woods

and I jump to my feet, straining to see what made it. However, all I see in every direction is more sand and dirt.

The sound comes again and Asher stands and mutters under his breath, "That's not good."

What did he say? I ask myself, but before I can ask aloud he's kneeling in front of me.

"I'm sorry, Evie. I—I don't think he's coming."

"We don't know that yet. He'll come. Any minute now."

He glances over when the strange sound splits the air again. "We can't wait any longer. That sound? It's coyotes. And they're going to be hunting soon. We need to get somewhere safe."

The name makes my blood run cold. Gavin said something about them last night. If he was afraid of them, then I know I should be, too.

"What about Gavin?" I demand. "He needs somewhere safe, too. He's going to be looking for us. We can't just leave!"

"*If* he's alive, he'll survive. He's a hunter. He knows how to survive out here way better than we do. He'll be fine."

He touches my leg when I don't move. "He'd want you to go, Evie. He made me promise to keep you safe. He's going to look for us someplace safe, right? He sent you away to protect you, not get eaten by coyotes because you're too damn stubborn to listen to reason."

I open my mouth to refuse again, but then shake my head, the logic of that finally entering my heat-addled brain. I don't know what coyotes are, but that sound makes my stomach twist with fear, and Gavin hadn't wanted to run into them either. He knows what they are and how to get away from them. I'm sure. And Asher's right; Gavin would want me somewhere safe. That's where he'll look for me.

"No. Of course, you're right." I hold out my hand to him. "Let's find somewhere safe."

CHAPTER EIGHT

Caution! Restricted territory. Nanite-affected area. Unauthorized entry banned.

—SIGN BOLTED TO OUTLAND CITY GATES

Evie

We don't push Starshine as fast this time, but Asher isn't exactly taking his time either. The sun is setting quickly and before long the entire area will be dark as pitch with nothing but the moon for our light. It's not even a full moon. I hope he slows down once the sun sets—I worry we will push Starshine too fast and something we can't see will cause her to trip and fall. I voice my concerns, but Asher brushes it off.

"The sooner we get to shelter, the safer we'll be," he tells me, not even glancing over his shoulder at me.

Left with no choice but to agree, I shut my mouth. I have to trust him to get me to where we need to go. Gavin obviously did. At least enough to send me away with him. And I trust Gavin.

As the sun disappears, so does the heat, and while the cool was a relief at first, now it has gone almost too far. Goose pimples prick my exposed flesh. I keep my arms wrapped around Asher's chest and press myself closer to him for warmth. It doesn't help all that much.

Another howl echoes in the air. It's a sad, lonely sound, but it chills me just the same. I realize that they're getting louder and more frequent. They sound like they're just behind us. I look around to see if the animals are close, but there's nothing but darkness.

Asher pats my calf. "It's all right. We're a moving target and, unless they're starving, they won't come after us."

"And if they *are* starving?"

He pauses, then says, "Then we'll have to hope Starshine's faster than they are."

I swallow. I don't like the sound of it, yet we don't have much choice.

"How far until we find shelter?" There is a small quaver in my voice. I hope he doesn't hear how afraid I am.

"Not much. A couple hours. Probably."

I fight back a groan. Hours. Of riding a horse. In the dark. With carnivorous animals at our heels. Lovely.

I immediately feel guilty. Gavin's probably having much worse problems. He doesn't even have a horse, or any gear, or food. Medical care. My chest aches for him.

For what feels like forever, we ride. Starshine is moving fast, blowing wind into my eyes so I squeeze them shut. My whole body aches with the effort of staying on her back and holding Asher. If I weren't gritting my teeth, they'd be chattering in the cold.

My shivering isn't helping my fatigue. My head throbs with each of the horse's footsteps. I suspect I'm dehydrated—my tongue keeps sticking to the roof of my mouth, and my lips are chapped and sore—but I don't dare ask Asher to stop for a drink of water. Who knows how far back the coyotes are. I imagine them pursuing us with pointed teeth, foaming mouths, and red eyes, their bodies as tall, if not taller than, Starshine's. I don't know what came over me earlier, but it's obviously not dependable. I can't rely on those instincts to appear again and help us out if we need it. So, I cling. I shiver. And I pray we get wherever we're going just a little faster and that Gavin isn't too far behind us.

When I tremble for what feels like the thousandth time, Asher rubs his hand up and down my leg, quickly.

"I'm sorry," he calls over his shoulder. "It shouldn't be long now."

Afraid to speak in case I bite off my tongue, I nod.

When I shudder again, he says, "Maybe you should sit in front of me. Like before. You'll stay warmer."

It's tempting, but I'm not sure I should. "No," I say.

"Are you sure? I don't mind. You'll be a lot warmer."

I can't even respond because I'm shaking so hard, so when I can finally say something, I murmur "Yes" into his ear.

He slows immediately, but then, without warning, I hear another howl, practically right next to us. I start, then glance over in the direction of the howl. This time I see something. A set of yellow, glowing eyes.

Then I hear it—just under the sound of the horse's hoof-beats is the sound of other animals running and panting for breath.

"Asher?" I say.

"I see 'em," he responds back between clenched teeth. He digs his heel further into Starshine's sides and she jumps forward, running as fast as she had before.

One of the dog-like creatures makes a leap at us, just barely missing my leg. I bite back a scream and cling to Asher.

"Don't panic. They'll sense your fear."

I try not to, but when another one lunges at me, its claws scraping over the exposed skin of my leg, I can't help but scream. My leg is on fire and I can feel and smell the blood dripping down it.

"Evie!" Asher yells back. "Did they get you?"

Before I can answer, another dog jumps at us and I kick out with everything I have. I feel my foot connect with something fleshy and the dog yelps.

"Evie! What happened? Are you hurt?"

I can't speak over the pain so I just nod, but then I realize he can't see it, so I force out a "Yes" through gritted teeth.

"How bad?"

Before I can answer, yet another dog leaps at us, this time grabbing onto Starshine's backend.

She rears with a high-pitched whinny that sounds disturbingly like a scream, and it's everything I can do to hang on to Asher. The dog is shaken loose and falls with a yelp to the ground. Starshine lands with a bone-jarring thump, and if it's possible, she runs even faster.

Burying my face into Asher's back, I hang on to him as tightly as I can. Through his back I can hear him murmuring. "Come on. Just a little more. Almost there."

The dog-beasts are still behind us—I can hear them—but they're falling back by the second. I turn and watch as their yellow eyes grow smaller and smaller until they disappear completely in the dark.

Relieved and perilously close to sobbing, I press my lips together and my body even closer to Asher. He doesn't slow down for several minutes, only letting Starshine drop to a fast walk when the horse's breath is chugging like an engine ready to fail.

He turns to me and his eyes are wide in the moonlight.

"Are you okay?"

"I—I don't know. They clawed my leg."

He glances down, but I doubt there's enough light for him to see anything.

"We're almost there," he says after a minute. "Just a few more minutes. I think. Can you make it that long?"

"Of course," I say, although I don't know for certain. But I know now why he wanted us to get away from where we were so badly. There is absolutely no way I'm letting him stop to take a look at my leg. I'd rather lose it completely than give those . . . things time to catch up.

Gavin flits into my mind again. I seriously hope he found

a safe place before we did. Those things were not playing around. I don't even want to think what they'd do to him if they found him.

True to Asher's word, it's only a few minutes before I see what looks like the shadow of buildings rising up out of the dark. Asher lets out a relieved sigh and pushes Starshine to put on an extra burst of speed, racing toward them.

He stops short when he sees a tall wall surrounding the town, like the one surrounding our village. He follows it around until we find a large gate. It's closed, as it should be after dark, but unlike in our village there is no sign of a guard.

Asher pulls Starshine to a halt and then jumps off. "Stay here," he says, and I nod, trying to rub warmth into my arms and looking around to see if I can see any of those dog-beasts again. It terrifies me, standing out in the open like this, but I don't see that I have a choice. There is a protocol we have to follow, I'm sure. There always is.

"Hello?" Asher calls. "Anyone here?"

There's no response but the echo of his voice. I tremble again and curl into myself, trying to make myself as small as possible. It's entirely too quiet for my tastes. The only sounds are the echoes of Asher's voice.

"We're from Black Star Cove. A village a few days' travel east of here. We just want some shelter for the night as we pass through to Rushlake City."

Nothing. Not even the sound of wind.

Asher turns back to me and shrugs before turning back to the gate. He presses on one of the gate doors and with a loud squeal it swings open. It's worse than the proverbial nails on a chalkboard. I slap my hands to my ears, then wince when the movement causes my head to feel like I've split it open.

He freezes, waiting for an alarm to go up, but when it doesn't, he pushes the gate wider. It squeals again, but nothing else happens. He then comes back to me, and takes the reins, guiding Starshine through the gates before shutting them again.

"Guess no one's home," he says.

I don't say anything. Even though I should feel better that we're not just standing outside the gates waiting to be those animals' next meal, the whole place has my nerve endings tickling. I worry my pendant between my fingers. The village is dark, made darker in some spots because of the buildings that block out the moonlight. Almost all of the buildings reach for the stars, jutting out of the sand like fingers. I cannot believe how tall they are. They are at least three or four times taller than the mayor's house in the village. Not to mention intimidating, with their yawning doorways and hundreds of dusty windows that show us nothing but inky darkness. The shadows are so thick it's almost like I could reach out and feel a solid wall.

"What is this place?" I shudder as I stare into yet another pitch-black opening.

"It's a city."

"Not the one we're going to, right?" Please tell me this isn't the city that was supposed to cure me.

"No. This one is smaller. And probably abandoned, from the looks of it."

Asher jumps back into the saddle and continues farther into the city, slowly. It's still too quiet. Disturbingly so. The only sound is Starshine's hooves making clacking sounds on the hard ground. I shiver, but this time it has nothing to do with the cold.

"Asphalt," Asher murmurs. "Interesting."

I glance around, and that's when I see them. People. A bunch of them, standing in strange poses—as if time stopped and they were stuck in whatever move they were making at the time—just outside the doors of one of the tall buildings. I straighten and my hand tightens on Asher's shoulder.

"What's wrong?" He turns to look at me when I don't respond. He follows my gaze and pulls Starshine to a halt. "Is that a person?"

"People. I think." I keep my shaking voice quiet. I don't know why, only that I'm almost scared to talk. As if the people are only sleeping and I'll disturb them if I speak at a normal volume.

"Hello?" he calls to them, making me jump. "Can you help us?"

They don't so much as budge and we exchange a look before he dismounts and cautiously proceeds toward them. When he's within touching distance, he pauses, then starts laughing.

"What?" I demand. What could possibly be funny about any of this?

"They're just statues!" he says.

"Statues?" I rub a hand over my forehead and look again. The placement is odd. And why in Mother's name would they make them in such odd poses? It makes me wonder who lives here.

"That's weird," Asher says, tilting his head sideways as he studies the statues.

"What?" What I really want to ask is *What now?*, but I don't.

"They're all wearing real clothes. They're a bit torn and dirty, but they're real clothes." He tugs on one of the sleeves of the closest statue. I try to come up with an explanation, but can't. The whole thing is sort of creepy.

Asher comes back and vaults onto Starshine, prodding her forward with his heel. It isn't long before we see more of the eerie statues. They're placed so haphazardly, I start to wonder if they were positioned to make it appear as if people are living here. Like, maybe this town was meant to be some strange museum of what the world was like before the War. Some are clustered around doors leading into buildings, others at the cross streets we pass. The closer we get to the city center, the more there are.

"Whoa!" Asher exclaims as we get to a large, squat structure made of metal and glass, standing in the middle of the path.

"What is that?" I ask.

"It's a car. Like they have in Rushlake. But it's all rusted and falling apart."

Peering over his shoulder, I see more of them. They line up in an almost straight line behind the first one, reaching as far as I can see. All in various stages of falling apart. I try to get a good look as we pass; then I gasp.

"Asher!" I say, pointing excitedly. "Look. Inside the cars. More statues."

Even in the dark, I can see his eyes widen. "What the hell?"

But there's no ready explanation and we continue forward, ogling at the strangeness of it all. As we continue, we see more dispersed between the cars. Some are posed as if running from something. Running in the *opposite* direction we're moving. Others are holding smaller, child-sized statues in their stone arms. Some are huddled close to their cars, their arms over their heads. I can't understand why anyone would build something like this. It's creepy.

I shudder and wrap my arms around my body. "What *is* this place?"

"I don't know," Asher responds, and even he has a slight waver in his voice. When he squeezes my knee in comfort, there is nothing comforting about the tremor in his hand.

And while I can't help but think we should turn around, curiosity has me gripped tight. We push forward. The closer to the center we get, the more haphazard the placement of the cars and statues. It is as if the child playing with his toys got tired of setting them straight and just tossed them about and left them however they fell.

I stare at yet another statue as we pass by so closely I can see the expression on its face. Its mouth is wide open as if screaming and terror is etched all over its face.

When we finally get to what appears to be the center of town, the building that stood there is completely gone. The only thing left is a huge crater where it stood. Bits of metal, concrete, and glass litter the circle.

Asher leaps from the horse and strides toward the crater. Curious and unwilling to be left alone in this morbid city, I follow at his heels. When I make it next to him, he reaches out and grips my hand tightly in his. And this time I don't pull away. In fact I squeeze harder, clamping both my hands around his. In this dead city of fake people, it's nice to have a connection to someone alive.

Together we walk to the center of the crater, then stop. He releases my hand and kneels down in the dirt to sift through the wreckage. After a minute or two he lifts something up and studies it, then sighs, and hands it to me.

I take it and look it over. It appears to be a human hand, carved in stone and cut off at the wrist.

"What is this? A piece of one of those statues?" I scrutinize the piece. It feels like stone, but it's different. More porous. It makes my skin crawl just holding it.

"Yes. And no," he says, studying more of the debris. "They're not statues."

"Then what are they?"

"They're . . . they *were* people."

I drop the hand, a sour taste filling my mouth. When he

looks up at me, his eyes are filled with horror. I almost wonder if it isn't just a mirror reflecting back what I'm feeling.

"This town was destroyed with a nanobomb."

"Nanobomb?" For some reason the term sounds familiar to me, but I can't place where I heard the term.

He stands, brushing the dirt from his hands. "They were used during the War when they wanted to overtake an entire city, but didn't want to completely destroy it, or wanted to keep it useable. It was the quickest way."

"How?" I wheeze out. My chest feels like there's a band around it compressing until I'm breathless.

He meets my eyes and I know what he's going to say before he does. "When the bomb explodes, it disperses nanobots—tiny robots so small that they're invisible to the human eye—into the air like an aerosol. When a person breathes the aerosol in, they breathe in the nanobots, and they start attacking the body from the inside out. Sort of like a virus. In this case, it caused the body to calcify at an accelerated rate. Virtually turning them into stone statues."

CHAPTER NINE

Toward the end of the twenty-first century, nuclear weapons were almost completely abandoned in favor of the more effective bioweapons. These weapons could easily clear out entire cities, without making them uninhabitable for invading soldiers.

—EXCERPT FROM *A BRIEF HISTORY OF THE 21ST CENTURY,* "BIOWARFARE"

Evie

Oh, Mother," I gasp, but a band of fear must be compressing my chest, because when I suck in a breath it catches in my throat and I start coughing. Coughing so hard that blackness creeps in the sides of my vision until all I can see is a pinprick of the scene in front of me.

Asher slaps my back as if I'm choking, but it doesn't help. It only makes it worse, a metallic taste coating the back of my tongue. But finally I stop and, while I'm catching my breath, I look around at the statues that stand outside the circle. It's all so hard to believe, but explains a lot of things. The way they're dressed in real clothes, the poses, the looks of terror.

"But . . . why are they still here? Why did they just leave them like that?" Tears sting my eyes and my voice shakes, but disgust is almost as prominent as the sadness ripping through me that anyone could be so callous.

Asher won't meet my eyes when he says, "I don't really know, but considering how much damage there is to the surrounding buildings, I have to think this was one of the sites where they tested the prototypes. They probably realized that this city was too far gone to do anything with it and left it."

Now the disgust is definitely more prominent than the sadness. It makes me speechless. The lack of respect is just mind-blowing.

Asher is watching me with a strange look. "Did you ask for your mother a minute ago?"

At first I have no idea what he's talking about and the change of subject is a little jolting; then I realize he means what I said before I started choking.

I wince and slump my shoulders, ducking my head so I don't have to look at him when I say, "It's just something I say . . . sometimes. When things surprise me."

"Why?"

It doesn't sound anything other than curious, so I relax a little. "I don't know. Gavin says it's something from . . . before. One of the things that stuck in my head even after I lost everything else. I don't know why I do it, and Gavin doesn't tell me . . ." I trail off when I realize how silly that sounds. My saying something and expecting someone else to tell me what it means. It's ludicrous. I hate it. Feeling helpless like this.

Asher stares at me with this strange look on his face, before he shakes his head. I think I hear him mutter, "Despicable," but before I can question him, he smiles at me and says, "You're a strange one, Princess. Come on. We need to find somewhere warm to sleep before you shiver yourself into pieces."

It's then that I notice I'm a bundle of tremors. Every muscle in my body aches, especially my heart, which is beating furiously in my chest. My lungs feel like they're being compressed against my ribs. I rub the heel of my hand against my rib cage.

My teeth are chattering again, but I can't tell if it's from fear or the cold. Either way, I just want to leave this city. There's no way I'm staying here. Not with these statues watching over us.

When I say as much to Asher, he says, "We don't have much choice. This is the safest place until sunrise." As if to punctuate his claim, a howl disturbs the quiet of the town. I rub absently at the scratches on my legs. "Besides," he continues, "this is where I told Gavin we were heading. *If* he's coming, he'll try to meet us here."

I can tell he doesn't really believe Gavin is coming, but I'm not willing to take the chance. If waiting in some creepy town is what I need to do, then that's what I'll do. "Where do we start?"

"Let's try to find a spot inside one of these buildings."

That, of course, proves easier said than done. Almost all of the structures are so badly damaged they'd either provide us no protection from the elements, or are in danger of falling over. It isn't until we get to the other side of the town, as far from the bomb blast as possible, that we find one relatively intact. It's the smallest of them. Just a squat block building with a flat roof.

Asher kicks open the door, and peers inside, like he has at least a hundred times in the last hour. But this time, when he emerges, he has a smile in his voice.

"Found one." His voice is scratchy from exhaustion.

While I get down from Starshine, he pulls a flashlight from one of the packs. "Come on, we'll check the rest of this building out together. I don't want to leave you out here all alone."

I don't want to be alone either, but . . . "What about Gavin?"

He frowns. "What about him?"

I make a disgusted sound in my throat. "What if he comes while we're inside? How will he know where we are?"

He rolls his head on his shoulders and rubs his eyes. "Evie . . ."

I know what he's going to say, but I don't care. I cross my arms over my chest. "Look, I don't care what you think. He got away from the birds. All right? He got away and you're not going to convince me any different. Now how is he going to know we're inside?" Even I can hear the desperation in my voice, but I ignore it.

His eyebrows have winged up under his hair and he just stares at me. Finally, he sighs. "Starshine. She'll wait here until we get back."

"Wait." I glance over at her and see her staring at us with sad eyes. "We just can't leave her out here."

He mutters something under his breath, but says aloud, "We won't. We're just going to check this place out and make sure it's safe. We'll come back out for her in a few minutes. I'm sure no one's around here to care whether we bring her in the building to stay warm. And by that time," he continues when I open my mouth, "I'll have figured out a way to mark that we're here."

Uncomfortable with leaving her out here and still doubtful Gavin will find us, I don't immediately follow when Asher disappears through the open door.

Only when he pokes his head back out and asks "Coming?" do I make up my mind and follow him in. It's only for a few minutes. We'll be right back out.

Inside, our flashlight reveals glimpses of the place. It's a strange mishmash of a house and some type of military outpost. As if someone lived here until the very moment the army took over. I wonder if that happened before or after the bomb drop. If it was before, that would explain a lot— the calcified statue people, and how they were just left. They were probably used as a deterrent to keep people away from this area. The statues certainly gave the abandoned city a creepy feeling and if I could have avoided it, I would have.

I follow Asher as he wanders around the tiny building

until we locate a steel door set into the wall of a long hallway.

He hands me the flashlight and forces the door open. Surprisingly it opens without so much as a squeak or squeal. I hand him back the flashlight, then follow closely behind him as he walks through the door.

It's nothing but a pitch-black corridor. No light reaches in here, and my nerve endings go into overdrive. I try to focus on the area illuminated by the flashlight, but a memory is tugging at my mind.

Without warning, the lights flicker and go out throughout the complex. The red emergency lights stay lit, but ahead the hallway is dark. I reach into my pack and pull out my flashlight pin.

When I click it on, the light cuts through the darkness. It's actually brighter than the lights that would have lit the hallway, but it isn't big enough to dispel all of the gloom.

We keep our guard up, sticking close together. Our arms brush together, and at first I have to fight the urge to jerk my arm away. I bite my tongue, hoping the pain will be enough to distract me from my homicidal thoughts, but it isn't until he squeezes my hand—a simple gesture of his promise to protect me—that I'm able to push the thoughts to the side.

I can't fight this much longer. I hope we reach the submersibles soon.

After a few minutes, he releases my hand and I have to resist the urge to grab out for him again. It's the only thing grounding me from going crazy, but we can't take the chance of holding hands. We don't know what's ahead.

Suddenly my foot slides in something wet and I almost fall to the ground. I throw my hands out to the side to catch myself with the walls.

When I lift my foot, my shoe makes a sucking sound. I tap Gavin on the shoulder, then point to the floor. "There's something here," I say.

He nods and stands watch over me, while I kneel to shine the small light onto the floor, careful not to let my knee dip into whatever the sticky mess is. It's a puddle of something dark red, almost purple. I tilt my head, then stick my finger in it and bring it nearer to me to study. It's slightly tacky, like wet glue or drying paint.

Bringing it to my nose, I sniff at it. It has a metallic scent, like rust. Then it hits me. I know exactly what this is. It bothers me that it took me that long to figure it out.

When I turn to show Gavin, he's already staring at the puddle with a look of horror on his face. "Blood?" he asks.

"Oh, Mother," I whisper, staring at my hands. They're covered in blood. "No. No. It's not real. Not again."

"Evie?" Asher asks, turning toward me. When he does, he illuminates the walls, revealing a patchwork of gory handprints.

I shake my head. "No. No."

I stare, unable to blink while a rivulet of blood escapes and trickles down from the tip of one print's thumb. They're fresh. Whoever made these isn't far away.

A sound comes from behind me and I spin around, finding more prints. Some of these are near the floor and aimed upward, as if someone had crawled up from the ground. I press my hands to my eyes. This can't be real. Not again. My hands are wet—tacky—and I remember the blood on them. I yank them away with a whimper.

"Evie?" Someone touches my arm. It must be Asher, but the voice warps like a record slowing down. "What's wrong?"

It isn't Asher. It's Gavin, and he's smiling at me. His chin is already red, and more blood oozes from the space between his teeth. It's not a smile. Not at all.

"Gavin!" I can only whisper because fear has robbed me of my voice. I can't breathe. My chest feels like a horse is sitting on it.

His jaw drops, almost as if he means to speak, but instead blood spills out to patter wetly into the congealing puddles at my feet. He raises one hand to me, stretching his fingers like he can't decide if he wants to caress my cheek or grab my face. The action splits white cracks into the blood coating his palm. I want to run, but all I can do is lean away from him, my muscles tight and protesting.

"You must be starving," he says with that same strange smile. When he lifts his other hand into view, he's holding a severed arm.

Finally, my body frees me from its paralysis. I spin around and try to race away, but I find myself looking into the face of a girl about my age. Her blond hair is stained pink and red, matted to her head. There's something gray clinging to her temple that for some reason I'm certain came from inside her head. Her scalp is split open there, showing a glint of bone, but she doesn't seem to care. She stares at me, unaware of the trickle of blood running into her right eye. I have the strange thought that her eyes are a lovely sapphire color, but it's obscured by the hate in them as they bore into mine.

Macie! my mind whispers. And for a second, I'm overjoyed, but— "You're dead," I say.

"You left me," she says. "You left me to die. You didn't even try to help me. You're selfish, Evie. How could you?"

"I tried. I wanted to. But . . . you—you were already gone," I say, fighting the urge to cough. I can't seem to catch my breath and every time I inhale I hear a high-pitched wheezing sound. "I—I avenged you."

"You took my life, then you took my love." Her eyes roll back up into her head so only the white shows, yet she still walks toward me. "I trusted you. I *helped* you. And you left me to die, then killed the only man I ever really cared about. You're a murderer, Evelyn. A cold-blooded murderer."

"No, no," I whisper and back up, right into someone. I whirl and see Gavin again.

Up close, I see deep gouges in his cheeks and forehead. *The birds.* Blood runs freely from his injuries, making his face a mask of blood.

"You left me, too. You said you loved me, but it was a lie. You've done nothing but want to go back home since you got here. Then you ran away with Asher when I needed you the most."

"No, no! That's not true. I—I wanted to help you, Gavin,

but I couldn't get down. It's Asher's fault! He wouldn't let me down. I tried! Really I did."

"Liar," he and Macie yell, both of them stepping forward and trying to pin me between them. "You didn't care. You never cared."

Shaking my head, I try to slip out from between them. Their voices grow louder and louder, until it's just one horrifying scream. I slap my hands to my ears and run as fast as I can away from them. The walls are just a blur of black and red.

I run as fast and as far as I can, but they're chasing me, the sound of their footsteps echoing behind me.

"Evie!" they call after me. "Wait!"

But I don't stop. I can't stop. No matter what, I can't stop.

I can't breathe. My lungs are on fire and my legs are shaking from exhaustion. I don't know how much longer I can run. I don't even know where I'm going.

"Evie! Stop! Please!" a familiar voice calls after me.

White lights bob ahead of me. The ghosts of the people I killed. I'm a murderer. A killer. I turn down a corridor, and for a minute they're gone, but that relief is short-lived. They spring back up in front of me. Taunting me.

"There's a poor wee little lamby . . ."

They want me to follow them to my own grave.

"The bees and the butterflies pickin' at its eyes . . ."

Screaming, I take another turn, desperate to get away, but the voices echo off the rusting walls. *"The poor wee thing cried for her mammy."*

"No!" Without warning, my legs give out on me and I crash onto the ground. The skin on the palms of my hands and knees tear, causing tears to prick at my eyes. The floor is wet, sticky, and the stink of iron clogs my nose. My lungs heave, pulling the metallic smell—fresh and old mingled—deep into my body. I can smell it, taste it, feel it inside me like a sickness.

I try to push myself up, but I can't. My legs and arms are shaking too much. So I just lie there, coughing and wheezing, tears pouring from my eyes.

A hand touches my back and I jerk up, trying to force it away. Again, it's no use—I don't even budge it. "Evie. It's okay. I'm here," the voice says. "It's not real. Whatever it is you're seeing, it isn't real, but I am. And I'm going to help you. I just need you to trust me."

The voice is familiar, so I turn slowly to see who it is. The person is kneeling over me, the light in his hand facing down into the pool of water I'm lying in and reflecting up enough that I can see his face clearly.

"Asher?" I ask, feeling a huge amount of relief. There's no blood on him. His eyes are clear, if a little worried, but he's normal. *Normal!* And I can't hear the voices anymore.

He nods. "I'm right here. Don't worry."

Forcing myself to muster all the energy I have, I throw myself at him, burying my face into his shoulder. He falls back onto his butt, but holds me to him, his arms tight around my back. "It's okay. You're okay. Nothing is going to hurt you," he repeats over and over again, patting my back as if I were a fussy baby.

I can only sob and gasp into his shirt as the terror fades away and I remember where I am.

After a long while, I pull away and wipe my face on my sleeve, embarrassed by my behavior. *Tears are a weakness.*

He watches me for a moment, then says, "Are you okay?"

I nod and refuse to look at him. "Yes. I am. Now. I'm sorry. I don't know what happened. I saw . . . Gavin and a girl—Macie, I think . . ." I trail off when I realize he will have no idea what I'm talking about. *I don't even really know what I'm talking about; how can I expect him to?*

"It's okay. It's my fault. I shouldn't have brought you in here."

We sit quietly for a few minutes before he stands. "Can you walk?"

"I think so." Despite the fact that my legs still shake and burn as if they're on fire, I push myself up. No more tears. No more weakness, I promise myself.

"Don't worry. We'll figure a way out of here."

We try to retrace our steps, but I don't remember how I got to where I was, and Asher was too busy trying to keep up with me to pay attention. So we find ourselves exhausted, in pain, and thoroughly lost.

We eventually find a large supply room and Asher shines his light around it. One of the walls is stacked to the ceiling with boxes, but is otherwise empty. He shuts the door and shoves some of the bigger boxes in front of it, preventing anyone from entering without our knowledge.

"We should try to get some sleep," he says, and I nod. I'm absolutely exhausted. My head is foggy with it.

He goes through a couple of the easily reachable boxes, and dumps their contents onto the floor. It's nothing useful, of course. I don't even know what any of it is. However, he takes the now empty box and starts tearing it apart.

When he's finished doing whatever it is he's doing to it, he lays it down on the dusty floor, and gestures for me to lie on it. Exhausted, I curl up in the middle of it, surprised by how comfortable it actually is. It isn't exactly a feather bed, but it's a hundred times better than the cold, hard floor. However, even though it's not as cold in here as it was outside, I continue to shiver—huge shudders that wrack my body. It's in that moment that I really, really miss Gavin. My throat is thick with unshed tears.

He's never going to find us. When he finds the city, he's not going to find us and he'll think we left him and it's my fault again. A tiny voice in my head whispers that it doesn't matter because he's dead anyway, and *that* is my fault, too.

I curl tighter into a ball. No. He's not dead. I refuse to believe it.

Asher shuffles closer, looks down at me for a moment, then seems to make up his mind about something and crawls next to me, lying on his back and obviously taking care not to touch me. Instantly, I feel warmer with his body heat licking at my skin and I crave more of it. And even though a voice yells at me in my head not to, that skin-to-skin contact is punishable by death, I roll over and curl into his side, resting my head on his chest. He tenses immediately, but doesn't push me away. After some hesitation, his arms come around me, holding me to him.

Soon, our combined body heat makes sleeping bearable and I fall asleep, soothed by the sound of his heartbeat.

CHAPTER TEN

Due to possible biohazard or nanobot contamination, all personnel must exit through the decontamination stations and submit to a full body scan.

—SIGN BOLTED TO WALL IN UNDERGROUND FACILITY

Evie

I wake when Asher gets up. Although it's still as dark as before, my eyes are already adjusted and I can see fairly clearly now. It's obvious he's trying to be as quiet as possible, and if I hadn't noticed the drop in temperature between us, I probably wouldn't have awakened.

"Where are you going?" I sit up and rub at my scratchy eyes.

He starts, then turns around. "Sorry to wake you, Princess. I was going to try and find a way out of here."

"Without me?" That stings. That he'd just leave me all alone here. Especially after what I went through last night. I draw my knees up to my chest and hug them to me.

"Only temporarily. As soon as I found the exit, I would have come back for you."

I can't help but glare at him. "And if you ended up more lost? Then what?"

From the way his face twists up I can tell that wasn't something he'd considered. He confirms it when he doesn't say anything. It worries—terrifies—me that he'd leave me like that, but then again, I guess I can't really blame him either. I suppose after what happened last night, if I'd been in his position, the thought of trying to find the exit alone would have crossed my mind as well.

I push myself shakily to my feet and sway for a second when my head spins. It's not long, but obviously long enough to scare Asher as he rushes to me and slips an arm around my waist. I push him away.

"I'm not helpless. I can walk by myself. I just got up too fast. And I'm tired."

He removes his arm, but narrows his eyes at me, then turns back to the door. He moves the boxes out of the way, then flicks the flashlight back on. We try retracing the steps we took the night before, but it's hard. All of the corridors look the same, especially in the dark, and with all its corners and twists and turns it feels like a gigantic maze. I almost expect to wind up face to face with a sphinx, with a riddle to figure out.

We take our time, trying to remember each hallway we go through and create a map inside our heads. Asher keeps mumbling "Left, right, left, left" under his breath every time we turn a corridor or go down a set of stairs, and I'm tempted to be perverse and ask him which way to go. Left? Or right? Just to see him get flustered when he forgets the pattern. But I don't because I've lost track of the pattern myself and if he remembers it, it may be the only way we get out.

There's still a chill in the air, and it causes goose pimples to rise on my skin. The scent of mildew and something worse—something that I can't place—is thick and causes my already sore lungs to fight each and every breath. The light from Asher's flashlight is dim, and only reveals meters and meters of gray walls. The lack of color makes me feel like my eyes aren't focusing, and I find myself blinking too often. Sound travels strangely as we walk, sometimes echoing, sometimes seeming to swallow even the soft sounds of Asher's mumbles, my wheezing, and our shoes scraping against the debris on the floor. It has me on edge, but I don't say anything to Asher, just stay close to him. The only other sound is the occasional plop of water as it drips onto the floor, startling me every time.

In the back of my mind, I hear the echoes of memories trying to force their way up to the front, but I shove them back every time.

I won't have another attack. Not if I can help it.

As we walk, curiosity causes us to push open some of the doors. We use the flashlight to illuminate as much of the rooms as it can, which isn't much. Each one shows us something new. Some look like some sort of lab. Others are obviously sleeping quarters. And others are like nothing I've ever seen before. Even Asher has no clue what they could be. One of these rooms has odd machines set in a half circle around a strange bed. The machines look to be made of plastic and are really tall. At least as tall as Asher. All sorts of tubes and wires are hanging off each one and there's an accordioned attachment on the side of the machine. Silver metal boxes rest on top with the words "Halothane," "Isoflurane," and "Desflurane" on the side of them.

I frown and enter the room, trying to get a closer look.

"Evie! Get back here," Asher whisper-yells.

I ignore him and continue toward the machine. To the right and slightly above the strange metal boxes, there's a thing that looks like Gavin's television screen. Below the boxes there are four or so dials. Each dial has numbers and letters below it that look like some kind of chemical compound. And I have *no* idea how I know *that*.

There's a thick layer of dust on the contraptions, so obviously this place has been abandoned for a while. I open the top drawer of the machine and find syringes, medicine vials, and tubes. With a shudder, I quickly shut the drawer and turn toward the bed. Straps crisscross over the top and, like the machine, it's covered in dust.

"What is this?" I ask, trailing a finger over the strange machine.

"Anesthesia. It's used to put people to sleep for medical procedures and . . . experiments . . ."

How odd, I think and go back to join Asher, who takes my arm, firmly leading me out of the room.

Looking up at him, I ask, "Do you suppose that room was used for sexual experiments? Like a study in sexual response, perhaps?"

He stops in his tracks and looks down at me, his eyes wide. "What? No. Why would you think that?"

I shrug. "There was a bed, and the straps . . ." I trail off, blushing at the smile crawling over Asher's face.

"And what, pray tell, do you know about sexual practices that involve straps?" There's laughter in his voice.

I straighten my shoulders and lift my chin. *"I am well-versed in the ways of mating."* I frown. Where did that come from?

"You are, are you?" he says, still laughing. He threads my arm through his. "Well, then, do tell. I'm obviously not as 'well-versed' as you."

I have to laugh and lightly punch his arm. "You wish."

He laughs back. "Yes. Yes I do." But he drops it and we continue on our way.

Finally I spot a pinprick of light, growing brighter and brighter the closer we get.

Asher and I grin at each other, then rush to what looks like it could be the outdoors, but when we get to where the light is coming from, it's not an exit. It's a large wall-sized window. Curtains cover it, so it's impossible to see what the window shows, but we frown at each other. The confusion in his eyes mirrors my own. If we're underground, how is there a window?

We creep to it, and when Asher pulls the curtain away, I gasp. It's a window that looks directly into water. From the murkiness of it, it's easy to tell it's some kind of lake, though the glow of the surface isn't too far overhead. Asher looks over at me, then places a hand on my shoulder. "You okay?"

"Of course." But I swallow at the lump in my throat. This view reminds me of something, and it has my nerves tingling. I can't recall what it is, and that has me even more nervous. I'm grateful for Asher's presence. He studies me a bit longer, then shrugs and goes back to peering out into the water.

"I wonder why this is here," he says.

I don't have an answer, but I don't think he was looking for one anyway. My legs feel weak and it takes almost all of my strength to continue forward, but I step closer to get a better look. The water is a really light green and if I look up high enough, I can see through it to the surface. It's too dark to see the bottom.

The blood rushes out of my head and I feel a bit dizzy. I press a hand to the glass to steady myself.

I shift so I can see Asher. "I've never seen water this color before. Have you?"

He shakes his head—the way he does it makes me think he didn't really hear me—and goes back to staring at a metal nameplate on the side of the door. Just as I turn back to the water I hear him say, "Oh, Jesus."

Before I can ask him what's wrong, something slides across the glass. I jump, but figure it's probably just a fish. It *is* a lake after all. Maybe it's even a mermaid. I saw an old water stained and torn picture of one in Ann Marie's room and I've wanted to see a real one ever since. But when I eagerly lean closer, I scream.

And scream. And scream. I can't seem to stop myself from screaming.

The dark object sliding across the glass is a body. Well, what's left of the body anyway. The bottom half of it is missing and a lot of the skin appears to have melted away.

Asher spins me around so I'm facing away from the glass and forced to stare at him instead.

"Don't look, Evie. Just . . . don't look."

I stare into his eyes, trying to focus on them, but I can't. I can't think. Everything in me is telling me to run. I try to fight it; I know the thing on the other side can't hurt me. But despite that, I can't help but think—know—the body is going to break the glass, trying to get to us, and we'll either drown, or end up being eaten by it.

Asher rubs his hands up and down my arms, his voice soothing, even though I can't understand what he's saying, yet my mind still screams at me to run.

So that's what I do. I run. Back into the dark, and as far away from the window as I can get. Asher's behind me; I can hear his feet pounding behind me and I *want* to stop. But my body won't let me. It's like I'm on a runaway train with no way to get to the controls and stop myself from hurtling through the Tube at Mach 10.

"Evie!" Asher calls, and while I can hear the desperation, I can't even slow.

I just keep running, placing one foot in front of the other, as I try to locate the exit. Even when my lungs burn and spots flare into my eyes, I keep turning corners and pounding up stairs and banging through doors, hoping each one will bring me closer to the one that will set me outside.

Then, without warning, I burst out into the sunlight. My feet stumble when they hit the different texture of the sand after the concrete of the hallways, but surprisingly I don't fall. I just continue to run.

The light blinds me, but even then I don't stop. I can't. If I stop, even for a second, the monsters will get me.

"Evie! Stop! Don't go any further!" Asher yells from behind me. From the echo of his voice, I can tell that he's outside like me. There's even more desperation to his voice now and the pounding of his feet speed up.

Suddenly the ground underneath me slopes and I lose my footing just as something hits me in the back—hard. I land chest-first on the ground, all the air rushing from my body.

Whoever landed on me stays on my back and we're rolling down a hill, our limbs flailing wildly and getting caught on each other.

"Shit. Shit. Shit," Asher grunts in my ear and suddenly there's a jarring motion and we stop rolling, but we continue to slide for a few more meters before we're able to stop completely.

I immediately roll over onto my stomach and try to push up on my hands and knees, but I can't breathe, and can only manage a few strangled gasps.

Asher is yelling at me again, but I can't respond and the sunlight is still blinding me so I can't see him.

Finally, just as I feel I'm going to pass out, I manage to pull in a shaky breath, and collapse onto the ground, squeezing my eyes tightly shut as sweet, sweet oxygen fills my lungs.

Asher speaks directly into my ear. "Are you okay? Did you get hurt? Do you have any burns?"

I shake my head, and just continue to lie there, sucking in all the air I can get. It doesn't stop the burning in my lungs, or my pounding heart, but the spots in front of my eyes are slowly fading.

"Okay. That's good. That's very good." There's a thump next to me and he says, "I'm just going to lay here for a minute and catch my breath. Okay?"

I nod again.

For several minutes we lie next to each other, our breaths panting out before they slow and even out. I just want to lie here forever, but unfortunately, the foulest stench is assaulting my nose. I can't even describe it, but considering what I just saw, I'm sure it's dead bodies.

When I can breathe normally again, I slowly open my eyes, blinking against the bright sun, and even though it's bright and the sunlight stings my eyes, I can see. Frantically

I look around for the bodies to make sure they're nowhere near me.

But I don't see a single one. I frown. The smell is getting stronger and now it reeks exactly like the rotten eggs Gavin's mother found in the hen coop.

"Oh, Mother, what is that *smell*?" I sit up and cover my nose with my hand.

"Sulfur," Asher gasps, pushing himself up to a sitting position. "The lake. It's not a lake."

I look at him, wondering if he hit his head on a rock or something on the roll down. "I don't understand."

"There's no water in it. There must be a lava vent under it or something because it's all sulfuric acid now." He gestures to the lake, mere centimeters from our feet. "And if I hadn't tackled you, you would have run right into it."

CHAPTER ELEVEN

No admittance into Rushlake City will be authorized without this visa. Please safeguard this document as a replacement will not be issued if lost or stolen. Use of this visa constitutes acceptance of Rushlake City Community Standards. Only those individuals listed on visa will be accepted into the city.

—INSTRUCTIONS ON VISA

Evie

To say the thought that I would have run blindly into a poisonous lake doesn't terrify me would be a lie, so I decide it's better not to think about it at all.

"Thank you." My voice is so soft I almost can't hear myself.

Asher continues to look out over the acid water, before pushing to his feet. "We've got a long road ahead of us without Starshine and our supplies."

"Where's Starshine?"

"Probably waiting for us back at the town." He holds his hand out at me.

I take it and let him pull me up. "Aren't we in the town?"

He helps me up the slope, then gives me this lopsided smile. "See for yourself."

When I look at where I presume we came from, I only see a tiny little metal shack not much bigger than the door itself. It's the only thing for kilometers in every direction. All I see is brown dirt and blue sky. It looks just like when we stopped yesterday and waited for Gavin. The only difference is the gross-smelling not-water lake and the metal shack a few meters from it.

"Where did it go?" As soon as I say it, I realize how stupid a question it is. Between last night and this morning we could have walked kilometers underground. It's not the town that moved, but us. I did it again. With a groan, I sit back on the ground. "I'm so sorry."

Asher pulls me back to my feet. "It's as much my fault as yours. I'm the one who pulled you into that space. I should've thought that through a little better. If I'd known . . ." He trails off and I want to tell him there was no way he could have known I would do that. *I* didn't even know I would do that. But he continues. "We'd better get going. We've already missed most of the morning."

He starts in a fast walk and I have to rush to keep up.

"How do you know which way to go?" I ask.

He gestures to the sun. "Sun always rises in the east. Rushlake should be southwest of us. This is approximately southwest according to the placement of the sun."

"But . . . we're going back for Starshine first. And to wait for Gavin, right?"

He gives me a look. "No. We're continuing on, because I have no idea where that city was or how long it'll take to get back there. We're working on limited time as it is."

I stop walking. "We have to go back. We can go back in through the tunnels. We found our way out here, we can find our way back there."

He turns around and frowns at me. "No. We're not. We're lucky we made it out of there alive the first time. And who knows what the hell we breathed in all that time we were stuck in there. It was an accident that you managed to run in the right direction and we didn't run into . . . anything that might be in there. If I'd known what that place was, we never would have stepped foot in there."

"Well, then we'll just need to take . . ." Then I hear what he said last. "Wait. What? What was that place?" A chill crawls over my skin.

"Nothing we need to worry about now. We're out and we're not going back in." Asher turns to walk away, but I rush in front of him and stop, so he has no choice to do the same or run into me.

"You will tell me." I cross my arms over my chest and lift my chin.

"You really are a princess, aren't you?" He sighs. "It's an old bioengineering outpost. The military used them in the War to design bioweapons and supersoldiers. That bed you saw? They strapped willing—and unwilling—participants to it and conducted experiments on them. Painful, appalling experiments. The straps kept them from escaping during the process."

The blood drains from my head, but I stand my ground, despite the fact that it doesn't feel as solid as it did a minute ago. "That's horrible, but that place has obviously been abandoned for years, probably decades. And we can't just leave Starshine and Gavin behind." There's a tickle in the back of my throat again.

"We can. And we will." He touches the back of his hand to my cheek. "I'm sorry, Evie. I don't want to leave them behind either, but we're not going back into that place. There are probably spores from their bio experiments just waiting for some idiot to come across them. Like I said, we're lucky we even made it out in the first place."

"So we're just going to leave Starshine out here. To die." My blood boils and I clench my fingers into a fist, holding them tightly to my body. "And what about Gavin? He'll be looking for us in that city."

"Gavin can find his own way. And we're only going to leave Starshine for now. I'll send someone back for her when we get to Rushlake. It'll only be a day, two at the most. She'll be fine."

There's a pressure in my chest and it hurts to breathe. "Is that all you ever do?" I whisper, half because I'm so mad I can't speak and half because even that is excruciating to my lungs.

Asher drops his hand. His whole face goes blank. "What?"

"Whenever something becomes too difficult to handle, you quit? Whenever someone becomes an issue, you abandon them?" He steps toward me, but I step away from him. "Don't touch me," I rasp.

His mouth firms into a tight line and anger flares into his eyes, but he doesn't say anything, so I continue, "Is that what you're going to do to me when I get to be too difficult? Are you going to leave me behind? Just like you did to Gavin? What you're trying to do to Starshine? Admit it, you're thinking of leaving me now, aren't you?"

Spots flash into my eyes and my head is tingling, like it did just before that last hallucination. I know I have to be careful or I'll have another one.

Despite that, I can see the muscle in Asher's jaw flutter and his hands curl tight into fists when he says, "Of course not! I wouldn't ever ditch you. I'm doing all of this *for* you!"

"You willingly left Gavin to die and now you're doing the same to Starshine. What makes me different?" I demand. He doesn't say anything, so I push my face into his as darkness leaks into the sides of my vision. Despite my efforts not to, I have to grab ahold of his arms to stop myself from falling. "Tell me!"

"You just are. I'm not going to ditch you, ever. Okay?" He shoves a hand through his hair. "But God, Evie, look at you!" He takes me by my shoulders and gives me a little shake. "You're standing here arguing with me and you can't even stand up straight, you're so exhausted. You had not one, but *two* hallucinations. One that almost got you killed, the other that could have. I don't even know if you're going to make it to Rushlake as it is, let alone if we take the time to go back who knows how far. I'm not going to watch you die in front of me. I won't go through that again. We're not going back." He grabs my arm and starts dragging me in the direction he wants me to go.

I wrench my arm from his and sneer at him. "I'd rather die fighting, than live as a coward."

He stops and turns. His breathing is just as hard as mine, and I'm sure my eyes are filled with the same conflicting swirls of wild fear and anger. His nostrils flare and he narrows his eyes at me. "I doubt Gavin would agree." His voice is soft and unwavering even if he is staring daggers at me. "Do you really want him to go all the way to Rushlake only to find that you're not there? And the reason you're not there is because *you're too damned stubborn to walk there?*" He shouts the last part, startling me.

Regretfully, I have to admit he could be right. Gavin's far from stupid. And I don't want to give him any more cause for worry. With a sigh, I say, "Let's go."

He spins on his heel, and starts forward again. I rush to catch up to him and he walks next to me, but doesn't touch me. We don't even talk. I don't question him again about what direction to go, I just take his word for it. I have to. I have no sense of direction, and no reference for where we are.

We walk for hours and it doesn't take long for my body to protest every movement I make. I just want to sit back onto the ground, curl up into a ball, and sleep. That, of course, makes me miss Starshine even more as I probably could have slept the entire trip if she were here. But I keep the thought to myself, not wanting to start another fight.

We pass a few trees along our route, but it's mostly just desolate desert for as far as the eye can see. And between the sand and scorching sun, I'm so thirsty that if I were still near that acid lake, I'd be tempted to drink some of it.

The worst part is Asher has not said one word to me that wasn't an answer to something I asked, or to warn me about something. I'm a little taken aback by how I've already come to rely on his all-the-time-positive attitude.

As the sun burns high in the sky, I see what looks like a lake ahead. It's blurry, but shimmering in the sunlight. I grab Asher's arm. "Asher! Water!" My throat is hoarse and hurts to talk.

He doesn't even look, he only shakes his head. "No, it's a mirage."

"No, it's water. I'm sure of it." I try pulling him, to move him faster, but he only keeps moving at his steady pace.

"No use chasing after it," he says, huffing a little himself with each step. "It's not real. You'll only make yourself more thirsty."

I ignore him, though. It's water; I know it. It's not just some delusion I've concocted in my head. Not this time. So I let go of him and race ahead. But no matter how fast I move, how hard I push my muscles, and how much my lungs beg me to stop, the water stays exactly the same distance away. I can't get to it.

Unable to keep my pace up, I slow to the point that Asher catches up to me. "It's okay," he says. "It's happened to almost every one."

I nod, feeling stupid on top of being hot, sweaty, thirsty, sore, and tired. My chest hurts again and my breath is racing as fast as my heart, reminding me that I need to stop being stupid and start listening to what Asher says.

To keep myself occupied and my mind off the never-ending and sweltering sand, I play with the sand. Of course I'm not stopping to build sand castles or anything, but with each step the sand makes this strange dry, squishy sound and I like it. So each time I step, I wiggle my foot around so it makes the sound again and again.

Asher startles me when he chuckles. I gape at him. "What?" I ask.

He shakes his head. "Nothing."

But I'm not letting him get away with that, especially since it's the first *Asher* thing he's done in hours. I slide in front of him, turning to walk backward.

"What's so funny?"

"You."

His dimple flashes when he grins at me, and a little bubble of relief floats into me, but I pretend to frown. "Me? What's so funny about me?"

"You're like a little kid bouncing around and playing in the sand. It's funny."

"I'm not a kid."

"Ah! But you *are* little." He taps my nose. "And you should probably turn around before you trip over something—"

Of course at that moment, my foot finds the only hole in the entire desert and my ankle catches, which causes me to fall hard onto my butt. Asher, unable to stop in time, follows suit and lands on top of me, pinning me to the ground underneath him.

A sharp pain shoots up my leg, but it ends as soon as my foot is free of the hole. Laughing, I try to sit up, but Asher's too busy trying to see if he hurt me and we end up bumping heads.

"I'm so sorry," we say together, and then just sit there laughing and rubbing our heads.

It's probably more the hysterical kind of laughter than anything else, but it feels good to laugh, even if it's only for a minute.

He smiles down at me and I smile back up at him, but something in his expression changes and he stares down at me so intensely, I stop laughing. I shouldn't be here, like this, I think and quickly slide out from underneath him. I clear my throat. "We should probably keep going." I turn away so I'm not looking at him.

After a minute he stands, but he doesn't hold out a hand for me this time and I'm sure we're back to silent Asher. With a sigh, I push myself to my feet on my own.

We keep going like that until the sun starts to lower in the west, leaving only a reddish pink sky and some violet clouds. The temperature starts dropping considerably the further the sun lowers.

"Any idea where we are?" I ask him when I realize we might be stuck in the desert with those dog beasts and no way to beat them this time. No way to outrun them. And no supplies or a way to keep warm through the night.

"No," he says, "but I don't think we have long. Those trees over there look familiar to me. See that tree in the front? The one that looks all twisty, like one tree is wrapped around the other? My father and I would stop there to rest every time we came this way."

I glance to where he's gesturing, and shiver. It's almost like the woods we stayed in the first night. "We're not going to go through there, are we?"

"Afraid so. No other way." He pats my arm as if to soothe my fears. Although he doesn't look very happy about our only option either.

I swallow. "But what about those birds?"

"They sleep at night, so if we go as far as we can tonight—hopefully getting on the other side of those trees—then wake up early, I don't think we'll have to worry about them."

"Are you sure?"

He looks down and at me, his eyes meeting mine. "No. I wish I was, but I'm not."

I can't help but compare Asher to Gavin in this moment. If Gavin were here, he would reassure me, even if he had to bend the truth. Asher always tells me how it is—always. Asher trusts me to be able to handle the truth. Even if it's bad. I like that. A lot. I'd much rather have the truth than have something sugar-coated to spare my "delicate" feelings.

To pay him back for his trust in me, I shrug and step forward. "Are you coming? Or are you going to stand there all day?"

We get to the tree line just as the sun is setting. I listen for the sound of wings, but the only sounds are crickets and the wind teasing the scrub oak leaves. As we walk, I wonder how the trees are getting water. Surely there has to be something nearby to keep them all hydrated and alive. I try not to spend too much time thinking about it. It's a waste of energy that should and could be spent on getting out of the small forest alive and well. But every time I lick my chapped lips, I'm reminded of exactly how dehydrated I am.

It's hard to tell when the sun actually sets, because the woods are so dark. The chill of the night is obvious though. My wheeze, which was easier to ignore in the heat of the day, sounds too loud in the tree-covered night. I worry I might cover up the sound of approaching animals, or worse yet, attract them to us.

"Maybe we should stop for the night."

"We have to keep going. Just a little bit longer, until we get to the tree line. If there are vulture-hawks, I want to be able to run into the light quickly."

"What about those beast-dogs?"

"The coyotes?" He continues before I can answer. "They *are* nocturnal, so let's try to stay quiet and move as quickly as possible."

I swallow at the lump in my throat, but do as he recommends. Hours later, when I'm continuing on nothing more than willpower alone, I hear Asher say, "Just a little further," for what feels like the thousandth time, but this time there's excitement in his voice.

I look up and gasp when I see the orange-black horizon of the rising sun just past the trees.

"Tree line," I whisper and dart forward to it, ignoring the aches and pains that cover my body.

Asher is close behind and we both make the same awed noise when we see the towers of buildings reaching up into the sky in the distance. It's probably less than five kilometers away.

"Come on!" I giggle, and tug on his arm. "We're almost there."

He allows himself to be pulled across the small plains before we get to a large body of water. A few hundred meters in is an island, where Rushlake city waits. There's a red footbridge that leads across the water to the island city with its huge buildings that sparkle and scrape the sky.

I trudge onto the bridge, nearly weeping at the thought of being so close. To sitting. To water. There's a guard station on the other side that I keep my eyes fixed on. I only have to make it that much farther, I am certain of it. But even these last fifty meters can't be easy. In my hurry, my foot catches on one of the loose planks and I crash onto the ground. I'm so exhausted I find it almost impossible to push myself up, but I finally manage, my legs shaking with the effort. The muscles in my jaw ache with thirst. I'm dizzy with it. There is water on the other side of this blasted bridge and I will crawl to it if I have to.

I take a determined step, but my energy is finished. My legs buckle, and I have a moment of thinking I might just have to crawl, when Asher swoops me up in his arms. He carries me across the rickety bridge, chest heaving with the effort. My stomach summersaults when the bridge sways wildly under his feet, but he keeps me held fast.

At the far end, two bored guards wait. Neither of them offers to help Asher, even when we're well within shouting distance. In fact, neither of them moves until we're at their station, and then it's only to demand to see our visa. Asher sets me on my feet to get out the letter from his father. The guard takes his time, inspecting each word as if he has just learned to read. I take the chance to study our surroundings. The guards' outpost is just a tiny wood building, not much bigger than the guard and his partner. It's set off to the side of a concrete platform, which has steps leading down to one of those large asphalt paths that were in the abandoned city.

When the guard is convinced our papers are in order, he lets us pass, then puts out a call to Asher's grandmother to come pick us up at the guard's station; she is going to keep us while we look for a doctor that can help me.

Asher tries leading me away toward the steps, but I pause. "What about Gavin?"

"What about him?"

"How will he get in? He doesn't have a visa. The guards won't let him in."

His eyes fill with something that looks like regret—maybe sadness—but then he sighs. "Wait here."

He turns back around and talks to the guard. His words slur in his exhaustion. "There was another member of our party. His name is Gavin Hunter." He pulls out the visa again, then points to Gavin's name. "He was separated from us in the Outlands. Will you make sure he's able to get into the city and call my grandmother when he arrives?"

"Yes, sir," the guard says. "I'll just place his name in the book. But, between you and me," he glances at his partner, "you might want to come up and check yourself for the next few days. Not everyone checks the book. . . ."

At first I'm not sure what he's getting at by letting his words trail off like that, but then the word *bribe* enters my mind. Without our supplies, we have nothing to offer the guards. Nothing to ensure Gavin's name will even make it into the book, much less earn him passage into the city.

"I understand. Thank you," Asher says, stifling a yawn. The guard appears disappointed, but says nothing.

I stare at Asher, desperate for a solution. I know he thinks Gavin didn't make it, but in my heart I know he's still out there. If I had any money, I would give it all to ensure his safety. I hate being dependent on Asher. I hate that we don't have anything to offer these lazy men. My eyes sting, but I'm too dehydrated to cry.

"I'll have someone from my grandmother's house bring them what they want," he whispers to me.

"Thank you." I press a hand to my trembling lips, grateful for even this small promise.

"Anything for such a pretty lady." Even though his voice

lacks the normal smoothness that he instills into each syllable, his eyes sparkle in amusement when he says it.

I laugh, grateful for the relief, and roll my blurry eyes.

We sit at the bottom of the steps on the other side of the guard station. My back aches from the hard stone beneath my sore hips, but the relief from sitting and making it to the city is sweet and, just when I find myself starting to fall asleep, a huge hunk of metal squeals to a halt in front of us. I pull my feet away from it, gasping and pressing a hand to my racing heart.

I glance up at Asher. "That's a car," I say, astonished.

He chuckles. "Yes, it's a car. It's my grandmother's car, in fact."

"It works?" I ask, dumbfounded and continuing to stare at the big machine. It looks the same as those other ones—the ones in the abandoned city—but it's shiny and actually moving. It's kind of pretty, really.

This time he snorts and his laugh is deep, seeming to come from deep in his chest. "I should hope so, or Grandmother wouldn't be a very happy woman."

As if on cue a person rushes around to the back of the car from the opposite side and pulls a lever on the side of it. A door opens and a woman with steel gray hair steps through the opening. She smiles when she sees Asher, then turns the smile to me, but it wobbles and her eyes widen when I smile back.

She shoots a glance at Asher. "This is her?" she asks in this deep, smoky voice.

He nods and slips an arm around my waist, pulling me toward him in a possessive manner I'm not entirely sure I like. "Yes. This is Evie."

She grabs my chin gently in her surprisingly smooth hands. She stares at me and I firm my lips into a line. I don't like how closely she's studying me, as if she recognizes me somehow. Then she startles me when her lip quivers and her eyes become shiny.

"Eli," she whispers.

I peek at Asher, who knit his brow together.

"Grandma?" he asks.

She steps away with a shake of her head. "I'm sorry, dear. For a minute, you reminded me of someone I used to know." She hugs Asher and pulls me into the same hug. "Come on. You'll both be more comfortable after a hot shower and some clean clothes."

Wary, but grateful, I step forward into the car and slither onto the car's backseat next to Asher's grandma and wait for Asher to slide in after me.

CHAPTER TWELVE

Adolescent female of European descent. Extreme pallor, signs of dehydration, multiple wounds in various stages of healing. Patient cooperative, but semi-conscious, unable to provide any details of how injuries were sustained.

—EXCERPT FROM TREATMENT NOTE OF RUSHLAKE CITY PHYSICIAN

Evie

Asher's grandmother hands both Asher and me bottles of water, but warns us to drink slowly. However, both of us are too thirsty to listen and we gulp down three of the bottles before the car even starts moving. My stomach clenches at first, but I will myself to keep the liquid down. I'm not going to waste a drop.

I'm just finishing my third bottle when we zoom away from the curb. Even though I haven't been in the car that long the heat inside makes me sleepy. It seems all the walking—stumbling—with little to no sleep has taken its toll. Even

still, I can't help but gawk at the city as we pass each building. I've never seen anything like it. With the sun rising over
the horizon, the sky is an orangish color that's reflected
directly on the glass structures, giving Rushlake City a lost-
in-a-rainbow look.

Rainbows are one of my absolute favorite things here. The
first time I saw one was right after getting home—Gavin's
house—after being in the hospital. Right before sunset, a
double rainbow arced across the sky. It was gorgeous. I had
to run to get Gavin and have him tell me what it was. The
city reminds me of that moment. Impressive. Simply gorgeous. And it takes my breath away to look at it.

As we travel, Asher leans over and points out different
buildings and landmarks. They're so completely different
from the ones in the village. Even though it's obvious they're
older than the newest buildings in the village—and much,
much taller—everything is practically perfect. There are no
cracks. The windows glimmer. They're actually pretty. And
clean. Really, really clean. As if they've never seen a spot of
dirt in their lives. With all the dirt and sand and mud I've
seen just in the last few days, I don't even know how that's
possible.

The tall buildings are called skyscrapers and they hold
a host of different businesses. From things called banks to
restaurants and everything in between. Interspersed between the skyscrapers are smaller single-business buildings.
On one corner there is a smallish building made completely

out of metal and glass. Asher says it's his favorite restaurant. He says it serves pizza, and the way he describes it makes my mouth water.

When we get to the city center, he points out a park. It's still foggy as the sun burns away the cold of night, but I can see the beautiful trees and shrubs. And, in the very center, a tall statue of a man.

I turn to Asher. "Is that a real statue?"

He nods, but doesn't smile like I expected. "That's Michael Rush, founder of Rushlake City." He gives me a look. "Well, he's sort of the founder. This was originally a part of a different, larger city, but during the War the main municipality was destroyed. I'm not exactly sure how the whole story goes, but he owned a lot of the land on this peninsula. When the city was destroyed, the connecting piece of land was severed and this part became an island. After the War, Michael Rush rebuilt the city and built walls around the entire island to protect it. He became the city manager and anyone who wanted to have protection from the dangerous Outlands could come here. If they could afford to pay the Tithe."

"Tithe?"

"It's basically a protection tax. You pay him a certain amount every month, or year, or whatever and he keeps you safe and sound." He looks past me, out the window. "It works, because this place is almost exactly like cities were before the War. Sure, some things are different as technology and everything gets better, but for those who wanted things to be the same—for the ones who wanted to pretend like it never happened—this is perfect for them. And they're willing to pay for it. Pay for the illusion of safety. For a false peace. Deceptive freedoms." He looks back at me, his eyes dark, hard, and cold. "Even if sometimes the cost is *more* than just money."

"Asher . . ." his grandmother says with a warning in her voice.

He clears his throat and as he does it, his eyes clear, too. "And . . . it looks like we're almost home."

I want to know more about the protection tax, but I'm sure I won't get any answers when his grandmother is around. So I turn my attention back to the passing landscape. On either side of the car are smaller buildings. They remind me a bit of Gavin's house, but they're squished closer together and they're taller, which makes them look thinner. I stare at them, but I don't pay them much attention. My mind keeps wandering to Gavin and I fight to keep it focused on what is happening now. If I think about him, I'll worry, and there's no reason to worry right now. He's coming. I know he is. He's just a little behind.

The driver pulls up in front of one of the larger houses and gets out to open the door as he did before. Asher's grandmother steps out first, then Asher scoots around me and turns to offer me his hand.

His grandmother's house is stunning. Easily the most amazing of all the houses on this street. Judging by the windows, it's three stories tall, which is the same as Gavin's house but this one seems larger somehow, more imposing. Concrete steps lead up to a set of magnificent wood and glass doors. On either side of that, two large windows jut out from the brick siding at strange angles.

"What do you think?" Asher asks in my ear.

"It's . . . it's amazing." I can't keep the awe from my voice.

"Are you going to keep the girl in the cold all day, Asher?" his grandmother asks.

He shakes himself and says, "Uh . . . no." He looks a little embarrassed, but offers me his arm to help me up the steps. "This way."

Just before I pass through the door a blast of freezing wind makes me shiver.

"Let's get you to your room," Asher says. "You can take a nice hot shower. By that time, I'm sure Cook will have breakfast ready."

I nod and let him escort me to my room. Along the way I stare, amazed at how much wood is in the house. Everything is wood. The stairs. The walls. The furniture in the rooms I pass. Even the floors.

The most surprising—in a completely fantastic way—is the bathroom. Two large wooden doors open into a large room at least twice the size of Gavin's bathroom. The walls have pretty gray tile crawling halfway up the walls. The rest of the wall to the ceiling, which is I don't know how many meters above my head and has a window in it that I can see through to the beautiful blue sky, is more wood.

Attached to this first room is another, smaller room, which has big black square tiles up the entire wall and along the floor. Upon closer inspection, I realize that the smaller room is actually a really large, luxurious shower. Glass doors section that room in half with one half being the shower, and the other holding white robes on hooks. Underneath the hooks, towels are folded neatly on a wooden bench.

In the main part of the room, there's a low-to-the-ground, egg-shaped bathtub where the faucet comes straight out of the wood paneling, allowing water to fall into the tub. It looks deliciously inviting, but I'm afraid I'll fall asleep if I use it, so I figure I'll shower instead.

Asher shows me where everything is and how it all works. It's different from the village. For one, we don't have to ration the water. I can take as long of a shower as I want. And there's a heater built into the ceiling. I don't even have to switch on a pump like at Gavin's house.

The hot water sluices away days of dirt and grime, stinging the fresh wounds on my leg and shoulder, while the old bullet wound just stirs with its familiar throb. As refreshing as the water is, I'm achy, and confused, and my heart feels heavy every time I think of Gavin. Which is pretty much always. I don't bother to look at any of the scrapes and cuts and bruises crisscrossing my body, and I specifically avoid looking at my shoulder.

When I finish, I slip into one of the robes, then limp into the bedroom. Asher's grandmother is waiting for me. She's sitting on the bed, holding something red and silky-looking in her weathered hands. She holds out the fabric when she sees me.

"Here, they're pajamas. They should fit you well enough."

With a murmured "Thank you," I take them, and hobble back into the bathroom to pull them on. They're cool to the touch and so soft I can't help but coo a little when the fabric rubs against my wind, sand, and sunburned skin.

When I come back, adjusting the top over the bottoms, Asher and his grandmother are sitting at a little table in the corner of the bedroom. There are bowls set out and when I sit at the empty seat, Asher ladles soup into the bowl in front of me.

At first I gobble it down, along with the bread his grandmother places on a plate next to me. Asher does the same and there's no other sound except the scraping of our spoons against the bowls and the occasional slurp as we drink.

But my mind keeps circling back around to Gavin. How he's still out there. Somewhere. Probably hungry and hurt. Burning under the heat of the sun as it shoves the chill of night rudely away. All of the things Asher and I were, but now aren't. I don't know what else to do about it, though, so I just keep eating. Keep feeling guilty. Keep aching for him.

Finally full, I push the bowl away and rest my chin on my palm as Asher and his grandmother get caught up. I'm trying to come up with a plan to find Gavin, but my eyelids feel so heavy I'm having trouble keeping them open. Eventually I stop fighting it and close them, promising myself that I'm just going to rest my eyes and let myself drift to the ebb and flow of their voices.

After a few minutes, his grandmother says, "Aw, the poor

dear. She's falling asleep in her soup." There's a pause before she continues, "You used to do that when you were a babe. It was so cute to see your little head bob and sway as you tried to stay awake, but couldn't."

"Grandma," Asher sighs. Then, even though I don't hear the chair move, I feel myself being lifted.

Asher grunts a little when he picks me up, then he places me in the bed and pulls the soft blankets over me. I fall instantly to sleep.

I wake in a panic, my mind swirling with images of Gavin and giant birds. Those horrible beast-dogs. I sit straight up, gasping and scanning for danger. It takes me a minute to calm down and remember I'm in Asher's grandmother's house and I'm safe. Well. Safe from anything other than myself. My mind immediately goes to Gavin and how we just left him. In the woods. With man-eating birds. To die.

"No! He isn't dead," I say aloud. He's a fighter. He's probably just slower than we were. We had a horse for most of it, after all. And we found that underground place. That probably cut off kilometers from our trip. Maybe he's just stuck outside the gates and they won't let him in.

But all my reasoning fails to silence the nagging voice in my head that tells me he's dead. And it's my fault. For being weak. For being soft. For being damaged.

Because, if I'd been none of those, we wouldn't have been out there in the first place.

There's a knock on the door and I sit up straighter in the

bed. I force a smile to my lips when Asher pokes his head around the door. "Hey, you're awake! Wonderful. I was getting worried there."

I give him a confused smile. "Why?"

"You've been asleep for almost thirty-six hours. The doctors said your body just needed the sleep, though. I guess they were right. Are you hungry?"

Thirty-six *hours*? An entire day and half of another? *Surely* Gavin's arrived by now. I peer around Asher to see if anyone else came with him. "Where's Gavin?"

His mouth draws into a straight, thin line. He picks at something on his shirt; then, when he realizes what he's doing, he shoves his hands in his pockets before looking down at this feet. "He's . . ." He clears his throat, and I want to throw something at him. Part of me already knows what he's going to say. ". . . he hasn't arrived . . . yet."

Even though part of me had been expecting that answer, I still have to stop myself from screeching *What?* "I've been here almost two days and he's *still* not here?"

He doesn't say anything, only stares at the ground as if it might swallow him whole. Maybe he wishes it would.

Unable to remain sitting, I thrust myself to my feet. Although my legs are shaky and weak, I stumble my way over to the balcony and shove open the doors with Asher not far behind me. It's cold, but I lean against the metal railing. My breath puffs out in plumes in front of my face. The balcony overlooks the house next door, but in my mind's eye I'm picturing the Outlands.

Too long. Entirely too long. No food. No water. Way too long.

Asher steps up beside me and places his hand on my shoulder.

I can't help it. I blurt out, "Do you think Gavin's just stuck outside the gates? That that's why he hasn't come yet?"

The hand on my shoulder tightens and I know what he's going to say before he does. I keep talking so that I don't have to hear it.

"Maybe we should have left the visa there with them. Maybe we should go there and see. Maybe he's waiting for us and wondering why we haven't come."

He turns me around slowly to face him, his face a mask of misery.

He can't be gone. He can't be gone.

"Evie. He's not there."

Panic rises up in me, and I try pushing it back down, but it's almost impossible. I know any minute I'm going to lose it. I'm going to fall apart. Right here. Right now. I wrap my arms around my waist as if I can keep myself together that way. "How do you know? You can't know that."

"I do. I've gone every day to check with the guards to see if he's shown."

I curl into myself. "But he could be there *now*!" I try to make it sound like I believe it myself, but even I know I'm not very convincing. "We should head over there and see if he's waiting."

He shakes his head. "He's not coming, Evie. The odds of him getting away from the vultures were extremely slim.

And even if he did," he barrels on, ignoring my open mouth, obviously knowing what I was going to say, "he'd have been hurt, with no food or water. In the Outlands it's been over a hundred degrees every day this week during the day, and near freezing at night. Not to mention the coyotes and the wolves. There's no way he made it through all that."

My heart lurches in my chest and I stagger against the railing. I have to close my eyes against the pain, but still I can see him perfectly. His golden hair blowing in the breeze from the birds' wings and his beautiful gray eyes staring into mine as Starshine raced from him. I can see, now, he knew then he wasn't going to make it. When he said "I love you," what he really meant was "Good-bye."

Suddenly I'm so angry, it wouldn't surprise me to actually see red seeping into the corners of my eyes. "And whose fault is that? *You left him!* You wouldn't let me go back for him! It's your fault. Yours!" I scream at him.

He only nods, which makes me even angrier. "I know."

I can't stop myself—I punch him in the chest. But he doesn't even stop me. Which makes me even angrier and I punch him again. And again. It isn't making me feel any better, it just makes me more irate with each hit. Because he doesn't even *try* to stop me.

Obviously I'm not hitting very hard, because he doesn't move, doesn't even wince. He only continues to stare at me with those pain-filled eyes.

That just infuriates me more. How dare he just stand there and take it? How dare he not even fight back—not even tell me I'm wrong. That it's really *my* fault that Gavin's gone. Probably dead. Why is he just standing there taking it?

My mind's a jumble of emotions and thoughts. Pain. Anger. Sorrow. Frustration. Back to pain.

It isn't until the tears I hadn't noticed blind me and I can't breathe that Asher stops me, taking my wrists into his hands.

Exhausted, I slump against him, sobbing into my hands. My heart is cracked in so many places, it's hard to imagine it ever getting put back together completely.

"He can't be gone," I whisper, not because I don't believe he's dead, but because I need him. And I know it's really my fault he's gone. He'd always been there when I needed him, but I wasn't there the one time he needed me.

Asher lowers us so that we're both kneeling on the floor. And despite the fact that I just spent the last who-knows-how-long hitting him, he gathers me into his arms and holds me. Not saying a word, simply holding me.

The doors to the room open, but he shakes his head and whoever it was leaves, shutting the door quietly behind them.

CHAPTER THIRTEEN

Not since the Gutenberg printing press has anything had such a profound impact on the peoples of this world as the nanorevolution. Nanotechnology, developed in part by Lenore Allen, changed the entire course of the War in favor of those in possession of the technology.

—EXCERPT FROM *A BRIEF HISTORY OF THE 21ST CENTURY,* "NANOREVOLUTION"

Evie

After a long time, I finally cry myself out. Asher still holds me tightly against him. I push gently away, brushing the tears from my face with my sleeve, and look up to the stars. I'm too tired to pull completely away from Asher and it feels so nice, I don't really want to anyway. It's the small comforts now. The cold wind bites and snaps at my skin, but I don't care.

"They're not as pretty here," I say, thinking of that last night with Gavin in the clearing. Just us two. Lying next to each other, discussing the stars. It makes me sad. They kind of remind me of myself with their faded lights, and I'm reminded that every day I'm fading. Without Gavin, I have nothing to anchor me to my old life. Who I used to be.

"No, they're not." His voice is soft. "It's all the lights. They're jealous of the stars, and try to drown them out."

I know it's not true, but it's a nice thought.

We sit, both of us lost in our thoughts. I know something is bothering him, but I also know that he'll tell me what it is. Especially if it has something to do with me. That's one of the things I like about Asher. His unwavering honesty. No matter how terrible—or how difficult—he will *always* tell me the truth. Even when I don't want him to.

My mind flits over to Gavin and my heart squeezes. I miss that stupid little smile he gets when he looks at me and doesn't think I'm looking. I miss the way just the touch of him makes my heart swell, and how he looks at me like I'm the only one in the world. Or at least the only one that matters. I miss how he paces every time he's frustrated, or trying to figure something out, or nervous. I even miss that he *doesn't* tell me everything. Even as frustrating as that can be.

"They did some tests. While you were out. The test results came back," Asher says, yanking me from my thoughts.

"Hmm?" I turn to face him. I'm numb now. I can't seem to find the energy to care about the results, but for Asher's sake, I try to force enthusiasm. "Oh. That's great. Any news?"

"Nothing we don't know already."

I nod and turn my face back up to the stars. That didn't

seem all that bad, but Asher still acts like something is bothering him.

"The doctor wants to draw more blood tomorrow. Talk with you, too. If you're up to it."

I sigh, but nod. That's not entirely unexpected, either. And again, I don't really care. "Of course. Whatever he thinks is necessary."

"Evie? Look at me." His voice is still low, but there's something in his tone that has fear pushing past the numbness.

I turn to face him, furrowing my brow.

"They want to study your nanos. They think that . . . that they might have something to do with you being sick."

"My . . . nanos?" Nanos were what destroyed that town. What turned living, breathing people into rock and stone. My hand shakes and I frown even more as terror makes my heart kick in my chest. "I have *nanos* in me? How do you know?"

"Gavin told me," he says without meeting my eyes. "I—I thought you knew that."

Another of Gavin's omissions. For a minute, anger chases the terror away. So, even though there's bad blood between Asher and Gavin, Gavin still told Asher things about me. Maybe even everything about me. *Asher* was good enough to trust with *my* secrets, but not me.

When Gavin gets here, I'm so going to tell him exactly what I think about that, and then I'm going to demand he tell me absolutely everything. And if he thinks he can talk himself out of this one, he's got another think coming.

But then I remember Gavin isn't here. Isn't coming. Ever. And that numbness returns, replacing the anger. Concealing the fear. And then I can only nod.

I knead my skirt in my hands, pulling and tugging softly at the fabric. "I see. So are they like the ones that killed those people? Am I going to turn into stone like they did?"

Something like sadness flashes before his eyes and he stretches out his hand. Probably to take my hand, but I slide it out of reach.

He rakes it through his hair instead and tugs on the ends. "Yes. And no. It's not the same kind, I guess. More . . . complex or something. They don't really know, but they want to find out."

"So . . . I won't turn to stone?"

He shakes his head. "They don't think so. From what Gavin said, you've had them a long time and they were meant to help . . . not hurt. They just want to do more testing to see if they're malfunctioning."

I'm grateful for the numbness I feel. Being numb is so much better than being afraid. Better than feeling your heart break into tiny pieces. Better than any of the emotions I could—probably *should*—be feeling right now.

"Of course. Whatever they think is necessary."

My voice is flat as I say it and I know Asher's worried, but he only sighs.

"You don't have to worry." He grabs my hand and squeezes it before I can pull away again. "I'll be there for you. I won't leave you by yourself. I promise."

For a minute, a spark of anger ignites in me again. I remember Gavin saying that in the village right before the trip. And, softly, in the back of my head like an echo of a memory, I hear someone else saying it.

I can't stop myself from saying, "I've heard that before." I turn away from him as self-pity pricks at my heart. "But it's a lie. It's *always* a lie."

CHAPTER FOURTEEN

The answer to our problem has fallen in our laps, gentlemen. One of my son's friends has made a marvelous find. A young girl, the heir to a throne it would seem, from a city under the ocean. I know what you are thinking, and at first I didn't believe it either, but I've watched this girl and talked with the village doctor. She is most certainly different from any young woman we've ever seen. She appears quite ill, although it's unclear whether it's emotional or physical, and I think we would find it most beneficial to bring this child under our wing and offer our help in return for hers.

—Letter from Mayor St. James to Dr. Trevin, couriered by Asher

Evie

Asher says he checks the gate, but I also know he thinks Gavin's dead, so who knows if he actually does. I'm fairly certain they're not going to let me go out on my own. I've asked twice already, and both times they've said no and changed the subject.

I don't pretend I don't know why, but I'm going to check for myself. So I plan. And I plot.

I walk slowly to the bedroom. Asher's grandmother's eyes bore into me as I do and she slowly puts her knitting to the side.

"Bathroom," I murmur, not meeting her eyes, but out of the corner of mine, I see her sit back and resume her knitting.

I slip through the crack in the door, then tread to the bathroom, making sure my steps are loud, but not so loud they sound like I'm making them that way. I open and close the door, then sneak back down the hallway. I'm still sore all over, but I grit my teeth and keep going.

At the front door, I edge out, keeping an eye out for Asher, or his grandmother, or the maid, but no one stops me. Still, I don't take a full breath until I'm blocks away from Asher's house.

It takes me a while and several stops to rest and ask for directions, but finally I find my way back to the bridge.

Panting, I force myself up the steps and to the guards' box. They're not the same ones we'd met when we first arrived, but they look just as disinterested. They don't even lift an eyebrow when I knock on the window.

"Visa," the one closest to the door says, his voice flat.

"Um . . . I actually don't have one, but—"

He points to a sign on the window.

"No visa, no admittance to the Outlands," the other one says, repeating what the sign says in a bored voice. He has red hair and skin even more pale than mine. I can't help but stare at him. He seems so strange-looking, like he has shred-ded carrots on his head. "Go to City Hall and get one, then come back."

I force myself to meet his green eyes. "I—I don't actually want—"

"Go get the visa and come back."

"I'm not here to leave, I just want to find—"

He leans on the windowsill and interrupts me yet again. "Look, little girl, I don't really have time for this." He points to the sign and turns around.

The way he says "little girl" sets my nerves on edge. I nar-row my eyes and purse my lips. "My *name* is Evelyn Win-ters. I am Daughter of the People of the great city of Elysium. I am a guest of the St. James family. You will not speak to me as if I'm some foolish young child . . ." I look down my nose at him. ". . . or an ordinary commoner."

Where did *that* come from?

The two guards exchange an anxious look while I try to ignore the questions flying through my mind about my sud-den confidence.

But, finally I see I have their attention when they turn back to me. "We apologize, Ms. Winters, we don't mean any insult to you or the St. Jameses, but we still can't let you into the—" the dark-haired one says.

This time I break into what they're saying, and wave them off. "I am here to see if an Outlander has attempted to enter. His name is Gavin Hunter."

Confusion crosses their faces, but the one with red hair

shakes his head. "No one has entered this way since we've been here, ma'am."

Dejection blows throw me and my legs tremble, but I force myself to remain standing. I turn toward the Outlands, squinting into the growing darkness. He's out there. He has to be. I take one step, then another before one of the guards calls out, "Ma'am! Are you okay?"

I mentally shake myself, my shoulders drooping. "Fine." I swallow and clear my throat. "I'm fine." Forcing my shoulders back again, I turn back around and slowly, achingly make my way back to Asher's.

Hours later, I open Asher's door, intending to go straight up to my room and back to sleep. But I stop dead in my tracks when I hear raised voices coming from one of the doors to my left.

"How could you just let her sneak out?" Asher yells.

I follow the voices and stand in the open doorway to see Asher glaring at his grandmother, who sits in a large wingback chair. He has his arms crossed over his chest.

"I didn't know she was going to sneak out, Asher."

"But you had to have seen her leave her room."

"Of course I did. She said she needed to use the bathroom." He makes a sound in his throat and walks to behind his grandmother. "I'm not going to keep the girl prisoner in her room, Asher." She turns to continue to watch him, then stops when she sees me. She smiles and folds her hands in her lap. "There. See? Everything is fine."

Asher spins around. His whole face lights up when he sees

me. He rushes across the room, tugs me to him, and hugs me so hard, I'm certain my head is going to pop off.

"Where have you been?"

I swallow. "I went to see if anyone at the gate has seen Gavin." I push away from him and hug myself. "They haven't."

The room is silent and heavy with it until Asher sighs. "Come on. Let's get dinner." He slings his arm around my shoulders and leads me to the dining room where food has already been set out. I don't want to eat. I don't even want to think about eating. Just the thought reminds me that Gavin hasn't had food.

Several minutes into dinner, I push from the table, interrupting whatever Asher and his grandmother are talking about. I have to get away from here. From them. I need to be anywhere but here.

I make it as far as the door before Asher catches me. He grabs my wrist and tugs gently, stopping me from leaving. "It's not your fault," he says quietly. "It's no one's fault. He was protecting you." He frowns at me. "You know that, don't you?"

I rub my hand under my running nose. "But he wouldn't have *had* to protect me if I hadn't been so weak. If I hadn't forced him to come here."

"Weak?" He laughs. "You think you were weak? You totally kicked ass! The way you took care of those vulture-hawks was like something out of a comic book."

I lift my brows at him. "You make that sound like it's a good thing, when all it does is make me a . . . freak." That was one of Gavin's little brother's words. It was a word he liked to use. A lot. I'd made him tell me what it meant and, ever since, I'd known it applied to me.

Anger flashes across Asher's eyes and he takes my face in his hands, forcing me to look at him. "You are not a freak. You hear me? *Different* doesn't make you a freak. *Different* makes you special. And special is good. Special is what makes you *you*. That's who Gavin loved. He thought you were amazing and wonderful and . . . perfect just the way you are."

He's saying it to make me feel better, but all it does is make me sigh and try to look away. "My brand of perfect is what killed Gavin." I sigh and wave away what he opens his mouth to say, "Besides, I wish people would stop saying that. Everyone is always telling me how perfect I am. How beautiful. How *lucky* I am. To be this amazing, perfect person. How Mother hand-chose me, *because* I'm perfect. But I'm not. I'm not amazing. Or wonderful. I'm not perfect. I'm damaged," I whisper.

I'm not sure what I'm saying, where any of this is coming from. I don't know who told me so. Certainly no one here, but it's true. And it only proves my point . . . I'm *not* perfect.

His face blanches. "What did you say?"

"That I'm damaged?"

"No. About being hand-chosen by Mother. Why did you say that?"

I'm about to answer that I don't know when I'm suddenly not in the foyer. I'm somewhere else. Somewhere very familiar.

Glass walls and marble floors surround me. Behind the glass is another wall, one of water. I have my hand pressed against it, staring into the endless blue. I'm sad about something, but I can't remember what. Only that my heart is heavy with it.

There's a gentle tugging on my hair. It's soothing. "Evelyn," a woman says from behind me. "You mustn't worry what that child said to you. Children have a way of hurting one another by pulling out the one thing that makes you unique. Makes you special. And you *are* special, Evelyn."

I turn slightly and she tugs my head back around with my hair and continues brushing it. Instead of trying to see her directly, I focus my gaze to her reflection in the glass instead. "Am I, Mother?" My voice is younger, not quite as strong. It wobbles slightly with the tears I see running down my cheeks.

"Of course, my child. I chose you, didn't I? That alone makes you special. But I chose you because you were different. Because you were perfect. And a perfect person shouldn't worry what inferior people say about them." Her face hardens for a moment and her hand tightens on my hair, making me gasp. Almost immediately she releases me and her eyes meet mine in the glass. "After all," she smiles, "I never do."

There's a knock on the door behind us and a girl not much older than me steps in, dressed entirely in black. Mother and I both turn toward her, but the girl doesn't focus her dead eyes on either of us. "The situation has been taken care of," she states in her wispy voice.

For a second, I'm sure she glances at me, but before I can

venture a guess why, Mother says, "Excellent." Then she dismisses the girl and turns back to me, forcing my head back around again while the door closes behind us. "See? Things have a way of working themselves out."

CHAPTER FIFTEEN

Warning! Unauthorized exit from Rushlake City is prohibited. Violators will incur administrative penalty and criminal charges including, but not limited to, immediate and permanent expulsion from the city and forfeiture of all rights and property.

—SIGN POSTED AT ALL POINTS OF ENTRY OF RUSHLAKE CITY

Evie

The next day, I sit while a doctor does everything Dr. Gillian has already done at least a dozen times before. From the way he's not saying anything, and the pinch of skin around his eyes, I know he isn't coming up with any more answers than Dr. Gillian had, either.

He shines a light in my eyes. "You're completely healthy, Ms. Winters. Apart from a minor infection and some exhaustion. In fact, you're so healthy, I'm a little jealous. I don't know what could be causing these blackouts." He steps back and takes off his glasses to rub his eyes. "I'd like to bring you in for more testing. MRIs and PET scans specifically."

"What are those?" I ask.

"Sort of like X-rays, but more precise. I'll be able to see exactly what your brain is doing. That should tell us what's going on. If it's agreeable to you, I'd like you to come in as soon as possible. Say, tomorrow?" He glances between Asher and me. We both nod—what am I going to say? No?—and he continues, packing up his equipment. "Fantastic. We'll see you then." He pats my knee. "Don't worry, young lady. We'll figure all this out."

He leaves while I just stare at my hands. Asher nudges me. "Are you as tired of being cooped up in here as I am?"

I'm confused, but answer truthfully. "Yes."

"Great. Go get dressed. I'll meet you downstairs in twenty."

"Dressed for what?"

"We're going to see a bit of the city," he says. "Dress warmly. It's chilly."

As we walk through the city, Asher keeps pointing out different things, like he did in the car when we first arrived. I try to listen, but I can't help but keep an eye out for Gavin the entire time we walk. It just doesn't feel right to be out here with someone other than him. I sigh, then wince, looking over at Asher. It's amazing, the contrast between him and Gavin. Asher has this . . . perfect prettiness to him that makes him look just like everyone else here. His eyes are always smiling, showing his happy-go-lucky, nothing-ever-gets-me-down-for-long personality. Even dressed casually, like he is today, he looks effortlessly put together and fashionable, like the other people I'm seeing on the street.

He's wearing a hat. His dark hair sticks out on either side of it, the blue patch just barely visible under the lip of the hat. He's also wearing a long-sleeved dress shirt with the sleeves pushed up over his elbows and a gray vest. Of course, since this is Asher, his shirt is not tucked into his jeans. But it doesn't stop him from looking great, anyway.

Gavin, on the other hand, has a rugged—almost dirty, even when he's freshly washed—look that is simply the sexiest thing I've ever seen. No matter how nice and shiny Asher looks, it's Gavin that will always take my breath away.

I feel strange thinking of him like that, especially considering I may never see him again.

But, as Asher continues to show me around, my thoughts move to the city itself. I'm amazed how different the people look from the villagers. They're cleaner, but they've got the same shiny look to them that the city has. Like Asher, only the kindness in his eyes isn't reflected in anyone else's. It's as if they're really fake. Like dolls.

I don't belong here either. I don't belong anywhere.

Asher, however, seems at home. More so than he did in the village. It makes me think of what Gavin said about not trusting him. "We need to check the gates," I say.

He doesn't even argue. Just changes direction and leads the way back to the guards. They're the same as the day before. And they have the same news. "No one has seen him."

I wrap my arms around myself and shiver. Maybe he really is dead. Maybe he isn't coming.

Asher glances over, his features as sad as I feel. "Want to go and get something warm to eat?"

I let him drag me to the closest restaurant, where he orders something that sounds like absolute heaven. Hot chocolate.

We spend the next few hours talking. He tells me about his childhood, and Gavin's, remaining careful not to tell me anything of what really happened between them, keeping to lighter things like the time Gavin and him were fishing when they were fourteen and Gavin hooked Asher instead of the fish. And how he, Asher, had gone running off, screaming, before Gavin could take it out. When Gavin finally found him, it was dug deep into his skin, and Asher squealed like a little girl when they tried to remove it. To take his mind off it, Gavin had the bright idea to break into the Mr. Pok's back room and alleviate him of the shine he kept hidden in a closet. They'd both gotten so drunk that they'd stripped down to their underpants and ran through the town square yelling something about fish. I try to ask Asher why and he just shakes his head and grins, shrugging. They'd ended up grounded for a month.

Even when the conversation moves to the other things, like me, and what I remember, and laughing or gushing over things Asher and I have in common, Gavin is never far from my mind.

CHAPTER SIXTEEN

One of the most cunning animals of those in the Outlands is the coyote. The coyote's ability to adapt is the leading reason for its continued survival. Over time, coyotes have learned to hunt in small packs and stun their kill before dragging them to their burrow for consumption.

—EXCERPT FROM *FIELD GUIDE TO DANGEROUS WILDLIFE*

Gavin

A shout wakes me, and there's a flurry of movement around me. For a second, something sharp tightens around my arm; there's another shout, and the sound of a gun going off. Finally, something yelps next to me, and the sharpness in my arm lets off.

Coyotes! my mind screams at me. *Get up. Get up. Get up.*

I try to open my eyes, but I can't force myself to do it. Sleep just grabs ahold of me and pulls me in.

After what feels like no time at all, I'm being shaken awake again. I open my eyes, immediately regretting my decision.

The light stabs my eyes like rusty knives. I groan and slam them shut again.

"Nuh-uh, Sleeping Beauty. You've got some explainin' to do," a gruff male voice says. I open my eyes again as a rough hand yanks me up to a sitting position.

In front of me is a man. From the lines in his face, the gray in his scraggly beard, and what's left of the hair on his head, he's either fast approaching middle age or time has not been his friend. He's wearing all black. It looks like some kind of military uniform.

Immediately I tense. I reach for my gun, but it's gone.

The man barks out a laugh. "Did ya think I was goin' t' let you keep yer gun?" He scratches his chin and flakes of something dribble out of his beard like snow. "Not a very bright thing, are ya?"

"Who are you? What do you want?" I force myself to my feet. I'm grateful he didn't feel the need to tie me up.

"Ah, now, see, I said you had some explainin' to do, not the other way round, boy." He straightens up and I fight back a wince when I see that not only is he taller than me, but his arms are as thick as small trees.

Shit.

"So, now. Are yeh goin' t' explain what yer doin' here?"

Where *is* here? Glancing around, I notice I'm at the lip of a sulfur lake. I recognize it from the strange greenish-yellow color and the smell. How did I get here?

Then I remember. The birds. Barely escaping with my life only to run into a pack of hungry coyotes. One of them pouncing. Falling, hitting my head on the hard ground and blacking out.

But how did I end up here?

Something my father taught me ages ago when we found the chicken coop raided pops into my head. He said that coyotes have only managed to make it so long because they're smart enough to drag their food to their dens before eating, because otherwise they'd have been hunted to extinction.

So I look around for the den, but there's nothing visible except the lake. I take a small step backward, then two.

The man chuckles. "At least yer smart enough to stay away from that." He jerks his thumb at the water. Then he frowns again. "Come on, boy. I don't got all day. What ya doin' here?"

"I—I don't know." I rub my head. "I think the coyotes dragged me."

The man frowns and scratches at his beard again, making this scratchy sound like sandpaper, and it makes me want to shudder. He continues to stare at me, his eyes boring into me as if trying to read my soul to judge the truth of my words. "Ah, yeah. I can see that. Yer lucky, you are. I stopped one of them from eatin' yer face off." He smiles, showing off several gaps where his teeth should have been. "Ye'd better get goin' though. It ain't safe here, neither." He nods a head at the lake. "That ain't the only thing waiting to peel the flesh from yer bones."

My heart beats furiously, skipping a beat here and there.

I don't know what he means by that, and I'm not sure I want to.

Obviously, he's decided I'm not a threat and is allowing me to leave. I'm willing to take it without asking questions as long as that means I get to leave here alive and intact.

I start backing up, then stop. "Can I have my gun back?"

He frowns. "Now what would yeh think I was stupid enough to hand ye back yer gun fer?"

"I didn't say you were stupid," I say.

"Nah, but if yeh think I'm jes goin' to be givin' you yer gun back, yeh must think it."

I shake my head, trying to tell him I just want the gun to hunt for food, but he narrows his eyes at me.

"What'cha doin' out here all alone fer, boy? Didn't your mammy tell yeh the Outlands is no place for tots and green horns?"

Deciding I don't need the gun after all, I bob my head quickly. "Never mind. Keep the gun." I start backing away again.

His wide face wrinkles further when I do. "I wouldn't do that, boy. I'd be stoppin' now."

I do. Immediately.

"Yeh aren't out here alone, are yeh? Yer with someone else. Aren't ya?"

I hesitate only a moment before shaking my head. Evie and Asher are somewhere out here, I hope, but it's anybody's guess where. "No. I'm by myself."

He grins, showing those dark spaces again, but it isn't a

happy look. It's mean. I've only seen that look on one other person's face—Mother. It makes my veins drip with icy fear.

"Now, why would yeh do that?"

"What?" I slide another foot backward.

"Lie to me." He shakes his head, then pulls a gun from his back. My gun, actually. I recognize the large dent in the wood stock. "Hands on your head." He gestures with the gun when I don't comply. "Come now, don't be stupid."

I lift my hands and lace my fingers together behind my head. Plan after stupid, horrible plan bounces through my mind. None of them would work. They would all leave me with a nice-sized hole in my body.

I'm pretty sure that's going to happen anyway.

Something squawks and he jumps. He turns, looking to see what's made the sound, and I decide it's now or never. I pounce on him. I hope the surprise will help me avoid that hole.

It sort of works. I *do* manage to get my hands on the barrel of the gun, but he manages to keep a grip on it even as we fall to the ground.

That squawk happens again and this time there's a voice not far from my head. "Fred? You there? Did you find the source of the alarm?"

It's a radio. It's sticking out of the sand a few feet away, next to some kind of pack and a large gun. The gun is just lying in the sand, held up by a mini-tripod. I've never seen one like this before. Between that, the mention of the alarm, and his weird uniform, I figure Fred is a guard and he's protecting something. Not that I really care. I'm more concerned with not dying. But as we roll, I realize it might just be easier to go for that other gun after all.

We continue to tussle with the shotgun, but he throws a punch with his meaty fist that connects directly with my temple. Stars explode into my eyes and my ears ring. He rips the gun out of my hands, but I jump backward, immediately falling to the ground and rolling toward the other gun.

A shot rings out. The burst of sand just inches from my head tells me he's shooting to kill. I grab the gun and spring to my feet, bringing it to my shoulder and aiming at his midsection.

"Stop!" I gasp out. "Don't come any closer." This is a bigass gun and it's going to hurt like hell to fire it. Might even break my shoulder, but a broken shoulder is better than dead.

That is, if I can actually shoot the damn thing. It's heavy, and I don't even know if it's loaded. But, maybe, I'll be able to convince him to leave me alone long enough that he won't know I've never used something like this.

He lifts his hands in the air as he pushes himself to his feet, but there's a smirk on his face. "Yeh don't have the guts, boy." He spits on the ground and my eyes take in the bloody spittle that flecks the sand.

"Fred," the radio squawks again. "You okay? . . . Did you find out what set off that alarm? . . . Fred?"

I smile, just a small stretching of my lips. "Try me." I tighten my finger on the trigger. Given the size of the gun, it's surprisingly easy to press the trigger.

The smirk falls off his face. "Now, boy, yeh don't need to do that."

"Fred? . . . If you don't answer me, I'm sending someone out there. . . ."

That seems to bolster him, though. "Even if yeh shoot me, yeh won't get away with it. They'll find yeh." Then he lunges at me, and even though I'd expected him to try something, it startles me and I press the trigger. The gun goes off and knocks me onto my ass.

As I fall, I hear three distinct shots before I hit the ground, knocking the air from my lungs.

I was right. The gun hurts like hell.

I leap back to my feet, wincing as pain rips through my shoulder. I don't raise the gun. Even if I could, there's no need to. Fred is rolling down the hill. At first he's in one piece, with three large holes in his abdomen. But then, to my horror and disgust, as he continues to roll, the skin between the holes tear and he splits into two parts.

The friction must have been too much for those thin strings of flesh. I shudder when what was inside his body comes out and tangles around him before he splashes into the water with a hiss.

Both parts sink quickly and I feel like I'm going to be sick. Actually, I *know* I'm going to be sick. I collapse onto my knees and try hurling into the sand, but nothing comes up. I'm stuck just kneeling there, gagging, until the retching stops.

What the hell kind of gun was that? I've never seen bullets that could tear someone completely in half like that.

The radio squawks again and my heart kicks. I have to get out of here.

With a lurch, I shove to my feet, then throw the gun and radio into the water. A quick search of Fred's bag produces some much needed food and supplies. I toss the whole bag over my shoulder, grab my own gun, and run. Dizzy, with a fuzzy mind, and still a little green around the gills, I don't even know what direction I'm running in. I'll figure it out later. I just run.

As fast and as far as I can.

CHAPTER SEVENTEEN

Once upon a time, there was a queen who lived in an under-water kingdom. The queen was beautiful, but cruel. And although she had many subjects, they were only loyal to her out of fear. The queen did not know love, and she kept her daughter, the princess, locked away for fear that the princess would someday discover love and leave the queen and the underwater kingdom.

—EXCERPT FROM *SURFACE FAIRY TALE*

Evie

I wake with a scream trapped in my throat as the tatters of the nightmare drift away. The room is still dark, but I reach for Gavin. I just want him to hold me. To tell me it's all right. That they're not real. That *he's* real, that he's here. But he's not. He'll never be here.

For a good ten minutes, I stare at the ceiling, then sigh and sit up, letting my legs dangle off the side before placing my foot on the floor. But there's something squishy, and warm, underneath it. I squeal and jump back onto the bed. Whatever it is pops up and lunges at me, making me fall off the bed on the opposite side and onto my back end on the floor with a thump. It looms above me, looking down at me from its perch on the bed. It's too dark to make out what it is, but I'm suddenly sure it's the monsters from my dreams coming to get me.

I scramble back until I'm crouched with my back up against the wall. As it slowly comes nearer me, I hear that click in my head. Everything focuses, just like before.

So I can see the monster better, I reach out and grab a handful of cloth and yank it to me. The fabric rips, fueling my desire to hurt whatever this creature is and prevent it from hurting me. But even then, it's too dark to really see anything but a pair of wide blue eyes staring into mine. And, only because they look frightened, I decide not to kill it right now.

I tighten my grip on the cloth, tearing it farther and pulling the creature after me, dragging it to the lamp in the corner. With a flick of my fingers, I switch the light on and turn to see . . . Asher. He's staring at me, his eyes still wide as he watches me. His shirt is ripped practically from his shoulders, hanging by nothing but a few threads.

His tongue flickers out nervously and wets his lips before he says, "M-morning, Princess."

I scowl and release him. His shirt pools at his waist when he falls to his knees.

"What did you think you were doing?" I demand, my voice hard and hardly recognizable.

His tongue flicks out again, but he only says, "You squealed and I was trying to see what was wrong."

Things are starting to get blurry again and I feel exhausted. I let myself sink to the floor next to him as I recall what happened.

"I guess I must have stepped on you," I finally say. "I stepped on something warm and squishy and it scar . . . startled me." No need to admit I was scared. This is embarrassing enough. "Why didn't you say anything?"

He looks at me with an embarrassed smile. "I was too . . . startled."

He rubs a hand across his chest and even through my blurry eyes, I can see the distinct lines my fingernails left across his bare skin. Five distinct scratches across his chest that stretch out in a long line from his right pec to the center of his abdomen. Blood oozes down.

I touch his chest gently and bite my lower lip, wrinkling my nose. "Oh, Mother, I'm so sorry, Asher. I . . . I don't know what happened."

He takes a shaky breath, and his eyes swim with something other than pain when he takes my hand. "It's all right. My fault. Completely. I should've known better than to jump up like that." He squeezes my hand.

"Still." I try to pull my hand back. "That's no excuse. I could have seriously hurt you. I don't know what's wro—"

He cuts me off when he places his finger over my mouth. "It's okay. I'm not hurt. I'm just fine. Are you?" he asks. "Hurt, I mean? You fell off the bed pretty hard."

I take a minute to get my emotions under control—it's not like feeling guilty and angry with myself is going to change what I've done. Besides, hopefully, in a few hours, I'll know exactly what's wrong with me and how to fix it.

Gavin

I run until I collapse from exhaustion. Even lying in the dirt, my whole body shakes. My eyes are heavy, gritty and dry. They hurt almost worse than my shoulder. I tell myself I'll only close my eyes for a second. Just to catch my breath. But when I open them again, it's freezing, pitch dark, and there's so much cloud cover I can't even see the stars.

Cursing under my breath, I fight the urge to laugh, because I'm sure once I start, I'm not going to be able to stop. With my luck, the noise will tempt the coyotes back.

Coyotes. Shit.

I've got to get up. Have to keep moving, but I don't know where I'm going. I don't even know if I ran in the right direction. There's an empty, gnawing feeling in my stomach. My head swims and I'm having difficulty concentrating. I decide that I just don't care if the coyotes find me again. Maybe they'll carry me somewhere useful this time.

Until morning, I huddle into myself, trying to keep warm. By some miracle the coyotes don't find me. When the sun rises, I'm cramped and my body is reminding me how much it hates me. When I see the sun, I just stare at it.

"Damn it!" I yell and hear it echo for miles and miles—

hundreds of repeats of the word, reiterating my frustration back to me.

I went the wrong way. The completely wrong effing way. I run a hand over my face, still cursing myself over and over in my head, but I push myself to my feet and begin the long trek back the way I came.

For the next several days, I hike with the sun at my back in the mornings and follow it to its horizon in the afternoons. Nights are for lie-downs and fitful sleeps, while I try to keep one ear open for carnivorous wild animals and one hand on my gun.

Every day my muscles get heavier. It requires more and more effort just to keep walking. Even my bones feel like they're made of lead. Several times, I'm certain I hear voices. And once I even hear Evie's laugh. I spin around looking for the source; I even backtrack a few steps looking for someone, hoping it's Evie and Asher, only to find there's no one there. Which only fills me with bitter disappointment and makes it even harder to keep blundering my way forward.

Finally, I stumble upon another set of footprints. Two sets. One is about my size; the other is much smaller. It can't be them, though. They have Starshine. There'd be horse prints. Unless they ran into coyotes like I did.

It's impossible to know for sure, but I follow the prints anyway. Wherever they lead, there will probably be people on the other side, and I hope that means Rushlake, too. My thoughts are fixed firmly on finding Evie. She must be so worried about me. It's been days with no contact, and she has no way of knowing if I made it away from those vulture-hawks. I keep her face in my mind and put one foot in front of the other, knowing each step takes me closer to seeing her in person.

I panic a little when the footsteps lead into another set of trees. The vulture-hawks prefer forested areas, but they're diurnal. Thank God. I'll wait them out and slip into the trees while they sleep.

As soon as the sun sets completely, I step into the woods, keeping the shotgun drawn and cocked, but nothing happens and I push through the woods as quietly as I can.

The footprints disappear in the slightly marshy underbrush of the woods. There's not enough light, but I remember from the map that the city is just on the other side of a set of woods. So I just keep heading as straight as I can, hoping that I'm almost there. Then, as if I willed it to appear, I find myself on the other side of the trees and staring at Rushlake City.

Evie

I sit in the waiting room, my knee bouncing up and down and my heart beating almost in rhythm to it. I grasp my necklace and run my fingers over the edges of the rose. Whatever happens here at the medical facility, I know it's going to determine everything. I just have to hope that this time these tests will tell me exactly what I'm supposed to do. And the possibility of knowing the answers scares me almost more than not knowing them.

Asher puts his hand on my knee, but he's shaking almost as much as I am. For some reason that makes me feel slightly better. To know he's just as nervous as I am.

The door pushes open and the doctor stands there, silhouetted by the bright lights coming from the room behind him. My mind goes entirely blank and my mouth goes dry. Like I'm back in the Outlands.

"Subject 121!" a voice calls through a set of speakers set in the walls.

That's me. I know it's me. I know I have to follow the person in the shadows, but I can't make my legs move. I really want to cry and I really want my mom.

The woman next to me stands up. "Come now, Evelyn. That's you." She smiles down at me, but even I know it's fake. She doesn't want to be here either. That doesn't help my nerves.

"Mother does not tolerate dawdlers." She yanks me up. "You are not just any three-year-old, you are an Enforcer. And you are not off to a good start. If you wish to impress Mother, you need to follow orders implicitly."

I swallow and nod, forcing my legs to push me toward the dark person in the doorway. To the moment that changes everything.

"Evie, are you all right?" Asher asks right next to me, causing me to knock the top of my head into his chin.

He spins away, cursing, while I clutch the top of my head with both hands.

I jump up. "Are you okay?"

"Yes. Fine. You?"

"Yeah."

"I knew you were hardheaded, Evie, but I didn't realize how hard." He grins at me, still rubbing at his jaw.

"Evelyn Winters?" The woman at the door says, and not for the first time if her tone is anything to go by.

"Coming." My voice cracks and I clear my throat. "Coming."

Feeling faint and not a little nauseated, I walk through the door, letting it flap shut behind me. The room is completely white, and directly in the center, taking up most of the space, is this . . . well . . . I don't know exactly what it is, but it reminds me of Snow White's casket in the storybook I found in Gavin's house.

The image does nothing to help my fluttering stomach and heart palpitations.

I take a step backward, away from it, bouncing into someone. I twist around to see the doctor—the same one that had spoken with me at Asher's grandmother's house—peering down at me.

He explains the procedure, which consists of me lying in the glass coffin—wonderful—with it closed—even better—while they watch from another room. Fantastic.

"Ready?" he asks.

I don't answer. I only suck in a deep breath through my nose and settle myself into the tube.

The nurse places headphones over my ears, then presses a

button on the side of the box. The glass draws over my head and instantly I feel claustrophobic. As if it's not just glass crawling over my head, but thousands and thousands of liters of water.

Mother is speaking, droning on and on about etiquette and manners and my duty. Stand this way. Push your shoulders back. Head up. Make sure you smile!

I'm standing on a little pedestal while the Dressmaker walks around me, mumbling around a mouthful of pins.

"Evelyn, that pink is a wonderful color on you."

I smile even though I'm sure the color washes me out. "Thank you, Mother."

"I knew that it would." She tugs on her own sapphire blue dress. "I think that it's a little too short, though, don't you?"

It's just barely above my knees, but I nod. "Yes, Mother."

She nods at the Dressmaker, who starts pulling pins and adjusting the hemline.

Mother goes on about my schedule for the next week. Meetings I'm to attend with her to take notes. Another request day. My appointments with Dr. Friar. Another ball. Violin lessons. Vocal lessons. Suitor tea party. An event at the theater. A dinner.

"Ouch!" I call out when the Dressmaker pokes me with a needle.

Mother glares at me. "Evelyn. Do not interrupt me."

"Sorry, Mother," I mutter and the Dressmaker sends me a look of apology.

The glass top opens and the doctor peers down at me. "Everything all right?" he asks.

"Yes."

"Fantastic. Now we need to inject you with some dye. I'd like to see what those nanos are doing. We're going to stick a needle in your arm, okay?"

My stomach drops and I know this is a bad idea, but if it helps then I'll do whatever it takes. I nod.

He signals the nurse to come over and I roll my head to watch her. She walks over slowly with something in her hand, but keeps out of my sight. When she's next to me, she takes my arm and says, "This is going to sting a little. You might want to close your eyes."

I do as she says, but my stomach churns and my entire chest tingles. This is a bad idea. A very bad idea. I open my mouth to object, but a sharp pain stabs into the crook of my elbow. My eyes fly open, but I'm not staring at the white walls of the medical center.

The walls are a pretty light blue that instinctively I know is supposed to be calming, but it's not. It's terrifying.

Medical equipment beeps and buzzes. Air hisses from some-where nearby. The room is bustling with Medical Technicians. Their droning voices circle around me. "She's dangerous. Unpre-dictable. A killer . . . worse . . . a monster . . . a risk . . . must be eliminated."

Misery is my cloak and I wrap it around myself like a blanket. I deserve this.

I am a monster. A murderer. Betrayer.

A Technician leans over and sneers at me. "Traitor," he whis-pers into my ear, then pushes some sort of mask over my nose.

"This is too good for you." Straps are yanked across my body, biting into my skin, causing tears to prick at my eyes. But I don't cry out. I deserve this. I am a traitor.

My pulse beats a tattoo against my throat and my head swims. Black spots form in front of my eyes and no matter how much I blink they multiply and grow, so I let my eyes drift closed.

"Stand clear," a soft voice says.

Something pierces the skin inside my elbow and a deep aching fills my bones. The aching turns to gnawing, then to pure agony that travels from the marrow of my bones to the tips of my nerve endings. Within seconds every square centimeter of my flesh is being devoured slowly by fire. I scream out, but it doesn't sound like me. It's as if something primal has taken control of my body.

I thrash against my restraints, while people rush around me. Another needle is plunged into my other elbow. And yet another in my neck. With each assault the torture grows worse, until I'm nothing more than a writhing mass of torment.

Just when I think I can't take any more, there's a soft click in my brain and a mist films over the agony. I rip my arms from the straps, tearing the needles from my arms. Blood squirts across the nearest Technicians.

Shouts yell for someone—anyone—to get me under control before I hurt someone. Two Technicians advance on me and sink into a crouch. When they get near enough, I lunge forward, grabbing each by the arm and tossing them aside like dolls in turn. I'm moving before they even hit the wall to either side of me.

Another Technician jumps on me from behind, his arms tight around my neck. I flip him over my head. He lands hard on his back at my feet and his breath whooshes out all at once. I leave him there gasping as I run for the door.

As I wrench it open, two Enforcers appear on the other side of it. I strike out with my foot, kicking one in the chest. She flies back, hitting the wall on the other side of the hallway, but the other dashes forward and tackles me, shoving me into the ground and knocking the wind out of me.

Before I can even get my breath back, more people are crowding on top of me. My legs are tied together behind my back and to my arms. I have a moment to think that my limbs are going to be torn from my body when they lift me up and toss me onto the bed again.

They strap me to the bed again, this time facedown. A new voice speaks from the doorway. One I'd know anywhere.

Mother.

"What a mess. I told you to sedate her first."

My mind goes blank and my body seems to lose its connection with my brain as I blink and stare at the scene in front of me.

I'm not lying on my stomach restrained to a bed. I'm standing. Blood trickles down my arms from the slashes across them. Two men lie in a heap on the floor at my feet. The only sign they're still alive is the slight rise and fall of their chests.

The doctor stands only a few feet from me, another syringe in his hands. The nurse that talked to me just a few minutes ago is standing next to him, pulling jars of liquids from a cabinet.

Asher pushes past the two people in the doorway and we stare in shock and horror at each other. I don't have to ask to know I'm the one that did this.

CHAPTER EIGHTEEN

It's been a year to the day. I have to think that Eli's not coming back. To be honest, I probably knew from the beginning that Mother wouldn't let him get away with what he did, but even if my head knew it, my heart wouldn't believe it until now.

—EXCERPT FROM LENORE ALLEN'S JOURNAL

Gavin

I'm not sure how to get in. I'm almost positive the guards won't let me in without that stupid paper, so I'm working on coming up with another way. It takes me a moment to realize that the bridge across from me is only large enough for foot traffic. That means there's another entrance. There has to be. How else do they get supplies in?

I wander around until I find the bigger entrance, and then I wait, hiding in the shadow of the concrete wall. Watching. Studying the patterns and duties of the guards at this gate.

After a few hours, I realize that they don't even look inside the large supply wagons. If I can somehow sneak over to one, I can slip underneath it and hang on until it drives into the city.

Finally, a horse-drawn wagon comes rumbling up to the gates. One of the guards comes out and speaks with the driver. Seizing my chance, I sneak over to it, then slide underneath the wagon and wrap my ankles around part of the wagon's frame and my arms around another part. It hurts to be stretched out like this, and my shoulder is screaming at me, but I can't think of another way.

They have an eternity-long conversation that I try to block out, and my legs and arms start to cramp from the exertion of holding on to the undercarriage. Eventually, though, the wagon pulls through the gates and into the city.

When the wagon stops at a crossroads, I let go, dropping to the ground and rolling out to the side, before jumping up and strolling away as if I didn't just drop out from underneath a supply wagon. After a few blocks, I stop and massage the knots in my arms and legs.

I may not know the exact layout of the city, but I remember listening to Asher talking about it when we were kids. I know about where Asher's family lives. It's just a matter of finding out exactly which house is the correct one. It's not like I can just go up to the people and ask them if they know where the St. Jameses live. I'll be reported for being an Outlander and arrested faster than I can blink.

But there's no way I'm going to be able to find Evie without some kind of help. Maybe I should just take the chance and ask one of the police. I *can* prove that I'm supposed to be here. What harm could it do?

Then I shake my head. Nope. Bad idea. The people of

Rushlake dislike outsiders almost as much as Elysium hates Surface Dwellers. Except they don't go quite so far as death to punish people for "breaking" in. Still, I don't feel like getting booted out. Even though when they find the St. Jameses, they'll see I have a visa and it'll be fine. Of course, that would depend on *if* Asher actually showed them the visa.

Maybe I could surreptitiously ask a few people, saying I'd come with the St. Jameses and went for a walk and got lost and need help finding my way back. I glance down to my filthy clothes. Nope. That'll just send me back to talking with the police.

I'll just have to take the chance and try asking a servant. They're less likely to care that I'm an Outlander. But it's not like I can just pick a house and ring the bell. I'll have to wait until someone comes outside.

Even that proves to be difficult. When I get to the area where I know Asher's house is, I manage to catch three servants on their way out of various houses, but only one even acknowledges I'm talking to him, and he just points down the street, which doesn't help me. At all. Apparently even the servants think they're better than Outlanders. Figures.

Evie

I don't suppose it's much of a surprise they decide not to let me go home. Considering what I did, I guess I should be glad they didn't have me arrested. They still don't know what caused it, despite all their fancy equipment. And they don't know how I knocked out two grown men at least twice my size with my bare hands. So, now I'm stuck in yet another hospital room while they try to figure out how dangerous I am. While Asher talks with the doctor, trying to find out how long they're going to keep me here, I let my eyelids drift closed. All the panic is making me exhausted.

After what feels like only a few minutes, Asher gently shakes me awake. When I blink my eyes open, his grandmother is there, watching me with a sad expression.

She takes the seat across from the bed, while Asher settles onto the chair to my left. I can see she's bracing herself to tell me something. It's quiet and I try not to fidget while I wait for her to speak. She seems lost in her thoughts and Asher and I exchange a look before he clears his throat. She startles and then her eyes focus on Asher.

She gives him a look of apology. "It's always hard to know where to start, but as with everything it's probably best to start with the beginning." She moves her gaze to mine, then gives me a small smile. "You and I, my dear, have a lot more in common than you think." She takes a deep breath and then looks into her lap. That's when I notice her hands. She's holding a small piece of shiny paper.

She gives Asher one more apologetic glance before handing it to me. I take it, dread curling in my stomach. Whatever this is, I don't want to look, but I do. Then furrow my brow.

It's just a picture of a group of six people smiling into the camera. They're all wearing lab coats and smiles. There are six of them. Four men, a woman, and a girl about my age, maybe slightly older. All have blond hair. The four men are split, two on either side of the woman, who has her hands on the girl's shoulders. Behind the group is what looks like the window from that creepy underground lab in the Outlands, or from the rooms in my hallucinations, only the water behind them is lit with lights and is dark blue—almost black. It's only recognizable as water because of the colorful fish swimming in it.

It's pretty, and . . . I feel like I know where it was taken. Like I've been there. The strangest part is that the two females and the youngest man look familiar. I'm sure I know them for some reason.

I look back up at her. "I don't understand."

"That's me." She points to the woman.

I go back to studying the picture and Asher leans against my knee to get a better look himself. And while at first I didn't get it, I can see the resemblance now. It's in the shape and color of the eyes—the same as Asher's. The picture must have been taken years ago, when she was much younger, because her gray hair is blond in the picture and her face is smooth and free of wrinkles.

"You were very pretty," I blurt out. I realize quickly that was probably very rude. As if I'm saying she's not pretty now, which isn't the case. She's a very handsome woman, for someone of her—

She smiles at me, cutting off the mortified rant inside my head. "Thank you."

Asher looks up at her. "Who are the rest of these people?"

She returns his look, then turns back to me. "Do you know? Does anyone look familiar?"

I slowly shake my head. "I feel like I should, but I can't figure it out."

She points to the girl. "That's the woman you know as Mother." Asher freezes and his eyes lock on to his grandmother, but she ignores him and continues. "And, as I'm sure you've guessed, this picture was taken in Elysium. It was taken right after we cracked the puzzle to the greatest scientific advancement of that time. Permanent sentient nanobots." She looks up to meet my wide-eyed gaze. "I'm one of the scientists who invented the nanos that took away your memories, Evie."

I can only stare at Asher's grandmother. "*You* invented them?" I finally ask. She nods and I can't help but blurt out, "All of this is your fault? I don't know who or *what* I am because of *you*?"

She shakes her head, then pauses and nods. "Ultimately, I suppose this is my fault. They were never intended for what Mother eventually used them for, but . . . yes, I, and the others in my group, created them, and in the end that's all that really matters."

Asher doesn't even look shocked.

"Did you know about this?" I demand of him.

He shakes his head. "Not until a few hours ago. I . . . I didn't know how to tell you . . ." he trails off, looking at his hands.

My hands clench into fists as my anger turns to burn at his grandmother. "You didn't think it was important to tell me right away when we arrived? Or when the doctors said it may be my nanos making me hallucinate?" She doesn't answer, only looks away from me. I slam my fisted hand onto the bed. "Answer me! Why didn't you say anything?"

She sighs. "Because I didn't want to. That part of my life—the fragment of time I was there—is over, and I wanted to keep it that way." She looks at Asher. "I wanted to keep that part of my life from touching you, but it seems that fate has made it your problem too. I've been responsible for enough people dying. I wasn't going to let my selfishness harm an innocent girl. I couldn't keep it a secret anymore." She gives Asher an apologetic look, then sends me one as well.

Still furious, I shake my head and try to connect the dots. If she invented them, she knows how to fix them. I lean forward, the first flicker of hope fluttering in my heart.

"You know how to make me better."

She shakes her head. "No, they've made a few improvements to the 'bots that I don't know how to fix. I've already spoken to the doctor about it. But I might know someone who can help."

"Same thing," Asher says. He gets up and stalks toward the window.

Her eyes follow him. They're sad when they turn back to me. "Eli and I—we were partners." She glances over at Asher before turning back to me. "More than partners, really." She sighs. "But that's neither here nor there. As I said, I'll start from the beginning.

"I was recruited to work in Elysium shortly after the War. She—Mother—hired me because of my work with the military here and my knowledge of nanite technology. Apparently there had been an outbreak of disease in Elysium and it had killed over half her people. She wanted to prevent it from happening again. She'd read of my success with sentient nanobots and had hoped by injecting nanobots, they would act like an immunization. That is to say, they would work along with the body's immune system to get rid of germs and viruses, on a permanent basis, so she wouldn't have to worry about something like that again.

"I took the offer almost before she stopped speaking. I saw it as a real opportunity to help people. After everything that happened during the War, I thought it would be a good way to repent for my sins."

I frown. "Sins?"

Her chuckle is full of derision, but I'm certain it's not directed at me. "A way to make up for things I thought I'd done wrong. And for a while, I thought I'd done it. I spent months with the others there, experimenting with the military tech I'd brought along, and finally came up with something that would keep people from being sick.

"I was so young, barely into my thirties. And stupid. But I never dreamed what happened would happen. I never realized what she really wanted the nanos for. Or what she would do. She was so young herself. A baby really. Too young, I suppose, to be running an entire city all by herself."

"How old was she?" Asher asks.

"Seventeen, eighteen. Twenty at the most. She said she was twenty-five when I met her, but it was obvious she was lying. I suppose that should have been my first clue. But I didn't think I had anything to worry about. If only I'd known, even though she was so young, what she was capable of."

"What?" I ask, but I don't think she even hears me. Her eyes are far away and I'm certain she doesn't even see me anymore. I glance to Asher, who returns to sit next to me, his uncertain expression telling me he doesn't know what she's talking about either.

"Eli and I both came from the Surface, but he'd already been down there from . . . before. Apparently she trusted him more than anyone else. She put him with me mostly to supervise because I was a Surface Dweller."

For the first time, she smiles at me as if we're sharing an inside joke, but while the phrase makes me nervous, I don't know why. When I don't smile back, she turns her attention back to her hands. "And, for a while, it worked out well, and she began to trust me. I liked her almost from the beginning. She seemed so sweet, and she was so *young*, barely older than you and Asher. I almost saw her as a kid sister. And Eli . . ." Her eyes take on that faraway look again. "He was so smart. And sweet. Attractive. He had fantastic ideas. We quickly became partners." She looks back up; her eyes darting back and forth between Asher and me. "Both inside the lab and out."

She shakes her head as if amused when Asher makes a disgusted sound in his throat. "We continued working on our project and everything was falling into place easier than I'd hoped. I'd never been happier. I was doing something I loved, helping people, living in the prettiest place on earth, and I was falling in love with a wonderful man. Life couldn't have been more perfect."

My life is just about perfect. The thought comes out of nowhere. I don't know why I thought it, but it startles me and reminds me of the way Gavin had reacted in the village when I'd said something similar.

But before I can think further on it, Asher is talking and I lose the thought.

"So what happened?" His voice is rough, but he doesn't seem angry anymore.

"Fate had other plans," she says, quietly. "What neither of us knew was that Mother—we knew her as Abigail then—had fallen in love with Eli, too. And while he never did anything to encourage her, she developed an entire relationship between the two of them in her head." She meets my eyes. "If I'd known how . . . not right . . . in the head she was, I would never have taken the job. Never."

She pauses and seems to be waiting for me to respond. As if she needs me to believe her because maybe she doesn't believe herself. But I nod, because I want to know the rest of the story. It's the most information I've ever had about the place that was my home for sixteen years.

She lets out a breath. "Then, a few months after we found

success with the nanos and finished injecting them into people, we saw they were working. *Really* working. Just like they were supposed to. Sure, all the data and tests we'd done said they would work, but we didn't know for certain until we actually put them into people and tested them on a large scale. People weren't getting sick, even when directly exposed to diseases that should have killed them. It was fantastic. We'd found a cure for almost any disease we'd ever faced, and with no side effects. It was a huge medical breakthrough. I couldn't wait to share it with the rest of the world. However, one night, when Eli and I were . . . um . . . celebrating . . ." She blushes and I almost smile. "She caught us."

"Then what happened?" Asher asks, without even batting an eye at his grandmother's admission. He's leaning forward eagerly, and I have to admit I'm dying of curiosity.

"Abby went crazy. She was sure we'd done it on purpose. That we'd known she loved him and were laughing at her behind her back, which of course we didn't and hadn't. But she didn't believe us. She yelled about paying us back and then ran off.

"She was only a child, really. What was the worst she could do? We thought she'd get over it. But we should have known better. There had been rumors—that I ignored or just flat-out didn't believe—that the people who she said had died of diseases had really died at her hand. Because they didn't fit her ideal vision. But I blew it off as ludicrous. She'd lost her entire family in the War, but she was still only a child. And even though people always seemed especially careful not to upset her, I didn't put much stock into any of the rumors. But she instituted a new law. Unmarried— un*Coupled*—people weren't allowed to touch, and she was the only one who could permit people to become Coupled. It was her way of making sure Eli and I couldn't continue our relationship."

"UnCoupled." The term rolls around in my head. Coupled. UnCoupled. *Touching between unCoupled people is forbidden.* I glance at Asher, wondering if that's why I'm so nervous when anyone new touches me. But his grandmother is still talking and I force myself to listen.

"So, we just figured we'd leave. There was no reason to stay. We'd finished our task. Sure, Elysium was pretty and peaceful, but that was it. We had the nanos inside us, and we knew how we'd created them. It'd be easy to share that knowledge with the rest of the world. So we got ready to leave . . . except she caught us. And then we realized what *else* the nanos could be used for. Torture. Control. Not all of the military tech had been stripped from the nanos, and she used that against us. She tortured us until I agreed to let her have him." There's a tremor in her voice.

Asher and I exchange a glance and he squeezes my hand. I have no idea what Mother did to torture her, but if Lenore loved Eli as I love Gavin . . .

Asher's grandmother takes a deep shaky breath. "The minute she left us alone, confident she'd made her point, we ran away. Eli and I snuck out using one of the submersibles. When we got back to the Surface, he told me he loved me, but he was worried about the rest of the innocent people. That he didn't want her to use the tech we built to hurt others, but he wouldn't be able to live with himself if she killed me, which he was certain would happen if I stayed. Then he kissed me, and jumped back into the submersible before I could stop him. I never saw him again."

"Why?" Asher asks, voicing the question in my head.

"No way to get down there. No one believed me that it existed, and I couldn't find a different way to get that deep on my own. Eventually, I met your grandfather and it didn't seem to matter as much." She looks off into space. "I'd begun to wonder if I hadn't just been making it all up myself. A city underwater? It didn't seem possible. How could they be there without anyone knowing about them? So I just did the easiest thing and pretended to forget about it." Her eyes meet mine. "Until I met you, my dear."

"Me? How did you know?"

She gives me that soft smile again. "You reminded me of Eli. Then Asher told me where you'd come from and I knew."

"Knew what?"

She opens her mouth, then closes it and sighs. "Knew I couldn't pretend anymore."

"But . . . why didn't you use your technology to help people here?"

She gives me a level look. "Twice unscrupulous and murderous people corrupted the technology I invented to help people. Twice I was ignorant and naive enough to be used to hurt innocent people. I promised myself never again. I would never again be manipulated or let my knowledge cause pain for any reason."

"So . . ." I say, still not understanding.

She closes her eyes, and I get a sick feeling in the pit of my stomach when she reopens them and focuses directly on me. "I think you need to go back. To Elysium."

"You want me to go back?" My voice cracks with surprise. I don't know why, but I never saw that coming.

She nods. Then pauses and shakes her head. "No, I don't really want you to go back, but I think it's the only way. Go to Eli. He'll help you. If he's even still alive. . . ." Her voice trails off and she goes back to twisting her wedding ring around and around on her finger.

Asher turns to me. "You don't have to go back, but it sounds like it's the best bet. Even if we can't find Eli, there has to be *some*one there who knows how to fix the nanos."

When I hesitate, thinking of everything Gavin feels about the place, Asher's grandmother speaks up once more. "I know you want to go back, Evie."

"No . . . I . . ." I sigh. What's the point in lying? Despite everything Gavin said about it, I do want to go back. I want to go home. "Yes. I want to go back." Looking first at Asher and then at his grandmother, I say, "Thank you for helping me."

She gives me a sad smile. "It isn't just for you I'm doing it. It's for me, too." Without any further explanation she stands and walks from the room, leaving Asher and me to stare after her.

CHAPTER NINETEEN

I found a letter today. From Eli. From . . . back then. I found it in one of the books I haven't looked at since then. I don't even really know why I looked now, except I needed to clean out that room. The baby is due any day now, and she'll need it. Anyway, the letter warns me to never go back. Not until he gives the signal. I can only assume he never got the chance to send one.
—Excerpt from Lenore Allen's journal

Evie

Exhaustion pools into me and I let myself fall back into the bed. Asher turns toward me, but I wave him off. "I'm fine. Just tired." I'm beyond tired. I feel like a husk of myself. Every time I feel that click in my head, or have a hallucination, or wake up somewhere other than where I thought I was, it's followed by this crushing fatigue. I feel as though I'm being dragged to the floor by invisible hands.

He watches me for a minute, then nods as if he just came to a decision. "We're going to have to leave tonight," he says.

Shock makes me speechless and he continues, either not noticing or not caring that I'm completely flabbergasted. "They're not going to just let you walk out of here. Not after you KO'd everyone in that room. And if we go late, there won't be as many people walking around. We should be able to sneak out."

Sneak out? Gavin's stories of Elysium dig at me. "I don't know. Maybe we should wait and see what your doctor comes up with."

He blinks at me. "No. They're not going to come up with an answer, Evie. You've intrigued them. They want to know more about *you* and how *you* can do what you did. You'll be nothing but a lab rat now. I can't let that happen, which means we need to leave tonight."

"But . . . why? What's the hurry? Why can't we wait?

He sighs. "Remember those errands my father wanted me to run in exchange for helping you here?"

I'm not sure what that has to do with anything, but I only say, "Y-yes . . ."

"Well, one of the errands was to take a letter to someone in the city. I'm not stupid enough to give someone a letter without reading it first, at least, not anymore." He looks extremely sad for a minute, but when he continues his voice is just as strong as it was. "Well, I read it and it was about you. To someone I know very well." The way he says it suggests that he may know him pretty well, but liking is another matter entirely. "My father wanted this person to find out as much as they could about you. To do some tests and everything to figure out just what you could do. He said you could be useful to the city in ways we could never imagine."

"I-I don't think I understand. Are you saying that *you* gave a letter to someone to have them *experiment* on me?" I can't decide if I'm angry or shocked or some other emotion all together.

"No!" he says forcefully. "No. I didn't give it to him. I ripped it up and threw it away. My grandmother made sure we could trust the doctors who were helping you. But after your testing today, I went to find the doctors to figure out what our next step was. I heard them talking with someone really familiar. The exact person I was supposed to give the letter to. And they weren't discussing treatment plans. They were talking about what tests to run and they were excited about what that could mean for Rushlake's security force and technological advances over the other cities."

This time I don't have to have him explain to me what he means. I get it, and besides, the quicker I get to Elysium, the quicker I can get my memories back. It's not like they can really do anything for me here anyway.

"All right," I say. "What's the plan?"

"I'm not exactly sure, but I've got some ideas. Give me a little time to pull things together and get everything ready," Asher says, pausing at the door. "Rest until I get back."

Left with no choice, I stay where I am, but I don't want to rest. Even as spent as I feel, my body is tingling with nerves and anticipation. If I weren't so exhausted, I'd probably be pacing the floor like Gavin used to do all the time.

My thoughts are filled with him. What if he's really gone for good? What if he's not? What if he shows up after we leave?

For the next two hours I sit in the chair, dozing while I wait, while Asher runs around getting things ready. I consider writing a note for Gavin, but what would I say? He'd never support returning to Elysium. I don't even know that he'd ever get it. If he's alive *to* get it.

Finally Asher steps into the room. "Everything's set. We should go."

"What's the plan? How are we going to get to Elysium?"

He looks over his shoulder, before stepping closer. "When Gavin came back with you, he had a submarine. I guess that's what he used to escape with you. My father confiscated it, for safety, of course." He rolls his eyes.

"Of course," I say.

"Anyway, I know where it is and I know it's still working. We're just going to steal it."

"Your father doesn't have it protected?"

Asher gives a cynical laugh. "Yeah, right. My dad's too sure of himself to think anyone would steal from him right under his nose."

It's not perfect, but it's the only plan we've got. We're going to have to make it work . . . but there's just one more thing I need to know. "What if Gavin is still looking for us?"

He gives me a sad look, but his eyes are determined. "We don't have time to wait. My friend is guarding the gates right now." He glances at his watch. "For only another twenty minutes. If we're going to go, now's the chance. We can't wait for a slim-chanced maybe."

My stomach lurches. "But . . ."

He leans down so his face is close to mine. "Evie . . . you know as well as I do, he's *not* coming. We've been through this and we have to leave now before it's too late."

I don't say anything and he turns and starts walking toward the door.

"But what if he's right? What if it is far worse to be there than here?" It's barely a whisper.

Asher spins around. "Evie! You do not have a choice! I wasn't kidding when I said Dr. Trevin would use you as a lab rat. Sure, they probably could fix your problems. But then they'll perform experiments on you. Just to see how well they work. They'll cut you open to see how long it takes you to heal. Give you different poisons, bring you to the point of death, only to revive you and bring you back. Force you into situations like what happened today, but maybe next time you won't pull back. Maybe you'll kill someone, Evie." I look at the ground. I know all too well, that's a definite possibility, but he doesn't stop. "Then, when they have all that, they'll torture you to get information about Elysium. Information you don't remember. And do you think they're going to believe you don't know the answers to their questions?"

Again I shake my head, as visions of what he's talking about play in my mind. My breath hitches, but as much as I don't want that to happen, I'm almost positive that if we leave, Gavin will show up. I'm not sure why I'm so sure. Maybe it's wishful thinking.

"I don't know, Asher—"

"Evie!" he yells, startling me into shutting my mouth. He's never yelled at me before. "If we don't leave in the next five minutes we won't get another chance until tomorrow night and by that time it may be too late."

I close my eyes and nod. He's right. Gavin's not coming and if I wait, it may be too late. Not just for me. For everyone around me.

Asher leads the way out of my room and around the corner to a stairway. He was right about there being no one around. It's almost as quiet as that horrible empty town we rode through. The clatter of our footfalls on the concrete stairs terrifies me as we run down them. I'm sure someone is going to hear, but then we're bursting out into the moonlight.

He glances left and right, then jerks his head to the left. "Come on. This way."

We run through the streets and I'm glad he knows where he's going, because by the time we've turned three times, I've no idea where we are or how to get back to where we were. Finally, a building looms in front of us, large enough to be at least two levels, but I can see through the open doors that it's just one large one. A smell that reminds me of Starshine blows out and I feel my stomach sink. I still don't know what happened to her. Lights suddenly blaze out as we approach, blinding me. Someone's going to see us. I try ducking back out of the path, but Asher lunges at me and yanks me back before I can.

"Relax," he says with a half smile. "The lights are automatic. They turn on when someone walks near them." He drags me into the building, which I can see now is lined on either side and as far as the eye can see with horses in boxes.

In the aisle between them, four horses are already prepared and tethered to the bars of the closest boxes. The leather of their saddles creaks as they shift from foot to foot. Almost the instant we step in, the horse on the left makes a familiar whinny sound and stomps at the floor. I can't help the grin that slides across my face. It's Starshine. I race toward her, and wrap my arms around her large neck.

"Told you I'd send for her."

At that moment, two men step out from an aisle. They're dressed in black with two guns crisscrossed on their backs. I can see the barrels peeking over their shoulders. I instantly tense when I see them and try backing away. I'm not letting them put me back in that hospital.

But Asher touches my shoulder. "It's okay, Evie. I hired them to protect us in the Outlands." He glances at my leg. "I'm not taking any chances this time."

I'm still a little wary of the guards, but I grin at Asher. For the first time in days I feel like maybe this will be all right. That everything is going to get better.

Starshine makes another sound and picks at the back of my shirt, tickling me. Giggling, I say, "I missed you, too."

Asher laughs. "Long way from the girl who was terrified of her just a few days ago."

I just shrug. "Transportation?" I put my foot in the stirrup and try to hitch myself up.

He gives me one quick nod and pushes on my butt to shove me into the saddle. "Transportation."

CHAPTER TWENTY

They came again today. Somehow my past has caught up with me, but, as before, I've told them nothing. Even if I have a few bruises on my person for my troubles. I don't know where they heard about Elysium or why they want information on it, but it can't be anything good, especially when they're willing to resort to torture of an old lady to obtain the information.

—EXCERPT FROM LENORE ALLEN'S JOURNAL

Gavin

I've just about given up. Despite my careful rationing, I'm out of food, and I've been hungry for hours already. I've just made up my mind to come up with a new plan when the door in the house across from where I'm sitting opens and Mayor St. James emerges.

I glance around, sure this is some weird set up. It couldn't be that easy. Could it? And why the hell is Asher's dad here? He jogs down the steps, then gets into a car that's waiting at the curb. The car pulls smoothly away, moving in the opposite direction from me.

I wait until I'm sure he's gone to rush up the front stairs and knock on the door. It takes a minute, but when the door opens, I recognize Asher's grandmother. At first she looks shocked to see me, but then she opens the door wider. I can't help but notice that her eyes don't look all that friendly.

"Gavin, isn't it?" She firms her lips into a thin line.

"Yes, ma'am."

She leads me into the warm kitchen. It's uncomfortably hot compared to my hours outside in the cold, but I forget all that when she introduces me to the cook, who beams at me and plies me with cookies and milk to eat while she cooks me something warm.

While I appreciate it all, and I *am* starving, I really just want to see Evie.

"Is Evie sleeping?" I peer around her to the door that leads to the living room. "I'd really like to see her."

Mrs. St James doesn't answer right away and I shift uncomfortably in my chair. Something's wrong. Something is very wrong.

"Eat, then come find me," she finally says, and leaves the room before I can argue.

I don't want food, I want Evie, so I try to follow, but it still takes me a few minutes to find her. She's sitting in the parlor and reading a book. I feel awkward going in—I'm pretty sure she doesn't like me very much—and even more so when she looks up at me. It's as if she's appraising me and I'm not up to her standards.

Nothing I'm not used to.

"They were here five days," she says at last. I open my mouth, but she gives me a look—one that tells me to shut my mouth, so I do. She continues, "In those five days, we've hired only the best physicians to work on her case. Asher has spent practically every waking moment with her making sure she was comfortable and happy. Despite all this, the hallucinations did not improve. The doctors were, for lack of a better word, stumped."

I lift an eyebrow. I'm so confused right now.

"She never gave up hope on you. She either snuck out to see if you made it to the gate or forced Asher to go with her to check. Every day. She cares for you very much."

This time, my eyebrows wing up. Evie snuck out to look for me? I have to grin. Of course she did.

She leans forward, the book falling to the floor, forgotten. "It's obvious she loves you and you love her." She pauses as if expecting me to argue, and a tiny bit of warmth creeps into her eyes when I don't. But there's sadness there, too, when she says, "Keep in mind you're not the only one."

That's not surprising really. My mom fell in love with Evie almost immediately. So did my sister, and my brother. Evie just has that way about her. I don't even know what it is exactly.

Maybe it's how strong she is despite everything that's happened to her. She's a fighter. That's for sure. And she's nice and polite to everyone, even when she's pissed. Especially when she's pissed. It's like she's trying to actually kill you with kindness.

I realize Asher's grandmother is still staring at me, waiting for my answer, so I nod.

"They went back to Elysium."

The blood drains from my face. I can feel it. My head spins and I have to catch myself on a chair next to me to prevent myself from falling. I lower myself to it slowly.

"No. Absolutely not." It's all the words I can muster. I can't seem to remember how to form sentences.

She finally meets my eyes. "The nanos are malfunctioning. It's probably what's causing her issues. Her memory loss. Her blackouts. Her hallucinations. If they don't get them fixed and/or removed, she'll die."

I shake my head. "The nanos are only in her to prevent pressure sickness and to promote healing. That's what she told me when we were in Elysium. They're not making her sick." I pause at her expression. "What?"

"No. They're not. That's not at all what they're for."

"How do you know?"

She won't meet my eyes. And that bad feeling comes back with a vengeance. "I helped invent the nanos. I lived in Elysium. For a time."

My whole body trembles. And black spots swim in front of my eyes. *No. That's not possible. That can't be possible.* "You're from Elysium?"

"I am."

He betrayed me. Again. And I trusted him. I clench my hands into fists, red spots replacing the black ones. I can't believe I fell for it again. I knew better! Damn it! I strike the arm of the chair so hard my entire arm aches from the force. I shove up from the chair.

"Where are you going?"

"To get her back. I'm not letting her go to Elysium." I say it like I'm challenging her, and I think I am. Challenging her to stop me from going after Evie.

She sighs. "I understand why you wouldn't want her to go back, but it is her only option. Eli—my partner—can help fix her."

"That's a lie," I shout. Then something even worse occurs to me, making my stomach roll with terror. "That's why Mayor St. James was here. Why Asher was so willing to help us. He knew. He *knew* from the beginning and he had *no* intention of really helping." I glare at her. "You're one of *them*. One of those . . . those monsters, and you're going to get Evie killed. Just like my father."

Her voice is soft in comparison to mine. "Yes, Kristofer was here. And yes it was because of Evie. But I would *never* let them hurt her, especially my son-in-law. You don't live this long, with the secrets I know, by being foolish, boy. Even though Kristofer thinks he's calling the shots, I always have strings to pull and an ace in the hole. I wouldn't have sent her back to Elysium if I didn't think it was the only option." She shakes her head. "I'm not one of them, but your ranting sounds just like them . . . Surface Dweller."

I stop and spin around, my heart thudding in my ears like a drum. "What did you say?"

"I lost someone important to me, too, because of *her*. I

know how horrible Mother is. I don't think anyone but you and I know exactly how much of a monster she is, Gavin. But you have to understand how important this is. Going back is Evie's *only* chance. *Eli* is Evie's only chance. He made those nanos what they are; he'll be able to fix them to get her back to normal."

"I don't believe you."

"I don't blame you," she says with a sad smile. "I wouldn't believe me either." It's said so matter-of-factly, I'm suddenly sure it's the truth. I blink dumbly at her. "Do you even know what nanos really are?"

I shake my head.

"Sit. Please. You make me nervous when you hulk over me like that." She laughs softly, but I don't. I don't find anything funny about any of this. She sighs and gestures to the chair again. I lean against it instead, crossing my arms over my chest.

"Nanos are short for nanorobotics. Robots so small you can't see them unless you have a microscope. They're built on a nanoscale, which is why they're called nanobots. A nanometer is something like one billionth of a meter."

"Okay, so they're really small. I got that already."

Her entire face pinches, and I think she's finally going to lose her temper, but she takes a deep breath and continues. "Yes. They're really small. They were originally invented long before the War for medical purposes. At first simple things like site-specific medication delivery, microsurgery, and diag-

nosis. Then certain electronic companies started experimenting to make them smarter by adding propulsion systems
and the ability to control them remotely."

"I don't get what this has to do with Evie. . . ."

"I'm getting there. Mostly, nanites were used for peaceful purposes. And while they were important, most funding
went to less . . . out-there . . . programs. So, as you can imagine, progress was slow. But then the War started and the old
governments realized that nanotechnology wasn't just for
science fiction. They started an arms race with each other.
To find the most cost efficient, yet effective weapon possible
to turn the tide and win. They spent billions on technology
and scientists and engineers. I was one of those engineers.
Hired straight out of engineering school. I'd invented the
nanites that were used in the warheads that took down almost
every major city in the world by the time I was twenty-five."

I plop back into the chair, because my wobbly legs can't
hold my weight anymore. "Holy shit."

She cracks a smile. "Indeed."

"How . . . how did that happen?"

She shrugs. "Vanity." She waves her hand at me. "But that's
not important. What is important is that technology is the
same technology I took to Elysium when Mother hired me."

"She hired you?"

"Yes. She wanted me to develop permanent sentient
nanites that would protect her people from disease. I did it,
too. With the help of Eli, my partner. But Mother turned it

against us. She didn't want to prevent diseases, or not totally. She wanted control. Complete control, and she got it. All because of me."

I'm more confused than anything. "I don't get it."

"The nanites do whatever they're programmed to do. Prevent disease. Repair body tissues. Destroy them. Rewrite neuropathways." She gives me a meaningful look. "But the program only works if it's functional. Something broke Evie's. She needs it fixed, and I'm fairly certain Eli's the only one who can do it. Before something worse happens."

I stare at her. I can barely wrap my mind around what she's saying. This is insane. Then again, maybe I shouldn't be surprised. If there's one thing I know for sure, it's that Mother is insane.

Then another thought hits me. I remember this story. And I remember exactly where I heard it. Elysium. In the journals Evie found in the secret room in the abandoned sector. Except the story came from a different person.

Eli.

Who was killed. By Mother.

He's not even there. They're going back to Elysium to get help from a guy who's been dead before Evie was even born.

I shove to my feet, the chair falling over with a clatter.

"When did they leave?"

She frowns at me. "An hour or so, I think. I don't know. They snuck out."

I curse under my breath and rush to the front door.

"Where are you going?"

"To stop them."

"Didn't you hear what I said about the nanos?"

I don't even turn around. My mind is swirling with ideas of how to stop them. "Yeah. I heard you. And I also know that Eli is dead."

"Wait. What?" Her breath catches. "How do you know?"

Grimacing, I turn to look at her. "We found his journals. And then we found Mother's. He tried to start an uprising." I swallow and lick my lips. "Mother put a stop to it."

Her shoulders shake and her lips tremble; then her eyes grow wide. "You have stop them. Mother will kill them, and with Eli gone . . ." She shakes her head.

I yank open the door.

"You'll never catch them on foot," she calls out to me.

"I don't plan on running all the way there."

"Then how?"

"I'll figure something out." I push out the door.

"Good luck."

Whether or not luck is on my side, I will do whatever it takes to get to Evie before she leaves for Elysium.

Chapter Twenty-one

When traveling the Outlands, it is highly recommended to travel in groups of no less than three people. Should you need to travel in smaller groups, make sure to pack appropriately in case of emergency situations, keeping in mind the severe climate changes that take place in the Outlands. Travelers would also not go amiss carrying firearms to protect themselves from the wildlife.

—Excerpt from *Safety Guide to Traveling the Outlands*

Evie

The thud of the horses' hooves and the jingling of their reins and saddles are the only sound as we rush back to the village. We've been riding all night and I'm exhausted and sore and my skin is completely numb from the cold.

Asher is riding next to me and he looks just as tired. "How long?"

He sighs, and looks at the rising sun. "A few more hours until we stop to eat and rest the horses."

My stomach growls at the mention of food and he laughs. "Maybe only another hour."

The entire time we're riding, I try not to think about what's waiting for me under the ocean. There are too many unknowns. So instead, I let my mind drift.

It's so different from the trip to Rushlake. It's freezing for one. Plus the two guards with their guns and whatever else they have in those large packs. And we're moving much faster than a walk. Not as fast as when we were running to get away from the coyotes, but fast enough. Also, the air is so much drier. Even though our packs have water and food in them, my mouth and nose feel caked with sand.

Despite my discomfort, it doesn't take long for me to be dragged down into another dream. But this one is different. It starts as so many of them do, with me covered in blood and terrified, my mind filled with pain and misery. Something horrible has obviously happened, but I can't remember what as I sit on the floor of a shower stall and let the freezing water sluice over me.

I'm hoping the water will wake me, but even when I'm completely clean and shivering, I still feel weighted down. The water soaks my bandage and burns the wound, but I can't make myself get out. I just sit in the corner of the granite stall and bury my face in my hands. I've cried myself dry, but that doesn't stop the sorrow.

Eventually, Gavin comes to check on me. He knocks at first, but I ignore it, hoping he'll just go away. I should have known better, because when he receives no answer he pushes into the room. Then rushes across the bathroom, practically ripping the curtain from its hooks in his hurry to check on me.

His expression changes from worry to sadness when he sees me curled into the corner. He turns off the water with a flick of a wrist, then bundles me into a fluffy white—and dusty—towel and carries me into the bedroom. Then he starts chafing me with the towel, trying to rub warmth into my freezing body.

Even when I stop shivering, I still feel cold. I wonder if I'll ever feel warm again.

"How are you feeling?" he asks after several minutes.

I jump. I hadn't expected him to talk. "I don't know," I say. "She was my best friend. And she died because of me."

"Not you. Never you. Mother. She's the one who started this."

"I'm an Enforcer," I say without any emotion. "A monster."

"No, Evie. Not a monster," he says quietly.

"I killed those people. I've killed lots of people. All in the name of Mother's 'peace.'"

"Because Mother programmed you to do it. And Nick. Apparently." He takes my chin in his hand and forces me to look at him. "You also saved me. And you tried to save Macie. You only killed the guards in self-defense and you stopped yourself from killing the innocent people in the hallway. That's not a monster."

There's nothing to say to that.

"You're not afraid? Of me?" I ask finally, averting my eyes.

He waits until I look back up at him before he shakes his head and smiles at me. "No. Never."

Gavin pulls me into his arms again and kisses me. Gently at first, then more aggressively. As if he can't help himself. And the minute of panic fades as if it was never there. The kiss has the effect that nothing else has—it warms my blood and soothes my soul. I don't want it to stop.

Starshine veers and bumps into Asher's horse, who nips at her and startles me awake. I stare around for a minute, lost as to where I really am. The dream felt so real, I could swear I'd really been there and not here.

And then I realize.

It wasn't just a dream, it was a memory. A real memory. Not the stitched-together ones.

And I still remember it.

I smile as I savor it. It's the first memory I've been able to keep. And it's of him. My Gavin.

The smile fades when I remember I'll never be able to tell him.

The final two hours are a misery. No matter what I do, I can't get comfortable and we've only stopped long enough to rest the horses and fill our bellies and theirs before moving on again. I have no idea how they can keep up the pace, but they don't so much as neigh a complaint.

When we finally pull up to the village, it's dark with only the stars and moon to guide us. It looks just like it did before we left, and I almost expect to see Gavin waiting at the gates. But, of course, he's not.

Asher jumps out when we get to the gate to talk to the

guards. I watch as something passes between the two men; then the gates open and Asher signals me forward. The gates shut again behind us, while the guard stubbornly looks in the other direction and we continue into the village. Asher guides his horse to a stable like the one in Rushlake.

He helps me down and turns to our escorts when they step up to us. He talks with them for several minutes and, like with the guard, he hands something to the two of them. More bribes.

They promptly put it into their pockets and take the horses from us, while Asher guides me gently but firmly away.

It's still quiet, with only the occasional howls from outside the gates that I now recognize as coyotes. I shudder, remembering how vicious they were and how lucky we'd been to avoid them this time. Then again, Asher had a shotgun like Gavin's, so maybe it wasn't luck at all. Maybe they just knew better.

Asher leads me through the village, past Gavin's house. I don't look at it; I do not want anything to stop me from what I've decided to do. It doesn't take long before the lights from the village fade and our path is only illuminated by moon and starlight again. I glance up and watch the stars twinkle in their black canopy.

I'll miss this. I stop and take a few minutes to savor it.

Asher turns when he realizes I've stopped and returns to my side. "We'll see them again." He sounds so sure, I almost believe him.

"Of course we will." I shift so I'm looking at him.

He watches me for a moment, then turns and continues on. "We'd better hurry."

Without saying a word, I follow.

We're quiet the entire way to another large building. "Welcome to our boathouse," he says, tossing out his hand in a grand gesture.

"Boathouse?"

"Well, that's probably giving it too much credit." I have to agree. It's not much of a house at all. The wood has rotted away entirely in places. I'm not entirely confident the whole thing won't collapse on top of us the minute we step inside.

The door is unlocked and Asher pulls it open with a squeal of hinges. The sound is deafening in the quiet. We hold our breath as we wait to see if the sound has given us away.

After a few minutes, it's obvious no alarm has gone out, so we slip into the building. There, next to a rotting dock, is a shiny silver vehicle. It glows in the moonlight streaming through the holes in the roof.

"Here it is," Asher says. "Dad hid it away in here after you and Gavin showed up in it. He had a bunch of guys from Rushlake studying it, but they never could figure out how to open it." He shrugs.

Hesitantly I reach a hand out to the sleek silver machine and feel the cool metal and glass under my touch. I'm not sure what I expected, but nothing happens. Not even a hint of a memory.

Asher is watching me expectantly, so I shake my head. He lets out a breath. "Let's just get this show on the road."

"Road?" I frown. "Elysium is underwater."

He laughs. "Just an expression."

I turn my attention back to the boat, trying to locate the mechanism that will open the door. Asher kneels next to me, his thigh bumping mine as we run our fingers over the glossy surface.

After a few minutes, he straightens in triumph. "Here it is." The glass top opens with a hiss.

I lift an eyebrow and he grins at me. "They never figured out how to open it, but I did."

He turns and holds his hand out to help me up. I grasp it and let him haul me to my feet, wobbling slightly as the blood rushes from my head. "Why didn't you tell them?"

"They never asked." He looks away from me and I know that's not the real answer.

"Evie!" a voice says behind Asher. Asher spins and I peer around him, my heart somersaulting in my chest.

Gavin is standing there, his skin pale in the moonlight.

I tug on Asher's clothes. "Please, *please*, tell me you see Gavin, too. Please tell me I'm not just hallucinating." My voice has a pleading, almost hysterical, edge to it.

Asher stares if he can't believe his eyes, but then he shoves his hands into his pockets. He gives me this smile that I can't decipher before he nods.

"I see him. He's real."

Even then, I can't seem to make my legs move. Gavin's breath is coming out in ragged gasps and he's leaning over as he drags in more air, but he takes another step forward, tripping a little over his feet. "You're all right. Please tell me you're all right."

This time I can't stop myself—the desperation in the plea breaks through the shock and I rush to him.

He tucks a strand of hair behind my ear before cupping my cheek in his hand. I lean into it, letting my eyes drift closed and breathing his scent like air. Then his lips brush mine, and my stomach flips, like it does every time I kiss him. There's just something about that initial touch.

Then I'm pressing my lips harder against his and pulling him closer to me, as if even the tiniest space between us is too much. Tears flow down my cheeks, and he just keeps brushing them away with his thumbs.

Asher clears his throat, but I'm not ready to let go yet.

"Where were you?" My voice is still thick with tears and muffled in Gavin's chest. "We thought you were dead. *I* thought you were dead."

He's silent for a long moment, but his voice is filled with emotion—regret, pain, terror—when he finally says, "I'm sorry, Evie. I'm so sorry." He pulls me tighter to him and I don't have the heart to make him tell me the whole story right now.

"How did you get here?" I decide to ask instead.

He rests his forehead against mine. "I thought I was going to be too late," he whispers.

"I'm —" I start, but he interrupts me.

"I can't believe you just took off with him." He glares at Asher. "What were you thinking? I told you what it's like down there. You can't go down there. *She* can't go back. Mother will *kill* her. The nanos—"

Asher cuts him off. "Grandma told us about them. They're broken. And Eli—"

"Eli is dead," Gavin says. He glances down at me. "We saw him die, Evie. In Mother's diary. There was a link to a video. It showed the lead scientist, Eli, being killed by his nanos. Him and the majority of his sector."

I knit my brows together, my eyes searching his face. "That can't be true."

He hugs me. "It is. I'm sorry."

"Even if it is," Asher says. "There has to be someone there that can help."

Gavin gently pushes me away. "Are you stupid? There's no one there to help her. The only thing you'll find there is death." His eyes are wild. I can see his pulse racing.

"Gavin, calm down."

He takes me by the shoulders. "No. Not until you say you're not going to go."

I want to say I'll stay. For him. To make him happy. But I can't, because I'd only be staying for him. And that's not right for either of us. Closing my eyes, I say, "No, Gavin, I'm not. I made up my mind and I'm going to Elysium. They're the only ones who can help me."

"There's not anyone who *can* help you. Eli's gone. I wouldn't be surprised if Mother killed everyone who worked on nanos. The minute you set foot back in that freak show, Mother is going to be all over you like white on rice. We barely escaped last time. I'm not letting you go."

Anger makes my heart beat faster. I lift my chin. "Letting me? You don't *let* me do anything. I choose. Me. Not you. And I *choose* to go to Elysium." He opens his mouth, but this time I don't let him speak. "I *have* to go back. I'm tired of having bits and pieces thrown at me, and not being able to hold on to any of them." I take his hands in mine. "I just . . . I don't belong here. I've felt lost since I got here."

He squeezes his eyes shut. "I know. But going back isn't going to help you."

"It might. I have to try."

Gavin turns to Asher, his eyes feverish. He starts pacing, his movements short and jerky, to Asher and then back to me. He's muttering something to himself, a look of intense concentration on his face, and it terrifies me. I've never seen him like this.

I don't see it coming until it's too late. Gavin throws himself at Asher. The two fall onto the wood dock and it makes an ominous creaking sound. Before I can do anything more than avoid being pulled down with them, Gavin swings his arm back and throws his fist into Asher's face.

Despite the shock of being tossed onto the ground, Asher throws his own punch, and pretty soon the boathouse is filled with the sounds of Gavin and Asher fighting.

"Hey. Stop!" I whisper-yell. Of course that doesn't do

anything, so I step closer. "Asher! Gavin! Stop it. You're going to give us away. Stop it!"

Nothing. Hoping for the best, I step into the fray and try to pull them apart. But it's as if they don't even see me, and I get a fist to the side of my head for my trouble. My vision swims with red and black spots. I'm not sure which one did it, but Asher immediately stops, his eyes glued to my face.

"Evie, are you okay?" he asks, but Gavin evidently hasn't noticed what happened, and takes advantage of Asher's distraction to hit him in the face again. Asher tries to brush him off and stand, but Gavin keeps coming.

Suddenly there's that click in my head again, and all the pain I'm feeling disappears. My vision clears and the hatred on Gavin's face is clearly visible. *Surface Dwellers are dangerous.*

I grab him by the shoulder and spin him around. Shock widens his eyes when he sees me, but before he can do anything more than that, I punch him in the stomach. His breath whooshes out with an *oomph* and he bends over, clutching his abdomen. Then I straighten my hand and chop him in the back of the neck. Not too hard, just enough to knock him out.

He immediately falls to the ground, out cold. It's as if a light is switched off, and I fall to my own knees as all the strength and energy I just had pours out of me. Asher kneels next to me.

"Are you all right?" He presses a hand to the side of my face and I hiss. He makes a face. "That's going to bruise. It's already turning colors. Come on." He shoots a disgusted look to Gavin. "We'd better go before he comes to."

Repulsed by what I did, I say, "We can't just leave him

here. He could be hurt. *I* could have hurt him." My stomach rolls. What is *wrong* with me?

Asher opens his mouth like he's going to say something, but then stops when he sees my face. He sighs. "Fine. He'll just have to come with." He smirks. "Boy is he going to be pissed when he wakes up and realizes where we are."

That only makes me feel worse. Asher sighs again, then helps me to my feet. "Let's get you in first." He helps me into the seat next to the driver's seat, before unceremoniously dragging Gavin through the hatch until he's crumpled onto the floor behind us.

"Asher!" I chastise, but he only skirts around Gavin to go to the console.

I rush to Gavin and kneel beside him, adjusting him so he's not just piled onto the floor like so much unwanted rubbish. Brushing the hair out of his face, I see dark shadows under his eyes, not to mention a slew of other bruises, cuts, and scrapes, some of them in the process of forming because of his altercation with Asher just now. And there's an ugly yellow bruise peeking out from under the collar of his dirty and torn T-shirt. I tug it down to see that the bruise covers pretty much his entire shoulder and upper right chest. Guilt tears at me for knocking him out, but it wars with relief and utter joy at seeing him again. Alive. Knocked out because of me, and pretty beat up, but alive.

"Better get buckled up, Evie. This will probably be a bumpy ride," Asher says, startling me. I'd all but forgotten he was there.

At first, I consider ignoring Asher, but then I realize if I do lose my balance and fall, I'll land on Gavin, causing more harm.

I press a gentle kiss to his forehead and run my fingers along the side of his face, before sighing and pushing myself up to walk to my seat and buckle up.

Seated behind the console, Asher frowns and pushes a button, but nothing happens. He pushes another. No response.

Finally, his face lights up. "This *has* to be it," he says, and tries one more. The glass top shuts over the top of us and he leans over the console, more confident now, before pushing a lever forward. We move, the nose dipping down so we can pass under the broken doors leading to the open water.

Soon we're completely under the surface. My breath catches in my throat when it closes over our heads. For a terrifying few seconds I'm dead certain that we're going to drown, but then Asher says, *"With hands held high into the sky so blue, As the ocean opens up to swallow you."*

"I'm sorry?"

He turns to me, and shrugs. "It was from a song back before the War."

"Ah."

He turns back to controlling the sub and the way he's competently pushing buttons I have to think he knows what he's doing. I turn to ask how, but he only smiles at me, obviously anticipating the question. "I . . . ah . . . kind of played with this when you first got here."

I laugh, roll my eyes, and shake my head. Of course he

did. "Didn't your dad know you were playing around with this thing?"

He gives me a look. "My dad doesn't know anything unless his assistants tell him. And he doesn't know anything of what I do, unless I screw something up."

I wrinkle my nose and go back to staring at the water. I try to control the flutters in my stomach that seem to grow stronger with each passing air bubble.

It's hard to tell how fast we're going since it all looks the same and I don't know how long it'll take to get there. I decide to ask Asher, since he seems to know where we're going. He's probably gone down there a lot while "playing around."

He shrugs. "Don't know."

"But . . . you *do* know where we're going, don't you?"

He shakes his head. "Not a clue."

I lift an eyebrow and sit up straighter. "Then . . . what . . . how are we going to get there?"

Even in the dim light from the console, I can see him blush. "Uh . . . the buttons are labeled and this one here says 'autopilot.' When I pressed it, it gave me a list of choices. I chose Sector Three."

I stare at him for a minute, then burst out laughing. "Cheater," I say.

Asher winks at me, then goes back to studying the panel, while I look over at Gavin. He's still breathing, so that's a good thing, but I'm worried about him. He's been out awhile.

But I can't find it in me to feel too bad about it when I

think how close I am to answers. To getting my memories—and my mind—back.

Asher looks over. "You okay?"

"Just excited." It's not *entirely* a lie.

From the look he gives me, I can tell he doesn't really believe me, but he only says, "Okay, just let me know if you need anything."

I don't respond, but when I turn to face out the window, I gasp and stand to walk closer to the front of the sub and get a better view. Asher gasps behind me.

There, rising in the murky depths, like Atlantis, is Elysium. I've never seen anything more beautiful. The feeling of rightness returns with a vengeance and I smile.

"I'm home," I say and press a hand to the glass in front of me.

Chapter Twenty-two

PRIVATE PROPERTY.
TRESPASSERS WILL BE PROSECUTED
TO THE FULLEST EXTENT OF THE LAW*
*The Law in Elysium permits the use of lethal force.
—Sign in submersible bay

Evie

The computerized voice of the submersible says to have a seat and buckle up to prepare for docking, and while I do sit, I can't stop staring openmouthed at everything as we drift slowly down a trench. From a distance, it looks like an overgrown, lopsided octopus. In the trench, though, you can see one entire side is lit up like a strange glow-in-the-dark honeycomb. Directly below us I can see more lights. The sub slows and I have a minute of panic about what we'll meet when we dock. A memory pushes into my brain of a glass-walled room filled with blue-eyed, blond-haired girls, all wearing the same thing.

Black dresses and hooded capes, with black gloves and black boots covering up every square inch of visible skin.

Enforcers, my brain supplies not so helpfully, and I shiver. Something about them makes my blood run cold.

Another flash: I'm standing in the center of the room and all around me are the charred remains of the girls . . . the Enforcers.

I blink when I hear the computer voice again reminding us to remain seated. That was the same memory I had in the Outlands. So that was probably real, too!

My breathing is ragged and I recognize the signs of an impending attack. Despite the ominous computer warnings, Asher pushes himself up, leaps over the few centimeters separating us, and tries to shove my head between my knees. I push him away.

"I'm fine," I rasp, trying to swallow the cough away. "I'm not having a panic attack. Promise."

"Then what's wrong?" he asks.

"I remember them," I whisper. "We were there, trying to find a way into the submersible, and they were trying to break down the door." I look up to meet Asher's eyes. "Mother. I think. Her Enforcers. And, before that, these strange, murderous men. Gavin was right." My heart speeds up. Oh Mother. Gavin was right.

I shove my own head between my legs this time.

"It's okay, Evie. We'll be fine. It's been weeks. It's doubtful they're still there. I'm sure your mother took care of them.

No way she's going to let murderers run around and destroy her perfect city, right?"

After a minute, I nod. "I hope you're right."

We're all jolted as the submersible docks to what, according to the computer, is Sector Three. The seat belt digs painfully into my ribs, but Asher gets the worst of it when he flies into the front of the submersible, then back. He lands on top of Gavin, who groans.

Poor Gavin.

Asher quickly shoves himself to his feet and brushes himself off, before giving me this cocky grin that says, "I meant to do that."

Snickering, I disconnect myself from the seat belt and turn to face the rear of the sub, where another door I didn't know existed is open. I can see what appears to be the room from my memory.

I exchange a look with Asher, who takes a deep breath and starts forward. "Stay here," he says. "The big red button on the console closes the door. If I shout, shut the door."

I narrow my eyes at him. "I'm not letting you go out there alone."

"But I—" He points to himself, then hesitates and adds helplessly, "And you . . ."

I use my best no arguments voice. "I don't seem to recall you tearing vulture-hawks apart with your bare hands."

He flushes. "You're injured."

"So are you." Gavin gave him a good walloping on the dock. There's still a bit of blood trickling from his nose.

He sighs. "Will you at least let me go first?"

"A gentleman always lets a lady go first." I push out of my seat and lead the way onto the concrete deck.

There are bloodstains and burn marks on the floor. I don't even know what could have left the divots in the concrete, and I don't think I want to.

"Nobody's here," Asher whispers from behind me.

I scan the room, wishing I could have the clear vision I experienced every time I've had to protect myself. "Yes, but *something* happened here."

"Obviously," someone says behind me, and I whirl around, my heart flying into my throat.

Gavin stands just inside the submersible, rubbing the back of his neck. "Damn it, Evie. Did you really have to knock me out?"

I open my mouth to apologize, but Asher beats me to it. "You should know better than anyone that she didn't mean to. Besides, if you hadn't attacked me like a maniac, she wouldn't have had to subdue you."

" 'Subdue'? Fancy word for coldcock." Gavin glares at him, then turns his attention to the room. He shudders and gets that wild look in his eyes again. I swallow and worry that he's going to do something to Asher again, but he takes a deep breath and his eyes focus. He looks around, zeroing in on the doors. "Looks like someone did some clean up." He turns his attention to me, his eyes traveling up and down my body. "How are you feeling? Anything different?"

I assess myself, then shake my head. "Everything feels the same."

He gives Asher a smug look, even though it's easy to see the worry lines spreading across his brow. "See? Nothing has changed. Now let's get the hell out of here before Mother figures out we're back."

He takes a step back into the sub, but Asher says, "Nice try. We have to find someone to fix Evie."

"No one here can help her. Everyone here is *trained* to *hurt* her," Gavin points out. He shifts slightly to one foot and almost instantly transfers his weight back.

"Someone here has to know *something* about nanos. They wouldn't keep using them if no one here knew how to make them work or fix them if they malfunctioned." Asher tilts his head to the side, his expression saying, "Just try to argue with me."

Gavin stares daggers at him and I'm terrified they're going to get into it again.

"Come on, Gavin. We made it this far," I say. "We can't quit now." And I have no plans of doing so either.

He crosses his arms over his chest. "We need to go back."

Asher looks at me, then shrugs. "Then go. No one is stopping you." Then he turns back to the door. "Come on, Evie, let's go find some help."

Gavin still has his arms crossed, but he's watching me now, his eyes pleading with me. I look back to Asher, who has his hand on the door, then back to Gavin.

I let out a breath and give Gavin a look of apology. "I have to." It tears me up inside to do it, but I go to Asher, who opens the door and glances around quickly before stepping into the hall. Second-guessing and regretting every step I take away from Gavin, I follow Asher into the hallway.

My mind whirls with déjà vu, but I can't remember what exactly is familiar about it. Other than it reminds me a bit of that strange complex Asher and I got lost in, back in the Outlands. My body tingles a bit as I wait for some kind of panic attack, but when nothing happens, I release the breath I didn't know I was holding.

"Where to?" Asher's voice echoes. There are only two options, but it's pitch-dark one way and the other dead-ends several meters up ahead.

"I guess this way." I start moving down the pitch-dark hallway.

Asher follows, and we're a ways down the hall when we hear a door open. Because of the echoes it's hard to tell where the door is, but when we hear footsteps, we push ourselves tight against the wall and try to breathe as shallowly as possible.

The footsteps tread slowly, and a light flicks on to our left—the way we came from—but I can't see who's holding it. I hope it's Gavin, but I doubt it. Where would he have gotten a light?

The light sweeps from side to side as it continues forward and my heart pumps furiously. I wonder if anyone else can hear it. I'm afraid to move, but if we stay where we are we'll be caught for sure.

Finally, I decide I have to move. I slide my foot out, then move my body to join it.

The light immediately swings in my direction and shines in my face, blinding me. "Evie?" Gavin says, the same relief I feel in his voice.

"Oh, thank Mother," I say, wrapping my arms around him in a strangle hold as he steps next to me.

"I'd rather not, actually," he says, but he holds me just as tightly. The stuff in his hands presses painfully into my back, but I don't care.

"You stayed," I say, my voice muffled by his chest.

He pushes me away a little and tilts my chin up with his finger. "I won't ever leave you again."

"Promise?" I ask.

"Promise." He smiles, but before I can smile back he's kissing me. My stomach flips and my heart trips, but I kiss him back, breathing in his scent like air and holding on to him as if my life depends on it. And it might just. I don't think I could handle it if he were gone again. Thinking he was dead had just about killed me, too.

Behind me, Asher clears his throat and regretfully I peel myself from Gavin, but I wrap my hand around his forearm. I'm not letting him go again, either.

"Where did you find that?" Asher cuts in, gesturing to the light in Gavin's hand.

"It's from before. We needed it the last time we were here because the Enforcers cut off the power so the murderous monsters running around the Sector would have an easier time killing us. Thankfully we had plasma and machine guns." He shoves something at Asher. "I left them in the submersible. I guess it's a good thing, too. If I can't persuade you not to go, at least I can try to offer some kind of protection."

"What is this?" Asher stares at the silver contraption in his hand.

"It's a gun, dipshit. It's called a Reising and it's fully automatic. You do know how to work a gun, don't you? I'm all out of knives."

"Knives?" Asher asks. I'm a bit perplexed myself.

"I figured with all your backstabbing experience a knife would be your weapon of choice, right?"

Asher makes this sound in his throat and I step between the two of them, trying to prevent another fight. This isn't the time or the place.

"Great! We have weapons. Let's keep moving, shall we?"

At first no one moves, and then Asher puts a hand on my shoulder. "Lead the way. I'll be right behind you."

Gavin snorts. "Typical. Hiding behind someone." He slings the Reising over his shoulder by the strap and palms the smaller one, holding it and the flashlight in the same hand and taking my hand with the other, before he starts walking, leaving Asher to follow or not.

Gavin

The Sector is so quiet it's almost creepier than the first time we were here. It's hard to believe that it *is* the same place.

But I don't drop my guard. I'm sure those . . . things are still here somewhere and the minute I turn in the wrong direction they're going to jump out and claw my face off.

I don't want to be here. What I really want to do is grab Evie in a football hold and run straight back to the submarine. But Evie is nothing if not stubborn, and with Asher feeding her stubbornness, there's no way I would win. So it's on to plan B. Which . . . I haven't quite figured out yet. Being here makes it almost impossible to think.

The dark is playing tricks on my mind. There are times that I'm positive something is right next to me, so close it could breathe on me, but when I flash the light, there's nothing there. And then there's the horrible creaking sounds. It reminds me of when I used to climb around the old wrecked warships as a kid. The sound was unnerving when I heard it then; it's even more terrifying now. It's making me jumpy, and my nerves are so tight I'm afraid they're going to snap at any minute.

We turn down another corridor and I pause, trying to remember which way to go to get to the elevators. I focus on bringing up the map I have in my head from when I was here last, and I'm concentrating so hard I don't see what I'm walking into until my foot catches on something and I land with my nose just inches from something that smells incredibly disgusting. Evie tugs on me to help me up, asking if I'm okay. I quickly shove to my feet, thinking the worst of what I almost landed in. A body. *Part* of a body? Something worse? I don't want to look at whatever it is but I know I don't have a choice.

I expect to see blood and body parts, like last time. But what I see when I shine the light down totally confuses me. It's definitely a puddle of something, but it's a greenish color instead of red.

"What's wrong?" Evie asks.

"I almost fell in something weird." I squat down to examine it and she does the same, placing a hand on my thigh when she teeters a bit. She reaches out, but I grab her wrist. "Don't," I say. "Who knows what this stuff is."

Asher peers over her shoulder. "Yeah, it could be acid or something. We wouldn't want you to lose a finger."

She yanks her hand away and I peer at him over my shoulder. "Really, Asher? Really? Do you just say every little thing that pops into your head?"

"Not everything."

Even though I can't really see him in the dark, the smirk in his voice is obvious and it sets my teeth on edge.

"Well, the next time you want to open your mouth, use that tiny thing in your head that passes for a brain, will ya?"

"I think you're confusing my brain with your—"

"Enough!" Evie says, and the heat of her gaze burns my face. "Can you two just pretend to get along until we get back to the Surface? *Please.*"

We both mumble "Sorry," but I'm sure we both know she's asking for too much.

"What do you think this is?" I can feel her watching me again, so I'm pretty sure she's talking to me.

"I don't know. I don't want to touch it."

"Does it really matter, guys? I mean, it's green goo. So what? Let's just keep going so we can get somewhere there's light," Asher says.

"What's the matter? Afraid of the dark?" I say, smiling.

"Gavin," Evie warns. "Asher's right. Let's keep moving." She places her hand on my thigh again to push herself up.

I stand and hop over the puddle, before turning to shine the light on it so Evie can see her way around. As soon as she's over, I turn around and start walking away, keeping her hand in mine.

"Hey!" Asher says. "What about me? I don't want to step in that stuff."

I pretend not to hear him and keep going. A few seconds later I smile when I hear, "Ugh! Gross!" Music to my ears.

But then, Asher says, "Uh. Guys? I'm stuck."

I laugh as I turn back around to see him pulling on the leg that's supposedly stuck in the puddle. "Seriously, Asher? Now's not the time to pull that shit. Stop kidding around."

He looks up at me and I don't see the glint of amusement in his eyes, I see anxiousness. "I'm not joking. It's really stuck."

"Really?" I stare closer at his arms pulling on his legs. He's definitely straining to yank his foot out.

Releasing Evie, I bend down and start tugging too, but it's really stuck. No matter how hard I pull, it doesn't even budge. Then I realize something that sends chills down my spine. The muck is actually creeping up his shoe.

"Take your shoe off. Take it off now," I shout, yanking at his laces now instead of his leg.

He starts pulling at them, too, and for a minute we're battling each other for the laces until we finally get them loose enough for him to wrench his foot from the shoe. The three of us share a glance, but can only stare in horror as his entire shoe is consumed.

"What. The. Hell?" Asher says, still staring at the spot his shoe was.

"I have no flippin' clue," I say, more shaken than I want to admit.

"Those were my favorite shoes." Asher rips off the other shoe and throws it at the crap. It floats on the surface for a minute before it too sinks. "Damn it."

Evie grabs my hand and tugs on it. "We should get away from here." Her voice is soft, but I can hear the nerves underneath and her hand is sweating. She's never shown her nerves this much. She really must be scared. If she can keep going, as scared as she is, so can I.

I nod and start forward again.

We continue walking, every so often running into more puddles. We're careful to avoid them, each of us working with the others to make sure everyone makes it over them, especially the larger ones. And especially Asher. It's bad enough he has to walk around barefoot; we don't need him to lose them, too. The puddles are strange, though. It's too dark, even with the flashlight, to see them completely, but I've never seen liquid pool in the shapes that these are collecting in. There's no sign of a source, so we ignore them as much as possible and keep going.

It's entirely too quiet again, the only sounds the scrape of our shoes against the concrete, that odd groaning sound, and Asher's occasional mutterings about me purposely getting us lost. And while it's definitely not purposeful, I have to admit we probably are. Lost, that is. I'd only traveled this way once, and we'd gotten a little distracted running for our lives from the insane cannibals. It's a wee bit hard to remember where to turn.

Eventually, with more luck than anything else, when we turn yet another corner—I'm *sure* we didn't turn this much last time—I see a tiny bit of light peeking around a corner.

I rush forward, reaching behind me to grab Evie's hand and tug so she'll follow me. As unrealistic as I know this is, my mind begs for the light because light equals safety. Her feet drag a little until she sees why I'm rushing. She speeds up a bit and I don't feel so much like I'm dragging her behind me.

"Hey! Wait up!" Asher calls from behind us, but we ignore him. I stop only when I get into the light. The hallway looks just like I remember it. Long, and empty. Concrete walls with the occasional door. Every so often down the hall there are more piles of gunk, and their shapes are starting to click in my head. They almost look like bodies, or parts of bodies, but I'm almost positive my memories of this damned place are making me imagine it, like when you see shapes in the clouds. This makes me especially grateful for the light.

I follow down the corridors with the lights working until *finally* I see a set of elevator banks. I rush to the button and press it, then press it again a few seconds later. Then again. Over and over again, until Evie places her hand on mine, stopping me.

Come on. Come on. Come on.

Inside the shafts the car clangs and bangs as it gets pulled up. My mind flashes on those monsters from the last time. I shudder as I remember how the whole hallway had been filled with blood. Sprays of it on the walls, dripping from the ceiling. And a carpet of bodies strewn across the floor. It dawns on me that I should be more careful. Just because, so far, we haven't seen hide nor hair of them, doesn't mean they aren't waiting. An elevator would be just the place to hide.

I usher Evie and Asher back to wait behind a corner, where I watch for the elevator to arrive while they both stare at me like I've lost my mind. Maybe I have. I've never been more terrified in my life.

Asher shoves past me. "What are we waiting for? Let's go."

I grab him and yank him back. "Stay still," I hiss. "Those things could be in there."

Evie and Asher exchange a look and he wrinkles his nose. "You've lost it, dude. We haven't seen anyone in the entire time we've been here. There's no one here."

He steps forward again, and I snatch him back, shoving him to the wall so hard his head smashes against it. He yelps.

"Gavin!" Evie says, tugging on my arm.

I ignore her, shoving Asher into the wall again. "Damn it, Asher. Just flippin' listen to me for once. You're going to get us killed."

He scowls at me and rubs his head, but doesn't say anything. When the doors finally slide open and no one steps out, I palm the plasma gun and double-check to make sure it's loaded before stepping out into the hall.

It's a relief to see there's nothing in there. Not even any of the green goo. I signal for the others to come, and while Asher glowers at me when he gets to me, he gets into the elevator without saying a word. I ignore the concerned looks Evie keeps shooting me and press the button for the bottom floor. I'm pretty sure that's where the Tube station is anyway. I can't really remember where we'd started from when we were here before. I just know it was a relatively long elevator ride. But it's not like we can't start at the bottom and work our way up until we find the right floor if I'm wrong.

Snakes roll around in my stomach as my nerves act up. I *really* don't want to go back to the other side of Elysium. It makes the most sense to go there, but I don't know how we're going to get past the turrets and cameras. Even if we're not shot, the cameras will catch our every move. Evie might have been able to delete us from the targeting systems last time, but it seems unlikely Mother hasn't had her little trick undone by now. And there's no way Evie can get us back in the system now. Not without her memories.

We'll just have to use those maintenance tunnels again and hope we don't set off any of the turrets as we run from the Tube to the tunnel. Of course, the problem with that is, Evie has no memory of how to break the security on the doors. Maybe it'll come to her. Maybe just being in the area will spark some of her memories.

The way she's looking around like she's never seen an elevator before, I don't hold out much hope for that.

When we're finally about to hit the bottom level, I step in front of Evie and hold the plasma gun out in front of me. This is where our luck runs out. I'm sure of it. Evie makes a frustrated noise, but doesn't argue. Behind me Asher cocks the Reising, and steps up next to me.

I lift an eyebrow at him.

He shrugs. "You're not the only one who can protect her."

Evie makes that sound again. "I don't need protecting," she says, but her voice wavers. There's no doubt in my mind that if she was herself right now, this wouldn't even be up for discussion. She'd be in front of both of us, strapped to the teeth and ready to take no prisoners.

I grunt in response, but turn my attention back to the doors as they slide open. I'm not sure what I expect, but it isn't what I get: freezing cold water flooding into the car. It gushes in so fast the only thing I can do is inhale a single breath before it closes over my head.

Chapter Twenty-three

EVACUATION GATHERING LOCATION!
PLEASE PLACE SAMPLES INSIDE NEXT TO
PALM READER!
—Sign on storage room door

Evie

As the water closes over my head, the memory of something similar flashes in my mind, but I shove it away. There's no time and it's not like it'll help. I force my eyes open, then wish I hadn't when the seawater sears my eyes, but I have to be able to tell which way is up.

Something tugs on my hand, pulling me out of the car, and I almost scream, but manage to clamp my lips together to keep from letting loose and losing the much needed oxygen. The familiar roughness of the hand tells me it's Gavin and while I try to look around for Asher, it's a lost cause. It's too dark and I can't see anything.

My lungs burning, I kick as hard as I can, letting Gavin pull me. Just when I can't hold my breath any longer, we burst through the surface, our heads hitting the ceiling. Seconds later, as Gavin is practically begging me to tell him I'm okay, Asher surfaces next to us, gasping for breath. He frantically looks around and when he sees me, I can see him relax. He swims closer, panting a little.

"You okay?"

Coughing, I nod and ignore the pain in my chest. "Just in a little bit of shock."

He turns to Gavin. "What the hell, dude? Are you trying to kill us?"

Gavin only gives him a look. "If I'd known that was going to happen, I wouldn't have brought us down here. It wasn't like this before. I don't know what's going on, but we have to get out of here," he says.

We all turn around in circles, but I can't see anything. None of this looks familiar to me, though I'm starting to get small flashes. Gavin running, me slung over his shoulder. Shooting some kind of blue light at people running behind us. Clouds of ash where the people stood.

Something brushes my leg and I scream as my imagination forms the image of one of those blood- and gore-covered brutes, wrenching me under the water. Then, because I still haven't caught my breath, I break into harsh coughing.

"What?" Gavin pulls me behind him and looks around frantically.

"Something . . . brushed my leg. I don't know what it was." I accidentally inhale a mouthful of water in my panic and nearly choke.

Gavin shoves a wall of water at Asher. "Come on. Stop playin' around."

Asher holds up his hands before slamming them back into the water to paddle. "Don't look at me. I didn't do it."

"What the hell was it then?" Gavin's eyes are taking on that frenzied look again, but it doesn't take long to find out his answer. An obviously dead body floats by just under the surface, its eyes wide and unseeing. We all watch as it continues its meandering path past us. And I'm pretty sure the reason it's moving is because wherever the leak is, the water is still coming in.

"Oh Jesus," Gavin says, while Asher starts gagging and flapping his arms around in an obvious attempt to get away from it. He only ends up drawing the body closer.

My body feels numb and there's a pressure deep in my head as it buzzes from the shock.

Gavin focuses on me. "Can we go back to the Surface now?"

I want to say yes. I want to say forget this, forget all of it, but I shake my head. "I can't. I need to find the answers."

He sighs, but looks resigned. "Well, we have to get out of here at least."

"If this is like any of the buildings in Rushlake, there should be stairs near this elevator," Asher says, trying to stay calm, and Gavin nods. "So who wants to look for it?"

Another body floats by and I shudder so hard I bite my tongue.

They both stare at each other; then Gavin holds his

hand out in a fist. I open my mouth to tell him he can't force Asher to try and find it, but then Asher holds his out too, just short of touching Gavin's. I watch, completely confused, as they lift and lower their hand three times; then Gavin splays his hand out flat at the same Asher brings out his index and middle finger in a sideways V.

Gavin nods. "Right." Then he takes a deep breath and his head disappears under the water before I can say anything.

I paddle over to Asher. "What was that?"

"Rock, paper, scissors. The ultimate decider." He manages a shaky smile and I shake my head and wait, metaphorically holding my breath until Gavin's head appears again.

He pops up, sucks in a breath and goes back under before anyone can say anything. He does this five more times, taking longer and longer and making me more and more anxious until he finally comes up with a look of triumph.

"Found it!"

Relieved, I swim over to him. He takes one hand, and Asher takes my other. We all suck in deep breaths, and go back under, letting Gavin guide us to the stairwell.

It takes both Gavin and Asher working together to open the exit door, but then we're slipping through the crack and swimming up. This time when we surface, we're in a much smaller space and there are stairs leading up.

We swim over to where the stairs meet the water, and start climbing. I go much slower than them, though, because no matter what I do I can't get these visions out of my head. They're just flashes. I can't make out what they are, but they slow me down, nonetheless. Gavin and Asher pause to wait for me, and so I suck in breaths and go as fast as I can.

Each time we reach a new floor, Gavin pokes his head out the door to check if we're at the floor with what he calls the Tube station. According to him, he'll know it when he sees it because it's the only floor that is completely open. That kind of terrifies me. Open to what? We've already been almost drowned. I don't really want to try that again. Maybe Gavin's right. Maybe it *is* time to head back to the Surface. Between the stuff that almost ate Asher's foot and now practically drowning in a sea of dead bodies, I have to admit that Gavin was right about it being dangerous. He was probably right about a lot of things. Yet . . . we're so close to the answers I want. The answers I *need*. I can feel it. If we leave now, I'll never know who I was. Who I am.

So I don't say anything about turning back. I keep going, but when we stop for what feels like the hundredth time, a huge wave of déjà vu hits me. My head swims and I have to lean against the wall.

Asher turns around to smile at me, and a hallucination hits me so hard, I stumble.

The hallway is so dark I can't even see Timothy, but I know he's there. His uneven gasps blow across my cheeks.

"Are you going to tell her?" he asks.

"First thing in the morning," I reply, feeling a familiar tickle in my stomach, and smiling.

"You won't forget," he teases.

Before I can reply, he kisses me again, pressing me back

against the cold concrete. I push harder into the warmth of his body, closing my eyes.

When I open them again, I'm back in the stairwell, gasping for breath, those black dots back in my vision. Asher is watching me warily.

"Everything okay, Evie?" he asks. Gavin must have slipped out of the stairwell to do his quick look-around.

I wave Asher away, not wanting to waste what little breath I have to assure him I'm fine when I'm not completely confident I am.

His brows furrow, but he doesn't say anything. He only continues to watch me. Gavin returns and I push quickly off the wall, as if I've only been biding my time and not trying to figure out what in the world that was all about. He shakes his head before heading up the stairs to yet another level.

Between the ordeal at the hospital in Rushlake, the race back to the village, and now almost drowning, exhausted doesn't even begin to explain how I feel. I want to groan, but I still haven't caught my breath and I'm sure even that would be too much, so I just put one foot in front of the other. I stumble when I don't lift my foot up high enough. I put my hands out to catch myself, but Asher catches my arm and pulls me back up to my feet. I give him a grateful smile before I turn back around to try that step again and notice Gavin watching us.

That hallucination—me, pressed against another boy—makes me feel incredibly guilty, and I duck my head and start trudging up the steps again.

I can feel Gavin's curious gaze, but he keeps moving after a second or two.

At the next landing, Gavin looks out the door and whoops. "Found it!" He dashes out the door.

"Finally," Asher says, and follows.

I follow, just at a bit slower pace. When I step out the door, I can definitely see the difference between the other floors and this one. It's absolutely gorgeous, for one. The floors are all concrete, but the walls! The walls are floor-to-ceiling windows, the outside is all lit up and I can see the ocean. It's so peaceful, I think, walking over to it. I press my hand against the cool glass, and watch as a school of brightly colored fish swim by.

A grouping of brightly colored and strangely shaped rocks gather on the bottom of the window sills. *This*. This feels right. *Finally*, I think. The glass feels so marvelous against my hand, I decide to press my face against it too. A moan escapes me at the feel and I hear a chuckle behind me.

"That good, huh?" Asher asks.

Gavin clears his throat from the other end of the large hallway and I open my eyes to see him smiling at me. "If you're done molesting the glass, we should get to the Tube."

Asher chuckles and, flushing, I push away from the wall, but keep a hand to it as we walk toward where Gavin is.

Just before the hallway turns, there are more splashes of that green goo again. Almost the entire floor, from wall to wall, is spotted in the strange pools. But when I get close to them, I shudder. Each one looks like a body. Flat, green, liquid bodies. As if someone painted them onto the floor. Some are larger than others, like some are children and some are adults. Some have their arms close to their torsos; others have them stretched out as if reaching for the puddle next to it. I don't know why, but the scene has a lump forming in my throat and tears stinging my eyes.

Gavin frowns down at them. "This is so weird."

"What is?" Asher asks.

Gavin looks up at me and I blink the tears quickly away so he can't see them. "This is where all those people were, remember?" he asks.

"No," I say flatly, trying not to let it bother me that he obviously forgot I don't remember *anything* from here except those flashes.

His eyes close for a minute. "That's right. I can't believe I forgot." I shrug and he stands, brushing his hands together. "Never mind. It's not important. Come on, let's get to that Tube station."

I stare at the green bodies for a bit longer, letting his words tumble through my mind, trying to remember something, anything, so I can begin to understand, but nothing comes and Asher tugs on my arm to get me to go. I have to practically run to catch up with Gavin in the next room, but when I do, I stop short.

I remember this room. Or at least one similar.

I'm waiting in the dark, peering out over a thousand faces. I'm leaning against a brick wall. The area around me looks like the streets in Rushlake City, only with short squat one-story buildings lining each side of the street instead of the several-stories-tall buildings that were in Rushlake. The street in front of me is filled with people with identical faces, all staring up at a woman. The woman who frequently stars in my nightmares.

Mother.

She's making a speech on the platform in the Square about working together and how everyone is just one cog in a giant machine. A commotion to my left draws my attention. A man close to me is arguing in whispers with the woman next to him. She's vigorously shaking her head and glancing in my direction.

In response, I step out of the shadows and up to the couple. The crowd around them disperses quickly, watching me as carefully as I watch them and the pair I'm walking to. They're both taller than me, but when they see me looking up at them, they freeze, identical expressions of terror on their almost identical faces. I don't say anything, I don't have to and I know it.

But the man suddenly glares at me. "Monster," he whispers. The woman's face goes completely white.

I signal the two guards next to me to apprehend him. They each take an arm, but he shrugs them off, and follows me into the dark of the shadows. We walk into a maintenance tunnel and behind a stairwell. I lift the weapon on my side. He only lifts his chin as I press the trigger. The click of the hammer hitting the cylinder echoes throughout the stairwell.

Oh, Mother. I think I killed someone. Not accidentally, either.

Gavin starts swearing at something, but I don't look up.

My chest is squeezing like it did in the stairwell and my heart won't slow down. I can't seem to catch my breath. I bend over and shove my head close to my knees like Asher had done in the sub, but I still can't breathe.

"Are you okay?" Asher places his hand on my back and crouches down to look me in the face.

"Fine. Fine. Just need to sit and catch my breath," I wheeze out, but that proves too much for me and even as I suck in more air, my head spins. Then I feel like I'm falling right before the darkness comes.

When I wake, it's as if I'm hearing things from underwater. Their voices echo, bouncing around each other until they finally come together as they're supposed to.

"Did she hit her head?" That's Gavin.

"No. I caught her right as she fell forward." And there is Asher.

Slowly I open my eyes to see them both staring down at me. I try pushing myself up, but only manage to feel like a turtle on its back. Gavin and Asher help me up, then ask me what happened. I hesitate. Gavin doesn't want to be down here at all. If he knows I've hallucinated twice in less than an hour, and that I think I'm one of the monsters he was talking about, he's going to insist we go back, or worse, go back without me, leaving me.

But I'm sure these hallucinations, these flashes of memory, are proof I'm doing the right thing. So I lie. I tell them I couldn't breathe and that it must be left over from almost drowning. And instead of insisting we go back, they decide I need a short break. I try to insist that by passing out I already *had* a short break, but they won't listen.

"Besides," Gavin says, "we've kinda reached the end of the road." His voice is relieved and his eyes are bright. For the first time since we got here, his entire body seems relaxed, not rigid and tense. "In order to get where you need to be, we have to use the Tube. That's the track." He gestures to the sloping floor with the strange metal plates on it. Then he looks at me. "The last time we were here, we shut and locked the door to prevent Mother from sending anyone else over. But it didn't work. And now it seems they've sealed them back up." His lip twitches and I can tell he's trying not to smile.

I push myself to my feet. We've come this far, and I can *feel* we're getting closer. I walk up to the door and press on the red button on the side, but it doesn't budge. Make a noise. Anything. Frowning, I stride back up the sloped floor and cross over to the booth. I didn't make it all this way to give up so easily.

Inside it is a bunch of levers and knobs, but I don't know which does what. Gavin, on the other hand, does this indecisive little back and forth motion with his body before sighing, then taking my hand and pressing it against the cool glass plate. I jump when a light flashes underneath my palm, but he won't let me take my hand from it. He keeps it pressed against the glass. As soon as I realize it doesn't hurt me, I turn to watch Gavin, who is in turn watching the door, obviously expecting something to happen.

"Access denied," a computer voice says, startling all of us.

Gavin swears again under his breath and I can't hide my own disappointment. This can't be the end. "There has to be some other way to get to where we need to go."

Gavin shakes his head. "If there is, I don't know what it is. We came through here before and at the time, you said it was the only way. Considering how dangerous it was, I have to believe you were right." Again, I can't help but notice that he doesn't seem all that disappointed by the turn of events.

Asher kicks the console hard enough for an alarm to start screaming on it. I slam my hands to my ears, while Gavin punches Asher in the arm. He yells something at him, gesturing wildly, but I can't hear him over the shrill alarm.

Then, the entire thing turns off and a computer voice speaks. "Due to unauthorized tampering, this console will shut down until re-activated by an authorized service technician. Any further damage to the machine will result in harsh punishment. Vandalism will not be tolerated at the Elysium Resort and persons accused of such an act will be fined and sent to the Detainment Center until you are relinquished to Surface authorities. Have a nice day!"

We glance at each other, but before any of us can react to that, there's a mechanical humming sound. Gavin and I dash out of the booth to find where it's coming from, only to see that a wall is being lowered from the ceiling, blocking the way back to the stairs.

"They're locking us in!" Gavin exclaims. "Come on! We've got to go."

He yanks me down the hallway and to the corner and Asher is right behind us. I wonder if we'll make it. Considering how heavy that wall must be, it's moving fairly rapidly. When we get to it, we have to slither underneath. With no time to hesitate, I slide under followed by Gavin, and then Asher. Not even ten seconds later the wall slides into place and there's a loud clang of what I'm sure is a lock clicking.

Across the way, another wall slams, effectively locking us, and at least a half a dozen bodies of goo, between them in a square approximately ten meters by ten meters, with no way out, and nowhere to hide.

Chapter Twenty-four

CAUTION: THIS SECTOR UNDER QUARANTINE
DUE TO BIOHAZARDOUS MATERIAL.
TRESPASSERS WILL BE PROSECUTED.
—Painted on sign next to the Tube

Evie

Gavin and Asher each take a turn shoving at the wall while I look for some kind of button or lever that'll release it, but none of us are successful.

"Way to go, Asher," Gavin says between clenched teeth. He's adopted that tense, ramrod-straight posture again. "Now either we've alerted Mother that we're here, or she'll find out when she sends someone to check out what's going on."

"Me?" Asher says with a pinched laugh. "I'm not the one who shoved everyone in here! You're the one who decided it would be the smart thing to run under a *wall*."

"I didn't know there'd be another wall right behind it doing the same thing." He throws his hands in the air, prowling along the wall. "I was hoping to get back to the stairs or elevator!" He glances over to me and I try to give him an encouraging smile, but I can't hold it. I wrap my arms around myself instead.

"Maybe she'll just ignore it altogether," Asher says. "It's obvious this sector isn't used anymore. She could think it's a false alarm."

"Like that's better?" Gavin's voice sounds like he's fighting back a scream. "Then we get to starve to death or suffocate. I'm not sure which is worse." Gavin kicks the wall, even though that's exactly what Asher did to get us in trouble. "I told you this was a bad idea. I told you guys not to come here, but no. Does anyone listen? Of course not!"

I'm relieved when Gavin stops shouting and starts pacing. I thought for sure I would have to break them up again.

Asher looks to the floor. "I'm sorry. I didn't realize—"

Gavin spins around to glare at Asher. "That's exactly the problem, Asher. You didn't think. You *never* think. You just *do*, and ask questions later."

"It's better to beg forgiveness than ask permission," Asher shoots back.

"And screw anyone who happens to get hurt in the process, right? As long as Asher's happy, no one else matters."

"That's not true and you know it!" Asher practically yells. "This? All this? We're only here because I was thinking of Evie. Because *she* needs to be here. I didn't do this for me. I did this to help *her*."

"And this is helping her? We're trapped. And we're going to *die*! No matter what happens from this point out, that's going be the end result because Mother is going to *kill* us. And Evie is going to get the worst of it because she betrayed Mother to help me."

I stop twisting my hands together to gape at Gavin. "I did *what?*"

He winces. "You betrayed Mother. To get me home." He rushes on, his sentences running together. "But it's a good thing, because she was going to turn you into breeding stock, and there were those murders, and she was going to kill you eventually. I'm sure of it. You were much safer up there." He goes back to glaring at Asher. "Until *some*one decided to bring you back."

"I was trying to *help* her," Asher starts.

"You weren't planning on helping her! You were planning on using her. Like you do with everyone."

I shake my head. "You don't know that."

"Yes I do! I know him more than you ever could. And I know for a fact that he's just using you."

Asher butts in, face flaming. "When are you going to realize what happened was an *accident*? A horrible mistake. My mistake. I trusted someone I shouldn't have. He's a liar and a cheat. He gets people to trust him, only to turn around and not only stab them in the back, but take away the people most important to them. I lost my best friend because of it. Because in trying to help him and his family, I ended up betraying them, and not a day goes by that I don't regret it. And you want to know something else? The reason I was even helping you and Evie in the first place was because I was trying to make up for what I did to you."

"That's a lie," Gavin says, but he doesn't sound convinced. "You've said numerous times that you *weren't* doing this for me."

"For pity's sake, Gavin! I couldn't exactly *admit* I was doing this for you or you'd never have let me. You're as stubborn as a damn mule and have never taken help from anyone. I knew that the only way I was going to be able to prove anything to you was to take care of your girl. You'd have to be blind not to see how much she means to you and I knew you'd do anything, including letting me help you, to help her."

I gape at Asher, shocked. He's standing with his fists clenched at his sides, his whole body shakes with indignation and anger. I want so badly to ask what exactly happened. It's not hard to see it was bad—bad enough to split up two best friends—and my heart breaks for the both of them, but I don't know what to say. I wouldn't even know where to start.

Gavin doesn't say anything either, but at least his anger has left him. Instead, he looks thunderstruck. He lowers himself to the ground, staring off into space. Asher watches him for a few minutes, but when Gavin doesn't seem intent on saying anything to anyone, Asher turns back to me.

"So," he says as if he hadn't just been yelling at Gavin for the last few minutes, "what do you think that stuff is?" He points to the closest "body."

I watch Gavin a second more before turning to Asher. "I don't know. Maybe it was something they used to clean up the deceased Gavin said were here. They *are* in the shapes of bodies."

"But why did it try to eat my foot?"

"Maybe it likes the taste of chicken," Gavin mutters.

I have to stifle a laugh, but Asher ignores him completely.

"Hmm." Asher tilts his head as he focuses his attention on the green sludge. Eventually, he stands and leans over it, then kneels next to it. He rubs his hand against the floor, picks up a handful of debris and starts throwing it into the puddle.

Even from here I can see it suck up the pieces like a sponge.

"Hmm," he says again, then looks around.

"What are you looking for?" I ask.

"Something else to throw in it."

"Why?"

"Got any other plans to keep busy?"

I shake my head.

"Well, then, this is as good as any."

Since he's got a point, I dig into my pockets to see if I have anything hiding in there. I come up with a pen, a couple scraps of very wet paper, and a paper clip.

Asher takes the items. One by one he throws them in, only to have them get sucked up. Which is odd, because the muck can't be more than half a centimeter thick. The pen, at least, should be touching the floor and still visible. Instead the puddle looks completely unchanged. It seems to have eaten the items, just like the other mass ate Asher's shoe.

"I guess they're not coming," Gavin says when we run out of things to throw. "It's been a while. I'm sure if they were going to come, they'd have been here by now."

"I don't know whether to gloat, or be upset that I was right," Asher says, worry clouding his face.

What was it the computer said about being arrested until surface police get here? Asher's focused on me, but it's Gavin who answers.

"I think it's a holdover from when this was a resort. The journals Evie found made it really clear her dad had built this whole complex as a rich man's playground. It was never meant to be a self-sufficient city. Not until Mother killed him and turned it into one.

"She killed her own dad?" Asher asks. "That's sick."

Gavin presses his lips together and nods, not saying anything.

I decide I don't want to continue this conversation and step closer to the green stuff.

I step as close to the goo as I can without getting a foot full of whatever it is.

Just as I squat down to look closer at it, the whole puddle lurches toward me. Screaming, I fall back onto my butt at the same time Gavin and Asher shout, "Whoa!"

Asher, the closest to me, yanks me away, shoving me behind him. I peer around his shoulder.

"What was that?" Asher asks.

But Gavin doesn't get a chance to respond before it moves again, its arm stretching toward Asher and me.

All three of us run to the other wall, as far away from it as possible, but it doesn't do anything else.

"What the hell was that?" Gavin asks.

Asher shrugs. "I have no clue. I have never seen anything like that before."

They both turn toward me. "Evie?" Gavin asks.

I shake my head rapidly. "How should I know? I don't remember seeing anything like that. I don't remember *anything*, remember?"

Gavin steps up to it again, but when he apparently gets too close, its arm lunges at him again and he jumps back with a yelp.

"Okay, I take it back," Gavin says. "Mother isn't going to kill us. That thing is."

Asher and I both nod, our eyes wide as the arms of several of the piles slide slowly across the floor toward us. But before we can do more than think about reacting, the walls start to rise. The three of us exchange a terrified look. It appears Gavin was wrong again. Mother did come, and she is going to kill us.

Asher slides underneath the still rising walls and pulls me toward the stairwell with Gavin close on our heels, but before we can get there, a male voice yells, "Stop! Don't move any further."

We keep running, but the voice yells, "Evelyn! Gavin! Wait! Please."

Both Asher and I stop in our tracks and Gavin plows into the back of us. "What are you waiting for? Come on!"

"He knows your names," Asher says. His face is crumpled into a look of confusion and I'm pretty sure he feels the same warring emotions of fear and curiosity as I do.

"So . . . we were here before, it's not surprising," Gavin says, tugging on my arm.

I start to turn away, to listen to Gavin, but the voice shouts again. "I'm not here to hurt you. I promise. I know you don't trust me, but I promise I'm really here to help you."

I'm not sure why I turn around, but when I do there's an older man with blond hair streaked with gray coming toward us. He appears to be in his sixties or seventies, but he carries himself as if he's younger. He looks . . . familiar.

"Who—who are you?" I ask, narrowing my eyes.

"Don't you remember me, Evelyn?" the man asks. I shake my head and he sighs. "It's me. Father," he says with a smile.

I exchange a look with Gavin, who purses his lips and says, "Father is Coupled with Mother. He's the second-in-command, which means he's lying about not turning us in."

But Asher steps forward, his eyes narrowed. "Eli?"

Chapter Twenty-five

Due to the recent infiltration of a Surface Dweller and subsequent kidnapping of my daughter, Elysium is now under a mandatory curfew. All Citizens, minus those designated by Mother, must be in their residences no later than 8:00pm. All doors will be locked and will be checked nightly. Anyone with their door unlocked or caught outside their residences will be persecuted to the full extent of the law. We understand that this is an inconvenience and appreciate your cooperation.

—Letter sent to all residents of Elysium

Evie

My mind instantly goes back to the picture Asher's grandmother showed us and I realize why the man looks so familiar. He's one of the men from the picture. The one that was closest to Asher's grandmother. Asher's right. It *is* Eli. A huge weight lifts from my shoulders as I realize we actually found the man we were sent here to find. And he's alive! Now to see if he can actually do what Asher's grandmother thinks he can and help me get my memories back.

Eli, who's been staring at me, turns his full attention to Asher. "Yes. Yes, but that is not a name I've heard in a long, long time."

"But . . . you're dead!" Gavin bursts out. "We saw the video. We read the journals. Eli was trying to escape, but he was betrayed by someone and Mother killed anyone who tried to escape. She *killed* Eli. You can't be him."

Eli raises an eyebrow. "Well, she tried anyway," he says, but before Gavin can argue further, Eli turns his attention back to Asher. "Who are you and how do you know who I am?"

"I'm Asher St. James. My grandmother—Lenore Allen— sent us here to ask you for help."

Eli stares at Asher for a long time. There are so many emotions flickering across his face you can't even make one out before another is flashing into place.

Finally, he steps forward, bypassing the green goo, which has stopped moving as if it never had started. His eyes are focused completely on Asher, who shifts as if uncomfortable. When Eli gets within touching distance, he stops and tilts his head this way, then that, studying.

Gavin and I exchange a look. A smile slowly spreads across Eli's lips. There is definitely sadness in his expression, but relief as well.

"You have her eyes," he says after a minute. He presses his lips together and I think for a minute he's going to say something or do something else, but then he shakes his head. "No time for regrets."

Eli catches the look Asher sends me and raises his brow at Gavin, who only stares back at him, distrust clear on his face. Then Eli turns his attention to me. And this time, I can make out the emotions running over his face. Relief, happiness, and, finally, sadness. Gavin slides his hand into mine and squeezes. I squeeze back to let him know I'm fine.

It's not exactly true. My head feels like it could explode at any moment from all the stress, but he doesn't need to know it.

Eli reaches out toward me and both Asher and Gavin shout and block his advance. Gavin draws his gun and Eli puts his hands up, palms out.

"I just wanted to touch the necklace." He keeps his eyes steady on mine. "I meant no harm. I can't believe you still have it. I meant no harm."

Gavin jerks his head around to face me and there's understanding in his eyes. He lowers the gun and steps back. "You're the one who gave it to her?" he asks.

Eli hesitates for a moment, lowering his hands to let them hang at his sides before saying, "No, not I. Her mother . . . her *real* mother. But I gave . . . I'm pleased to see she kept it."

He's not telling us everything. I don't know how I know, but I know. From the expression on Gavin's face, I can see he's thinking the same thing.

"But the scents? You're the one who gave her the perfume bottles, right? You're the one who helped her every time she got her memories erased?"

Asher jerks his head around and narrows his eyes at

Gavin, even as I watch Eli and Gavin wide-eyed. I had my memories erased before? This isn't the first time? Why didn't Gavin tell me? If it happened before and there was a cure, why didn't we come to Elysium earlier?

Eli nods. "Yes. I did what I could at the time. Even if it wasn't nearly enough."

"But now you're here to actually help us?" Asher asks, his face scrunched up in confusion.

Eli looks around. "Yes, but not here. There's a place in the Residential Sector that I can take you to. I assure you, it's safe. Then you can tell me what you need help with." He turns to me with a smile. "There's someone there who really misses you and wants to see you again."

"Oh no," Gavin says, and all of us turn to him. He crosses his arms across his chest. "We're not going anywhere. We came to find you and you're here, so you need to help us now, so we can back to the Surface."

Asher nods, agreeing with Gavin for once, but I ignore it and ask, "Who's waiting for me?"

Both boys turn to me. "Evie . . . ," they warn, but I ignore them.

"Who?" I demand.

Eli takes a deep breath. "Your mother. Your *real* mother," he says, quietly.

My heart trips in my chest and I raise a hand to my necklace again, trying to remember something about the woman who birthed me, but nothing comes. Not even the tiniest of memories.

But . . . I do feel *something*. And I want nothing more than to meet this woman.

I open my mouth to tell him we'll go, but Gavin interrupts. "Nice try, but no. We came to get her memories back. That's it, and then we're gone."

Eli turns toward me, his eyes really focusing on me again. "You lost your memories?" I nod. "What happened?

I don't think Gavin will tell him anything—after all, he was dead set that coming to this place was the wrong idea—but he surprises me. "I don't know. She was having issues when we left. Small things. Like how to work the Slate, and where things were. But it wasn't until we got to the Surface that I realized she'd forgotten everything." He looks at the ground. "Including me."

"It's the nanos," Asher shoves in. "Grandma said that you and she developed the nanos, but they've changed. She couldn't help Evie, but she was sure you could."

Eli's face darkens. "They've changed all right. After all, we couldn't have our little prize giving anything away, could we?" he mutters.

Gavin and Asher exchange a look. "Huh?" Asher asks.

Eli shakes his head. "Nothing. Never mind. I can help her, but not here. She needs to come with me."

Gavin raises the gun and aims it at Eli. "I'm not sure if you're hard of hearing or just dumb, but she's. Not. Going. With you. Whatever you need to do, you can do it here."

Eli shakes his head. "You don't understand. What needs

to be done is . . . quite complicated. I *can't* do it here. Believe me, if I could, I would. It's going to be hard enough as it is." He looks at me. "I promise you I won't let anything happen to you. I *can* help you, but you have to come with me."

Gavin is about to say something, but I know it's another argument, so I start talking before he can. "The nanos? Are they what's making me forget everything?"

Eli hesitates, then nods. "Yes."

Gavin and Asher look between Eli and me as I say, "And will I get my memories back if you fix them?"

Eli at first doesn't respond, but then he starts firing questions at me. "Have you been able to recall anything at all?"

"I-I don't know. I'm not sure."

"How about any dreams that seem more real than usual?"

I share a glance with Gavin and nod. "Y-Yes."

Eli makes a hmm-ing noise. "How about hallucinations? Sleepwalking? Sleeptalking? Fugue states?"

I nod quickly, getting more excited with every question. "Yes! Yes, I have. All of those."

"That's the major reason we're here, actually. She's almost killed herself a couple of times with sleepwalking and the fugue states," Gavin interjects.

Eli's eyes widen. "Please explain."

Gavin tells him the story of me walking into his weapons room and then of me almost drowning myself, while Asher explains about my hallucination in the Outlands.

Eli tilts his head back and forth, obviously considering all of the information. "Yes," he finally says. "The memories are still there, they're just blocked. It's part of their programming for Enforcers. We've never tried to get memories back, but I think I can."

He doesn't seem confident, but I've heard all I need to hear. He can help. Probably. Before I can respond, Gavin asks, "How are you going to get her memories back if you've never done it before?"

"Well, we're going to have to reset the nanites."

"And how are you going to do that?"

Eli shakes his head. "We don't have time for explanations right now. It's not safe here. I'll explain everything when we get somewhere secure."

"Then let's go." I push past Gavin and Asher.

They grab at my arms, each saying something to try to make me change my mind, but they speak over each other and I can't understand.

Besides, I don't want to hear it. Eli says he thinks he can fix my memories. That's good enough for me. I pull away and step closer to Eli before looking over my shoulder. "I'm going. You can come along if that will make you feel better, or you can wait here with the goo."

Then I turn back around and start walking toward the Tube station again.

Eli laughs as they run to catch up after a long pause. "Still the same Evelyn, I see. Good. We'll need that spunk." Then he steps in front of me, leading the way.

Gavin

I don't know what to do. I can't say I'm surprised Evie made us follow Eli, but nothing good is going to come of this. I'm certain of that. I can sense Asher's unease as he walks behind me, and serves him right. He's the one who brought us down here. My only comfort is that even if Evie doesn't remember Father, I remember the way she'd talked about him and how he'd helped her stand up to Mother in the past. If anyone can help her now, it's probably him.

Of course, that doesn't mean I completely trust him.

"The train itself is out of service," Eli explains as we quickly walk through the Tube. "Due in part to a mysterious malfunction that ended up causing the entire tunnel to flood, killing six people." He gives me a knowing look.

I clear my throat. "And the other part?"

His look doesn't change, but it darkens. "I'm sure I don't have to say, but it has something to do with some . . . failed experiments, and that marvelous substance you were trapped with."

Asher dances in front of Eli, walking backward to face him. "What was that stuff, anyway?"

Eli shrugs and shakes his head. "We don't know yet. We're still studying it. It's been a bit of a challenge. It resists all our attempts to gather it by somehow mutating anything that touches it into its matrix."

"And that doesn't bother you?" I ask, shuddering as I think how close *Asher* came to "being mutated into its matrix."

"Of course it does. We've had to quarantine Sector Three." He passes by Asher, shutting down any further questions, while the three of us exchange a look behind his back. Just another reason on the long list of them: murderous experiments, entire floors flooded with seawater, green mutating goo—to get the hell out of here as soon as possible.

When we enter the Tube tunnel, dread hunches my shoulders. I expect the sound of rushing water and the icy chill of the ocean to pour over my head. Mother'd tried to drown Evie and me—not to mention the family that had been unlucky enough to have been in the train with us—the last time. There's no evidence of any of that now. It doesn't surprise me that the train—and bodies—are gone. Mother strikes me as nothing if not efficient. Even so, I'm glad Evie doesn't remember any of it. She doesn't need any more anguish right now. It's funny to see her gaping around at the water that surrounds us and the lava flows below us that turn the water orange. She's the one who grew up here.

Asher is doing the same and I have to wonder if that's what I looked like when I first came. I hope I didn't look as stupid as he does, with his mouth hanging wide open. I can't imagine I did. Evie wouldn't have tolerated it.

Then again . . . I chuckle to myself as Eli barks at Asher to stop gawking and keep up. *That* sounds exactly like what Evie had said to me.

The tunnel slopes upward and for the first hundred or so feet, everything seems to be okay. But then Evie stumbles.

I rush to help her up, but she says, "I'm fine. Just a bit

tired." Her voice is all breathy and her tone confused. She had another hallucination. I know it. I can see it in the way her eyes aren't completely focused.

Eli looks over her head at me with worried eyes. He turns his attention back to her. "We can rest if you need to, but we really need to get you somewhere safe as soon as possible. You'll probably experience more and more of your . . . hallucinations the further we go. Especially back in Sector Two. The more familiar surroundings are likely to act as triggers, and we can't risk you doing something to endanger yourself."

I know what he didn't say, "and us." Then something he said clicks in my head.

"Wait. If she'll get her memories back just by being here, why do you even need to do anything?"

"I didn't say she'd get her memories back by being here. I said here might *trigger* more *hallucinations*. And the hallucinations, as you well know, are dangerous. She's been lucky—mostly because of you—up until now, but there's no guarantee that she'll stay lucky. Without my intervention, she could end up injured or worse." He gives me a steady look until he's satisfied I understand what he means, then he turns back to Evie. "Again, we can stop if you need to rest, just let me know."

She must see how worried he is, because she shakes her head. "I'm fine. Let's just keep going."

We do, but after another couple hundred feet, she stumbles again. When I reach for her this time, she just leans against me. Her body is shaking, and even through that I can feel her chest heaving with each breath she takes. Whatever she's seeing, it terrifies her.

"Are you okay?" I ask.

She nods. "Yeah. Perfect."

Asher shoots me an uneasy glance. He knows as well as I do how far from perfect we are right now.

"Do you want me to carry you?" I ask. I don't know if it'll help, but at least we'd be able to keep going.

She looks up at me with the look of "Are you insane?" She shakes her head. "No. I've got it."

For the next several minutes we continue up the constantly sloping floor until even I'm winded. The last week of running all over the Outlands has taken its toll. At least for the trip from Rushlake, I had a horse. Even if I did have to steal it. My whole body aches and I just want to collapse right here and sleep for a month. But I don't trust Eli enough to close my eyes even for a second. Looks like sleep is off the menu until we leave.

And then we come to the open doorway that leads into the main part of Elysium. Up ahead, I can see the pools of light in the center of the Square, though the shops and businesses around it appear dark. Closed up for the night. It looks peaceful, like my own village after dark, but I know it's nothing like that. Everything in this place is manufactured. False peace. Fake plants, a fake moon overhead, and a weird smell like baked goods. But even that isn't quite right. It's more candy-like—a sickly sweet—instead of real spices and sugar.

I have to fight not to turn and run in the other direction as every cell in my body warns me of the danger. Eli gestures for us to get into the shadows made by the lights just outside of the tunnel, so we slip around the corner and press ourselves against the walls as he goes on ahead. My mind screams that we can't trust him, that he works for *her*. He's not bringing us to help, he's bringing us to Mother.

With a small shudder, I push the thoughts away. I don't have a choice. Evie is determined Eli can help and Asher's the classic case of curiosity killing the cat. Even as I think it, he steps into the light to look closer at *something*. I bark at him to get back into the shadows. Which he does with an "oops" expression, but doesn't look all that concerned. I have to remind myself, he doesn't know what could be watching him. Literally. And he doesn't realize that his silver tongue isn't going to be able to talk him out of any trouble he's gotten into.

We wait and I look around, trying to find the turrets, but I can't see any from my angle. I take slow, deep breaths to calm my own unease. What if Eli's going to get an Enforcer? Or Mother? What if he doesn't come back at all?

It's so quiet around here. Last time we were here, this street—the whole Sector—was filled with people. So much so we couldn't walk from one end of it to the other without having to weave between them. Where are all the Citizens? The Enforcers? Guards, even?

Something's wrong. I can feel it.

A few minutes later, Eli reappears, alone, and gestures for us to follow him. "Keep quiet. The city is under curfew."

"Curfew?" Asher asks with raised eyebrows and Evie knits her brow together as if that doesn't quite make sense.

Glancing at her, Eli says, "Mother instituted it shortly after you . . . left. In fact, she started a lot of new, more restrictive laws using you as an excuse."

"Wonderful," Evie murmurs. Guilt drips from every syllable and I can't help but feel for her. She shouldn't be here. She shouldn't know what happened after we left. This isn't at all what *should* have happened. I clench my fists, then force myself to relax them.

Just then Eli curses under his breath and yanks Evie deeper into the shadows. I immediately do the same, knowing better than to take longer than a second. When I turn, my back pressed as tightly as possible against the wall, I see someone that makes the blood in my veins turn to ice. An Enforcer stepping out of the shadows. I thought—wanted, hoped—I'd never see one again, but she's unmistakable with her all-black clothing. The short dress that falls to just above her knees. The long boots, the tops hiding under the skirt, and the gloves and cape that cover the rest of her exposed skin. She's looking right at us. Right at Evie.

Her eyes flick to Asher, who was the slowest of us getting to the wall, and I want to hit him when he whispers, quite loudly, "What's going on?"

"Enforcers." I barely breathe the word. It's probably still too loud, but if I don't answer him, he'll just keep questioning. Next to me, Evie shifts from one foot to the other, and grasps my arm tightly. She's shaking. Or maybe that's me.

The last time I saw an Enforcer up close, she was trying to put a bullet in me.

But then she—the Enforcer—steps backward into the dark. It's almost as if she's melting into them, becoming part of just one large Enforcer shadow. My muscles spasm at the thought.

Eli narrows his eyes, but doesn't say anything. After a minute, he continues forward. Cautiously, I follow, sticking like glue to the walls. Last time, the shadows meant for the Enforcers kept us safe from the turrets. Not that running into more Enforcers is on my list of priorities—that last one is still causing my nerves to spit sparks throughout my body—but maybe with Eli here, they'll ignore us.

I won't get my hopes up.

I think he's going to lead us to the maintenance tunnels Evie and I used the last time we were here, but instead he walks right past them.

"We aren't going to use the tunnels?" I ask, tense.

He doesn't even spare me a glance. "She's too weak to crawl up the ladders on her own. Now hush and keep up."

I glance nervously at a section of the ceiling that has a black pole protruding from it. "What about the turrets?"

This time he stops, but only long enough to give me a look. "Do you think I didn't already think of that, Surface Dweller? I would not let harm come to my daughter, even if that means protecting someone like you. Now hurry, before another Enforcer sees us and all my precautions were for naught."

I bite back a nasty comment, because he's right. While

the Square appears to be deserted, it doesn't mean we can drop our guard. Enforcers could be anywhere. Didn't Evie teach me that?

We move quickly through the spookily quiet city. Every once in a while an Enforcer steps out of the shadows, and every time they look in our direction, I think we're busted. That it's all over. But they just slide back into the shadows.

"What the hell," I whisper.

Eli turns to me with an equally confused look, but his eyes are filled with worry and not a little fear. He mutters, "That's not good." Then he speeds up, but it still feels way too slow for me.

If Eli is worried, "that's not good" is an understatement. My heart gallops in my chest and I feel cold, like I've just drunk an entire gallon of ice water in one shot. The only thing not stopping me from running straight back to the sub is Evie. Even though it's obvious she's terrified with her wide eyes and colorless face, she also looks resolute. There's no way I'd get her out of here without a fight. Which would only draw more attention to us.

"This is insane," I say as quietly as I can. "We're going to get caught. The Enforcers *know* we're here. I know they do."

Eli only nods. "We must hurry. It's safe where I'm taking you. I assure you."

I'm not "assured," but Evie follows, leaving me no choice unless I hit her over the head and drag her back with me. I have to admit, that's looking more and more like a good option.

Suddenly, there's a giggle and shout.

"Meredith! No. *Stop!*"

A little blond-haired girl darts by, and we all stop in our tracks. Eli's face goes from worried to full-out terrified. He lunges forward, trying to grab the child, but she only laughs harder and slips right out of Eli's outstretched hands. I reach for her too, but she only twists her body around, dodging me, still giggling.

"Meredith!" a woman calls. We can't see her yet, but I don't need to see her to know she's in a full-out panic.

I focus in on Eli. The panic he's obviously feeling is practically pouring off him in waves, which makes the dread pooling in my stomach weigh like a stone. He seems torn— undecided—but then he straightens his shoulders and takes a step out of the shadows. Evie makes a short squeaking sound, then slaps her hand against her mouth, her other hand reaching out to him. As if she's willing him to come back.

But it's too late. An Enforcer has beaten both of us to it. Eli steps back into the shadows almost instantly.

The Enforcer is holding the girl, who isn't giggling anymore.

Somewhere in me, I know what's about to happen.

A woman rushes around the corner, then stops in her tracks at the sight in front of her. Her eyes shut and even from here, I can see her swallow. But she straightens her shoulders and walks calmly forward. I have to admire that even though she's obviously terrified, she doesn't turn tail and run.

"That's my daughter," she says, her voice only wavering slightly. "I apologize. She just learned how to open doors. She doesn't understand the curfew. It won't happen again. I promise."

The Enforcer doesn't say anything. She looks down at the child, who is shrieking now.

The mother is still blabbing on, stepping forward, but Eli is mumbling something too and I can't make out what either is saying. I want to do something, grab the girl and run, but I know what would happen. I'm a Surface Dweller. She'd probably kill the girl, then come after me next.

But Eli could do something. Right? He could stop what's happening. Why doesn't he?

Without warning, the mother's body jerks as red spreads across her chest. Her eyes widen, but I can see the light in them die before she even hits the ground. I turn back to the Enforcer to see the glint of a gun in the Enforcer's gloved hand.

Her voice is as dead as the woman on the floor when she says, "Curfew is for the safety of all Citizens. Failure to comply will result in severe punishment."

Then she turns and disappears with the girl into the shadows. The girl's howls slowly fade away.

Chapter Twenty-six

Citizen Evangeline Summers, you are hereby summoned to report to the Medical Sector, tomorrow, March 15, to initiate fertilization treatments.

—Summons for Procreation Duty, dated seventeen years prior

Evie

The memory comes so fast and so hard, I almost feel like it's pulling me from one world to another.

"*Congratulations! Evelyn has been chosen for Mother's special program.*" The woman behind the desk smiles. "*You two must be so proud. It isn't every family that gets the privilege of serving our city so completely.*"

"*Special . . . program?*" My mom, my real one, clutches me tightly to her chest. Dad is staring at my mom like something horrible has happened and it's all her fault. I can see him clearly, but when I look at her, her face is just a smudge of smoke.

She turns back to the woman behind the desk. "*But—but we thought Evelyn was meant to be a scientist, like her father and I.*"

I fidget in my seat and try not to look at the woman, but fail. She makes me nervous. I want to suck my thumb even though my mom says big girls don't do that.

"Mother requested her personally," the woman says, her voice notably cooler. Then she laughs and her blue eyes sparkle with fake happiness. My parents don't join her. They're too busy having one of their silent conversations. "Her genomes have proven superb." She forces her face into a serious expression, one that makes me even more scared of her. "Of course," she says, "you will be fully compensated for your contribution."

As if summoned, a young woman slips out of the shadows, startling my parents and terrifying me. I cling to my mom's neck as the shadow woman walks directly to me.

"She is in my charge now," the new woman says. Her emotionless voice causes my little body to shudder and I cower even more into my mom's chest.

"Now?" my mom asks. "But—"

"She must begin immediately. There is no time to waste." The monster takes my hand and rips me from my mom's lap.

"Mommy," I yell, tears rolling down my cheeks. But she doesn't get up, and the monster doesn't even pause as she removes me from the room.

When I come out of it, I'm staring at a woman's body and the small pool of red forming around her. I feel like I'm going to be sick.

Everyone is still gaping and Eli looks shell-shocked. After a second he yanks me down the hall in a full out run. Gavin is pushing me from behind as if he's terrified I'm still not moving fast enough. Finally we reach what Eli calls—and a little voice tells me is—the Residential Sector without further incident.

I can tell Gavin thinks this has been too easy, despite the scene we just witnessed. He's watching Eli warily as if he thinks we're being led into a trap, but I hope he can shove down his paranoia enough to let Eli help me. If it is a trap, then we'll just have to deal with that when the time comes. I don't have to tell Gavin to be prepared. He's got his fingers wrapped tightly around the gun.

We take a set of stairs and by the time we make it up the half dozen or so flights, I think my heart's going to explode the way it's banging against my ribs. Finally we reach the right floor and go through a door and down a hallway. We stop at a door at the very end and Eli knocks loud enough to startle everyone.

"What's he trying to do?" Gavin whispers to me. "Wake the dead?"

I wince. Not exactly the right wording there.

A few seconds later, the door opens slowly and blue eyes peer out from the crack. Then it jerks open slightly more as those eyes catch slight of Eli.

"Father?!" The woman bows her head, the only part of her body I can see, but her hair covers most of her face besides her eyes. "To what do I owe the pleasure of seeing you so late this evening?"

"Evangeline." His tone—one I've heard Gavin use when talking to me—has everyone glancing at him, before Eli shakes himself. Suddenly he's all business. "Evelyn has returned. These Surface Dwellers have brought her back to us, but her memories are wiped clean. The nanobots have done their job. Too well, it would seem."

The woman's eyes widen; then she follows Eli's gaze over to me, and the door flies open, banging against the wall. It makes me jump, but the woman ignores it.

She leans against the door and I'm surprised to see how familiar she looks to me. As if I've seen her before, but I can't remember where.

"Come, come. Get in here before someone sees you," she demands.

We step inside, and she immediately shuts and locks the door behind us. She starts toward me, but Eli brushes her off. "No time for that now. We need to get her memories back or she'll never be able to help us. Where's the best place?"

She gives him a bland look. "The Medical Sector," Evangeline says.

"You know we can't risk that," Eli says.

She gives him another look, but sighs. "Follow me." She pushes past him, leading the way down a hallway painted a pretty lavender with wood wainscoting on the bottom. It reminds me a little of Asher's house in Rushlake. Pictures of a little girl are framed on the wall and I tip my head to the side to study them closer. I think I recognize her from somewhere.

Eli clears his throat. "Come on, Evelyn. We should get started as quickly as we can."

I follow him, though I keep glancing back at the photos until I get into the room. It too is purple with the wood wainscoting. The pictures in this room are all of flowers. Disappointment pricks at me. The answer to where I've seen that girl before had been just at the edge of my memory.

"Lay here." Eli gestures to the bed. "I'll be right back. I need to get some things. I hadn't been expecting to do this."

He starts to walk past me, but I place a hand on his arm as the question I should have asked first finally comes to mind. "How did you know we were here?"

"The nanite substrate."

"Excuse me?"

"The nanite substrate. The green substance? It moves. I'm sure you noticed." He lifts his eyebrows. "Mother has me studying it. I told you. And we've been trying to figure out what it is. We've figured out it has something to do with the nanites of the deceased bodies, but we're not sure exactly how they went from"—he glances at me—"human bodies to that substance. We'll figure it out eventually. Anyway, it sets off the alarms in the Sector. As you can imagine, Mother hated that the alarms were going off every time the stuff migrated." He shrugs when Gavin scoffs. "So I rerouted them to send an alert to my slate. That included *all* the alarms for the Sector. Including when the sub docked, and the alarms for the Tube station. I knew the minute you came back." He glances at Gavin. "You weren't as secretive as you thought you were."

"I wasn't trying to be secretive. Just stay alive," Gavin mutters.

"Anyway, as soon as I realized you were back and got over the initial shock of that," he smiles at me, "I made sure I'd be able to get you into Sector Two and up here without setting off the other alarms. Then I went to find you and ensure you made it to safety without causing the uproar you caused before."

"And the Enforcers? What about them?" Gavin asks. His arms are crossed over his chest.

"That, young man, is the exact reason we can't be sitting here talking." He focuses back on me. "Sit tight. I'll be right back."

Before we can ask any more questions, he rushes out the door and the four of us—Asher, Gavin, Evangeline, and I— sit there in an uncomfortable silence. Gavin is studying her. She's studying me.

I nudge Gavin—hard—with my elbow and give him my "stop staring" look. He gives me a "what?" look in return. Evangeline grins at me.

I shift my gaze to my hands while Gavin sits next to me, still watching Evangeline while trying to look like he's not. Asher walks around the room, picking up picture frames and putting them back down before moving on to the next one.

After a few minutes, he says, "So? Evangeline? How are you involved in all this?"

Before she can answer, Eli bursts through the door. "I've got everything here to help you." He swallows and I see how nervous he is. "But there's a problem."

"What? What's the problem? I thought you said you could fix this," Gavin demands, his voice and movements panicky as he jumps from the bed.

"I can," Eli says. "But she . . ." He focuses back on me. "You'll have to be awake for the procedure. I'm sorry, but I don't have the equipment I need to put you to sleep. I'm sorry," he finishes weakly.

"Mother," Mom says, and presses her hands to her mouth. "There's nothing you can do?"

"I'm going to give her a sedative, but there's no guarantee she'll stay asleep during . . . everything." He looks over at Gavin. "You need to keep her still. Can you do that? If not, I'll have to tie her down. It's bad enough that I have to gag her; I don't want to do that, too."

Gavin blanches. "Why does she need to be held down? What *exactly* are you going to do to her?" His voice has a hint of panic in it, which makes me feel a little panicky.

Eli sighs as if he really doesn't want to spare the time telling us, but he says, "I'm re-injecting her with working nanites, or nanobots. They'll go in and they'll repair the bots that aren't working and hopefully restore the parts of her neuro-network that have been destroyed to access those memories again—"

"Hopefully?" Gavin interrupts, disbelief tainting his voice.

"You've said repeatedly you could fix her and we're actually working with a hopefully?"

Eli glares at him. "I've never promised anything. I've promised to do the best I can, and I'm fairly confident this will work, but there's never any guarantee. We're working with human biology here, not machines."

"Well, actually we are," Asher says. "Aren't nanobots tiny robots?"

"Yes." Eli sounds exasperated. "But the main part we're actually restoring is her neuronetwork inside her brain. So yes, we're working with machines, but the machines are working on the biology. Now are we going to sit here discussing what we're going to do or are we going to do it before Evie has another hallucination that could kill her?"

I finally pipe up. Ultimately I don't really care what's going to happen as long as I get my memories back. "Let's get moving."

Eli gives me a grim smile, then turns his attention to Gavin. "Can you hold her down? Or not?"

"I can."

"Are you sure? I can't—"

"I said I could do it," Gavin says between clenched teeth.

"Me, too," Asher says, swallowing hard.

Eli nods and turns back to me. "I'm going to give you a shot. Okay? It's going to sting, but it should make you sleepy after that. It should . . . help."

I'm about to nod when Asher says, "Uh . . . maybe we should hold her down for this? She kind of took out like six full-grown men at the hospital back home when they tried taking her blood."

"What?" Gavin demands. "Really?"

Eli's eyes grow wide, but there's something in them that makes me think he's happy to hear this. "There's no need. It's not a real needle. Just a pressure syringe. She won't feel it."

I look away anyway. I really don't want to hurt the people in this room. But Eli was right. I don't feel it. I don't even know he's done it, until he says, "Done."

Eli disappears and comes back again with an armful of supplies. He lays them all out on the dresser next to the bed. It's a handful of syringes that make my mouth dry. I recognize those syringes for some reason and they terrify me, but the shot he gave me already is masking it and I watch with an increasing amount of numbness as he lays out different machines, vials with a silvery liquid in them, and other things that I don't recognize. Then he removes his jacket and rolls his sleeves up past his elbows, before turning to me with a piece of cloth all twisted together. "I'm sorry, Evelyn, but this has to go in your mouth. If anyone hears . . . anything, we'll be in trouble. Okay?"

I know I should feel something. Panic. Fear. Anxiety. Something. But all I feel is an odd floating sensation, and so I do as he asks and open my mouth without even so much as a question.

He places the cloth in my mouth and ties it behind my head, then disappears from view again while the pungent smell of rubbing alcohol scents the air. When he returns, he peers down at me. "Scream all you want. Okay?" he says, and looks away.

My eyes widen. Something in his tone makes panic tingle in my veins for the first time.

I shake my head rapidly back and forth. But they all ignore it and it's only moments before a sharp pain tears through me. My chest, lungs, shoulder, leg. They're all on fire. I jerk, trying to scream, but the gag prevents it. There are voices in the background, but it's hard to understand over the screaming inside my head.

I struggle harder, but they're pinning me down. I open my eyes to see Gavin with a determined look on his face. Asher stands at my side, leaning over my chest, holding my arms down. More pain rips through my body and it jerks. My head spins opposite of my stomach and I think I'm going to be sick, but neither Gavin nor Asher will let me up.

Without warning, I feel bugs crawling over my feet, burrowing into my skin, slithering across my muscles and nerve endings. I try pulling away, but it only gets worse and worse. Those nasty little bugs crawling up over my feet, past my ankles, my shins, knees, until more than half my body feels like it's infested with the horrible burrowing insects. I scream, wiggling and struggling to get away. But the firebugs continue to ravage my body, over my chest, up my neck, until I'm gagging on them, fighting to breathe.

Voices crowd around me. Shouting, whispering, rising and falling around me like waves.

Then, just when I think I can't take any more, it stops and I feel nothing. No pain. No burrowing insects. Nothing but the strange floatiness I felt before. My eyes drift closed.

My eyes fly open. Every bone in my body aches. Sweat clings to my skin and blood bubbles on my mouth where my teeth tore into my lips. My whole body feels like it's encased in ice.

I'm lying naked in a room of all white, strapped down to the bed, Technicians floating around me, murmuring.

"Excellent candidate," one says. "Procedure went perfectly. Tell Mother. She'll want to watch this one."

One of the female Technicians helps me sit up, wrapping a robe around my shoulders. She smiles at me. "Congratulations, Evelyn. You're officially an Enforcer."

I kneel, careful not to get too close. He's quite obviously a Surface Dweller and therefore unpredictable.

"Hello," I say softly. "I won't hurt you."

He shrinks away from me and narrows his eyes, but adjusts his body, bracing his legs. It's obvious he's positioning himself to run again.

"Yeah, right." His voice is scratchy, as if he's swallowed too much saltwater.

I try again, using a smile this time—a woman's best weapon is her smile, unless there's a loaded Beretta 9mm nearby. *I frown. What an odd thought. "I don't blame you for not trusting me. You don't know me, but I assure you, I mean you no harm. My name is Evelyn Winters. I'm the Daughter of the People."*

"Gavin Hunter," he answers warily.

I smile again, a real one this time, and he blinks, as if surprised.

"Gavin. It's a pleasure to meet you."

"Faster," the woman says, mashing a button on the box in her hand.

Suddenly my blood's on fire and I scream, collapsing onto the ground. Almost instantly the pain stops, but I'm still gasping for breath, even as I lurch to my feet and jump onto the rope swinging from the ceiling, pulling myself up hand over hand. Even as I push the button to ring the bell at the top, I know it's my fastest time yet. I let myself drop, bending my knees as I was taught to absorb the force of my weight.

"Good." The instructor smiles. "Faster." She presses the button again.

"Aren't you coming?"

"Of course not. Why would I leave? This is my home. I'm just going to make sure you get back to the door that leads to the Surface. You're all healed, so you should have no problems getting out okay after that."

"But what about the Enforcers? Won't they kill you for helping me?"

"A chill tickles my spine and I suppress a shudder, but I say, "I'm the Daughter of the People. Mother will never believe it was me who helped you."

He doesn't look convinced. "I'd feel better if you came with me," he says.

"If you're really concerned about me, you won't argue with me. The clock is running and the sooner you get out, the less chance they'll figure it out."

"But the guards saw you."

"Who will Mother believe? The Guards? Or her own daughter? Now come on!"

"Fine, but this conversation isn't over," he says, and I fight the urge to roll my eyes. "So, we're on the run now, right?"

"Yes."

"Great." He grabs my arm and spins me around, and then pushes me back with his body so I bump into the wall. Before I can say anything he leans down so his mouth captures mine.

At first I freeze, afraid of the punishment that's surely coming. I start to struggle to get away from him, but then, as my mind fogs from his scent and taste, I melt in his arms. If not for his hands holding me steady at my hips, I would be a puddle on the ground. His lips are sweet and soft, but insistent. The kiss makes my head spin. As far as first kisses go, I can't imagine a better one.

A girl lies at my feet, her face covered in blood, her arm twisted by her side at an awkward angle. She's older than me and almost a complete Enforcer. Sweat covers every inch of skin and my body is bruised and battered, but I held my own. I stand there as straight as I can, wanting to pant as my body craves oxygen, but I will maintain control over myself. No one will know how I almost lost. How winded and exhausted I am. Especially not Mother.

She watched the entire thing, and now she strolls over to us both, flicking a gaze down at the girl who's trying to push herself up on her good arm before turning her attention to me.

My lips want to pull up in a smile as she inspects me. Instead, I pull myself straighter, ignoring the excruciating pain in my ribs from where the girl kicked me. Mother's gaze travels from my head to my feet and back again, before she turns away without saying a word.

I close my eyes against the dismissal and let my shoulders droop.

I struggle to remain standing. I'll kill him before I go down. Again, I raise the gun, aiming for his head. I won't miss this time. I won't fail again.

He closes his eyes and steps forward, pressing the gun to his own head.

"What are you doing?" I ask. Panic is tearing through me and I don't know why. I should be grateful he's doing my job for me.

"Making it easier for you. With that arm, you wouldn't be able to hit the broad side of a barn."

"Are you crazy?"

He nods and there's a small ghost of a smile. "Yeah. I think maybe I am. I've fallen in love with a girl who's programmed to kill me. Not a very sane thing to do, is it?

My jaw drops. "What? What did you say?"

He looks straight into my eyes. "I love you, Evie."

"This is your chance, Evelyn. You won't get another one like it today. Failure will not be tolerated," my mentor says. We're standing in the Square, waiting for Sorting. The water is dark blue over our heads and I can hear the low moaning of the whales in the distance. The Square is decorated in black and purple.

"I understand," I reply, determined that this time, Mother will notice me. She won't be able to ignore me this time.

My mentor leaves me to wander the slowly growing crowd and takes her station somewhere on the other side of the aisle left open for Mother. For a loud few minutes, people talk around me, not even noticing me. I don't look like an Enforcer. Not yet, I think. But soon. Very soon.

Excitement boils in my blood. Butterflies flutter in my stomach but I squash all emotion. Emotion won't get me noticed. Success will. I will *not* fail.

Then a hush draws over the crowd. Mother walks through the crowd, and on either side of the aisle, Citizens bow their heads in reverence. Except the Citizen right next to me. An older man. He refuses to bow his head. The Citizens next to him are hissing at him to do it, but he stares straight back at Mother without so much as a nod. She lifts an eyebrow and stops for the briefest of seconds before moving her gaze to me.

I know what I'm supposed to do. It makes me sick to think about it, but failure will not be tolerated. I sneak behind him, then grab him by his arm and pull him into the shadows.

Although he struggles, it's a simple matter of injecting him with the syringe of medication Enforcers use to calm the unwilling. I place my hands around his head and twist. The popping sound his neck makes leaves me nauseated and for a minute, I lean over, pressing my sweaty palms on my thighs.

After a few minutes of breathing shallowly through my nose, I leave his body for one of the disposal crew to clean up. They should be around any minute. I rejoin the crowd with my stomach still rolling. They part for me now and when Mother sees me, she smiles from the stage set in the middle of the Square. I'm disgusted and queasy, but I fight a smile. I've been waiting five years for this.

Memories flash by in an endless series of bodies and blood and pain. The minute one ends another starts, filling my body with sorrow, regret, disgust, and anger. For myself. For the woman who did this to me and for the one who let it happen. But there are certain memories I'm grateful for. Ones that make up for every single one of the bad ones. Memories of Gavin.

CHAPTER TWENTY-SEVEN

It is a privilege and an honor to serve as an Enforcer, Elysium's most prestigious designation . . . Conditioning is the ideal training method as it is safe, quick, and completely painless.

—EXCERPT FROM *SO YOUR DAUGHTER HAS BEEN CHOSEN TO BE AN ENFORCER. CONGRATULATIONS!* PAMPHLET

Evie

When I wake, my whole body is sore. Just like in the memories. This is a pain I know well. How many times did they do this before? Too many to count. Enough for me to lose myself, though. Enough to turn me from a normal little girl who wanted to play with dolls and have tea parties to a monster who killed people to impress a different monster. To make *someone* proud of me.

I open my eyes and survey the people grouped around me. My eyes land on Evangeline. The woman I now realize is my mother. My real mother. I must have been an idiot not to see the resemblance between us. It's there, slapping me in the face in the color of our eyes. The tilt of our mouths. The upper lip that's slightly fuller than the bottom. Her face is almost identical to the one I see every time I look in the mirror.

Unlike my reflection, though, she won't meet my gaze. She knows that I know and that's just fine with me. I firm my mouth into a straight line. "So, where's my real father?"

Evangeline's eyes widen and stare daggers into Eli. "You didn't tell her?"

Eli looks down at the ground and mumbles, "I thought we should tell her. Together."

Evangeline—I don't know if I can think of her as my mom—shakes her head. "You mean leave it to me." She lowers herself to the bed and tries to stroke my hair, but I jerk myself away from her. She sighs. "Father *is* your real father."

I don't know how to respond to that. Evangeline is obviously my real mom. Eli, on the other hand . . . I tilt my head to study him, but looking at him, there really isn't anything physical we share. But . . . there is something similar. Our mannerisms. Our facial expressions. Even the way he's looking at me, obviously trying not to let me know how nervous he is about what Evangeline just told me, is something I would do, and I doubt anyone else would even know he's nervous.

More than that, there's some kind of connection between us. More of one than I feel toward my mom, and enough of one that I trusted him to get us here. My memories are like leaves fluttering on the wind. No order yet, but something tells me I still don't have the whole story of what happened between Eli and Evangeline.

I sneak a look at Gavin, who doesn't seem that shocked. But Asher is gaping at Eli, and a considering look crosses his face when he turns his attention to me.

I frown at him, wondering what he's thinking, but I say, "This isn't right. He's not my dad." I focus back on Evangeline. "I remember someone else. I never met you until . . . until after I became an Enforcer."

Eli has this half smile on his face, but Evangeline shoots a worried look at him. He nods at her to continue, and for a minute she looks like she's going to refuse, but then she sighs and stands as if she's too nervous to just sit and do nothing.

"You're right, Evie. This is all very complicated, but there *was* someone else. His name was Nathaniel. We were Coupled and he . . ." She stops and closes her eyes, taking a shaky breath before continuing. "He's the one who raised you, but he wasn't your real dad. Not genetically."

My heart starts pounding in my chest and I know I don't want to hear the rest of the story, but I can't make myself tell her to stop. It's as if my body knows I need to hear the rest.

"I was so young. Just barely sixteen. But Nathaniel and I were in love. I was already approved as a breeder, so it was simply a matter of obtaining the license to Couple. So we went to Mother and applied for it. We were approved, but there was a stipulation." She looks at me, and lets out this short, humorless laugh before glancing down to her hands. "For me, anyway. But I didn't know it. Not until after Nathaniel and I were Coupled. Nathaniel and I decided we wanted to start our family right away. We said it was to do our duty for Elysium, but we really just wanted to have children." She smiles at me, but I can't smile back, so she looks back at her hands. "I remember that day perfectly. It was two months after our Coupling and I was in what was to be your nursery. Getting it ready in the hopes that it would give me good luck." She looks at me. "I'd failed to conceive up until this point and she—Mother—came to find me personally. She told me that my genetics were a perfect match for something she was hoping to do. She'd chosen me to be the mother to a new breed of Enforcers. A breed designed specifically for the task. At first I was flattered. Who wouldn't be?"

She smiles at me, but I'm not amused. She was *flattered*? Really? How fantastic for her.

She clears her throat. "Um . . . it was short-lived. She went on to say that the father of the baby I would carry would not be Nathaniel, but would be her own partner. Father."

Everyone looks at Eli and he shifts from side to side, looking at the ground.

"I don't understand." Gavin moves his gaze back to Evangeline. "If she wanted you to Couple with Eli, why did she allow you to Couple with Nathaniel?"

"To force her to agree," Asher says, and I shift my attention to him. He's looking at Evangeline. "Right? She gave you what you wanted, then threatened to take it away if you didn't do what *she* wanted."

Tears fall from Evangeline's eyes, but she nods. "Yes.

Exactly. When she told me that she wanted me to breed with Father—" She looks at each of us in turn. "Not Couple," she clarifies. "Coupling would mean she would have had to give him up. And there was no way she was going to allow that. No, she only wanted him to breed with me. Anyway, when she told me, I refused. I said that I was Coupled and that I wanted children with Nathaniel. So she threatened me. She told me that Nathaniel was sterile. A failure. He wouldn't be able to breed, but she had allowed me to Couple with him anyway, because he would make an excellent father to the child she wanted to create. Since Father wouldn't be there to be the dad, somebody else would have to stand in. And because of my genetics, I would make the perfect mother.

"So I had a choice. I could either allow her to artificially inseminate me and keep my mouth shut, letting Nathaniel think he was the father. Or I could refuse and Nathaniel and I would disappear. She'd take what she needed from me and 'gift' some other woman with being the mother to the perfect Enforcer. She gave me twenty-four hours to think about it. I didn't have any choice but to accept. The next day when she came, she brought the doctor with her." She shrugs. "She knew I'd accept. We started treatments and a few months later I was pregnant with you."

"So," I say, anger boiling up in me like a volcano, "I was . . . just a means to an end." I look between Eli and Evangeline. "For Mother I was . . . the beginning of a perfect race of assassins. For you, Evangeline, a way to stay alive, and for you,

Eli? What . . . what was I to you?" My voice gets higher and louder with each word. But I don't let him answer before asking, "I was never wanted? None of you wanted me? Only *Mother*?"

"Oh hell," Asher says.

"It wasn't like that, Evelyn, you have to understand—" Evangeline starts to say.

"I understand perfectly. No one wanted me except Mother, and she only wanted me for my . . . DNA." I swipe my palms together as if to clean them. "I'm just a bunch of spare parts waiting to be assembled into something better. What a terrible inconvenience for you all that I turned out to be a real person!"

"No, no—" she starts to say.

"Evie—" Eli starts to speak but I cut him off with a glare.

"You're the worst of them. You *knew* what she was capable of and you let her do it anyway. To your own *daughter*." My chest aches and my eyes burn miserably. "You didn't even care, did you?"

"Don't answer that," Gavin says to my parents, then turns to me. "It doesn't matter. It doesn't matter the motivation of any of *them*. Look at me." He peers into my eyes when I do. "*I* love you. *I* want you. And no matter what you were created for, that will always be true. Okay?"

His words are like a balm on the open wounds Evangeline just broke open, and I nod, but it doesn't stop me from needing to know the answers. I turn back to Evangeline, who is watching me.

"We loved you, Evie. Me. Nathaniel and—"

"Me," Eli says, and I jerk my head around to look at him. "I loved you, too. We still do."

"But you still sent me to *her*. Sent me to be an Enforcer. Let them"—I search for the word Gavin used—"brainwash me. If you loved me, how could you do that?" I look between the two of them. "How could *any* decent human being do that to *anyone*? *You're despicable*." The burning in my eyes melts into tears, but I refuse to let them fall.

They glance at each other and I can almost see them asking each other how to answer the question. I push myself up to my feet, but stagger when the blood rushes from my head. Both Gavin and Asher rush to catch me before I can fall. My parents exchange another look.

This, of course, makes the volcano of anger boil over and I shout, "Answer me!"

"We didn't have a choice," Evangeline finally says. "Being an Enforcer was . . . is a privilege. Mother's most prestigious designation. We didn't know what would happen."

"Bullshit!" Gavin says.

"Watch your tongue, boy," Eli says. "She wanted answers, she's getting them."

Evangeline looks at Gavin. "We did know about the Conditioning." She turns back to me. "But we *didn't* know that your brain would be able to fight it. If we had, we might have done things differently."

"What?" I demand, crossing my arms over my aching chest. "What would you have done?"

She shakes her head. "I—I don't know. Something. Anything." She meets my eyes and takes my hands in hers, frowning at them. "But you have to know—I loved you. Love you. Very much. It didn't matter to me why you were here, just that you were. You were always *my* daughter, even when she thought of you as hers."

"But you gave me up! You didn't fight for me at all! You let her take me. I *lost* myself before I even knew who I was! How could you do that?" My voice is a whisper. A husk of itself.

"You've seen her," Eli says. "I know you've seen her in those memories. Even if they don't all make sense at the moment. You know what she's like and you also know she's the one who did this to you. And you're not the only one. You're not even the last. But if you want this to stop . . . you know what has to be done."

"What?" I ask, sniffling and running a hand under my running nose.

"You have to eliminate Mother."

Chapter Twenty-eight

Elite Enforcer Testing Requirements
In order to pass training, an Enforcer must:
- *Lift 8 times her own body weight (minimum)*
- *Master all forms of martial art techniques*
- *Be able to name, repair, and correctly use all weapons modern or archaic, while also adapting easily to new technologies*
- *Endure emotional, pain tolerance, and healing tests, while being able to make snap judgments that benefit the whole, even if sacrificing the few*
- *Demonstrate knowledge of all computer skills including but not limited to: extensive knowledge of all operating systems (past and present, and adaptation to new technologies), coding, software for the express purpose of "hacking," forensics, and electronic bypassing*

Evie

I push myself up to my feet. "Absolutely not. I can't kill someone."

Eli keeps his gaze on mine. "You're the only one who can, Evie. You've had Enforcer training—"

"I don't remember it!" A lie. Bits and pieces of those memories crowd my brain, making me dizzy. But it's all jumbled, just like all the rest.

"Your body does, even if you don't."

I flash back to the path in the woods, how I tore the birds' heads from their bodies without even batting an eye. The attack on Asher. And then again when I knocked Gavin out.

The blood rushes from my head, and I have to sit back down. He's right. My body *does* remember what to do. But still . . . "I can't kill her. Then I'm no better than she is."

Gavin squeezes my hand. "Of course you can't kill her." He glares at Eli. "How can you even ask that of her?" He stands, pulling me up with him, and I let him. I don't care that I just found out who my parents are, I just want to get away from these psychotic people.

"You can't leave here," Eli says, stopping Gavin and me in our tracks.

"Yes we can, and we will," Gavin says, his teeth and fists clenching.

"You can. She can't. She'll lose everything again. There's an EMF field around the city. If you leave, the field will cause the bots to hardlock. They'll automatically suppress Evelyn's memories again. It prevents people who've managed to . . . leave—not that it happens very often—from telling our secrets to the Surface Dwellers. But if you help us, I'll figure out a way to bypass that so you can go. Both of you."

I exchange a glance with Gavin. As much as I don't want to believe Eli, there's something that rings true about what he's saying. I think I knew this. Somehow.

I don't say anything, but Asher says, "What if we come up with a compromise?" He glances to me. "We don't have to kill anyone. We could just . . . exile her."

Evangeline's eyes light up. "Yes. To the Surface. For her *that* would be a fate worse than death."

Eli furrows her brow. "How are we going to do that? She's never going to go without a fight. And who's to say she won't find a way to come back in when we're not expecting her? It's too dangerous."

The room becomes quiet again, but I don't care. "I'm not killing anyone," I say. "No matter how horrible she is. Or how I was trained. I'm not taking someone's life. It's wrong. And I refuse to do it again for you or anyone."

Eli holds my gaze for a long minute. "Fine," he says finally. "Exile could work, but we need to remove her from office and find a way to get her out of here and onto the Surface, while figuring out how to keep her from returning. And for that we'll still need you. Your training will still be the best advantage we have, especially if things go wrong."

Gavin shakes his head. "No. This isn't our fight anymore. We appreciate you helping her, but we can't stay. I'm not going to let her get herself hurt again. Mother doesn't know she's here, as far as we know, and I'd rather it stay that way." He looks up at me. "Right, Evie?"

I don't know what to say. My mind is still chaotic. I'm

starting to put together all the information that I've regained access to, but not all of it makes sense. A lot of it doesn't, actually. It's like putting a puzzle together without having the box to tell you what the whole picture is supposed to look like. I can't be certain of anything. I can't even be sure the memories I have are real memories or ones my brain has supplied to fill in the gaps. All I really have is what they've told me. Is that enough for me to risk my life for people I don't even know anymore?

Gavin may be right. This isn't really my fight anymore, and Mother is surely out for my blood. It'd be much better for us—Asher, Gavin, and me—to just leave now.

But that doesn't feel right either.

If what they're saying is right, and there is anything I can do to help, I don't think I'd be able to live with myself if I just left them to fend for themselves. I'd probably end up like Asher's grandmother, trying to get rid of the guilt years later.

They're all still staring at me, but I don't know what to do.

"I don't know," I finally say. "I—I need a few minutes. To think." I press a hand to my pounding head.

Immediately Evangeline jumps up. "Of course you do. You're probably exhausted. After everything you've gone through." She starts leading me down the hall and to the first room on the left.

She pushes open the door to reveal a bedroom decorated in pink. She gestures to the bed. "Please. Rest. You know where to find me if you need me."

I nod and sit on the side of the bed while she stands awkwardly in the doorway. After a minute, she turns and leaves, looking lost.

I know the feeling. I feel lost myself. Engrossed in my thoughts, I don't hear the door open, and when Asher's head pops into my line of view, I have to stifle a scream.

He laughs when I swat at him. "Asher! Don't *do* that!"

"Sorry," he says, still laughing.

I make room for him on the bed and he sits next to me.

We sit in easy silence, until finally he breaks it by saying, "You know that I'm *not* on the side of you dying, right?"

Surprised, I jerk my head up to look at him. "Of course!"

"And that I didn't bring you here to betray you?"

I blink. "Of course you didn't. I've known from the beginning that the only reason you brought me here was to help me. You've been incredibly kind. Thank you."

"Don't thank me," he says. "It wasn't entirely selfless on my part."

"You mean how you're trying to make up to Gavin by helping me?"

"No. At first that was the reason. Then I got to know you and I was doing it for you. You seemed to be able to see right through me and yet . . . you still liked me. I think." He looks up at me and I nod. He smiles; then it falls and he continues. "That doesn't happen to me very often. Even my own father isn't exactly fond of me. I thought I was falling in love with you. I kind of hoped I was because it would have made things so much easier. And I convinced myself that it was mutual." He sighs. "And if it wasn't, that with time, maybe it would be."

My eyes widen as I stare at him. I open my mouth to say something, but I'm so shocked that nothing comes out.

He only laughs. "Yeah. That's what I thought. Don't worry. I've realized that's not gonna happen. And it's okay. Because I do love you. It's just not that kind of love."

"I—I don't understand."

He takes my hand, running a thumb over the back of it. "You didn't realize what Eli was saying back there. Did you?"

"About him being my dad? Yeah, I get it."

He shakes his head. "No. Not exactly. Remember what my grandma said about him? About *them*?" He emphasizes the "them" and stares at me as I frown.

Then slowly I get it. "About them being lovers?"

He looks uncomfortable, squirming a little in his seat, but nods. "What if she was pregnant when she left here?" His eyes bore into mine. "What if my mom is Eli's daughter, too?"

"No. That can't be right." Can it? Do I have family out there I didn't even know about? I stare at Asher. Is *he* part of my family?

He smiles when he sees I understand and his hand grips mine. "You get it now, don't you?"

I slowly nod.

"When Eli said that you were his daughter, it surprised me that it didn't bother me as much as it should have, you know? Because he was my grandma's boyfriend, for God's sake, and that meant you were—well, you could be . . . I realized that it could mean you were family. And it should have been so disgusting, but it's not, because I see you more like my sister than a girl." He laughs. "That didn't come out right. And that's why I get so pissed off at Gavin for the way he treats you sometimes. I'm not jealous—" He bumps my shoulder with his. "—I'm just watching out for my sister."

I stare at him, my heart bursting with happiness. Family. *Real* family. Someone who actually wants to be my family, instead of just tolerating my existence.

I smile at him, then hug him tightly, tears brimming in my eyes. He hugs me back.

"Do you think it's true?" I ask.

"I don't know. It seems possible." He shrugs. "I kind of like the idea of you being my sister."

"You realize I'd actually be your aunt, right?" I ask, grinning.

He rolls his eyes. "Please. You're little-sister material all the way."

Laughing, I feel lighter than air. I can't wait to tell Gavin this new revelation. I've no doubt he'll be happy for me. And maybe this will help him bridge that ridiculous gap between them.

He nudges my shoulder again, before standing and walking to the door. "I know this is probably the hardest decision you'll ever have to make, but I just want you to know that I'm behind you. No matter what you decide." Without saying another word, he steps out of the room.

For a few minutes, I just stare at the open door, trying to

gather my thoughts, until Gavin knocks. He steps in without waiting for an answer and joins me on the bed, linking his fingers with mine.

"You're not seriously thinking of staying, are you?"

"I don't know. If Mother has done half the things they say, I can't just walk away."

He opens his mouth, then shuts it, before sighing. "We can't stay, Evie. You know that. I won't take the chance of you getting hurt again, and Mother is dangerous. There's no way she's just going to let you stroll in and tell her she can't live here anymore."

"But there's no one else to help them. You heard them. I'm the only one."

"So they say. What if you never came back at all? What would they have done then?"

"But I did."

"But what if you didn't?" He pushes off the bed to pace, then stops in front of me. "You are under no obligation to help them. In fact, they have no right"—he balls his hands into fists—"*no right*, to ask this of you. They're your family. Any parent would have saved their daughter's life without asking for *payment*. And they lost the right to ask you for help when they gave you to the psychotic woman and let her *brainwash you*, repeatedly." He goes on, getting louder and more animated by the second.

Finally I cut into his diatribe.

"Gavin?" I ask, looking at him.

He stops, frowning at me. "What?"

"You're not helping."

He stares at me. "You're not just going to make me watch you walk into that black widow's lair. I won't do it, Evie. Not this time. I've already had to endure being back here. I won't let you do this."

At that, anything I would have said flies out of my mind. "You're not going to *let* me?" I push up from the bed.

His eyes widen at my tone and he starts to say something, but I interrupt. "Gavin, I appreciate everything you've done for me. I understand this hasn't been easy. But just because I don't remember much about my life before we met doesn't mean I'm your property. *You* don't let me do anything. If *I* choose to help them, I will do so and there will be nothing you can do to stop me." I turn around so my back is to him, then gesture to the door. "You may leave."

"But, Evie, wait. That's not what I—"

"You may leave," I repeat, swallowing the lump of rage and hurt balling in my throat.

He sighs, but I hear him leave the room, his shoes dragging across the floor. He pauses at the door momentarily, but then he keeps going without saying anything.

An hour later, I've made my decision. I carefully make my way back to the living room to stand at the doorway, being a silent observer for the minute or so before anyone sees me.

Evangeline is talking quietly with Eli in a corner of the

room. Their backs are to me, and I can't hear what they're saying, but they look nervous. Gavin sits on the couch, curled into himself.

I take a deep breath and instantly feel everyone's eyes on mine. Waiting for an answer I don't want to give because I know what it'll mean and what I'll have to do. When I look up, I meet Asher's gaze first. He nods once and I close my eyes in relief. At least someone is standing by me.

When I open them again, I look all of them in the face, stopping last on Gavin. His eyes narrow, but I don't look away. I want him to know this is something I have to do. I can't just let Mother's tyranny continue. She's already taken everything from me; I can't let her destroy any more lives. Not if I have even the smallest chance of stopping it.

I turn to my parents. "I'll do it. For Elysium." To Asher. "For my family." Then to Gavin. "For us."

A war of words breaks out around me. Gavin is the first up and I expect him to start on me, but he pushes his face into Eli's, screaming as loud as I've ever heard. Eli is screaming right back, gesturing to where I sit. I can't hear anything as everyone is fighting to talk over each other.

The only one not yelling is Asher, who is watching me intently. So intently I wonder if he's trying to tell me something. For a minute, we just sit there watching each other, letting the words crash over us before he breaks it with his signature smile. As if to say, "I've got this."

I smile back. "Thank you," I mouth, and he nods again,

then tips his head toward the door, gesturing for me to exit while everyone is preoccupied.

Then he stands and enters the fight, while I slip quietly to my room to contemplate how to take Mother down.

Chapter Twenty-nine

My daughter has returned to me, as I knew she would. After all, she is my creation. And like anything that requires programming by an outside influence, it is inevitable that she should return to her creator.

Especially when programmed to do so.

—Excerpt from Mother's Journal

Mother

I watch the monitor and smile. They actually believe they got into Elysium without me knowing. I didn't become the Governess by being a fool. I *am* Evelyn's Mother. Everyone's Mother. And nothing escapes me.

I turn to Dr. Friar behind me. "You made sure he got everything he needed?"

"Yes. I made sure the staff was otherwise entertained so all he had to do was 'sneak' in and grab it." He tips his head to the side, that sly smile twinkling in his eyes. "Poor man. Seemed in such a hurry. Didn't even notice it was unusually quiet in the Medical Sector. I do hope nothing is wrong."

I laugh and lean against the back of my chair. "Fantastic." Then a thought occurs to me. "How much of her memory will he be able to recover?"

"Not much, I'm afraid. With the reactivation she may get them all back eventually, but it will be very slow. You'd probably have more success planting new ones."

I nod and lean into my mirror, checking the line of my eyeliner. I press a light finger to the small wrinkles to the side. "Make sure you have everything you need to make that happen." I look at him through the mirror. "She's probably already said yes. They won't wait long. And I'm eager to continue Evelyn's training now that she's passed her test. I must say, I'm pleased that she's brought these fabulous new specimens with her." The side of my mouth lifts. "Such a lovely surprise."

There's a soft knock on the door. "Come," I say.

One of my Maids pokes her head through the opening. "Enforcer Lydia here to see you, ma'am."

I clap my hands. "Wonderful. Send her in."

The Maid quickly disappears to be replaced with the girl Evelyn's age who has taken over as lead Enforcer since Evelyn and that Surface Dweller killed my last leader. She stands just inside the door, staring over my head with her trained gaze. I know she sees everything, even when it looks like she sees nothing.

"The situation is under control," she says, her voice as flat as the floor my chair is sitting on.

"The girl?"

"She's been relocated to Enforcer training."

"And her poor mother?"

"Eliminated."

My smile creeps across my face. "Very good. You may go." I waggle my fingers at the door and spin back around in my seat to look in the mirror again.

"Problems?" Dr. Friar asks.

"None. Everything is going exactly according to plan."

Acknowledgments

As always, turning a manuscript into a novel takes many more people than just the lonely author, writing in her garret. I will never be able to thank everyone who's helped make the mess of words that was originally *Revelations* into the book it is now without making this a novel itself, so I'm not even going to try. *smiles*

A huge thanks to my wonderful agent, Natalie Lakosil, for being in my corner when I needed her the most. And to my editor, Mel, for her awesome insight and for seeing once again the story I was trying to tell and helping me pull it out. And as always, a huge thanks to the cover artist, Eithne, and Tor's art director Seth for yet another beautiful cover.

I definitely couldn't have done this without the support of my family, specifically, my husband, for all those late nights helping me see the simple solutions to the problems I was trying to make more complicated than they needed to be, and for my children for putting up with all the time my imaginary friends took all my attention.

And to my crit partner Liz Czukas for all the brain-storming sessions and for talking me down from all the last-minute freak-outs. Thank you so, so much.

And to my crit partner Larissa Hardesty for making sure my story had heart and soul and wasn't just a mess of words.

A special shout-out and thank-you to Ryan Campbell and his daughter Cordelia for being my first "outside" readers. Your excitement and enthusiasm for my characters and writing gave me the courage to persevere through the dark until I saw the light. You both rock!

And, of course, thank you to God for giving me the talent and perseverance to make my dream a career.

And last but not least, a huge thank-you to all my fabulous readers that loved *Renegade* and loved and rooted for Evie and Gavin. I hope you enjoy the new chapter of their story. I couldn't do this without you. XOXO.

WOMEN
ON DIVORCE
A Bedside Companion

WOMEN

ON

EDITED BY *Penny Kaganoff*

AND *Susan Spano*

DIVORCE

A Bedside Companion

Harcourt Brace & Company

New York   San Diego   London

Library of Congress Cataloging-in-Publication Data
Women on divorce: a bedside companion/edited by
Penny Kaganoff & Susan Spano.—1st ed.
p.   cm.
ISBN 0-15-100114-6
1. Divorce. I. Kaganoff, Penny. II. Spano, Susan.
HQ814.W64   1995
300.89—dc20   95-20287

Text set in Galliard   Designed by Camilla Filancia
Printed in the United States of America   First edition   A B C D E

CONTENTS

Special thanks go to our friend Linda Yellin,
the godmother of this anthology; to Lisa Bankoff,
our wonderful agent; and to our editors: Claire Wachtel,
whose vision and enthusiasm gave our project life,
and Ruth Greenstein, whose grace and patience
shepherded us through to the end. We are also grateful
to our many generous friends, colleagues, and relatives
who helped us bring this book about in more ways
than we can enumerate.

INTRODUCTION

$\mathcal{S}$o OFTEN, in casual conversation, women make mention of their divorces to us—whether or not they know that we have been through the dreaded experience ourselves. And when they do, this signals the fact that they've undergone one of life's major changes, increasingly on a par with the other milestones: menarche, marriage, motherhood, menopause, and death.

We are just two of the millions of women who divorce each year. In America today nearly a third of all women who marry between the ages of twenty and forty-four get divorced. What is more, half of all second marriages end in divorce.

Divorce is a radical rupture in a person's life. It leads us to wonder why we marry in the first place, why marriages go wrong, and what it takes in these times to make a marriage endure. Divorce raises issues such as monogamy,

morality, feminism, sexuality, misogyny, loyalty and betrayal, love, self-respect, and self-delusion. It asks us to question the way we see ourselves as children, siblings, and parents, and changes the way others perceive us—be it as failures, pariahs, threats, comrades, or role models.

For Susan, enduring the process of her divorce compelled her to recognize how her romanticism led her into a disastrous marriage. She had met her husband in college and for the next fifteen years never wavered in her love for him—or doubted his for her. But then one day he confessed that he'd been betraying her almost all along.

It was at this point, when Susan was in the thick of her divorce, that she met Penny through a mutual friend who was also a divorcée. Susan was shell-shocked, full of anger and pain; but more than anything else, she needed to talk about her divorce with others who had similar experiences. Sharing stories was a source of catharsis and the key to making sense of the confusion of her breakup.

Penny had more distance on the subject: Her divorce had occurred several years before and under different circumstances. She had married the proverbial handsome and successful Jewish professional—and their union was a misery. Her decision to divorce him was a moment of triumph, a brave and healthy act. But it caused a rift in her relationship with her family and the Orthodox Jewish community that had been at the center of her existence. Why couldn't she learn to compromise and make her marriage work? they wondered.

Although our marriages ended in different ways, we were surprised and gratified to realize how many of our

issues aligned. For example, although we both married after the women's movement had galvanized others of our sex, we still put the very concepts of husband and marriage on a pedestal.

As we read the divorce stories we commissioned for this volume, we were repeatedly impressed by how the various pieces aroused memories of our own experiences. Ann Patchett's essay particularly resonated for Penny. In the story of Ann's severance of a Catholic marriage that properly should have ended only in death, Penny found patterns that suggested her own situation: alienation from a beloved heritage, the shame of a failed relationship.

In fact, the more we considered the essays in this book, the more patterns we noticed, never identical, but there nonetheless to fascinate, twist the heart, make us laugh, and complicate prevailing notions about the how and why of divorce.

That marriages often go awry—sometimes even before the vows die on the lips of the bride and groom—comes as no surprise. But for many of the writers in this collection the question is why. "Why do we make these crazy marriages that end in tragedy or divorce?" Ellen Gilchrist asks in "Meditations on Divorce." For her the answer is bound up with the way people often repeat cycles established when they were young—taking wives and husbands who are like their mothers and fathers, failing to understand the "unconscious strivings and yearnings" that compel them to do so. In "A Tale of Two Divorces," Anne Roiphe tells the story of her mother's bad marriage, and then of her own, finally realizing that "I had married a man more like my father than not and

that, more like my mother than not, I had become a creature to be pitied. Like moth to flame I was drawn to repeat."

When ill-considered or simply ill-fated marriages fall
apart, children are the innocent victims; this truth echoes
throughout the essays. "I wish that we could marry a new
mate, repair, go on to undo the worst of our mistakes
without leaving ugly deep scars across our children's psyches, but we can't," Anne Roiphe writes. "And furthermore the children will never completely forgive us, never
understand how our backs were against the wall." Feeling
this, Alix Kates Shulman let a bad marriage go on until it
finally went sour; in "A Failed Divorce," she suggests that
breakups involving children may "take about as long to
get over as the age of the children when the breach occurred."

Though not divorced herself, Perri Klass ("The Divorces of Others") watched divorce after divorce strike the
families of the children in her son's play group, following
them with more than a little titillation—until her son's
fears of divorce toppled her from a "lofty peak of secure
coupledom." In "Divorce as a Spectator Sport," Francine
Prose notes a similar irresistible interest on the part of herself, her friends, and the culture at large for the kinds of
big, splashy, celebrity divorces reported by the media—
the great public battles of the sexes that incite happy husbands and wives to take sides. And in "The Marriage
Survivors," Carol Shields remarks on the fact that—
for fiction writers, at least—divorce has tended to seem
simply more engrossing than marriage. "Six hundred fast-turning pages without a single marital breakdown; now there is a challenge. Man and woman meet,

fall in love, and integrate their unspotted histories. Crises of all sorts arrive, but their marriage holds firm. Really? You expect readers to believe that kind of fairy-tale stuff?"

While onlookers thrill to each new page in messy marital ruptures and scrutinize their own relationships, the divorced live through the process. This is harrowing enough in itself, without the further complications, ironies, and endless delays created by divorce law and lawyers—and the essayists in this collection have a good deal to say about them. In "This Is What You Need for a Happy Life," Jane Shapiro interviews a preeminent New York City divorce lawyer who has never even contemplated getting divorced himself; unfortunately, he finds most of his colleagues a needy and mediocre lot. "And when you marry need with mediocrity," he says, "you get an awful hybrid."

Daphne Merkin confides that she went through two lawyers before she found one she could feel comfortable with—and even that match was far from perfect. "My lawyer is involved in the feminist end of law, which initially alarmed as much as it attracted me: I wanted to make sure she understood that I was not getting my divorce on behalf of the women's movement and was not interested in taking a rhetorical—if right-minded—position that would endanger my chances." Those "chances" had partly to do with child custody, which she notes is being granted with increasing frequency to fathers when the mothers have careers of their own. "In this regard," she writes, "the more vociferous and unyielding claims of the women's movement (which include the devaluation of motherhood and the insistence on a theoretical egalitari-

anism at home) have done an inadvertent disservice to divorcing professional women who also happen to be passionate mothers."

And in ways beyond this, the advances achieved by the feminist movement have had surprisingly complex effects on divorcing women. In the vanguard of the movement, Alix Kates Shulman drew up a marriage agreement based on complete gender equality ten years into her second marriage; but as the relationship fell apart, she found that the agreement "rested on nothing more substantial than . . . floating goodwill." Our marriages—that is, Penny's and Susan's—came after the major thrust of the women's movement in the 1970s and should have been informed by feminism. But instead, we married the wrong men for the same old wrong reasons.

Diana Hume George ("The Gender Wars") made a different sort of mistake. She chose a feminist man who had adopted "a conscious program of personal growth and transformation"—one of "the good guys." But when their common-law marriage finally broke down, it was, at least in part, says Hume George, because his feminism had provoked his misogyny. "Such men often feel deep if suppressed anger over what they gave up when they relinquished privileges that would otherwise have been theirs. And in some feminist men this rage is directed toward women. If you get in the way of it, you can be in big trouble."

Getting out of a bad marriage seems to some a great escape, managed desperately and just in the nick of time. This is explored by Ann Hood ("It's a Wonderful Divorce"), who married a man she could love as a friend, but couldn't abide as a spouse. Not long after her divorce, she

visited a psychic who read her cards and knew right away what she'd been going through. "Funny thing is," he said to her, "you're not at all upset. In fact, you're glad." Jane Shapiro fled a marriage, too, while pregnant with her second child. Years later she finds that she and her ex can't recall ever having had an argument.

Divorce also affords women the chance to imagine what a good—or at least, enduring—marriage would look like, how it would work. For Daphne Merkin, "psychic bartering" makes a marriage run; for Susan, it takes constant adjustments and tinkering. Interestingly, Anne Roiphe and Ellen Gilchrist both contemplate the value of arranged marriages—practical, mutually beneficial unions, in which love might develop only as an afterthought. And for Mary Morris ("Grounds"), another non-divorced writer, the failure of an important relationship in her past has made her understand why she won't divorce her husband, even if the marriage doesn't fulfill all her needs. "Because I'm the kite and he's the string. Because I can't stand the paperwork. Because he'll read this essay and laugh."

Nonetheless, most of the essayists in this collection find that divorce must exist; indeed, that it is as vital as marriage itself. Awful for children and the psyche, never simple or painlessly managed—but a necessary option. As Ann Patchett writes in "The Sacrament of Divorce," "Make marriage harder if you want to. Outlaw those Vegas chapels with the neon wedding bells, require marriage applications modeled after tax forms, but leave divorce alone. It's grueling. I have never known anyone who went into a marriage thinking that they would have to get out, and I have never known anyone who got out simply. To

leave, you have to involve the courts. You have to sue the person you live with for your freedom. You have to disconnect your life from another life and face the sea alone. Never easy, blithe. Never."

How hard divorce is! We found this sentiment expressed in almost every one of the essays in this book. From Daphne Merkin who, stranded "in the country of divorce," finds herself without an identity, to Ellen Gilchrist, appalled by the ugly twists of divorce ("How terrible we feel to be walking around thinking dark thoughts about someone we used to *sleep with*"), to Anne Roiphe, who "felt as if the skin had been stripped from my body the first months after my divorce, and I was only twenty-seven years old."

It is our hope that the essays in this book will reverberate for readers, too—whether they have been divorced, are contemplating the deed, or are witnessing the pain of a divorcing loved one. We offer them as consolation, as inspiration, and above all, as fine examples of writing by contemporary women.

NEW YORK CITY
April 1995

WOMEN
ON DIVORCE
A Bedside Companion

THE

SACRAMENT

OF DIVORCE

BY *Ann Patchett*

$\mathcal{I}$CALL HIM my husband half of the time and my
ex-husband the other half, but when I think of him it is as
my husband. This isn't because in my secret heart I want
to be married to him (there is nothing I can think of wanting less), but because I only have one husband and that's
him. Like it or not, he has an important place in my personal history. He has a title. I suppose I must be his ex-
wife, since somebody told me he married again. It's been
six years now. Enough time has passed that I wish him
well, in a way that is so distant and abstract it doesn't even
matter.

My divorce began less than a week before we were
married. We had to drive out to Donelson to the rectory
at Holy Rosary, where we had an appointment with the
priest who would perform the service. It was a good thirty
minutes from Nashville, my hometown, but marriage was

a booming business that year and the more convenient priests were already booked solid. We got lost once we got off the interstate and twisted through the dark and identical streets of tract houses with cinder-block foundations. We didn't talk about anything more important than directions. My husband thought I should know where we were, Tennessee being my state, but I hadn't been to Donelson or Holy Rosary since I was ten years old. I also have a notoriously bad sense of direction.

It was June, because that was the month to get married in, and it was buggy and hot. We had been through the weekend of Catholic marriage seminars, nightmare classes full of the nitty gritty of Natural Family Planning (the cool new way to say rhythm) and personality questionnaires ("Which tasks will you do? Which will your husband do? Which will you do together? A. Iron, B. Take out the trash, C. Make decisions about major purchases"). Now we had to see Father Kibby one-on-one, go over a few things. My husband and I were both Catholics. He wanted nothing to do with the Church but was willing to be married by a priest to make his mother happy. For me it was worth more. I was a Catholic shaped by twelve years of Catholic school. Marriage was one of the seven sacraments I had memorized along with my multiplication tables in third grade. Catholicism wasn't at the heart of marriage for me, but it was part of it. Marriage was one of the sacraments I was entitled to.

My hands were sweating from more than the heat when we got to the rectory office. We were late and shouldn't have been. Seeing a priest meant trouble, sin, confession, nothing good, but Father Kibby was young and put us at ease. He wore jeans and a yellow polo shirt.

He even said we should get together sometime for a beer and I was flattered. But that would be another evening. Now it was late and there were a few things we had to get done. He would read from the questionnaire attached to the clipboard and check off the appropriate boxes. The June bugs were thumping against the screen. At the end, he explained, we would sign the form.

Did we believe in God and the Catholic Church?

Yes.

Would we raise our children to be Catholic?

Yes.

Were we entering into marriage lightly?

No.

Was this a marriage that could only be dissolved by death?

Death?

Death. That meant that if the marriage didn't work my only way out was to die. He was asking me to swear to my preference for death over divorce. That was the question and I am no fool so I didn't even have to think about the answer. No, of course not. I would choose not to die. At that moment, before it had even started, I understood how my marriage could end.

I should have understood it anyway, because even going into things I was not happy with my husband. We had lived together for two-and-a-half years before we got married so I had a fairly good idea of how we got along. Not well. It's difficult to talk about divorce without getting into your marriage, and yet I'd just as soon leave my marriage alone. Our general patterns were much like those of any unhappy couple, periods of our screaming and my crying broken up by intolerable stretches of silence. We

were not helpful to each other. We were not kind. These are the facts: I married him when I should not have and later on I left. I ran out the door, got a ride to the airport, and bought a one-way ticket back to Tennessee.

People ask me, if you knew it wasn't working, why did you marry him? And all I can say is, I didn't know how not to. I believed I was in too deep before the invitations were ever mailed, before the engagement. Maybe it was inexperience or maybe I was stupid. The relationship had a momentum that was taking us to this place and I couldn't figure out how to stop it until four nights before my wedding when the choice was presented in very simple terms: death—my death—or divorce. I was twenty-four years old. My husband was thirty-one. The only way off a runaway train is to jump off, but at that moment the ground looked to be going by so fast that I was paralyzed. And so I lied. I said yes.

Yes, this is a marriage that can only be dissolved by death.

IT IS RARE, but sometimes I still dream about my husband and the dream goes like this: I am in a big, frothy wedding dress of the sort that I refused to wear when we were actually married. It is shimmering white. My sister, in bridesmaid's seashell pink, is fussing with my hair, my mother is bringing me flowers, the church has the sunny, festive air of the kind of wedding that would resolve a Shakespearean comedy. I am about to marry my husband again, after having divorced him, but I don't know how this has happened. I cannot remember the promise but, surely, I must have promised. I am set to marry him and laced inside this dress, I know I have to stop it, break the

world apart all over again. Sometimes there are variations to this dream. I am already married to him, or I am married to him for a third or fourth time and am having to divorce him and there is no explanation. I have no idea how I could have let myself get into this kind of trouble, but here I am.

I divorced my husband not much more than a year after I married him, a fact that I still find myself fluffing up by saying we lived together for four years. But that's a lie, too: it was less than that. Oh, I longed for five years of marriage. I craved ten. I wanted to say, See how I tried? I did everything I could, God knows, there was nothing left for me to do. Sticking it out that one year took every ounce of courage I had. But a year sounds like nothing, not a marriage but a breath, a long date. In my mind, women stopped me on the street and said to me, "Put your one year against my fifteen, twenty, thirty-eight. Put your slim, never-had-a-single-baby hips beside mine, four children. Look at the entrenchment of a lifetime spent together. Who owns this house, that photograph. What you had was nothing."

Of course, no one said this, at least no one who had been divorced. In fact, it was quite the opposite. Without knowing it, I had stumbled into the underground and was given the secret handshake to the world's largest club. The Divorced. We were everywhere. Our insurance man called me the week after I left to tell me my husband had removed me from all the policies and I had to sign in approval because I was, at that point, still married. Our insurance man said to me in a quiet voice, "You don't have to do this. You're going to need to take some time." The receptionist at my divorce lawyer's office called back the

next day to see how I was doing. It turned out that the receptionist's marriage had ended too, and this was her first job after having spent half her life as a stay-at-home wife. And when I applied for my own credit card and the woman on the phone said to me, are you married or single, and I didn't know the answer, the woman on the phone dropped the questions and called me Honey. "Honey," she said, "I know."

They had empathy. A word I understood for the first time, because suddenly I had it too. It was, perhaps, my only emotion outside of depression and guilt. Days after I left my husband I propped myself up on my mother's sofa and I watched the guests on *Oprah Winfrey*. I watched women with no education and six children, women without a single safety net beneath them who day after day got their heads bashed into the wall for cold food or misfolded towels or the sheer fun of bashing another human head into a wall. I watched men and women from the studio audience stand up and say, "I have no sympathy for you! Why don't you get out? If someone raised a hand to me even once I'd be out of there. Don't you have any self-respect?"

I leaned forward. I knew that voice. I had been that audience, so long ago I can't even remember it now. I had thought I would never stand for anything short of decency and kindness. I thought that anyone who accepted less must be a willing participant, must like it on some level. But at that moment I wanted to be up there on that stage. I would rise out of my soft bucket chair, unclip my microphone. I would put my arms around the shoulders of the guest and whisper in her ear, "Honey, I know. Things happen that you never thought were pos-

sible." I would tell her she was good and bright and brave just for getting out of bed in the morning, because the person downstairs was going to call her an idiot when he was speaking to her at all. I didn't have any children and I had a wonderful family who met me at the airport when I came home and kissed me a hundred times. I had a good education and a lot of friends. My husband didn't hit me, a fact he pointed out often. I was only married for a year and with all I had going for me I barely scraped together the strength to leave. You get so worn down it's hard to think of how you might find a suitcase, much less figure out where you'd go or how you'd get there once it's packed. So when I hold the woman on the *Oprah* show I say, "Don't listen to the audience. They don't understand. When the choice is to die or divorce, it isn't always the clearest choice in the world."

It wasn't just strangers I was starting to understand. My mother divorced my father when I was three. Two years later she remarried. My mother and step-father spent the next twenty years trying to decide whether or not they should stay together. Growing up, I had never faulted her for the divorce, but I hated what I thought was her weakness. My mother didn't want to be wrong a second time. She wanted to believe in all sorts of goodness that didn't exist. She wanted to believe in people's ability to change, and so she went back and back and back, every resolution broken by some long talk they had that made things suddenly clear for a while. I wanted her to make her decision and stick to it. In or out, I ultimately didn't care, just make up your mind. But the mind isn't so easily made up. My mother used to say the more lost you were, the later it got, the more you had invested in not being lost. That's why

people who are lost so often keep heading in the same direction.

It took my own divorce to really understand, not just to forgive her, but to think that she was doing the very best that could be done with the circumstances at hand. I understood how we long to believe in goodness, especially in the person we promised to love and honor. It isn't just about them, it is how we want to see ourselves. It says that we are good people, patient and kind.

IF I COULDN'T SEE my way clear to leave my husband before we were married, I hadn't begun to take into account the complications that were ahead. We had a job together, adjoining offices, a split position in an English department. We had an Oldsmobile, a stacked washer-drier. We had his family and mine. We had been married. I had promised, sworn, and I believed I was only as good as my word. But as I slowly began to realize that all the problems between us that I had counted on to change would never change, I started running over the list I kept in my head, a secret tally of things that stood between me and my freedom. The dining room suite? Don't need it. The job? I'll give it up. His parents, who I cared for, who would certainly never speak to me again? Gone. This didn't happen all at once. It was a row of obstacles, each one a little more deadly than the one before. At every turn I thought, not this. I can't give this up too, but then I would. It's remarkable when you stop and think how little you've been getting by on and how much you can do without.

The moment of choice changed everything for me. I did the impossible thing, the thing I was sure would kill

us both, and we lived. And I kept on doing the impossible. I moved home and became a waitress at a Friday's, where I received a special pin for being the first person at that particular branch of the restaurant to receive a perfect score on her written waitress exam. I was told I would be shift leader in no time. I was required to wear a funny hat. I served fajitas to people I had gone to high school with and I smiled.

I did not die.

Sometimes I would spend half the morning in the shower because I couldn't remember if I'd already shampooed my hair and so I would wash it again and again, not out of some obsessive need for cleanliness, but because I simply couldn't remember. I would get so lost on the way to work some days that I had to pull the car over to the side of the road and take the map out of the glove compartment. I worked four miles from my house. When I woke up at three A.M., as I did every morning, I never once knew where I was. For several minutes I would lie in bed and wonder while my eyes adjusted to the dark. After a while it didn't frighten me anymore.

In time, a lot of time, after I left Friday's and got a fellowship that allowed me to write my first novel, I came to see that there was something liberating about failure and humiliation. Life as I had known it had been destroyed so completely, so publicly, that in a way I was free, like I imagine anyone who walks away from a crash is free. I didn't have expectations anymore, and no one seemed to expect anything from me. I believed that nothing short of a speeding car could kill me. I knew there was nothing I couldn't give up. Even writing, which was my joy and greatest source of self-definition, I could give up if I had

to. Despite what anyone says, no one ever died from not writing. It was a gift. And like any gift that comes in lean times, I appreciated it wildly. I loved it with my whole heart.

I was still ashamed. I was a quitter, a failure. Whatever anyone said about divorce, I owned. One night, years later, clear on the other side of the country, I was giving a boring, obligatory dinner party. Among my guests were a man and a woman, both married but living apart from their spouses because of jobs. They must have been paired together at every social outing, though their missing spouses were all they had in common. Late in the evening the conversation turned to where we had lived in the past. It came out, after a long series of questions, that the woman had been married before, that the husband she had now was her second husband.

When were you married?

"A long time ago." She waved her hand, indicating somewhere back there, dark water. It was a gesture I knew. "Another life."

"I was married," I said. It is a deal I am always making with myself, and always breaking, that I won't tell people this. I don't hide it, but it isn't part of my story anymore.

"Well, there you go," the man said. I couldn't remember why I felt I had to invite him, what social debt I owed him. "Two out of three marriages end in divorce. I'm married, both of you are divorced."

But the woman had remarried. Where did that leave us? "I thought it was one out of two," I said.

And maybe because he was feeling secure with his wife who was a thousand miles away, he shook his head. There can be something cruel about people who have had good

fortune. They equate it with personal goodness. "Two out of three," he said.

When you think of the statistic, think of me. I'm the one who did it, I divorced. I pulled the moral fabric of this country apart. Selfish quitter.

Time magazine ran an editorial not long after that, a man crying out for "Super Vows" in this age of disposable marriage. Super Vows would show a higher level of commitment. It would be a more serious ceremony. There would be promises, legal and binding, that the couple would submit to lengthy marriage counseling before divorce, that they could only seek divorce after being married a certain length of time. Divorce, the writer said, had become too easy. Waltz in, waltz out.

Waltz in, maybe. Make marriage harder if you want to. Outlaw those Vegas chapels with the neon wedding bells, require marriage applications modeled after tax forms, but leave divorce alone. It's grueling. I have never known anyone who went into a marriage thinking that they would have to get out, and I have never known anyone who got out simply. To leave, you have to involve the courts. You have to sue the person you live with for your freedom. You have to disconnect your life from another life and face the sea alone. Never easy, blithe. Never.

Nor do I think we should have to wait three months or six or nine, depending on the state, for our divorces to take effect, any more than I think a woman needs twenty-four legally enforced hours between consulting her doctor and having an abortion. Termination is a serious business, but we do not need the state to mandate a waiting period so we can see if we really know our own minds. Three weeks after I left my husband he called to say I had a week

to come home or file for divorce. Oddly enough, I hadn't even been thinking about divorce, I wasn't planning any further than five minutes ahead. But since I knew at the end of the week I couldn't go back, I called a lawyer.

It turned out my husband was bluffing, thinking that a tough ultimatum would bring me back. When I told him I had filed for the divorce, he told me he would not give me one. He refused to sign the papers. In the state of Pennsylvania, where we had been living, contested divorces had a three-year waiting period. We would be married for three more years. What choice did I have? I settled myself in for the wait, but it wasn't so long after all. One day the signed papers just showed up. My life in the mailbox, stacked between catalogs and the electric bill. I never knew what brought on his change of heart. I never saw him or spoke to him again. We were divorced.

I JUST RE-READ *The Age of Innocence.* Poor Countess Olenska, so much more alive than everyone in New York. She was better than Newland Archer, whom she couldn't give herself to because she was married. It didn't matter to society that she had been wronged by her husband. They felt her life was over. Thanks to the modern age of divorce, my life was not. I was coming to see that as a blessing and not as something to be ashamed of. I was starting to think that my life was a good thing to have. I do not believe that there were more happy marriages before divorce became socially acceptable, that people tried harder, got through their rough times, and were better off. I believe that more people suffered.

I am still a Catholic, and in the eyes of the Church I

am still married. Perhaps I'm just not Catholic enough to care.

Divorce is in the machine now, like love and birth and death. Its possibility informs us, even when it goes untouched. And if we fail at marriage, we are lucky we don't have to fail with the force of our whole life. Sometimes I dream of an eighth sacrament, the sacrament of divorce. Like communion, it is a slim white wafer on the tongue. Like confession, it is forgiveness. Forgiveness is important not so much for what we've done wrong, but for what we feel we need to be forgiven for. Family, friends, God, whoever loves us, forgives us, takes us in again. They are thrilled by our life, our possibilities, our second chances. They weep with gladness that we did not have to die.

13

by
ANN
PATCHETT

A TALE
OF TWO
DIVORCES

BY *Anne Roiphe*

*E*VERY DIVORCE is a story, and while they can begin to sound the same—sad and cautionary—each one is as unique as a human face. My divorce is the tale of two divorces, one that never was and one that was. The first is the story of my parents' marriage.

My mother was the late fifth child, raised in a large house on Riverside Drive in New York City. Her father, who came to America as a boy from a town outside of Suvałki, Poland, had piled shirts on a pushcart and wandered the streets of the Lower East Side in the 1880s. His pushcart turned into a loft with twenty women sewing shirts for him and before he was twenty-five he owned a small company called Van Heusen Shirts. He was one of the founding members of Beth Israel Hospital and I have a photo of him, shovel in hand, black hat on his head, as the foundation stone is placed in the ground.

My mother grew up, small, plump, nervous, fearful of horses, dogs, cats, cars, water, balls that were hit over nets, tunnels, and bridges. She was expected to marry brilliantly into the world of manufacturers of coats, shoes, gowns, store owners, prosperous bankers whose sons attended the dozens of teas and charity events where she—always afraid her hair was wrong, her conversation dull, her dress wrinkled—tried to obey the instructions of her older sister and sparkle. A girl after all had to sparkle. She was under five feet. She was nearsighted. Without her thick glasses she stumbled, recognized no one, groped the wall for comfort. Her lipstick tended to smear. She chainsmoked. She lost things. She daydreamed. Her father died of a sudden heart attack when she was just thirteen. Her older sisters married millionaires, her brothers inherited the business. She was herself considered an heiress, a dangerous state for a tremulous girl, whose soul was perpetually fogged in uncertainty.

At a Z.B.T. Columbia University fraternity party she met my father. He was the Hungarian-born son of a drug salesman who bet the horses and believed that he had missed his grander destiny. My paternal grandfather was never able to move his family out from the railroad flat under the Third Avenue El. His wife, my grandmother, was a statuesque woman, taller than her husband but overwhelmed by the noise, the turmoil of her American days. She never learned English. She stayed home in her nightgown and slippers, sleeping long hours. My father was in law school. He was tall and handsome with black hair slicked down like Valentino and cold eyes set perfectly in an even face. He was an athlete who had earned his college expenses by working summers as a lifeguard in the

Catskills. His shoes were perfectly polished. His white shirt gleamed. He loathed poverty. He claimed to speak no other language than English though he had arrived in America at age nine. He told my mother he loved her. Despite the warnings of her siblings, she believed him. If she was not his dream girl, she was his American dream. They went on their honeymoon to Europe and purchased fine china and linen at every stop.

MY FATHER became a lawyer for the family shirt company. He was edgy, prone to yell at others; he ground his teeth. He suffered from migraines. He could tolerate nothing out of place, nothing that wasn't spotless. He joined a club where men played squash, steamed in the sauna, and drank at the bar. He stayed long hours at his club. He told his wife she was unbeautiful. She believed him although the pictures of her at the time tell a different story. They show a young woman with soft amused eyes and a long neck, with a shy smile and a brave tilt of the head. My father explained to my mother that he could never admire a short woman, that long legs were the essence of glamour.

My father began to have other ladies. He would meet them under the clock at the Biltmore, at motels in Westchester. He had ice in his heart, but he looked good in his undershirt. He looked good in his monogrammed shirts. He lost his nonfamily clients. They didn't like his temper, his impatience. It didn't matter. He took up golf and was gone all day Saturday and Sunday in the good weather. He made investments in the stock market. He had a genius for bad bets. My mother made up the heavy losses. She had two children and she lived just as she was expected to do,

with servants to take care of the details, to wake with the babies, to prepare the food, to mop the floors. She spent her days playing cards and shopping. She went to the hairdresser two, sometimes three times a week. A lady came to the house to wax her legs and do her long red nails. She had ulcers, anxiety attacks, panic attacks. In the evening at about five o'clock she would begin to wait for my father to come home. She could do the crossword puzzle in five minutes. She was a genius at canasta, Oklahoma, bridge, backgammon. She joined a book club. She loved the theater and invested cleverly in Broadway shows. She took lessons in French and flower arranging.

At the dinner table, as the food was being served, my father would comment that he didn't like the way my mother wore the barrette in her hair. She would say bitterly that he never liked anything she wore. He would say that she was stupid. She would say that she was not. Their voices would carry. In the kitchen the maid would clutch the side of the sink until her fingernails were white. My mother would weep. My father would storm out of the house, slamming doors, knocking over lamps. She would shout after him, "You don't love me." He would scream at her, "Who could love you?" She would lie in bed with ice cubes on her swollen eyes, chain-smoking Camel cigarettes. She would call her sister for comfort. Her sister would say, "Don't give him an argument." She would say, "I'll try to do better, I really will."

WHEN I WAS seven years old, she lay in the bathtub soaking and I was sitting on the rim keeping her company. "I could divorce him," she said. "I could do it." Her eyes were puffed. I felt a surge of electricity run through me,

adrenaline flowed. "Leave him?" I asked. "Yes," she said. "Should I?" she asked me. "Should I leave him? Would you mind?" I was her friend, her confidante. I did not yet know enough of the world to answer the question. I thought of my home split apart. I thought my father would never see me again. I wondered what I would tell my friends. No one I knew had parents who were divorced. I was afraid. "Who will take care of us?" I asked. My mother let the ashes of her cigarette fall into the tub. "God!" she said. "Help me," she said. But she'd asked the wrong person.

Then she did a brave thing. She went to a psychiatrist. I would wait for her downstairs in the lobby. She would emerge from the elevator after her appointment with her mascara smeared over her checks. "When I'm stronger," she said, "I'll leave him." But the years went on. He said she was demanding. He said, "I spend enough time with you. Go to Florida with your sister. Go to Maine with your brother. Stop asking me to talk to you. I've already said everything I want to say." She said, "I need you to admire me. I need you to say you love me." "I do," he said, but then they had a party and I found him in the coat closet with a lady and lipstick all over his face.

He talked about politics. He read history books. He hit on the chin a man who disagreed with him. He yelled at my mother that she had no right to an opinion on anything. He said, "Women with opinions smell like skunks." She said, "He's so smart. He knows so much." She said, "If I leave him no other man will marry me." She said, "If I leave him I will be alone forever." She said, "I can't leave him."

Week after week, she would say something that irri-

tated him. He would make her cry and then he would scream at her for crying. His screams were howls. If you listened to the sound you would think an animal was trapped and in pain. Dinner after dinner my brother and I would silently try to eat our food as the same old fight began again, built and reached its crescendo.

Finally I was old enough. "Leave him," I said. "I don't know," she said, "maybe." But she couldn't and she wouldn't and the dance between them had turned into a marathon. She quit first. She died at age fifty-two, still married, still thinking, if only I had been taller, different, better. He inherited her money and immediately wed a tall woman, with whom he had been having an affair for many years, whose hands shook when she spoke to him. He called her: "That stupid dame." "That dumb broad," he would say. He went off to his club. He went for long walks. He had migraines.

This was a story of a divorce that should have been.

WHEN I WAS twenty-seven I found myself checking into a fleabag hotel in Juárez. My three-year-old daughter was trying to pull the corncob out of the parrot cage and the parrot was trying to bite her fingers. I was there, my room squeezed between those of the local drunks and prostitutes, to get a divorce. This was a divorce that should have been and was. I had married a man whom I thought was just the opposite of my father. He was a playwright, a philosopher. He was from an old southern family. He talked to me all the time and let me read and type his manuscripts. I worked as a receptionist to support him. Our friends were poets and painters, beatniks and their groupies. I had escaped my mother's home or so I

thought. What I didn't notice was that my husband was handsome and thought me plain, that my husband was poor and thought me a meal ticket, that my husband—like my father—was dwarfed of spirit and couldn't imagine another soul beside himself. What I didn't know was that I—like my mother—had no faith, no confidence, no sense that I could fly too. I could even write.

My husband had other women and I thought it was an artist's privilege. My husband said, "If Elizabeth Taylor is a woman, then you must be a hamster." I laughed. My husband went on binges and used up all our money. I thought it was poetic although I was always frightened; bill collectors called. I was always apologizing. We didn't fight so I thought I had achieved matrimonial heaven, a place where of course certain compromises were necessary.

Then after I had a child I thought of love as oxygen and I felt faint. In the middle of the night when I was nursing the baby and my husband was out at the local bar I discovered that loneliness was the name of my condition. I noticed that my husband could not hold his child because he was either too drunk, out of the house, closed into his head, or consumed with nervousness about the applause the outside world was giving or withholding from him. I discovered that I had married a man more like my father than not and that, more like my mother than not, I had become a creature to be pitied. Like moth to flame I was drawn to repeat. My divorce was related to her undivorce, so the generations unfold back to back handing on their burdens—by contamination, memory, experience, identification, one's failure becomes the other's.

The courage it takes to really make things better, to change, is rare and won only at great cost. Yes, we are responsible for ourselves, but nevertheless our family stories course and curse through our veins: our memories are not free.

If my mother had been brave enough to go it alone I might have seen myself differently. I might have been brave enough to let myself be loved the first time around. At least I didn't wait for my entire life to pass before leaping up and away. So this is why I listen with tongue in check to all the terrible tales of what divorce has done to the American family. I know that if my mother had left my father not only her life but mine too might have been set on more solid ground. I know that if I had stayed in my marriage my child would have lived forever in the shadow of my perpetual grief and thought of herself as I had, unworthy of the ordinary moments of affection and connection.

IN TWENTIETH-CENTURY America we place so much emphasis on romance that we barely notice the other essentials of marriage that include economics and child rearing. My mother was undone by the economic equation in her marriage. Money, which we know to be a part of the bitterness of divorce, is in there from the beginning, a thread in the cloak of love, whether we like it or not.

History clunking through our private lives certainly affected my mother's marriage and my bad marriage. Woman's proper role, woman's masochistic stance, immigration, push to rise in social status, the confusion of

money damned my mother to a lifetime of tears and almost caught me there too. But history is always present without our always being able to name its nasty work.

The women's movement, which came too late for my mother, sent some women off adventure bound, free of suburb, unwilling to be sole caretakers to find, at the end of their rainbow isolation, disappointment, bitterness. The sexual revolution, which soon after burned like a laser through our towns and sent wives running in circles in search of multiple pleasures, freedom from convention, and distance from the burdens of domesticity, was a balloon that popped long before the arrival of AIDS. We found we were not, after all, in need of the perfect orgasm. We were in need of a body to spoon with in bed, a story we could tell together as well as sexual equality.

But there is more. Divorce is also the terrible knife that rends family asunder, and for the children it can be the tilting, defining moment that marks them ever after, walking wounded, angry, sad souls akimbo, always prone to being lost in a forest of despair. They can be tough, too tough. They can be helpless, too helpless. They can never trust. They can be too trusting. They can accept a stepparent for a while and then revoke their acceptance. They can protest the stepparent for a while and then change their mind, but either way their own parents' divorce hangs over them, threat, reminder, betrayal always possible. My stepdaughter, now a married woman and a mother herself, speaks of her own parents' breakup, which came when she was only seven, as the most terrible moment in her life. As she says this I have only to listen to the tightness in her voice, watch the slight tremble in her hand to know that

the divorce seemed to her like an earthquake. The divorce caused a before and after and everything after is tarnished, diminished by what went before.

I wish this were not so. I wish that we could marry a new mate, repair, go on to undo the worst of our mistakes without leaving ugly deep scars across our children's psyches, but we can't. And furthermore the children will never completely forgive us, never understand how our backs were against the wall: They may try to understand our broken vows but they don't. Of course there are other things our children don't forgive us for. If we die, if we withdraw, if we let ourselves drown in misery, addictions, if we fail at work or lose our courage in the face of economic or other adversity, that too will eat at their hearts and spoil their chances for the gold ring on life's carousel. There are, in other words, many ways to damage children, and divorce is only the most effective and perhaps most common of them.

For a while, in the seventies, divorce was everywhere, a panacea for the heart burdened. We were too excited by the prospects of freedom to see the damage that was done. The wounds are very severe for both partners and children. It may be worth it as it would have been for my mother. It may be necessary, but divorce is never nice. I felt as if the skin had been stripped from my body the first months after my divorce, and I was only twenty-seven years old. I felt as if I had to learn anew how to walk in the streets, how to set my face, how to plot a direction, how to love. I had to admit to failure, take back my proud words, let others help me. It was a relief, but it was a disaster. I had lost confidence in my decisions. It took a long

while to gain back what I had lost. I understand why my mother did not have the strength to do it, although she should have.

I cannot imagine a world in which divorce would not sometimes occur. Men and women will always fail each other, miss each others' gestures, change in fatally different ways. There are men who cannot love, who abuse their wives or themselves or some substance. There are women who do the same. There are some disasters that wreck a marriage, a sick or damaged child, an economic calamity, a professional failure. There are marriages that are simply asphyxiated by daily life.

But I can imagine a world in which divorce would be rare, in which the madness, meanness, mess of everyday life were absorbed and managed without social cataclysm. It is perhaps our American obsession with the romantic that leads to so much trouble. If we were able to see marriage as largely an economic, child-rearing institution, as a social encounter involving ambition, class, money, we might be better off. Never mind our very up-to-date goals of personal fitness and fulfillment; we are still characters, all of us, in a nineteenth-century novel.

At the moment, now that my children are of marriageable age I have become a believer in the arranged betrothal. Such marriages could not possibly cause more mischief than those that were created by our free will rushing about in heavy traffic with its eyes closed. Perhaps we should consider love as a product of marriage instead of the other way around. Of course those societies that arrange marriages have other tragic stories of bride burning, lifelong miserable submission experienced by women, sexual nightmares, poor young girls and dirty old men.

We are the only animal species that cannot seem to figure out how to pair off and raise children without maiming ourselves in the process.

We can bemoan the social disorder caused by divorce until the moon turns to cream cheese, but we are such fragile souls, so easily cast adrift, wounded, set upon by devils of our own making, that no matter how we twist or turn, no system will protect us from the worst. There is cruelty in divorce. There is cruelty in forced or unfortunate marriage. We will continue to cry at weddings because we know how bittersweet, how fragile is the troth. We will always need legal divorce just as an emergency escape hatch is crucial in every submarine. No sense, however, in denying that after every divorce someone will be running like a cat, tin cans tied to its tail: spooked and slowed down.

25

~

by

ANNE
ROIPHE

OTHER USES FOR A WEDDING GOWN

BY *Penny Kaganoff*

I WINCE when I recall those bizarrely hand-decorated doors of the dormitory rooms of my alma mater, Stern College for Women of Yeshiva University. When friends express surprise that I graduated from such a parochial, conservative institution, I half-jokingly tell them that I don't regret having gotten married or divorced, but I do regret having gone to Stern. The truth is that the three are inextricably linked, cause and effect, cause and effect. My older sister Leah used to press my buttons by calling the school "Sperm" because even though I was trying my best to be a budding intellectual, Stern was known as the type of place a girl went to get her MRS degree. It was a fantasyland whose administrators scheduled classes on Christmas in the middle of a dead and deserted New York City and thought it perfectly all right to pay us dorm counselors less than our male coun-

terparts at Yeshiva College because, after all, the boys needed pocket money to take out the girls. It was the kind of school that pandered to rabbinic families like mine that felt a little inadequate for living in the Jewish boondocks and worried that their daughters might not otherwise meet the right sort of husbands. (Never mind that I grew up in the thriving Jewish community of Chicago and never even met a gentile socially until I left home—when it came to Jews and Jewishness in America, anywhere outside of New York City was considered diaspora.) So I was shipped off to Stern as a matter of course; Leah escaped her fate and thoroughly sealed mine by moving to Israel.

As Stern custom dictated, when a student became engaged—an event which seemed to take place with alarming frequency during my school years—her roommates would decorate their dorm door in her honor. If the girl's fiancé was a medical student, the roommates might fashion a pair of hearts from a stethoscope and write in calligraphy, "There's a doctor in the house." If you were marrying a lawyer there would be scales of justice or a judge's gavel on your door.

In the school newspaper, alongside my carefully reported articles on Israeli women soldiers or religious cults, was the ever-popular column, Rings 'n Things, that congratulated the newest brides- and bridegrooms-to-be. I and my brainy friends often felt like interlopers on Mars where all this hoopla was concerned. We might have felt alienated, but we couldn't help buying into it. As surely as Abraham and Moses believed that the Jews were the chosen people, we Stern girls believed that we would be chosen by a man who would remake us in his image. I remember seeing roommates working on their door

creations for hours, and I seem to recall lots of animated discussions about materials and themes and how to resolve the thorny issue that arose when two (or more) roommates were engaged at the same time. Whose decorations were awarded the door, whose got second billing on a wall in the hallway? A friend recalls that a higher status was conferred on a room whose door was decorated. (It was also rumored that if you slept in an engaged girl's bed you, too, would become so lucky.) Little about the girl or her career aspirations was incorporated into these elaborate door designs, and no one asked if the boys at Yeshiva College decorated *their* roommates' doors.

I wish I could tell you I went to Stern in the 1940s or 1950s, when women didn't know better, when a woman's sole career aspiration was to get married and make babies, and when college was just the best place to snag a better class of husband. But the truth is that I went to Stern in the late seventies, graduated, in fact, in 1980, years after the women's movement had changed the lives of others of my sex. I think of those doors and I am instantly helpless and ashamed to be an unmarried Jewish woman. I'm back in high school and my mother is telling me—her straight-A, honor society child, the last of three daughters in an Orthodox family that prides itself on its unbroken until now, fifteen-generation-long line of rabbis—not to act smart on dates because boys won't like me and I won't get asked out a lot. I'm back in grammar school and my loudmouthed buddy Susie and I have wangled our way into the boys-only Talmud class, and now I've placed first in a citywide Talmud competition. We'll give you the Bible prize (which I've also won), say the less-than-consistent powers that be, but there is no way we will

award a Talmud prize to a girl. I want my parents to storm the school, hold my principal hostage, and demand that the prize-givers reverse their heinous decision, their capitulation to religious decorum. Of course, nothing happens. My parents aren't thrilled but don't make a stink. I think they are genuinely puzzled—maybe even a little embarrassed—by their smart, troublemaking girl-child. Ah, how much simpler life would be if only I had been born a boy. I am forced to laugh it off and bury the memory. I wonder how the boy who plucked my prize rationalizes his victory; I like to think he's managing a dubious S&L now, but I know he became a rabbi.

Years later, Zack, my ex-husband, and I are in the process of our no-fault American divorce and have to talk on the phone to discuss some legal detail or another. He tells me he has a new girlfriend and like the well-brought-up woman that I am I make polite small talk and ask him what she's like. It's not the only occasion at which I am involuntarily made privy to Zack's post-marriage social life. She has the figure of a model, he says, knowing I'm battling to drop the pounds I put on when I was married to him. A control freak, he was obsessed with every morsel I ate. I was eating, if only he knew it, to fill the emptiness in my heart.

"And she's bright but not intellectual," Zack gloats. He means, of course, she's not like you, Penny. My mother's warning has come home to taunt me after all.

Some years after that, I bump into Zack's sour sister and she tells me my ex has remarried. *Mazel tov,* it seems that he has found my exact opposite: a Jewish gym teacher.

———

THIS IS the Orthodox Jewish world I came from. For a long time I tried to fit in — above all by marrying the perfect man for a Stern girl, a handsome Jewish lawyer on a partner track in a prestigious firm. But when my marriage became unbearable, and I was losing any sense of myself inch by inch, and I knew I had to leave my husband or disappear completely, I was more worried about telling my parents than I was about telling my husband because here was their pride and joy disappointing them by leaving their son-in-law.

After returning from a depressingly happy wedding of one of my Stern friends, I call my mother and tell her something terrible has happened but I can't discuss it on the phone and I insist she fly out that week from Chicago. When my mother and I meet in Boston and I try to explain the abusive nature of my marriage but I don't go into detail because it's too humiliating, she, who loves me very much, asks me what I did to provoke him.

My parents are devastated by the divorce, so worried for my future that they can't communicate their feelings to me. No one from my immediate family flies in to keep me company for the Jewish divorce, the *get*, which in its archaic ritual proves more debilitating than the antiseptic American version. My sister Leah is visiting my folks from Israel and I ask her to leave the kids with my parents and stay with me, but she tells me, "Mommy and Daddy are in a lot of pain right now and they need me." I'm in pain, too; after all, it's *my* divorce. But I accept what I believe to be a punishment I deserve. An aunt and uncle who live in Brookline, Mass., accompany me to the *get*, their certainty palpable that this will never happen to one of their five happily married children.

My divorce drives a necessary wedge between my parents and me. I learn to live a little more for myself and less for them and what I perceive as their overarching demands of me. I completely stop caring about what the Jewish community makes of me.

O U R   M A R R I A G E was like a bad Jewish joke: We were a perfect couple; I was always feeling guilty and he blamed me for everything. It was my job to make him happy; Zack did not take responsibility for his life. In his eyes we were glued together. Anything I said or did was a reflection on him.

A few months after our wedding, Zack and I move to Brookline. Near us in our apartment complex lives an old high-school friend of Zack's with his wife and son. Brad is one of the most popular and gregarious members of the synagogue, and Zack wants badly to join his crowd. Brad has us over for lunch our first Shabbat in the neighborhood but refuses our many subsequent offers to reciprocate.

Characteristically Zack blames me, rehashing every detail of our conversation that Shabbat afternoon and finding fault in everything I said or did in Brad's presence. They won't be our friends, Zack concludes, because you offended them in some way. I am the social half of the couple, the one who makes friends easily and with pleasure, but Zack makes me so self-conscious that I begin to doubt myself. I dread having guests over for Shabbat and holidays because as soon as they leave Zack begins to pick apart my actions and words, convincing me that I am crazy and unfit for company. (These wounds have never completely healed. To this day, I remain a strange hybrid:

On the outside I'm very outgoing and comfortable with myself, but inside hides a shy person who worries that she's intruding herself upon another, perhaps making a fool of herself.)

Late one night Brad ties the belt from his bathrobe around his neck and hangs himself from a pipe in his basement, leaving his pregnant wife to discover the body. At the *shiva* she apologizes for having evaded us, explaining that Brad had been severely depressed for months and couldn't respond to our friendship. Brad's suicide and his widow's sad apology slap me awake to the misery of my marriage. There are even times when Zack seems to be trying to choke me to silence me during a fight. I am terrified and unable to catch my breath. I never confide in friends; I can't even tell my shrink about Zack's behavior. Part of this is denial and shame, but I also feel that I owe him a measure of loyalty because I am, after all, his wife. You make your bed and lie in it. A good Stern girl to the end.

I light the Shabbat candles and pray to God to end my unhappiness. I begin to obsess that to get back at me after one of our awful fights Zack, never an original thinker, will copy Brad and hang himself to spite me. I make him promise that he won't do it; if he's in the bathroom for a long time, I pound on the door in panic. Then the worry passes and I fantasize about how wonderful it would be to be a widow, pitied and coddled by a warm and loving community, rid of a mean husband without the disgrace and mess of a divorce. Not long after that I leave him.

ONE DAY, several years after our divorce, I am startled to get a call from my ex-husband. He wants to

marry a woman, her name is Miriam, but she won't commit until she has talked to me. I am so caught off guard by the call that I say okay, and I am more than a little curious. By this time, during party chitchat, I have rewritten my marriage into a scenario of hopelessly boring corporate lawyer married to the restless bohemian writer. My conversation with Miriam brings me back to the unpleasant reality that was my marriage and makes me face facts.

She is an Orthodox Jew whose family emigrated from Syria. Her first husband, she tells me, used to beat her and she knows that Zack is a real catch. Her candor amazes me; I thought our conversation would be light and breezy. Apparently this type of premarital investigative phone call isn't all that unusual among Orthodox Jews. My parents later admit that a man whose daughter was dating my ex called them to check him out. My parents, incredibly, said he was very nice, just not for me. "What did you expect us to say? After all, you had married him so we didn't want to say he was so bad," they rationalized. Don't hang out your dirty laundry, so to speak.

But Miriam isn't interested in a casual, insincere reference from me. She frightens me and I feel sorry for her in equal measures. She says more than once that "we girls have to stick together." She asks me if his health was a big problem. Zack has a peptic ulcer, and I tell her I think his condition contributed to his general depression and moodiness. She asks me why we didn't have children. How dare she, I think. But then it sinks in that she must be desperate with fear or she wouldn't be asking. We didn't have children, I think but I don't tell Miriam, because I didn't want them to see how Zack treated me and hate and pity me for it. I'd once heard Zack's father tell

his mother to shut up and I understood my mother-in-law better than I had before, but I didn't resent her any less. We didn't have children, I think but I don't tell Miriam, because Zack was always so angry at me that he wouldn't make love to me. I finally tell her that we were very young and didn't want any just then. (I was twenty-four when I got married and twenty-seven when I left Zack; twenty-four may have been ancient according to my Orthodox Jewish family but was a baby to the rest of the world.)

Then she circles in for the kill: Was he ever abusive? The memories rush back of a marriage that was like a war: numbing boredom interspersed with horrific episodes. And so, I admit to her, and to myself, how bad my marriage really was. (Whatever she heard may have scared her off; she never married Zack.) She thanks me politely but impersonally, as if I have just shared my grandmother's sought-after recipe for potato kugel, and promises she will never tell Zack what I have told her.

The next day Zack phones me yelling and demanding to know what I said because Miriam wouldn't share our conversation with him. I ask him what he expected and tell him never to call me again. He never does. I hang up, trembling, remembering how frightened I had been during our marriage of him and his unpredictable, explosive anger. For weeks after Miriam's call I have nightmares that Zack is stalking me and retaliates for my disobedience and disloyalty.

I CAN'T even tell you the exact date when a Massachusetts judge finalized my divorce. It was anticlimactic because the one that really counted, the Jewish ritual *get*, took place months before, precisely three weeks after I

decided I didn't want to be married anymore. I had to get a *get,* so to speak, because without one any children I might give birth to in the future would be ostracized from the Jewish community and, according to Jewish law, would only be able to marry other offspring of similarly "adulterous" unions.

A *get* is particularly demeaning for women because the Jewish laws that consecrate marriage and divorce also subjugate women to a passive role in these essential life rituals. Apologists are quick to point out that the law served to protect women in the world of the Ancient East, but at the turn of the twenty-first century I could only see these laws to be a cruel anachronism. As a rabbi's daughter, I had known of several cases in which men virtually blackmailed their wives for a fortune of money or for custody of their children. Zack even told me that a relative had encouraged him to extort some sort of financial compensation for letting me go free. I believe he didn't because he was still in love with me and also a bit stunned by the speed with which I set our Jewish divorce in motion.

The rabbis who preside over the *get* also are surprised and duly uncomfortable about dealing with a woman and an assertive one at that. Because Zack has said that he won't lift a finger to arrange the *get* but will, nice guy that he imagines himself to be, show up if I do all the work, I call the local board of rabbis and plead my case. I am informed that they can't assemble a *beth din,* a small rabbinical court, during the summer and can't I wait until the busy fall season? I castigate them for their insensitivity, tell them my husband is hardly enthusiastic now and may withhold a *get* if we wait. Then basically I steel myself and bulldoze them into importing a *beth din* from outside.

But not before they ask numerous and pointless questions about our sex life and other issues that are not their business. I do the begging myself, without my father or any of my many rabbi relatives as my advocate.

During the proceeding, the head rabbi, who had been a great admirer of my grandfather and knows my father as well, never looks me in the eye, obsessing over the letter of the law—he must ask me at least ten times to verify the spelling of my name—and never offering me a word of consolation. The bill of divorce is handwritten in Aramaic, the document is folded, and I am asked to hold out my hands: I look like a supplicant. Zack is told to drop it in my hands but not to hand it to me—no touching allowed for those passing out of coupledom—and I am instructed to lift the document in the air, and then walk several steps with it stuck awkwardly under my arm, my back to the man who was my husband moments before.

After we leave, the rabbi will take a knife to our *get* and slash it in the criss-cross fashion established by Jewish tradition. In reality, this is a small perforation—somewhat like a ticket being cancelled by a conductor—that prevents another couple with our identical names from passing off our *get* as theirs. But intoxicated by the ritual, I have mythologized even this mundane legal detail, bloated it with significance, and feel cheated that I'm not privy to that deed. I once read a book in which a woman scheduled to have a tumor removed from her breast makes the doctor promise to show it to her before disposing of it. I need the catharsis and finality of this *get-wounding,* and I imagine I am stabbing the *get* until it bleeds like a husband would.

SOON AFTER my divorce, my mother calls and asks me what I did with my wedding gown. At this time in my life, I have little patience for smugly married, oblivious couples, my parents included, and fantasize that they are all getting divorced. My mother tells me that a young woman in my father's congregation is getting married and why don't we lend her my gown? Over my dead body, I think. I don't want everyone in the synagogue to say as the bride walks down the aisle: There goes poor, divorced Penny Kaganoff's wedding gown. I tell her I gave it to charity, but I really gave it to my friend Karen who says she wants to dye the satin a vivid color and go dancing in it. She never gets around to it, and besides, even if tinted crimson, an old wedding gown would probably still look like a wedding gown. Ultimately Karen and I donate it to needy Russian Jewish immigrants, but when I close my eyes before sleep I see my transformed wedding gown dancing away the nights, and the vision sustains me.

MY DIVORCE is still recent when a moneyed cousin of mine throws a weekend bar mitzvah on Long Island. I am tired of these affairs, where no one asks what books I've read, only a handful of relatives are interested in how I'm advancing at my job, and everyone quizzes me about my dating life. Indeed, I seem to be the only single person at the hotel who is not in the bar mitzvah boy's class at school. Afterward, I get a ride back to the city with a couple whom I've just met, but that doesn't stop them from asking personal questions. Single people just don't have a lot of rights in the Orthodox Jewish milieu. The bored suburban wife perks up considerably when she learns that

I'm divorced, pries all the particulars out of me, and then pops the big question: "Didn't you feel like a failure when you got divorced?"

And there in that overheated, candy wrapper–strewn Ford, creeping along on a crowded expressway, I have an epiphany, and I cross some threshold through which I'll never be able to return. The bad feelings about myself and my husbandless state, generated by the family gathering, evaporate as I tell her from my heart that my divorce was a brave and healthy act, a moment of triumph that I'll always cherish.

Mrs. Nosy is disappointed, for sure, but I'm still singing when I walk through the door of my apartment.

THIS IS WHAT YOU NEED FOR A HAPPY LIFE

BY *Jane Shapiro*

I WANT TO BE married to one man for life. So far this has eluded me—that's the way I think about it: *so far.* As if, after two marriages and two divorces and many quick, interesting years alone—during which years I've lived exactly as I wanted—it could still happen now. I'll be twenty-one and my sexy, considerate boyfriend and I will marry on a blue day, surrounded by an elaborate, loving, familial community that will ratify and then proceed to sustain our union, and he and I will live productively side by side for six decades, growing daily more tranquil and enmeshed. We'll move to a hot climate and sit in twin lawn chairs and telephone our many grown children. Our gold rings will wear and our fingers will shrink. We'll die married! Still this story seems so real to me.

———

ONE WAY I've been thinking about divorce these days has been in discussion with Raoul Lionel Felder, the famous New York divorce lawyer, whose matrimonial firm is the largest and most successful in the country.

Q: Do people first arrive in your office with great ambivalence about divorcing?

A: Not really. Because by the time they come here, they've been to the priest, the minister, psychiatrist, psychologist, the yenta next door—all these people. So while it's not a Rubicon beyond which they can't step back, the fact is they've usually played out all their hands.

Q: So you don't see people who aren't sure—

A: I see them. I see them. But that's not the profile of the majority of clients, no. Because even the people who say "I just want information"—they don't want information, they want to see if they can get up enough courage, or enough money, and so forth.

Q: Have you often thought "These two people should not get divorced"?

A: What I have seen is two misfits. Where you say "Jesus, they're made for each other in heaven! Why are these people ever getting divorced? Who would want to put up with either one of them?"

FIFTEEN YEARS back in time, Ed's and my divorce is imminent. He phones, from a resort in South Carolina. "It's terrific here!" Ed cries, forgetting he and I are estranged. There are 125 tennis courts. There are lavish plants and lawns. Meanwhile I'm thinking: This guy owes me money. Ed has been my second husband—my real one, as I think of him; every divorced woman has had one real husband. Before the kids get to the phone, Ed has

filled me in on the layout of his suite. Two giant bedrooms, a living room, a dining room, and an immaculate,
gargantuan terrace now house my lonely future ex-
husband as he struggles in South Carolina to get perspective on his confusing, tangled, ongoing life with
me.

Divorce, like other traumatic events, causes time traveling—like me, many divorcing people, I imagine, find
themselves vividly living in other time places: years ago, or
years from now when all this will be over, when what is
broken will be fixed. Or you feel like two people at once—
an old woman who has lost everyone and a girl whose life
is beginning at last.

I'm an ordinary divorcée, vivaciously mourning. I rise
in the morning peppy and sanguine; only hours later, a
heaviness grows in my chest and I'm near sobbing. I weep
for hours, fall asleep still snuffling, then wake in the night
with tears running into my ears. The next day, I'm shaky
and refreshed; at midnight, I can't sleep because I'm excited, planning my moves.

I call my friends to make crude jokes, talk urgently,
overexplain and guffaw; I keep them on the phone too
long and call again too soon. Daily, I have ideas! I impul-
sively introduce myself to new people, make plans to
change careers or adopt some children or leave town,
write sudden letters to friends from high school, sleep
with wrong men: a merry widow, every day.

ED TAKES THE KIDS for the weekend. I can't
bear two days without the kids. So I travel to Fire Island
to see Benjy, my childhood friend, and his wife and their
children—to visit them and their family-ness. On Ben and

Alice's redwood deck, in hazy sun and wet air, I know I've been cast off the planet. How can I be among that vast company, the divorcing or divorced, and be so alone? Morosely, Ben introduces me to three sunburned couples: *"This lady is estranged, poor woman."*

All fall, when not working or cooking, I look at television. A week before our divorce is final, a Tuesday evening finds me intently watching the interviewing of some cover girls. Outside, it's darkening fast. The phone rings and I grab for it—could be my husband. But the line is dead. In pearly voices, the cover girls unanimously maintain that having your image appear in a magazine does not change your life.

I have never understood this construct: does not change your life. If these women are right, then divorce doesn't change your life either. I try saying this to myself, but with a convincing sense that my life is (for the second time, this being my second divorce) about to be over.

People who have gone from poverty and obscurity and struggle and despair to being famous movie actors and best-selling authors will say this too: It doesn't change your life. When patently it does. When anyone can see your life is changed beyond recognition.

THE IMMINENCE of Eddie's and my divorce brings back to me my old tormenting feeling of not belonging to any group, family, or clan. A raucous call from a divorced girlfriend reminds me I'll soon be joining a new family—that of women alone, making bawdy jokes, asserting their exhilaration at controlling their lives, and looking, wherever they want, whenever they choose, for fresh mates.

I want to steal some husbands.

I imagine some married women—my closest friends—dying. Right now they're young, lovely, strong. Suddenly they get painless illnesses and swiftly succumb. Their bereaved husbands and I, linked in shock and grief, begin having dinners together. Helpless, in extremis, each husband and I tell many truths. In a dignified way, we bond. At last, hesitantly, then robustly, he and I have brave, profound, elegiac, joyful sex; tears drop from our four over-informed eyes onto afternoon sheets. *Astonishing, life's bounty. We have found each other.* Except that the identity of the widower changes daily, my fantasy is almost pornographic in its extreme specificity: We take our several children to the Phoenix Garden, and then to the movies on Greenwich Avenue, where we chew jujubes and hold hands in the flickering dark and light. We borrow an eight-room condo at Sugarbush, ski hard and eat chili for lunch; at night the kids sleep curled together like pups.

I actually sit at married couples' tables around town, indefatigable in my frantic loneliness, accepting condolences and advice, and thinking, Do I want him? As if I might slip poisoned powder into my beloved girlfriends' Cabernets.

I see what this is: I don't want to have to begin again and set out and endure trial and error and finally make a husband out of an actual person loose in the world. I want someone who *already is* a husband.

I ASK RAOUL FELDER if he has in mind a profile of the ideal client.

A: No, *I* don't. But generally a divorce lawyer would like a stupid rich woman. A stupid *compliant* rich woman.

It doesn't mean the woman is going to be exploited. It means that there's enough money to get well paid, that the client isn't going to question you, and that the client will follow your advice. It's not pejorative, it doesn't mean you'll do something bad for your client—actually, it's the reverse, you'll do better for her; you'll just do your job and not be bothered. You can't blame a lawyer for wanting those three attributes.

MONTHS PASS and I am still thirty-eight—still young. While waiting for my best friends to die, I start dating.

When you first turn your attention from your husband, your judgment is wild and you can't tell potentially suitable people from entirely wrong ones. As we've learned, there are days almost any man (or woman) in the known world looks like a real possibility.

I find a man. I think he's a possibility. I support this idea with the contention that he and I are culturally similar. Our fathers both went (before the Second World War) to Harvard; the new man and I share a longing and admiration for our dead fathers, those darkly handsome, clever boys bucking the quota up there in foreign Cambridge so long ago. The correspondences between the new man and I are so unlikely as to appear significant: We are grandchildren of Latvian Jews who settled in Newark and sold rags until they got ideas and promptly made, in dental equipment and real estate respectively, two modest fortunes. The new man and I get stoned in his Jacuzzi and I make a fool of myself crying, "*From rags to riches!* I never understood what it meant!"

He's a surgeon and I'm ready for a lover; watching

him cut a bite of steak is pretty much a sexual thing. We love meeting in the hospital lobby and rushing to a restaurant. All summer we sit on banquettes in chilled air, plates of pasta before us, trying to get to know each other, not too fast and not too much. We watch ourselves dialing for reservations, chatting at the theater, moving confidently through a lavish world, availing ourselves, without guilt or regret, of its pleasures—he and I share some romantic dream of being well-heeled grown-ups. This makes us appear to be in love.

The new man is great—competent, energetic, alternately solicitous and remote, well paid. After a couple of months, he suddenly appears distracted and says we are not the lovers I had assumed we had become. He needs to think. He wants time off. You are a passive-aggressive shit, I tell him, and our shared passion vanishes like day breaking.

I sob to a friend about our breakup. She says: "This always happens. This is a typical opening salvo: doesn't hit the target, just starts to define where it is."

My friend Ben, though married, knows many single men. When I beg him, he tries to think up a guy for me, suggesting in quick succession two rich, sentimental drug dealers and a never-married mathematician with a heart condition.

Not long after this, I stopped worrying about remarrying and promptly enjoyed fifteen interesting single years.

Q: I ask Raoul Felder: is there a difference between a man's divorce and a woman's divorce?

A: The dynamics are different if you represent a man.

Q: There's probably more crying with a woman —?

A: More crying. There's more emotionality in a woman's divorce and less punching numbers in a computer. It's much harder when you represent a woman. Because today, in divorce in America, the business is at stake. If you represent a man, you're sitting with a party who has all the records, knows what he's doing, has the business accounts in his control. With a woman, you're outside knocking on the door, trying to get in.

Q: Has a woman ever come in to see you and not cried?

A: Oh, sure. *Sure.*

Q: Who? Women who are just completely fed up and finished?

A: [Looks at me sympathetically] Oh, there are fortune hunters and adventuresses in the world.

JUST THIS YEAR—just this month—I woke early, in darkness, with the fully formed intention to talk to my first husband. Since our parting thirty years ago, I've laid eyes on him three times: twice, we spoke awhile; once, I happened to see him run past in the Boston Marathon (even before I recognized his face, I felt an access of pride: his legs were springy and he was breathing well). My first husband and I had never discussed our divorce, as we had never discussed our marriage—we've never mentioned what we were doing all those years ago. Recently, I gave him a call.

JANE: I have very little recollection of what happened when we got divorced. Do you?

DAVID: Well, I've always had three important recollections. I recall coming home from work one day and the

apartment was cleared out: not only you and the baby but also furniture.

JANE: What furniture?

DAVID: Not a lot. We had some furniture. One of your father's trucks came for it.

JANE: I didn't take the furniture!

DAVID: The baby's furniture. And I remember a knock on the door about seven at night, I don't know what month. Two cops were there, and I remember the shine, the light reflecting off their leather jackets. And they handed me something—I think it was a court order.

JANE: It's not in your divorce folder?

DAVID: I couldn't find it. But I deduced that the court order was to pay child support of 125 dollars per— must've been a week.

JANE: Could've been a month. It was 1966.

DAVID: Yeah, it could've—

JANE: Sounds like a month.

DAVID: And I also remember going to New York and not being able to see the kids. Those are the three recollections that have stuck with me over the years.

JANE: Why couldn't you see the kids?

DAVID: One time you weren't there when you were supposed to be. And another time—

JANE: You mean I knew in advance you were coming?

DAVID: Oh yeah. In the folder I found a log, it was interesting, of when I went to see them. Strange pieces of paper, with dates. It says: "January: Jane to Europe. February: Jane asked to delay visitation because of her marriage." And then apparently I saw the kids March

22nd, 1969. And then: "April: Delayed because of death." I have no idea whose death it was—

JANE: My father's.

DAVID: That was your father's death, in sixty-nine?

JANE: Yeah, I got married in February and my father died in April.

DAVID: And then that May: "Not there." You weren't there. I remember knocking and there was no answer. And then in June: "Jane said no because of erratic behavior."

JANE: Whose? [laughing]

DAVID: Well, I don't know! I assume you had determined that my behavior was erratic—

JANE: Oh, this is terrible, this is—

DAVID: And then the visitation stops. I think you were still living then in Washington Square. And the Mexican divorce had been—

JANE: Yes, when was that? When *was* the Mexican divorce?

DAVID: I have a copy of it, so I assume you must have the original.

JANE: I don't have the original of anything.

DAVID: And I've also got all these papers from Ephraim London and all your high-powered—

JANE: He was a civil rights lawyer, I don't know why he—

DAVID: He was your attorney! You had all Park Avenue—

JANE: I know. London had an elegant office. I mainly remember the dresses I wore when I went to see him. I have a sartorial record of that time, nothing else—

it's really embarrassing. But I went to Juárez, I had to fly to El Paso, so—

DAVID: I know that.

JANE: Well, when did—when was that?

DAVID: Hold on. I've got it here—

JANE: [laughing] I'm pretty excited about this—

DAVID: You're "excited." This is just like a reunion then, isn't it?

JANE: This is great!

DAVID: "This is *grreatt.*" Is it?

JANE: No, but it's—it's important, for me anyway, because who's going to be able to tell me about my life?

DAVID: I'll tell you about your life.

DAVID: Yeah, after reading these papers over the weekend, I had so many strange feelings. Okay. How do you want to proceed?

JANE: Well, we *are* proceeding. My memories from that time are so hazy. And one reason I don't remember much, I think, was that I'd been suddenly thrust into another, completely consuming life. Because of course when I left I had one baby and I was pregnant, and then soon I had two babies, and I moved alone to New York, where I got no sleep, I didn't have time to eat, I got up at five in the morning and took care of the babies and I went to school at night. So I was hurled out of the life I had lived with you, you know?

DAVID: Yes.

JANE: Into another life, all alone. I just don't remember a lot from that time. Do you recall anything

about our marriage? I mean—how did we *decide* to get married? And who brought it up? And how did—

DAVID: You brought it up.

JANE: I did?

DAVID: You brought it up.

JANE: That's what I figured.

DAVID: One day, I think, you called and said Let's get married. So we did.

JANE: Sounds plausible.

DAVID: Late December.

JANE [gloomily]: I know we had anemone and ranunculus.

DAVID: Do you want the Hebrew date?

JANE: Yeah, I'd love that.

DAVID: The sixth of—either "Teves" or "Jeves."

JANE: Probably a *T*, don't you think?

DAVID: Rabbi Stanley Yedwab.

JANE: Doesn't Yedwab sound like one of those invented words, or like a name backwards?

DAVID: Absolutely.

JANE: "B-A-W-D-E-Y," it is, backwards.

DAVID: Bawdy. We said that at the time.

JANE: Oh! We did? At the time? So that was a memory, what I just said?

DAVID: It was a memory.

JANE: Now, do you remember anything about our marriage?

DAVID: Uhh. I—

JANE: I mean, did we have fights? Probably did.

DAVID: I don't remember fights.

JANE: I don't remember *any*.

DAVID: None. I remember feeling pressure from your father and, less so, from you: "What are you gonna do with your life?"

JANE: But you were in graduate school.

DAVID: No.

JANE: Oh.

DAVID: I was only in school when we first got married, in Ithaca.

JANE: Well, how long did we live in Ithaca?

DAVID: Two semesters. A calendar year.

JANE: I've often wondered. Well, what was our— did we have any relationship, that you recall? I know we did, but do you specifically recall anything about it?

DAVID: I remember a dock we used to walk to. On Cooper River.

JANE: Do you remember having discussions about anything, ever?

DAVID: About me: "What are you going to do that's respectable?"

JANE: That was scapegoating—it seems so now. It was neatly structured. I was sinking and dying. And nobody was saying to *me*, "What're you gonna do?" Also, when I got pregnant, nobody said "Gee, isn't it a little early?" In those days, y'know, it seemed sensible.

DAVID: Well, I don't recall if you were taking birth control pills. I think you were, weren't you?

JANE: Well, obviously at some point I must not've been.

DAVID: It was a conscious choice, therefore, not to continue with birth control. Okay.

———

DAVID: I would have to say I did not know the kind of turmoil you were going through. I had no idea of the psychological pain you felt.

JANE: Did I ever mention anything? I can imagine I didn't. I'm just wondering.

DAVID: I don't think so. But it could've been my insensitivity.

JANE: Oh no no no, I doubt I did mention it, actually. Did I talk much? I think I was silent.

DAVID: You were quiet.

JANE: Did I attack you? I can imagine that too.

DAVID: Attack me? Physically?

JANE: Emotionally. I mean did I get mad?

DAVID: I still don't recall *ever* having an argument.

JANE: Isn't that interesting. I don't either.

DAVID: And that was part of the difficulty I had in understanding why there was a breakup. I suppose retrospectively it seems our marriage was meant to be an escape for you.

JANE: Yes, it was.

DAVID: I was a way out.

JANE: Well, I didn't know what else to do with my life. I didn't *have anything* I could possibly do with my life. And I couldn't work, I couldn't study, I couldn't think. There was this blind pain in my head. For many years. And I guess—it was a desperate thing: "Okay, I'll get married, what else can I do. Because I can't think straight."

DAVID: It's a shame we have to have our conversation by phone. There's so much here, real and imagined. And maybe the prelude to your writing about our marriage and divorce is for us to—

JANE: Well, y'know, I'm not writing about *our* divorce. I'm doing a piece about divorce generally. Which is just one of those things in my professional life. And I could imagine our conversation might end up a paragraph, or a sentence. And I'll interview Raoul Felder, the big divorce lawyer, and that'll be another paragraph. And I'll write some very emotional thing about—maybe what I recall of Juárez (which is almost nothing).

But really, the main thing is, this is about thirty years later. Our lives are moving fast. I thought I'd like to— know what happened.

Q: for Raoul Felder: What qualities make an excellent divorce lawyer?

A: Well, the field attracts a mixed bag. Some of them are good lawyers—very few—and some are just cesspool types. Some are control freaks and some are exploitation people. It attracts the worst. (And sometimes some of the best, but very few.) It's not a complicated area of law. I think it's fair to say of most divorce lawyers that you wouldn't want to have a cup of tea with them. And you wouldn't want to kiss them. There's just nobody home.

Q: So it attracts an unsavory group?

A: "Unsavory" is a strong word. A needy group of people. And when you marry need with mediocrity, you get an awful hybrid.

AS DAVID AND I reminded ourselves, I secured our divorce in Juárez. At once, I forgot it; decades later when I tried to remember, what returned so strongly was an odd constellation of things—heat and pale sunlight and dust blowing, and a grim feeling of timelessness and

urgency and sadness, and air-conditioning and the scent of martinis and whiskey sours transpiring from iced glasses. I remember the experience both vaguely and intensely, as if this divorce had been a childhood milestone, which of course it almost was — I was twenty-four.

My younger sister flew down with me to El Paso. (The family, I think, assigned her to do this; it's still astonishing to me that she was there. My sister must've stayed in a motel with me and the next morning ridden with me across the border along with the other charges of our local Mexican lawyer. Down in El Paso, we were this morning's bunch of New Yorkers about to be unhitched fast, in concert, in Spanish. We crossed and recrossed the border in a van, through clouds of dust that hung in Texan, then Mexican, then Texan air.

Later, I think our group drank cocktails in a freezing hotel bar in the middle of the afternoon, me and my sister and the other divorced people. Dark red glow of the bar's interior, relief and camaraderie and pain. The others were older than I and either hectically pleased to be unencumbered or despondent about it or both. In farewell, our lawyer said to my sister, who was twenty-one and engaged to be married: "I'll see you in a couple of years."

I ASK Raoul Felder how many years he has been married.

A: Thirty — I don't know, thirty-one years, something like that.

Q: Could you imagine getting a divorce?

A: I'm not a divorce person myself. I'm not a divorcing kind of person. If people leave me alone, I leave them alone.

Q: But let's say yours and your wife's paths diverged?

A: Things don't bother me, I'm into my own head. I don't get bothered if somebody makes a lousy meal — so you eat out. You don't like the perfume — so you sniff other people's perfume. That's all. It's a simple life.

Q: Right. So why is it that other people are coming in this office, their paths have diverged and they've got to —

A: Because most of the time, I think, people are narrow intellectually; they've put too much investment in marriage. You put a lot of investment in marriage, it doesn't work out. You don't put a lot of investment, you roll with it as it comes.

Q: Like anything else. If your expectation is at the correct level, it's going to work?

A: That's right.

55

by
JANE
SHAPIRO

1995

MY LOVER and his former wife still own together, for tax reasons, the house he lives in. When we met, this seemed okay — sensible and modern. But my lover sleeps on the futon they shared, under his wife's childhood counterpane; nearby sits her dressing table, holding makeup and combs and perfume; on his desk is a silver box with bracelets and earrings inside. The bathroom (dual sinks) is a gallery of photographs: They have no children, so over and over, in black-and-white and color, it's just them. She graduates from law school, he catches a fish. Every time you step out of the shower, you meet again the annoyingly fresh-faced couple at their wedding in 1978. One of the pictures is so prized that a duplicate appears in his study, pinned as if casually on the wall. They are splashing in the Caribbean sea! Enjoying honeymoon

water play! My lover says: "That picture is not characteristic of us. I don't know who stuck it there. I never look at it." He says about her clothes in the closet: "I don't notice them."

"Well, do you notice when she's sleeping with you?"

This is a tough one. Sometimes she drives the two hours from the city and sleeps in their former bed at his side. It isn't often, but it does happen. They don't make love, or touch at all. (I believe this; they hadn't had wholehearted sex in years anyway; why would he need to invent this, after the amazing stuff he's cheerfully confessed?) They just lie there. Probably he clings to the futon's edge and immediately drops unconscious. Maybe she falls quickly into her own dreamless sleep and wakes wondering where she is. She walked out of this house, for somebody else, five years ago.

Well, it turns out they're not divorced yet—haven't gotten around to it. Almost every day, some of the mail that arrives is addressed to his wife. "Do you notice her mail?" I demand. "Not this again," he says. "No. I don't. It's an occasional piece of *mail*."

And of course she used to cook once in awhile, and his kitchen is still hung with her omelette pans, and her spices are lined up, alphabetized and fading, above the sink. One night while I'm standing under the copper-pot ceiling, the phone rings, and he cries, "Don't answer it!" I answer it. She asks for him: "This is his wife." When, midsentence, she realizes who I am, she hangs up. So is she gone?

He's sick of me. He says *Yes, sue me, I was sad when she left*. He says she left regretfully but irrevocably. He says their interdependence is the merest vestigial convenience,

their emotional contact nil. (On alternate days, he says she's his best friend for life.) He says the distance between them is vast and unvarying and immutable and he's so fucking tired of being badgered. He says it means less than nothing that they're not divorced yet; not being divorced yet is fundamentally a clerical oversight; of course they plan to divorce, they can divorce any time.

"How about now?"

"Man, you make trouble, don't you?"

Anybody can see I'm stupid in romance and inclined to believe just about anything. We both want me to think my lover's story adds up. Still, I've learned a simple thing in my complicated travels: If you're not divorced yet, you're married.

DAVID: You gonna interview your second husband too?

JANE [puzzled]: Of course not. I know what happened with him. I talk to him once a week.

RAOUL FELDER tells me: In the beginning when you married somebody you were twenty-five, all you did was pound away; you're two sweaty bodies—that's what the marriage is. And then you realize, "Why'd I marry this one?"

Q: So you meet someone else, or you just decide to leave.

A: And most of the time people end up marrying the same people. A little younger, or sexier, or richer, or this or that. But basically the same people again.

Q: Have clients come back to you repeatedly?

A: Of course! As many as four times—a man I talked to this morning, I've done three divorces for. [Pauses. Reflects.] Give 'em a nice divorce, they keep coming.

Q: That's very interesting—it makes the divorce sound nicer than the wedding.

A: It's more expensive but sometimes nicer. You're giving them freedom. At the wedding, they're selling themselves into bondage. With the divorce, you're giving them happiness, release, a chance to make a better life for themselves. How many times can you say to someone, "Here: This is what you need for a happy life. Go. [glumly] Have a happy life."

DIVORCE has left me high and dry. The other day, after, as I've said, many years of excellent single living, I surprised myself with that thought.

I tell my married friends: "I've changed my mind—I want to live with a man." They all say the same thing: "No you don't."

Whenever I have dinner with another single woman, after a decent interval we say what we want in a husband. We name popular qualities, always the same ones, as if men were truly commodities. Potent, we say. Rich, we say. We all claim to want to mate with independent, mature men, and later in the evening all claim to want younger, gentler, more passionate and malleable ones with beautiful arms and legs.

Everybody always says her cherished fantasy is to be *with* a man but to live in a separate house. Okay, maybe that's impossible. So everybody rushes to say she wants a man who is "very busy." This is a universal wish: busy. I am often the first to assert that I want a busy man—

somebody who has his "own life," who doesn't "cling," who will leave me alone and so on. Who can sit nearby without leaning into the edge of my vision or even glancing my way. Of course we don't want to marry a cold or hard or distant man, but somebody as anomalous, fantastic, as a satyr or unicorn: so independent, so warm. And we'll live with him forever—we'll never divorce.

Rich, we say.

Let him live across town, we say.

We are hard-hearted hannahs. We laugh like maniacs and order more wine.

Nobody says: somebody to care for me alone in the world.

by

JANE

SHAPIRO

THE

MARRIAGE

SURVIVORS

BY *Carol Shields*

*W*HEN I WAS a young child back in Illinois my Aunt Marjorie and Uncle Fred came over for supper on Wednesday evenings. My mother made meatloaf on those nights, with lemon pudding for dessert; this was Uncle Fred's favorite meal. Once in a while Aunt Marjorie came alone. After a while she *always* came alone. The ghost of Uncle Fred grew thinner and thinner, though his name oddly persisted. "When's Uncle Fred going to come?" I asked Aunt Marjorie one night. "Hmmmmm," she said, and looked down at her hands, frightened.

Later my mother explained about the divorce. Sometimes married people didn't stay married. You could change your mind; it was allowed. Uncle Fred had turned out to be a "rolling stone." He'd rather be on the road than be married to Aunt Marjorie, who, naturally, was very, very sad about the way things had worked out. She

didn't want to be reminded of it; it hurt her feelings. It would be better if I didn't mention Uncle Fred to her again. And I mustn't tell anyone else either; the neighbors, my school friends—they didn't need to know.

This was in 1942. The word *divorce* felt hard, ugly, full of suffering and secrecy. Some people at that time associated divorce with movie stars, with glamour, but I didn't. My aunt, a woman in her late thirties, went to night school to learn typing and shorthand, and later found an office job with Magnavox. She lived alone in a small Cleveland apartment; she sent her nieces and nephews birthday cards with dollar bills enclosed; she grew old, developed severe osteoporosis, moved to a Florida trailer park, and died in her bathtub. In all those years the only contact she had with Uncle Fred was a valentine he mailed from California—no return address—in the midfifties. The thought of this whimsical greeting fills me with horror: Uncle Fred's careless act of sentimentality rattling down on my aunt's smashed heart. She bore that as she had borne her other injuries, and the divorce—*her* divorce—seemed almost to disfigure her with time, its molecules joined to her fragile bone structure, her powdery skin, her humility, her lack of ease in the world.

Divorce in those days was rare, and its scattered victims were stamped with failure. Today's higher divorce rate dilutes blame, some believe, invoking the old raspberry jam analogy: the farther you spread it the thinner it gets. It's no one's fault. The stresses of contemporary life are cited. People's expectations are too high. Or too low. There's too much intervention or not enough. Power struggle. Communication problems. Cost of living. Sexual dysfunction. Co-dependence. Inability to establish intimacy.

Victim, victimizer. A subtle inversion has taken place in our thinking, and we remark what a wonder it is, really, considering all the pungently labeled enemies of conjugality, that marriages sometimes survive.

And yet they do. Despite the fact that the divorce rate in North America stands near the 50 percent mark, almost all the people I know are married. Not only married, but involved in long, established, ongoing marriages, thirty years, forty years. Is it by accident that theirs are the faces I find most often around our dining-room table, conversing, reminiscing, toasting each other's anniversaries, and giving an altogether convincing performance of people who are at ease with one another? And news comes from the wider world, too, as year after year Christmas greetings arrive from Tom and Marvie in Toronto, Judy and Sam in London, Dot and Al in California. Our married friends. Still together. Still breathing the old trusted oxygen of matrimony.

I understand the textures of these particular seasoned marriages; after all, they're very like my own. I apprehend the compromises, the unspoken bargains, the rituals, and the jokes, too—the biggest joke being that a good many of us are astonished to find ourselves citizens of the undivorced world, part of a robust kicking chorus, the fortunate few who have fallen through a rent in today's statistical charts. We've had a lucky escape—and we know it—from the tug of social evolution and can't help feeling that there's something just a little bit ludicrous about our situation.

There's something worrying about this, too, for what is it that draws us toward those whose domestic arrangements mirror our own? Surely we don't consciously, or

62

The
Marriage
Survivors

unconsciously either, reject the company of the single and the divorced. What could be more unpardonably smug? And yet, there does seem, when I sit down to review my various tiers of friendship, a preponderance of those like ourselves, the marriage survivors, our comrades in a baffling demographic warp. Why?

Might our flocking together suggest egregious self-congratulations? Did we "try harder"? Did we unwind with greater care the skeins of consequence or were we simply fortunate enough to marry at a time when there were fewer guarantees for parts and services? Are we less sexually imaginative? Or too complacent to countenance disruption—putting the house on the market, breaking the news to the children? Is it a question of temperament that draws us together, a willingness to shrug and put up with things while *they* had the courage to cry halt?

Or is it the thought of the emotional gulf that divides us from the divorced? The divorced and separated know, as we can't possibly know, that dark zone that surrounds the cessation of love. We've never had our life cleft by a moment of decision, that particular morning—I always imagine *it* happening on a Monday morning in November, wind, sleet, the window rattling in its frame—when it is understood, finally, that the shared life, that which has been pledged, sealed, and witnessed, is about to be withdrawn.

IF THERE EXISTS a negative statistical deformation among my own circle of friends, there is an inverse bulge in the world of fiction. Here the divorce curve runs wildly out of range. In literary novels, in works of popular romance, in mysteries, in science fiction, from genre to

genre and sparing none—the line on the graph climbs straight up, leaving America's 50 percent divorce figures in the shadows of an impossibly innocent time.

Ask yourself when you last read a novel about a happily married couple. For one reason or another, enduring marriages find little space on the printed page. How is a novelist to pump the necessary tension into the lives of the happily committed? Even the suggestion of a sound marital relationship posits the suspicion of what is being hidden and about to be revealed in a forthcoming chapter. Couples who have good sex, who discuss and resolve their differences, and who care deeply about their bonds of loyalty are clearly as simpleminded and unimaginative as their creator. There they sit with their hobbies and their wallpaper and their cups of decaffeinated coffee, finishing each other's sentences and nodding agreement. She sends his winter coat to the cleaners and frets about his asthma. He continues to find her aging body erotic and he's also extremely fond of her way with grilled peppers. This is all very well, but what can be *done* with folks so narratively unpromising?

It might be thought that novelists would come running forward to pick up the gauntlet. Six hundred fast-turning pages without a single marital breakdown; now there is a challenge. Man and woman meet, fall in love, and integrate their unspotted histories. Crises of all sorts arrive, but their marriage holds firm. Really? You expect readers to believe that kind of fairy-tale stuff?

As a marriage survivor—thirty-eight years—I would like to write that book. I've tried to write it. The modern novel may not be a glass reflecting life back to us, but shouldn't we at least be able to find a measure of congruity

between what we experience and what we imagine? We depend on contemporary literature to bring us bulletins from the frontier, just as we look to the literature of previous centuries for an outline of societal patterns. Why then do today's novelists distort the state of marriage by concentrating on connubial disarray? To this I can only cry *mea culpa*, for, despite my long, happy marriage, my novels and short stories are as filled with divorce as any other writer's.

An early novel, *Happenstance* (1980), is as close as I've come to presenting a picture of married contentment. In this book Jack and Brenda Bowman have been married for twenty years. They speak to each other kindly, they honor their vows of fidelity, and they still have fulfilling sex; it's right there in Chapter 3. A number of their friends, though, have gone through divorce, and this casts a shadow over their own happiness. Brenda wonders how the divorced cope with the detritus of all those married years. Like all couples, she and Jack have built up a hoard of shared anecdotes, their private stock, exquisitely flavored by the retelling. The timing and phrasing of these accounts have reached a state of near perfection. Brenda wonders what happens to such stories when couples separate; do they cease to exist? How do people bear such a loss?

As the novel opens both Brenda and Jack are experiencing undefined feelings of restlessness, and, during a week spent apart, they toy with images of temptation. The two of them are as close as people can be after twenty years, and yet they remain, ultimately, strangers, one to the other. The distance between them is wide as a football field; it is also delicately gauged. Anything could knock

them off course. This novel about a happy marriage, then, is fueled by the fear of its loss and the possibility of a diminished life.

Tom Avery, the hero of my 1992 novel, *The Republic of Love*, has been divorced not once, but three times. His marriages lie strewn about him. Quickies. He tells himself he's been unlucky, but only half believes it. He lives in a small city where at any moment he's likely to run into his ex-wives or one of his six ex-parents-in-law. There isn't a day when he doesn't feel his three failed marriages pressing down on him. He hates the thought of meeting his old drinking mates who like to kid him about rice coming out of his ears, about going for the *Guinness Book of Records*, about buying the Wedding March on compact disk. Friday nights are spent, dismally, in a community center with the members of the Newly Singles Club, companion divorcées who long to repair their lives and perhaps meet someone new. The program rotates every six months, and by now Tom has heard a variety of lectures on such subjects as "The Ghettoization of the Single in Contemporary Urban Society," which introduces three key coping strategies: bonding, rebonding and disbonding. He is beginning to weary of these talks, and has grown skeptical of the way in which human behavior divides itself into categories of three. Nevertheless, at forty years old he's out looking, once again, perhaps foolishly, for the kind of married love that lasts.

Luckily he has a few married friends, but he's noticed that he's seldom included anymore in their dinner parties. Instead he's more likely to be asked for brunch, joining the family around the table for waffles, or to participate, perhaps, in a backyard project. He feels obliged now to

earn his invitations with gifts of fresh flowers or bottles of expensive wine. He admires his friends' babies and dutifully bounces them on his knee in hearty faux-uncle fashion. In return, these married friends dispense well-meaning advice, and occasionally fix him up with single women. Blind dates, though, have become a nightmare, since they lead straight to the agonizing moment when he must confess the details of his splattered history and brace himself for the inevitable response. "Three! You were married three times!" The novel is a love story, employing the classic pattern of enchantment, rupture, and reconciliation, but in the end it is driven less by love than by the failure of love.

Another early novel, *The Box Garden* (1977), should have been a warning to me of the danger of writing about unlived experience. Charleen and Watson, the divorced couple in the book, meet by accident after twelve years of separation, but the encounter felt flat on the page, so flat, in fact, that my two editors, both divorced themselves, asked me if I would rethink the scene. They urged me to show greater "intensity" and "strangeness," and the "bittersweet resonance" such a meeting would arouse. I took their advice, setting the scene up more carefully and turning the emotional thermostat to high. But today, re-reading the section, I find Charleen's reaction forced.

> A twisting breathlessness like a rising funnel-shaped cloud of anguish pressed on my lungs, robbing me of speech and, for a moment, of coherence.

Oh, my. More like a purple-shaped cloud of incomprehension!

STILL, THE FACT IS I *would* like to see more
marital equity in the pages of our fiction. And I'd be willing to honor the principle of mimesis and settle for a
straight 50 percent success/failure rate. Coupledom, especially when seen in an unsparing light, should not necessarily equal boredom, should it? It might be interesting to
see novelists look inside their own specific human packag-
ing and admit that a long marriage—the union of two
souls, the merging of contraries, whatever—can be as
complex, as potentially dynamic, and as open to catharsis
as the most shattering divorce. "It takes more courage to
stay together," a friend once said to me, "than to go our
separate ways."

We all know that a steadfast marriage can be disman-
tled in an afternoon, but how much is understood about
the aesthetic light that such a revealed arrangement can
produce? Long-term marriages do accrue a kind of com-
pacted understanding, and there seems every reason to
believe this material can be shaped to form a useful and
novel dramatic arc, the prickly, conflicted spine of narrative fiction.

Perhaps it is this notion of conflict that needs revis-
iting; we may find that conflict is centered not in the fiber
of human arrangements but in the interstices of human
thought. What exactly are we owed? What can we aspire
to? How well can we know another being? I'd like to begin
over again—a project for the late nineties—asking why
the rub of disunity strikes larger sparks than the rewards of
accommodation, and how we've come to privilege what
separates us above that which brings us together.

MEDITATIONS
ON DIVORCE

BY *Ellen Gilchrist*

$\mathcal{I}$ HAVE PUT this essay in the form of meditations because I do not have a theory to expound. I do not want to "lead you to an overwhelming question." All I have to offer are the ideas I have been entertaining for many years as I watched myself, my friends, and my children live through painful and troubled times in the courts of love. The higher the intelligence, the slower the rate of maturation. This is true in phylogeny, ontogeny, and in our lives. The more intelligent and sensitive the person, the more likely they seem to have their relationships end in chaos. Perhaps the intelligence and sensitivity make it more difficult for them to endure relationships that have gone bad.

Here are some of the things I have observed.

Divorce is caused by stupid marriages. By people getting married when they are too young or because they are scared or because they think a wife or husband will

"complete" them. And divorce is often a very good idea. It's certainly better than a loveless or ill-suited or painful marriage.

Children are the victims of divorce. Most grown men and women go on to other relationships and, except for wasting energy being angry at the person they have divorced or been divorced by, usually manage to learn a little something from the interchange. Of course, unless they are in some sort of therapy during the marriage or divorce, they generally go on to repeat the cycle, hopefully with someone at least slightly more suited to their real needs (which very few people ever acknowledge or examine, much less try to overcome or alter). Between them, my two brothers have married five women who look like my mother. Blond, blue-eyed, polite, quiet, gentle, inflexible. But neither of my brothers is interested in talking about animas or in seeing patterns in their behavior.

Not that years of psychoanalysis have made a dent in my program. Every man I have been involved with has been the oldest son of a powerful woman. In the deep and meaningful relationships, the ones that ended in marriage, they have usually been the oldest son of three brothers. My father is the oldest of three brothers and the son of a powerful mother.

Perhaps it does no good to know any of this. Perhaps it is impossible to choose who we love or want to breed with. Still, for me, the ability to articulate and understand my experience makes up somewhat for whatever inconvenience I have been caused by my unconscious strivings and yearnings.

"We can do what we want, but we can't want what we want," a wise man wrote, and this is, alas, the long and short and the *halter* of it.

Why do we make these crazy marriages that end in tragedy or divorce? Because we have mothers. When we are born we are held against the soft skin of our mothers. (Unless we are unlucky and lose our mothers, but that is another story.)

This sets us up to fall in love. The minute you take off your clothes and lie down beside the soft skin of another human being, the relationship is changed forever. This is the ground of being. This is the big, big story. I have often thought, now that I am in my late middle age, a time surely of reflection and surmise, that perhaps we were better off with arranged marriages. To allow our young men and women to go off and lie down beside anyone they find attractive is dangerous. It often leads to marriages where the partners are unequal in money, scope, intelligence, sophistication, culture. These inequities are of no importance to nature, who wants us to breed far away from our DNA (hybrid vigor, that mother and father of beauty, genius, stamina, brilliance), but they are fertile ground for disagreement when the initial attraction begins to wane.

I have known many wise and wonderful men and women who were good at everything but staying married. Well-meaning men and women, who entered marriages with the best and purest of intentions, have been shocked and stricken to find they could not maintain the love they felt for the person they married, or, worse, that they fell in love with "someone new," as the language so brilliantly

puts it. A marriage is altered by such yearnings whether the adulterous heart acts on them or not.

Even the best among us are subject to Cupid and his arrows, to our unconscious wishes to re-create and recast our childhood, to fall into romantic dreams that are doomed to fade and die and be repeated with new actors.

We reap what we sow. Divorce is the fruit of ignorance about our true nature. It is the harvest of ignorance. We cannot teach our children what we do not know. If we do not understand human sexuality and psychology, we cannot protect our young people from perpetuating the cycle of broken homes. We rush to buy our daughters elaborate wedding gowns and stage huge wedding parties. We feel like the bad fairy if we do not greet every engagement as a marvelous possibility, not to be questioned or probed. The minute two young people tell us they are getting married, we drop our judgment at the door and begin to ooh and aah.

IN THIS CULTURE of bad marriages, divorce is a good idea more often than it is a bad idea. But it is nearly always a bad idea for the children. The child nearly always sees it as a fault of his own. He thinks he has failed because his parents do not live together. He thinks he has not been good enough to deserve the American dream of an intact family. This seems to be true even when the lost parent was abusive or alcoholic. All around him the child sees images of families with both mothers and fathers, and it makes him feel impoverished if he has only half this loaf.

Perhaps there is nothing we can do about this. Perhaps we have to muddle along as we have been doing. Making

messes of our lives and then cleaning them up as best we can.

YEARS AGO, Margaret Mead figured out a plan to lower our divorce rate and keep us from damaging our children. She posited a system of marriages. Any two grown people could apply for a license to be married or to cohabit. If the relationship was successful over a period of time, perhaps two to five years, then they could apply for a second license that would allow them to have a child together.

God knows, I do not want government meddling in the private lives of citizens, but at least we should try to teach young people not to have children until they have achieved a stable home. This means we must fight against nature. Nature doesn't care about quality. Nature has cast its lot with quantity.

The young people of the middle class who have access to reliable birth-control methods seem to be working out a system not unlike the one Margaret Mead proposed. They have a series of cohabitations, and, if one sticks for a long period of time, they get married and produce one or maybe two offspring. Sometimes these arrangements continue to work after the child is born. Sometimes they don't.

I HAVE THOUGHT about these matters for years, trying to understand my own failed marriages and the harm divorce wreaked on my sons. I took them away from their father and tried to keep them from him. I was so young I believed they belonged only to me. They had come from my body. I had risked my life to have them. It

was impossible for me to think their father had any right to them. Now they are older and have divorces and broken homes of their own. Women have borne children for them and used the children to manipulate them. Women have taken their children from them and made them beg to see them. Because of this, they look at their father with new eyes and commiserate with him. I am glad that time and experience have partially healed a cruelty I thought I had a right to inflict.

I do not know how broken homes and divorces will be stopped. I know that knowledge is our only weapon. We must teach our children the history of our own divorces. We must warn them and beg them to be wiser than we were. We must do whatever is in our power to convince them not to marry until they are old enough to know themselves. How old is that? Thirty for some, forty for others, never for a few.

I AM ASKED all the time about how an artist can balance a family and work. And the truthful answer is that I do not know an artist of great or unusual talent who is married. I will revise that to say an artist of great or unusual talent who uses that talent fully. There is no room in the life of an artist for a husband or a wife or a normal family life. The hours an artist has to spend mulling around in solitude leave no time for the ordinary friendliness and courtesy that a happy marriage demands.

A happy marriage? I am so cynical I really cannot think of one. I know people who are married who have cut deals that allow them to live in relative peace with each other but I don't know any marriages that seem to be delivering

much happiness. Perhaps marriage was never supposed to make us happy. Perhaps it is just the price we have to pay to reproduce and make a nest.

THE WORST THING about divorce is how long it takes to achieve it. It takes as long to decathect as it did to create the problem. For every romantic thought you had about the man or woman to whom you were married, you must now add a cynical, mean, ugly thought. For every time you decided he was Prince Charming, you must now decide he is Evil Incarnate. For every rapturous account of his virtues you gave your friends, you must now add a general account of his impossibility as a spouse.

Spouse: there's a word to make one shudder. From the term, espousal, which means to promise. For every ill-thought-out promise, you must add the legal fine print. Thank goodness for sofas and jointly owned automobiles. As soon as the argument can degenerate into a battle over property, the personal emotional ground can begin to be abandoned.

How ugly all this seems to us while we are going through it. How terrible we feel to be walking around thinking dark thoughts about someone we used to *sleep with*. Just when we think we are making some progress, we run into the person we are divorcing at the grocery store. "Ill met by moonlight, Proud Titania," Oberon says to his queen in Shakespeare's *A Midsummer-Night's Dream*. He has come upon her in the forest, where she is dancing with her fairies and elves. She has with her a young boy, the possession of whom is the cause of her dissension with Oberon. Their conversation begins

with jealousy, moves on to Titania's blaming Oberon for everything that's wrong with the world, and ends with his throwing the blame back onto her. Especially with a subject as dark as divorce, it is good to stop and drink from the hands of a master.

TITANIA:
These are the forgeries of jealousy;
And never, since the middle summer's spring,
Met we on hill, in dale, forest, or mead,
By paved fountain or by rushy brook,
Or in the beached margent of the sea,
To dance our ringlets to the whistling wind,
But with thy brawls thou hast disturb'd our sport.

. . . .

The human mortals want their winter here;
No night is now with hymn or carol blest.
Therefore the moon (the governess of floods),
Pale in her anger, washes all the air,
That rheumatic diseases do abound.
And thorough this distemperature, we see
The seasons alter; hoary-headed frosts
Fall in the fresh lap of the crimson rose,
And on old Hiems' thin and icy crown,
An odorous chaplet of sweet summer buds
Is, as in mockery set; the spring, the summer,
The childing autumn, angry winter, change
Their wonted liveries; and the mazed world,
By their increase, now knows not which is which.
And this same progeny of evils comes
From our debate, from our dissension;
We are their parents and original.

Who has ever written a more perfect description of the way the injured party feels when a marriage has broken up? The winds have sucked up from the sea contagious fogs. Rivers have overborne their continents. The seasons have changed places. Hoary-headed frosts fall in the fresh lap of the crimson rose . . . And this same progeny of evils comes from our debate, from our dissension. . . .

SOMETIMES divorces are caused by children. Even a marriage that was consummated in the hope of having children may break down under the pressure of caring for and supporting the endless and expensive needs of children. Modern, educated women sometimes find the wear and tear of taking care of small children twenty-four hours a day is more than they bargained for.

I know of marriages that are breaking down because the children have become rebellious teenagers. The parents feel cheated. They have given their lives and the sweat of their brows for those ungrateful creatures. They feel they have wasted their lives. Perhaps they have.

Platitudes or shaky moral ground will not save us now. We have big problems in this culture. And all problems begin in infancy, in the home, in the mother-child relationship, and in the force field we call family.

Dustin Hoffman's brilliant portrayal of Captain Hook in the movie, *Hook*, is a lesson small children find easier to bear than most of the adults who see it. "They were happier before they had you," Hook tells the children. "They could do whatever they liked, without you always whining and asking for things."

Children know this is true. Why is it so hard for adults to admit it?

Some women make better mothers than others do. Some men make better fathers. This doesn't mean that some men and women are better than others, just that they are more temperamentally suited to the job of raising children. Where does this lead us?

One thing I know is that it is a bad idea to marry someone who had bad parents. If they hated their mother, if they were hated by their mother or father, your marriage will pay for it in ways both obvious and subtle. When the chips are down, when someone is sick or loses their job or gets scared, the old patterns will kick in and he will treat you the way he treated his mother or the way she treated him. If she yelled at him and compared him to others and blamed him for her own shortcomings, this is the treatment you will receive. If she expected to be constantly admired and rewarded, he will expect that. And this is just the problem with his (or her) mother. Before we even get to the father.

DIVORCES are also caused by people outgrowing each other or outgrowing the need for the marriage they have made. Sometimes marriages are broken down by events: the death or sickness of a child, the sickness or disability of one of the partners, sudden wealth, sudden poverty, all the things that the marriage ceremony in The Book of Common Prayer warned against. For richer, for poorer, for better, for worse, in sickness and in health, and forsaking all others . . .

The world that such marriages were made for no longer exists in the middle-class life of the United States. We *don't* depend on each other for food, clothing, hous-

ing, nursing, and are left depending on each other for company and emotional support. Most of the married people I know go to their friends for fun and gossip and long walks where everyone says exactly what they think.

Also, we live much longer than the people who wrote the ceremonies in the prayer books of our various religions. We don't want to forsake all others. We leave our troubled houses where children are sick and bills must be paid and travel to our offices where there are bright, well-dressed, good-natured people of the opposite sex, and we forsake. Oh, do we forsake! If not in physical ways, then in emotional ways, which are equally damaging to the marriages we left behind that morning.

W E L I V E so long we have time for two or three major careers, two or three or more transformations. We become someone new and the person we are married to feels betrayed. They have been betrayed. The person they married has ceased to exist and they feel cheated.

T H E O N L Y H O P E I can see for the unhappiness of divorce is knowing that it is better than a bad marriage. The unhappiness of divorce ends, in time, for healthy people. Healthy people refuse to stay unhappy. Sooner or later they wake up and decide to be happy again. They lose weight and start exercising. They dye their hair or get a toupee. They buy a red dress and go to a party and start flirting. They redecorate their living quarters. They get out their address books and start looking for old lovers to recycle.

Life goes on. They look back on their marriage and wonder who that person was who inhabited that troubled world. Time, the old healer, has erased the footsteps that led them to the altar and the divorce court.

*Meditations
on Divorce*

THE

GENDER

WARS

BY *Diana Hume George*

$\mathcal{H}$E WAS the great love of my life—I always knew we'd grow old together—sacred territory—desecration fears—feels like betrayal to write this." So begin my notes for this essay, jotted on Post-its over many months. Reviewing the inch-thick pile, I find I'm still genuflecting three-fourths of an inch into it, lighting candles, saying novenas to him, to us: "I will always love him, even if we cannot be together. Finest man and mind I will ever know." It sounds more like an elegy than an anatomy of divorce. We believed our own press, idealized ourselves.

We had assistance mythologizing our relationship. When we broke up, many friends actually said some version of "You can't do this to us." We were one of those sparkling academic couples known by many people in our business. No wonder I write this sort of dribble on Post-its. I wrote the last note in the middle of the night in the

dark, waking from another nightmare about him, one that left me vaguely nauseous throughout the next day. I can barely read the scribble, but I believe it says, "You stupid stupid man—infant—tyrant—grow up." I can't use his real name, so I'm going to call him Jason here, probably because he thought of me as a Medea, bent on destroying everyone I loved. Or maybe I was Medusa. Big hair.

I write about the breakup of my nearly twenty-year relationship from the perspective of a woman interested not only in telling a harrowing story about personal loss but also in figuring out how the story of my marriage intersects those of other women and men. I used to think ours was the greatest love the world had ever known, but I have come to see that we were enacting clichés, that the belief in our unique indissolubility was itself only a cliché. Had this been someone else's relationship instead of my own, I'd have known it all along.

Jason's perspective is diametrically opposed to mine. (His myth about himself is that he's always right. Mine is that I'm always reasonable.) Still, there are facts he would not dispute. He was once my professor and my mentor, although he did not believe that this influenced us to any significant degree. I saw a pattern of domination and submission in our relationship that he denied was there, and if he said it wasn't, then the subject wasn't up for discussion. He felt he'd changed quite enough as a male feminist and was not able to change any more. Though he ultimately agreed to counseling, he thought of it as "psychobabble." He believed that we should take care of our own problems rather than confiding them to a stranger and that talking about a problem was like digging into a

wound and opening it further; I believed that bandaging a wound when it's festering only makes the infection worse.

I MET JASON in his poetry class in 1969. Although I was only twenty, I was married and a mother. I was immediately smitten by him—and by John Donne and the other poets whose words fell seductively, dramatically, from his lips. He was a charismatic professor, a consummate performer. Many of his women students fell for him.

I took so many classes from Jason that I lost count. For years, we called each other by our surnames, Dr. X and Ms. Y. My marriage fell apart. Later his began to crumble. Eventually he left his wife and family, and although I'd never been involved with a married man, I was way beyond the ability to pull myself back on the basis of my moral reservations. We fell into each other's arms one night. It wasn't all that romantic—we were in his office in the dark, and somehow my foot got jammed in the wastebasket. We told that story for years.

Our intensity and passion didn't wane with those years. Instead it grew steadily, taking us through losses and difficulties. His children and parents wouldn't speak to him; my first husband went to jail for a serious crime; my best friend's daughter ran away from home, came to live with us, and gave birth to a daughter at the age of seventeen. My son also became a parent. We were a family that included white, Native American, and black members—and in the small town where we lived that made us a target for bigotry.

Jason and I were never legally married; we were common-law for all those years. We were always in deep

83
~
by
DIANA
HUME
GEORGE

financial difficulty because of his child support payments and the low salary I earned as a graduate teaching assistant while working on my Ph.D. And lord, we were busy. He was a professor and activist with a commitment to union politics and affirmative action. I was a grad student and then a young professor with growing activist concerns in women's issues. We wrote books. Yet it wasn't these pressures that did us in. Throughout these years, we found ways to get away from the tension of our lives by traveling around the country in the summer, camping in a series of leaky tents. We determinedly saved at least one long afternoon a week, often more, for being together. We worked hard. We raised good kids. And we loved each other madly.

When the trouble began, it hit us unaware because we'd been so busy, but also because we'd begun to believe our own press as a golden couple who represented love triumphing over all odds. For my part, I'd known early on that despite the feminist convictions we shared, we'd been backsliding. It wasn't about groceries—he bought them. It wasn't about housework—he helped, though I did more than he. (We had one of those arrangements in which the man concentrates on repairs and taking out the garbage and hauling heavy stuff, while the woman does more of the daily chores.) And it wasn't about cooking— we traded off. It wasn't even really about child care—he was involved with the kids, taking them on trips out West, helping with homework. I dedicated much more time to child rearing than he did, feeling it appropriate since our son was my child from a previous marriage, and our adoptive daughter was my best friend's child.

I'm still trying to figure out what happened, and he's still trying not to. His best revenge was leaving me to figure things out alone. After almost twenty years of loving each other, we didn't have a single real conversation about what had gone wrong. I asked him repeatedly to talk with me. Repeatedly he refused. Since he wouldn't talk about it, I had to reconstruct the accident scene by myself, make up the other half of the dialogue we're never going to have.

Here is how I see it. From the beginning, we allowed dangerous elements to creep into our relationship, even when it was healthy and alive. Jason had tremendous personal authority, a big voice, an imposing physical presence. He was quick to anger and equally good at turning on the deep freeze. He didn't have to do any of this often—a few times a year was enough, because it was scary and you remembered it well and didn't want to cause it again. I learned early on not to cross him. It was just too dangerous.

I can't rightly blame Jason for trying to stonewall me, because it worked so well year after year. Wouldn't you try that method if it worked, if it saved you pain, if you could avoid personal conflict by shutting down challenge or dissent? For years I was afraid of displeasing him. When I finally got up the courage—and even from someone as self-possessed as I normally am, courage is the appropriate word here—to try to speak to him of power inequities, he'd say there weren't any, that we were complete equals. He would simply refuse to talk about it further. Period. Scared, I'd shut up again. For years at a time. Now, what makes a woman do that if she's a feminist and isn't being

beaten and has analyzed traps such as this in literature and in the lives of her friends? I remain dumbfounded. I was writing feminist books on one hand, playing silenced daughter on the other.

Sex became an issue too. Remember the scene in *Annie Hall* with Diane Keaton and Woody Allen on either side of a split screen talking to their shrinks? "How often do you have sex?" the shrinks ask. The Woody Allen character answers, "Hardly ever, only three times a week." On the right, Keaton replies to the same question, "All the time, three times a week." Even the statistic matches Jason and me. Sometimes we'd laugh about that, but it was a deadly serious issue. My mother took DES, so I have chronic cervical problems. Sex was not always fun for me, and sometimes it was downright painful—if not at the moment, then afterward. It's stunning to me to recall how regularly both he and I expected me to put out. Amazing and unquestioned, that sense of entitlement on his part, loving duty on mine. Jason did not seem to understand that this young woman who had started out as his goddess of sex was all grown-up now, busy as hell, and sexually exhausted.

But I tried—it was the seventies and I believed that we were supposed to be liberated. We were supposed to lighten up. I lightened up. When we first got together, the agreement was that any time I didn't like what was happening, all I had to do was say so.

That's not what happened at all. What started out consensual became quietly, subtly coercive. He never forced me. There are ways other than physical force to get a person who loves you to do what you want. As I grew older, less daughterlike, less an acolyte and more my own per-

son, certain things became unacceptable. But each time I would say I was having trouble with them, that they weren't okay anymore, he would withdraw from me, punishing me with unexplained coolness that he, of course, denied; but I couldn't help noticing that when I acted the part of his sex goddess again, everything became warm and fuzzy. The emotional price for not playing was high — although he never acknowledged that he was exacting it.

I have asked myself a hundred times: How did it come to the point where I lost the right to set reasonable limits and boundaries, to satisfy needs of my own? How can I reconcile the me I know — strong, autonomous — with the woman who was so silenced, so afraid? The process of self-erasure in a relationship happens in small, almost imperceptible increments, one isolated incident after another. There is always, in any human relationship, the decision to let it go for now, not to disturb the peace with this need or that hurt. When you let that silence build, a pattern of self-denial emerges. Because you have not said, *"Wait. We must talk now,"* you can lose the "right" to speak at all.

This happens to people in love all the time. Take away the specifically sexual focus, and we all can name a thousand ways it happens in our lives. It's so subtle, and there's so much background noise, that you don't even hear the sound of the handcuffs going click, and you didn't know that it was your own hands, raised to your beloved in this small submission, that were now bound.

Jason meant me no harm. I really believe that. He loved me. He was just a pained man living in a patriarchy he himself fought against, though he didn't understand its outposts in his own head. By the time I found the

strength to meet his anger and disappointment with my own, mine was so concentrated from its long-term repression that it became destructive. Jason wouldn't discuss these issues, year upon year. Blue eyes gunning their warnings, he'd yell, "Go ahead and talk. I SAID GO AHEAD AND TALK. I'M LISTENING. SAY WHAT YOU HAVE TO SAY."

I finally found someone who would talk to me, who wanted to touch me in ways I did not find objectionable. Although he was no real threat to Jason in my eyes, Jason would say my affair caused our breakdown. We came completely undone.

I am fascinated by the way we remember, select, and devise "what happened" in a relationship, how we all rewrite the history of our lives, constructing our narratives so as to make ourselves whatever we want to be—heroes or martyrs or victims or visionaries. The "truth" about what happened at any given point in time recedes, or never existed to begin with, though it is enticing to behave as if there is a real "truth," a genuine, ultimately vindicating "what happened." On a bench somewhere in the universe sits a judge who can verify memories under dispute: She said what you remember she said; he turned from the table and put that piece of cake in his mouth and then sneered with contempt exactly as you recall; you behaved with long-suffering grace, and then with well-earned anger.

But of course, there is no such judge, which is why my truth and Jason's are mutually exclusive. Both of us are reasonable people and we were both *there*. Yet what he remembers is completely different from what I do.

Jason thinks that what happened is this. It's a script so simple and short that a gerbil could write it: He loved me completely and passionately and thought that I loved him

back that way; whereas, flighty woman that I must have been all along in disguise, I got tired of him for some arbitrary reason—probably connected to my whacked-out midlife hormones—then betrayed him with another man, and finally just up and left him. Ninety-nine percent my fault. (Recent revision under pressure: "Sure, I made some mistakes." But no elaboration. None.) He said to our son that this mess was "all your mother's idea. She just left me." That's it. He omits the part where he actually told me to leave, at least a dozen times, before I finally went. And I left and came back more than once.

One of his most recent revisions of his own first draft includes a tub. Always eager for any little detail to illuminate what he thinks occurred and why, I listen close. "You just got up out of the tub and walked out the door," he tells me. "Tub? What tub?" "The bathtub," he answers, giving me his you-know-what-I'm-talking-about-don't-play-dumb look. It seems he was sitting next to the tub talking to me, and suddenly I rose up, swept past him, and walked out the door. I guess I dressed first.

Then I remembered: From my point of view, it was not a silent or unexplained departure, but a sad, resigned, talked-about one, even if I did more of the talking. It had happened the winter before our final breakup when I tried to leave for a few weeks to figure things out, but only managed to be gone for twenty-four days, during which I came back and slept at our house with him several days a week, got in a car accident with him, injured my leg; and then our dear old dog lost control of his body functions, so I gave it up and came back home completely. The dog died in my arms and Jason and I buried him together, strewing roses, weeping, holding each other, singing

songs from the opera *Candide,* vowing to try again. I stayed for another six months, during which we tried to heal and could not. I had long since given up my affair and at Jason's demand was not even being civil to my former lover, which was very difficult. But by that time, Jason had introduced a new "family friend" into our home, the woman he later married, and with whom he was punishing me for my affair.

At that time, I felt so guilty and awful that I let him have her there, engaging in open physical affection right in front of me and our kids, cuddling our granddaughter to show off his good-daddy genes, and generally treating me like an irritating neighbor. Jason said he had to have her in his life because I did not love him like he loved me; she soothed the pain of my terrible withdrawal. I bought that crock all summer, comforting the grown kids when they cried, or reasoning with them when they begged me not to let this go on. Finally I left.

Yet according to Jason, the bathtub scene was the moment when I just walked out. What happened after that does not count. There's a gap in the narrative. I suspect that I, too, have engaged in similarly solipsistic narrative revisions, though I don't know what they are.

We'll never talk about it together. He'll be stuck forever in his simple martyrdom scenario about the man who gave all his love, his very life, to a woman who turned out to be—for no reason he could think of except perhaps racquetball hormones—a betraying liar who nearly destroyed him. He was the victim and I was the victimizer. Simple. But I wouldn't think a person could be content to let it rest with that. When the marriage of two complicated and decent people falls apart after two de-

cades, it's not likely to be such a simple bad-girl–good-guy story.

We're trying to get on with our lives. He's married, I'm not. I doubt I ever will be again. Neither of us wants to keep hating the other. We share a history, two kids, two grandchildren. We can't always avoid each other. It's been over five years since we split. He doesn't speak ill of me to other people. That's called "loyalty," which he also demonstrates by being essentially uncommunicative about "what happened." It's a shame, he might say, but it's over, so it goes, what's done is done. How about those Cubs?

Yet to one or two close friends, he confided a whole different scenario in which I'm not a bad guy but a hormonal depressive. (Read long-suffering, painful toleration of mental illness on his part.) One of them told a third friend how sad it was: Poor Diana. All those years I never realized she was emotionally ill. She hid her instability so well. The third friend called to tell me that one. We had a good laugh.

I HAVE THOUGHT long and hard about why my marriage ended, and have tried to put it into a broader perspective, to understand how it conforms to certain patterns. One of these has to do with feminist marriages involving men who came to their equity politics in the women's movement of the early 1970s, adopting a conscious program of personal growth and transformation. Such men formed their deeply held beliefs during adulthood, long after the massive machinery of gender construction had done its work in the unconscious. They constitute a socially, economically, and educationally advantaged elite. These men entered into marriages with

women of my generation on a basis of equality—striven toward, strenuously maintained. They're the good guys.

Surely many feminist marriages are exactly what they appear to be—successful partnerships between a man and a woman who live together in mutual recognition, respect, and carefulness. But judging from my own personal sampling, the country must be fairly crawling with women who have lived a weird double life for years, or are living it still, maintaining the fiction that they are in genuinely feminist marriages, when both husband and wife have long since backslid. Women in marriages such as this often take part in creating the myth that theirs are partnerships of equality (I certainly did), when they know deep down, and often say to their closest friends, that most of the change and transformation have been their own, that their men sometimes treat them with contempt and expect from them an enormously draining kind of dedication that is not fully mutual.

A great many feminist men are also misogynists *because of their feminism*. Such men often feel deep if suppressed anger over what they gave up when they relinquished privileges that would otherwise have been theirs. And in some feminist men this rage is directed toward women. If you get in the way of it, you can be in big trouble.

It has also struck me how my relationship with Jason contradicted gender clichés. In our culture, women are thought to be emotionally needy and vulnerable and more dependent on relationships for their identities than men. Research on female psychology supporting these generalizations cannot be all wrong. But has anyone out there noticed what my friends and I most certainly have? That

many middle-class men in their forties and older seem to be more emotionally dependent than their women? Am I making this up? Why are the women I know forever getting up from the dinner tables of their lives, from precious moments with their women friends, because *he* is waiting? Because he can't get to sleep without her? Because he needs her near him? Because he feels abandoned if she's gone too long?

It's no secret that many men dump older wives in midlife and take up with younger women. Indeed it seems to me epidemic, especially among men in positions of power in business, the arts, politics, and—like Jason—academia. I was one of the younger women on an older man's arm. I was Jason's midlife crisis. Men like him are mentor figures—younger women's bosses or superiors or teachers—and old patterns of domination and submission, of desire to please daddy, die hard. It's thought that father/daughter, domination/submission patterns exist even in normative heterosexual love when the man and woman are relatively the same age. When a man is a woman's senior, the difficulties of the norm become exaggerated. Partnering with a patriarch can be hazardous.

What is more, recent research on female psychology and moral development indicates that men tend to place a high value on hierarchy, autonomy, and authority, and don't appear to care as much about empathy or the perspectives of others as women do. There are exceptions, of course, but it's common for men to believe so deeply in their rightness, and to have so much difficulty admitting they might be wrong, that they often cannot take their share of the responsibility for failed relationships. Women, on the other hand, are normally enculturated to believe

93

by
DIANA
HUME
GEORGE

that nurturing relationships is their deepest obligation, and tend to internalize responsibility and guilt when relationships fail. In effect, the tendency is for men to say, "It's all your fault, you did it" and for women to reply, at least initially, "You're right. What a worthless human being I am." It's a tidy arrangement, but I can't imagine that it's good for our long-term chances as people trying to make it together on a fragile planet.

Beyond this, I've noticed that men are less likely than women to enter into marriage counseling, which by definition involves compromise. When pushed to do so, they often engage in the process with little real desire to change their own patterns of behavior, feeling on a basic level that it's only the women who *really* need to change or grow, so the process never has a chance.

We live in a patriarchy. Men have more power than women do, and many men have trouble sharing that power. Capitulation to authority is a major pitfall for women; the ability to be flexible and to change may typically come harder to men. We can all name exceptions—rigid and always-right women, empathic men—but they don't disturb the rule.

JASON BELIEVES I hate men. But I don't think this is true. I am sometimes afraid of men, and sometimes, in anger, I make sweeping generalizations I know aren't entirely true. But I like most men I know. And as a teacher of women's studies, I understand how both sexes have been shaped by the patriarchy.

Jason believes he does not harbor any significant misogyny. It's not a danger in his mind, so he doesn't challenge or examine himself. Like many feminist men, he

represses his anger at women, regarding it as inadmissible. Still, he has expressed his rage in both words and action, including fits of temper. He is a powerful man who has identified with the causes of oppressed peoples and fought for their rights for many years—and in some respects, beyond his conscious intentions, I think he resents them for it. He'd probably say that I simply drove him beyond the ability to cope—i.e., that a man can only stand so much.

He is now married to a woman even younger than I am. If I was almost young enough to be his daughter, she's almost young enough to be his granddaughter. But he would say this has nothing whatsoever to do with his need for a younger woman. She was "there to love me when you nearly destroyed me," he once told me. I have other interpretations, knowing that he desired me in part because he could make me his projection of a goddess of sexuality with whom he might regain his own sense of youth. It is no coincidence that he is yet again with a woman in her twenties, approximately the age I was when I first came to him. He needs the kind of love the young give their elders. He got it from me, too. I don't hold myself above that dynamic, which possesses its seductions and its beauties.

WHAT DOES it matter if Jason and I never figure out what really happened between us? I believe it matters; men and women need to come to some mutual understanding of what happened to them, how they damaged each other and themselves, what they might have done to avert their tragedies, might still do to avert the next one. I think Jason and I misunderstood each others' motives and intentions. In order that our time together should not be

written off as wasted—making us bitter and wary of other loves—we need to know what happened.

But now that we are separated, neither of us can understand anything beyond isolated, self-serving truths—and to me that feels horribly dangerous. If a man and woman who both care about a world larger than their own conflicts cannot make the effort to understand each other—or at least to listen to each other now that there is no primary relationship left to save, no flanks to protect—then what hope is there for peace and understanding in a broader context? Global conflict is personal conflict writ large.

If all I wanted was female martyrdom, aggrieved party status, support for not only my valid perceptions but also for my inevitable self-deceptions, then all I'd have to do is—well, nothing at all. I've gotten plenty of sympathy and confirmation of my version of reality from my friends. But I want something more, something better. I will always want to know what Jason experienced and felt. I want to understand what he was going through, now that I can see beyond my own pain. I want to take responsibility for the parts of this that belong to me. I can't really know what they are when he says it was *all* my fault, because that only makes me strike back defensively, or conclude that the fault was really all his. Neither of us can possibly be right about that.

The man I began living with a year after Jason and I separated was with me for several years. I chose him in part because he seemed to be the kind of person who could do what Jason could not—tear down with me, brick by brick, the walls that rise between people entangled in love. He said he could do it, but finally he could not. When I said it

was time to go our separate ways, he, too, decided it was all my fault. He was my victim. I was malicious. I abused him terribly. Like Jason, whose opposite he claimed to be, he will not talk to me about why our relationship ended. Like Jason, he says that perhaps he did make a mistake or two, though he does not say what they were. Still, he is glad to provide elaborate details on what I did wrong, which, apparently, was just about everything.

I know that none of us, male or female, can erase our unconscious drives. Our desires and needs were instilled in us early and are difficult to dislodge. But what I am desperately weary of is what I have always encountered in my personal relationships. It is not men's birthright to ask of women that we set no boundaries. It is not right that men's agendas, expectations, and needs so often become definitive of love relationships. It may be harder for men in a patriarchy to understand their limits, their relative powerlessness, and sometimes it may be almost impossible for them not to blame women for their defeats. I want them to try harder. Female conditioning may give some women an advantage—ironic as it is—in that they learn to be better at handling defeat and compromise. I know I cannot re-create myself to conform to a lover's image of me—and I am resigned, now, that the men I love cannot re-create themselves for me. I just hope that someday I will encounter a man who will take responsibility with me for whatever losses and pains we must endure together. In the meantime I'm taking a break from the gender wars.

GROUNDS

BY *Mary Morris*

$\mathcal{A}$ FEW MONTHS AGO I was standing in New York's Penn Station en route to Washington to visit a friend. It was a Friday afternoon and the station was crowded. Other travelers bustled about. Trains were announced and I listened to the various "All aboards" that rang through the station. When my train was called and I looked down, my leather backpack was gone.

The backpack contained student papers, a novel I was reading, my journal, some notes for stories. It also held my checkbook, credit cards, the keys to our house, my address book with all kinds of numbers, codes, secrets. All the things you aren't supposed to carry. In a panic I phoned my husband and told him to call the banks, the brokers, the creditors, the locksmith. Freeze the mortgage account, change our PINS. We had to cancel, stop everything.

I will spare you the logistical difficulties this produced: the deposits that disappeared into dead accounts, the changing of keys, the thirty-five checks my husband wrote on an account we had shut. What we had to open, what we had to close. But in the midst of a long, tedious bank session, I turned to my husband of five years and told him that now I knew I could never get divorced. I couldn't stand the paperwork.

First let me say that I have never been divorced, not legally. Not with documents, papers to file, custody battles, accounts to separate, not to mention books and records. I have never had to fiscally and on the dotted line divide myself from another. But I have suffered rifts, splits, separations, and breakups. I have lost a friendship that meant more to me than any friendship should. Most relevant to this essay, I've had to wrench myself away from a man with whom I'd spent several years, had a child, as well as assorted emotional ties. This must count for something. I have had to pick up the pieces, pull myself together, and begin a new life with an infant daughter.

When she was two, I married someone else, a jewel of a man, a gift, one of my closest friends said. He has adopted our daughter, Kate. We have a house, a dog, many records, and books and CDs and dishes and even some fine crystal and an antique bed we are both very attached to and rosebushes we love to prune and, of course, all that paperwork in common. Our books are merged into one good-sized library. Though we know this is conventional, I make the child-care arrangements and he pays the bills. We like the same movies and people and always order pad thai at our favorite Thai restaurant around the corner.

Yet every day I think to myself, this is it. I'm going to get divorced. I can't spend another minute with this man. I can't bear the way he scrubs the pots with those long tedious strokes, the way he walks the dog, always wary of letting it off the leash. I can't stand how he shifts his leg just when I'm cuddled in the right position. The way he puts things on the top shelf where he knows I can't reach. He does dumb things. Breaks the window of the hatchback before we leave on a vacation. Loses his keys. Hides the butter in the back of the fridge. I can't stand the pauses between sentences, the way silence sometimes creeps in between the cracks.

I know I am not fit for this marriage, any more than a stallion is fit for the corral. Orcas may swim in pods, but on the open sea. I can't live any longer in this cage, this trap. This accountability. I want to be able to walk out the door and not say that I'm going to the store and I'll be back in an hour. I don't want to phone in if I am late or apologize if something takes longer than it should. I don't want someone reading my thoughts or, worse, not reading them.

I used to be a drifter. I traveled where I wanted, when I wanted. For a year and a half I roamed through Central America and didn't tell anyone where I was. I crossed Siberia and no one knew how to reach me. Now, if I sneak out through my studio door, panic ensues. Wherever I am, like E. T., I have to phone home. I've come to admire the great escape artists—Houdini; the prisoners who swam away from Alcatraz; the distant cousin of mine who kissed his wife good-bye, got on his usual train, and was never heard from again. I am in awe of the ones who got away.

I have thoughts of moving west. Or east. Of packing up and starting over. Once I tried this. When I told my daughter's biological father that I thought we should make it legal, he said, "In what sense?" Since he is a professor of international law, I assumed he knew what legal meant. I decided that I needed to find a new place and begin again. I also needed a job because the same year Kate was born I lost mine, and there was one I could have in California. I packed up my daughter and headed to the other coast to start afresh.

As soon as I stood beneath the statue of the Duke at John Wayne International Airport, I knew I'd made the mistake of my life. There is a great tradition of people who moved to California to start over. A whole body of literature is dedicated to this theme, such as *Grapes of Wrath* or *Day of the Locust*. There is also another interesting motif that runs through California literature—deaths on the Pacific Coast Highway, car crashes, vehicles sailing over the edge. There is, after all, no place to go from there. It's the end of the line.

IN CALIFORNIA I lived in a house that over-looked the sea and every day as I walked my baby along the cliffs, I thought to myself, "I could just jump off and end it all here." I had no friends, no one to turn to. But, of course, as I watched the water battering the rocks, I knew that I couldn't leave my child behind because who would care for her? and I couldn't take her with me because even in my despair such selfishness was not an option.

I had no choice. I had to live. Besides, her father and I had not had to separate our books or our finances. It was

simply a divorce of the heart, one I was very slow in making. Nothing was made final between us. We were apart, that was all. I'd walk the cliffs weeping. Then return home to black smoke pouring out the window because Ramona, the woman I'd hired to help with the baby, left pots burning on the stove.

Mornings I hiked. Endless pacings back and forth through the hills above my house, baby on my back. There were mountain lions, coyotes, snakes up there. I took risks I shouldn't have taken. There were also butterflies, and Kate called them "Bye-byes." I should listen to her, I thought.

Because I had a baby and an automobile, two things I'd never had before, I began to drive. Through a series of strange events and journalistic curiosity, I became interested in coping. I infiltrated the California New Age groups and met with channelers, extraterrestrial walk-ins, goddesses, psychics, people who had been abducted by UFOs. I drove with my daughter all over Southern California, into the desert. Near the Nevada border we'd stop at chapels where we'd spend the afternoon watching people get married. Most of them had met the night before in Las Vegas and they all got in the car and headed west.

From pay phones in the middle of desert towns, I'd phone Kate's father. I'd tell him I wanted to get married. I'd tell him I loved him and we should try again. He said to be patient, to wait. He had finances to settle, his sons needed to grow. He would accept more responsibility soon.

One afternoon I drove to the Crystal Cathedral where, posing as a *New York Times* reporter, I interviewed

the angels who flew in their pageants—grown women in pink gossamer who flapped their wings forty feet in the air. Each angel had her story—divorce, betrayal, loss. And as Peter Pan's riggers flew me through the cathedral, too, I understood that if you don't flap, you flip.

I wanted to fly, to soar, but somehow I couldn't break away. He called. He visited. We went to Death Valley (no symbolism intended) for Christmas. We fought. Why not just say yes? I'd argue. Why not just try? At night we lay side by side, hardly touching. We tried to patch it up, not just the fight, but the whole thing. I wanted him to sell his house where he'd lived with his previous family and make a fresh start with ours. On New Year's Eve a woman phoned him, just after twelve. I told him to leave. He said he barely knew her. We patched it up again. He said he did want to try so we made Valentine's plans. He broke them. He said he'd promised his sons he'd take them skiing and could I fly from Orange County to Burlington, Vermont, with the baby for the weekend? Every night we talked. Long, painful conversations until at last we agreed. We would try again. Perhaps he could handle the responsibility. He loved us. "You are the sea in which I swim," he said. He wanted us. His life was complicated. Life was full of complexities. We would meet. Neutral territory. Florida where my parents have a place (relatively neutral anyway). He would bring his boys. I'd bring our daughter. I was stupid, everyone said. But I loved him. We would try again.

''ONLY CONNECT,'' E. M. Forster wrote in *Howards End*. I was in graduate school when I read that, and it has stayed with me. Only connect. I know that

longing and desire — and that need to make contact — are what keep fiction and life moving.

I have had this recurrent dream. That I am in a deep, dark hole. Words are my only way out. I keep trying to make the connections over and over again.

We talked. All the time. Our relationship was one endless dialogue, the same story told over and over again. Conversation is the erotic center of marriage, Dalma Heyn suggests in her book, *The Erotic Silence of the American Wife*. It is talk, dialogue, language that keeps us going. But in my case that talk was filled with cunning, deceit, betrayal. Perhaps because I am a writer, I was slow to see. Words are not actions, not really, when it comes to marriage.

A F T E R W E E K S of negotiating, Kate's father and I met in Florida, our neutral ground. I had not seen him in three months. He stood, flanked by his teenage sons, and I had our daughter in my arms. He looked very good to me. *What is wrong with this picture?* I asked myself. I was never very adept at that test in school, but now I wracked my brain. When you live with somebody, when you know them for years, you get to know their quirks. He won't eat oatmeal, hates crowds, and prides himself in not having been to a barber in over twenty-five years. I had cut his hair for the past five years. His ex-wife for seventeen years before that.

Now I looked at him. His trimmed hair and beard. I took a step back and remembered the voice of that woman on the phone New Year's Eve. "Who cut your hair?" I asked him. "Who cut your hair?"

———

JOYCE CAROL OATES writes in *On Boxing* that the boxer, like the writer, is always reestablishing the parameters of self. Many times I have had to reestablish my parameters, regroup, circle my wagons.

For example, I have asked my husband, if I put my book down at night and gaze dreamily into space, not to say to me, "What are you thinking?" Of course he views this as a double bind — only connect, but leave me alone. I say, "I'll tell you what I'm thinking if I want to," but I also think, "You let me go, you let me fall back down into that deep, dark hole."

He says this is a paradox. My hands are tied.

And I say I am reestablishing my parameters. I'm trying to get back in the ring.

I MARRIED my husband because the Navajo Tribal Police were going to arrest us for driving what they thought was a stolen vehicle (my brother's van) and found out that Larry was a Canadian living in the U.S. on an expired tourist visa. Three weeks later, we married out of fear of deportation. We also married because when I put my head on his chest, I could fall asleep. Because when I phoned him, he was where he said he'd be. Because life felt easier, not harder, when he was there, and when I talked, he listened.

Just before our wedding, my husband came to the marital suite and I handed him my wedding shoes. I need you to scuff these, I said. His best man was with him and they walked around Plymouth Court in Chicago each with one of my shoes in their hands, scraping the soles on the asphalt so I wouldn't slip on the rug.

As I waited alone in our bridal suite, I thought of my father's words: You can always correct a mistake; that's what divorce courts are for. Or Jeanette Winterson's about marriage being a plate-glass window and someone's always standing outside with a rock.

WHAT ENABLED me to leave one man and love another, I'll never know. Sheer force of will, the need to fly, my daughter's happiness. Something between a mother's strength as she lifts the car off her child and the delicacy of a hummingbird's heart prevailed. I met someone new. En route to our wedding, we stopped at Arcosanti, that utopian village in the Arizona desert. An announcement on the bulletin board said that the great minds of the twentieth century would be visiting and I saw a picture of Kate's father. I took a deep breath; I went on with my life. Love is never the same and no one replaces another.

After years of rifts, breakups, separations, and now marriage, I know that there are no fresh starts. There are only new problems. Perhaps one can avoid messy divorce (one can even avoid marriage and commitment as I did for years). Certainly one can make a mistake and marry the wrong person and find an easy or not-so-easy way out, but the truth of it all is you don't start again. Life is cumulative—both happiness and grief. You drag it behind you. It piles up in the attic. Other people notice. I also know that things tend to happen for the best.

Another man might not shift his leg when I've found just the right position, but he also might not come home when he says he's going to. He might let the dog off the leash, but he might talk on the phone in whispers and not

say where he's been. He might break my heart, or worse, my daughter's.

What's that movie with Ray Milland when the daughter cries to her parents that they can't know what she's suffering in love because they've always been in love and had such a perfect life? And they stand up and say, Do you know how many times I've thought about leaving him, how many times I've wanted to walk out on her? Marriage is work, my father always said. Just like anything else.

Years ago when I was a child, we got a flat tire. A man stopped to change it. It began to rain and that man lay on his back on the wet ground, whistling, changing the tire and explaining to me what he was doing. Later my mother said, "When you grow up, if you meet a man who can change a tire in the rain, whistle, and talk to a kid, marry him."

FOR YEARS I wrote short stories. I liked them better. Then I turned to novels. It became obvious to me right away that a short story was a fling and a novel was a marriage. A short story could happen on a two-week vacation, a brilliant passion that was soon over. But a novel was something you got up with every day. It was daily life, a process. Some days are good, some are bad, but you watch it build, slowly, over the years.

This is why I won't divorce my husband. Because while I take a shower, he makes the coffee. While he takes a shower, I get our daughter dressed. Because we dislike the same people and neither of us can put up a tent, nor wants to. Because when we walk down the street in a city where we've never been, he sees the light shimmering on

the buildings. Because in the face of an injustice, he will rant and rave. I always know where he is. I know when he will call. He has never disappointed me in any way that matters. Because the mystery of love remains a mystery to me and when he lies down beside me, I know I can sleep.

Because I'm the kite and he's the string. Because I can't stand the paperwork. Because he'll read this essay and laugh.

When I tell my husband I've got grounds, he thinks I mean coffee grounds for the compost, not grounds for divorce. And most of the time he's right.

THE
DIVORCES
OF OTHERS

BY *Perri Klass*

*W*HEN MY SON started at the day-care center, he met other babies, just as interested as he was in Cheerios and Jolly Jumpers. And I, of course, met the parents. Fair is fair; a peer group for the child, a peer group for the parents. All those I-can't-believe-I'm-really-having-this-conversation conversations that you can only have with people who have children the same age as yours, from Competitive Motor Achievements ("Well, yes, he does pull himself up to a standing position all the time, he just seems so eager to walk") to Toilet Training Tips (don't ask). And the way you report back at home, as if it were interesting gossip, the details of other families, other ways of raising children: "She still hasn't ever let him have anything with sugar in it!" "They play foreign language tapes while the baby is sleeping—they think she'll absorb French pronunciation!" "They're leaving the kids with

their housekeeper and going to Puerto Rico for the weekend!"

This is what we had, I suppose, instead of gossip. I have spent my life as a busybody and a gossip, and enjoyed a hundred vicarious personal dilemmas for each one that has actually unsettled my own somewhat tediously straightforward life. I have depended on friends and on the stories of friends of friends for a great many tortured love affairs and tumultuous passions, splendid acts of reckless abandon, and minor delicious perversities. All through high school and college and medical school, I drew interest and inspiration, tension and titillation, from the varying promiscuities and entanglements of my peer group.

But now I had landed on a plateau, a stage in life where there were no unexpected roughnesses in the landscape. No interesting gossip. Occasionally, I would call a friend who was single and childless, or lurching from relationship to relationship. "Tell me what's new," I would beg. But my friends got married and coupled off. "How are Larry and the baby?" they would ask, and confide that they were thinking of getting pregnant someday soon. Life became rather remarkably wholesome and familial on every side, and I grew increasingly desperate for dirt; I cannot speak for anyone else, but I know that I have never bought and read *People* magazine more faithfully than I did during those years.

And then came divorce. And though I have never been divorced, and for that matter, have never even been married, I found myself watching and discussing the divorces of others with various shades of fascination, titillation, and perturbation. Divorce, I suppose, comes to represent

some large and dangerous whirlpool at the center of the calm, mature (and occasionally monotonous) sea of domesticity-with-young-children. It's there, it's a hazard, you can only give thanks that you've escaped—but it makes for intriguing conversation and occasionally you find yourself venturing a little closer just to get a better look.

These, after all, are the people who could so easily be you, the people you have been identifying with for years. Parents talk all the time about peer groups and developmental stages, and they are generally referring to their children. But one unexpected aspect of childbearing, unexpected for me at least, is that having a child also generates for parents a set of people united by their similarly aged children, and drawn behind those children through a set of developmental stages in the unfolding of a family. In my circle, it turned out, divorce tends to come when the second child is preschool-aged. Call it some variant of the seven-year itch, call it the compound stress of life with two young children, but I have seen few, if any, one-child divorces from up close. The family breakups in my day-care center followed a definite and distinct pattern. Couples had one child, then another, usually two or three years apart, and then, when the second child was not yet in kindergarten, came the divorce.

And the divorces were ugly. Suddenly, I knew the names of local divorce lawyers: who's really easy to talk to, who's not too expensive because she's still getting established, who's the big-money power divorce lawyer—why, he won't even take your case unless he thinks it's a really hot one. But if he takes it, your spouse might as well give up right away. Everyone learned the new vocabulary:

the guardian ad litem thinks . . . temporary primary custody . . . joint physical custody.

Sometimes the day-care center would get involved in the custody battle; teachers would be called on to testify which parent picked up and dropped off. The not-divorcing (or, if you prefer, not-yet-divorcing) among the parents would whisper to one another, did you know, they subpoena the pediatrician to find out which parent brings the kids when they're sick! And not-yet-divorcing couples would look at each other narrow-eyed: ah-ha! I would mutter to Larry, who believes that because I am a doctor myself, I am the one best equipped to deal with our pediatrician. Take that! You might be sorry someday that you made *me* call the doctor that time *you* saw the funny-looking poop!

It was often strange and sad and even terrible to watch families come apart, families that were in some sense mirror images of my own—and yet, terribly enough, there was also wrapped up in all the sadness some small element of excitement, of change and possibility. No, this place we have come to, this plateau of family life, is not necessarily where we rest forever. There is still the possibility of drama and tragedy and metamorphosis; new conformations, new households taking shape. It is sad and frightening to learn that promises of forever are not necessarily about forever—and yet it can be slightly intoxicating to wonder, for perhaps the first time in years, whether you really do know for absolute sure the shape of your own life in the years to come. What if, what if—what if you broke your own promises? What if he broke his? What if the small irritations and exasperations of daily life multiplied and ultimately imploded? Oh, I clucked over the divorcing

couples, shook my head about the effects on their children, participated in the general pleasurable buzz of rising gossip—but there were moments too, I think, when I looked at those parents with fascination and fear, wondering whether I was just watching the bravest pioneers, the first to march boldly down a perilous path which would ultimately beckon many of those self-satisfied uxorious cluckers.

And yes, indeed, suddenly there was gossip. I had single, sexually active friends, who called and wanted the latest on my day-care center scandals. At the day-care center, I would scrutinize other parents for signs of personal change. A new haircut, a new clothing style—could it mean something? At pick-up time, you could, if you had the right kind of mind, hang around in the parking lot a little, letting your child say a slow good-bye to a good friend, and watch to see which parent of an acrimonious couple was doing the picking up, check to see if some mysterious stranger was waiting in the car. You could rush on home and tell the news: Karen got her hair cut short and curled and there was a guy waiting for her at pick-up time—in a silver Mercedes!

The divorces, I think, pushed many parents into overacting their roles. The still-happily-married-and-proud-of-it would nuzzle a little in the corridors, stagger out to their cars while attempting to embrace both each other and the cherished child: See how we love each other, see how tight and definite is our nuclear family! The recently-divorced-and-aware-of-the-scrutiny-of-others would parade defiantly past the cubbies in newly short skirts or unaccustomed contact lenses: I feel ten years younger and I know I've never looked better, and see how my child

runs to hug and kiss me! Instead of merely reacting to one another's styles of child-rearing, many parents were making larger, more global statements. There was: I keep my promises; I love my wife, my husband, my child; I am a good and honorable person with a stable family. And there was, also: Stability is not everything; good and honorable people do not always know what's around the next corner; I also love my child; *life is more complicated than you think.* Yes, I definitely had a sense, looking at those parents who were living through divorces, that they were the wiser ones, the ones who had learned the hard lessons that others were still trying to avoid, lessons about the sadness and uncertainty of life and the limitations of security.

I spent a day at the courthouse with a friend, offering support and my own wisecracking variety of comfort as she plowed through another stage in a particularly angry and difficult divorce. What I remember most about that day was the matter-of-fact parade of family fights, one after another, as we sat waiting our turn. The court-appointed guardians, the lawyers who all knew one another, the bustle in the courthouse halls. The estranged husbands and wives aware of each other's presence, meeting glances defiantly or avoiding one another's eyes. It was the other side of gossip, the institutionalization of emotion and human connection, the professional pawing over and sorting out of human complexity. Life is more complicated than you think.

And then I went home and even in private felt polarized into that extreme of demonstrative we-are-a-stable-couple-aren't-we overacting. This will never happen to us, will it? We will never join that parade, will we? No, no, no. We are different, you promise each other, and promise it

more fervently the less clearly you see the differences. In the end, we always fell back on the not-funny joke: We aren't married so we can't get divorced. Ha ha ha.

And then came the divorce that rocked the day-care center. Not another case of they-just-weren't-getting-along, not another she-says-he-has-somebody-else, not even she-got-a-better-job-out-of-state-and-he-says-he-doesn't-want-to-go. No, this was the grand passion of the four-year-olds' room: One little girl's mother and another little girl's father! Right there, in our day-care center, illicit passion! Adulterous love! Endless rumors flew: How long has this been going on and where did they meet and who found out when and who said what when who said which.

Now *this* was gossip, and with a vengeance. And it was vicarious thrills of many kinds: This too can still happen in families with young children, attraction too strong to resist, passion which carries away all before it, the world well-lost for love, and so on. There was intense disapproval, there was pity for the abandoned spouses (which became more complicated when the husband whose wife had left him moved in with the mother of yet another four-year-old in the same day-care room—but that's another story), there was intense interest in the unfolding drama. And I suppose there was also some complicated half-resentful envy, the envy of those whose lives seem to have lost all gossip value, and even any possibility of gossip value in the future. As you picked up your child, argued the winter boots on, and remembered the lunch box and the accumulated artwork, you could not help wondering, in some tiny base corner of your being, whether someday you too might be a public scandal. Yes, even this is possible, even for those grown well past adolescence, even for

those fully equipped with children and highchairs and car seats and lunch boxes.

I remember a day spent on the beach the summer before my second child was due to start that same four-year-old room, Larry and I and another day-care center couple. The children were burying one another in the sand, fighting over the waterguns, and generally carrying on; the parents were conducting a symposium: Which marriages will break up this year? Present company was, of course, excluded from consideration; we did successfully finger one couple who went on to have serious (and public) domestic problems over the course of the coming year, but they didn't actually separate. We worked ourselves up into crude hysterics imagining unlikely adulterous pairings among the parents—Jack's buxom loudmouthed mother and Leah's tiny little buttoned-up father. We imagined ourselves giving testimony against particularly disliked and self-righteous parents. But present company was of course excluded; no matter how well we might fit the profile (second child now preschool-aged), obviously we were all looking down on the foibles of our fellow parents from some lofty peak of secure couplehood.

My son is in the fifth grade now, and divorce has finally penetrated his consciousness. I found it fascinating that when he was younger, he didn't seem to notice that one good friend's father was now living with another friend's mother—the adult personae had changed radically, but I couldn't help wondering whether to four-year-old boys, all adults looked more or less alike. In my more paranoid moments, I wondered whether he could pick me out of a line-up. But now that he's older, he's aware that certain

friends of his have complex home lives—you can't usually see Danny on the weekend, because he goes to his father and stepmother, and they live a long distance away; if you want a sleepover with Greg, it has to be one of the two weekends a month that he's at his father's house, and it has to be there, not here, because his father doesn't want to lose one of his nights. Inevitably, one day, after an involved school vacation visit with Danny (pick up from mother, drop off at father—no, there's been a change of plan, but mother and father are not communicating directly, and all calls are funneled through stepmother), my son got disproportionately upset over a routine parental squabble in his own home.

"I don't want you to get a divorce," he said, and I had the feeling that he was trying on the drama for size, that this was less a sincere statement of loving anxiety than an attempt to say something about Danny and adults and the way they can mess up your life.

We won't, I said. We can't get a divorce, anyway—we aren't married. Ha ha ha. Look, you know me, I yell at everyone all the time and it doesn't mean anything. Look, I said, we love each other, we love you, and we'll stay together, even if we fight sometimes.

There are so many interesting promises, spoken and unspoken, that you make when you raise children. Some are the out-and-out impossible promises that you make even though they are not in your power: I won't die until you're all grown-up, nothing bad will happen in the night, I will protect you, always and forever. Some are the promises that seem reasonable and plausible, seem like they *should* be in your power: I will never hurt you, I will pro-

vide for you, our family will stay together. You don't stop making these promises just because you know that they, too, are not real promises, are only hopes and resolutions and small defiant plantings of the flag in what may be uncertain ground.

I make no apologies for relishing the details of other couples' marital discordancies, from the Prince and Princess of Wales to the parents at my children's elementary school. Yes, every fall when the school puts out the directory of parents' names and addresses, I still pore over it to see who has moved out on whom, who has dropped her husband's name off the end of the hyphen, who has remarried and now lists a stepparent. But I no longer speak from that lofty peak of secure couplehood, that above-it-all vantage point of amused distance. The lessons of my peer group, as we march through life, labeling our children's sweatshirts and signing up for teacher conferences, are in part lessons of complexity and vulnerability, the failure of good intentions, the transience of what was supposed to be permanent. They are also lessons of change and transformation and possibility, renewal and surprise. Adulthood and parenthood are not necessarily the known, safe quantities you thought they were, not for you and not for anyone else. Whether it is a warning or a titillation, a distant naughty frisson or a genuinely frightening premonition, you have to face the fact: Life is more complicated than you think.

IT'S

A WONDERFUL

DIVORCE

BY *Ann Hood*

$\mathcal{S}$HORTLY AFTER my divorce, I went to a psychic. He spread tarot cards on the table between us, studied them, and frowned.

"Recently," he said, "you lost a piece of jewelry."

I shook my head. I am not much of a jewelry wearer. In fact, I wore the same pair of earrings every day for three years until one literally fell off my ear.

The psychic continued my reading. I was in the arts, I was in financial ruin, I would move soon.

"Then there's that jewelry you lost," he said again. "The funny thing is, you're glad you lost it."

I thought about the jewelry box that sat on my bureau. It had been a gift from my ex-husband. Every year, on our anniversary, he gave me a box of some kind: one that played music; one that was made of glass; a painted ceramic one; and the large, square, wooden jewelry box that

held the pearls my mother gave me on my wedding day, the small diamond studs my grandmother gave me for my sixteenth birthday, my passport, and various oddities— earrings without mates, out-of-fashion earrings, things that needed chains to hang from, chains that needed things to hang on them.

"You know," I told the psychic, "I am in the arts, I do need to move, and I am broke. But I haven't lost any jewelry lately."

Puzzled, he tossed a few more cards on the table, looked down at them and then up at me in surprise.

"Yes, you have," he said. "You lost your wedding ring, figuratively speaking, didn't you? You just got divorced."

"That's right," I said, and glanced at my naked left hand.

"The funny thing is," he continued, "you're not at all upset. In fact, you're glad."

Glad. Not a word one usually associates with a divorce. But that psychic was right; I was glad.

The thesaurus gives joyful, light, lighthearted as synonyms for *glad.* I was all of those things. In the two years before my divorce I had become physically too thin, emotionally too heavy. I felt weighted, like a scuba diver about to drop backward off a boat into the ocean. Sometimes, my chest ached and tightened as if my heart was actually trying to send me a message. I developed insomnia. I stopped cutting my hair. In pictures from that time I am all bones and hair and tight lips. At night, every night, I dreamed I was dead.

As Faith Sullivan writes in *The Cape Ann,* "Being married was like having a hippopotamus sitting on my face, Mrs. Brown. No matter how hard I pushed or which way

I turned, I couldn't get up. I couldn't even breathe. Hip-popotamuses aren't all bad. They are what they are. But I wasn't meant to have one sitting on my face." Being unhappily married makes one think that marriage is the hippopotamus, when really it's only one marriage in par-ticular—your own.

On that January afternoon, as I sat in the psychic's apartment on Houston Street in Manhattan, it had only been one week since my husband and I agreed to a di-vorce. In that week I had grown lighter, lighthearted. One day I found myself walking out of my apartment, onto Hudson Street, and feeling something strange, yet oddly familiar. I had been sleeping well for the first time in years so it wasn't exhaustion. It wasn't hunger; I was eating all of my favorite foods. My work was going well and I had just finished a new novel. I was not yet tired of winter and I was not at all bored. In fact I was ready to leave for three weeks in Egypt. So what was this feeling pressing at my rib cage, demanding to be noticed? I kept walking up Hud-son Street, the feeling growing, getting larger, hugging me. A woman passed me and smiled. Suddenly, I recog-nized what I felt, as if from another lifetime. I was happy.

LAST MONTH my ex-husband called me for advice about his love life.

"What should I do?" he asked me. "You know how I think."

But do I?

I know how he takes his coffee, the type of underwear he prefers. I know when his birthday is and the funny little stories his family tells about him as a child. But after five years together, in many ways he remains an enigma. I am

uncertain why we moved from casual friends to dating, from dating to marriage. Why, I have asked myself, did he propose to me? And why did I say yes? Although they say that opposites attract, I have never read that they should marry. And, except for our careers and a love of old movies, there were never two more opposite people. Opposite in temperament, in the ways we live our lives day to day. He was Jewish, hated Manhattan, needed absolute quiet to work; I was Christian, thrived in the city, liked noise. Every summer, I went home to Rhode Island and rented a beach house; he did not like the beach or the noise my Italian relatives who populated the house made.

When reflecting on one's divorce, it is easy to overlook the good things and focus on the reasons why he is an EX-spouse. Certainly my ex-husband was kind and funny and smart and adventurous. On paper, in fact, he was just right. I remember nights back in college when my roommates and I would sit on our bunk beds and make lists of attributes for our perfect man. But how could I know at eighteen, at twenty-one, that there are intangibles that matter more than whether or not someone went to college or how tall they stand?

For years I had lived in an easygoing atmosphere. I had a boyfriend from California who epitomized the term *laid back*. I went to movies alone, enjoying the solitude of a dark theater in the middle of the day. A person who loves to cook, my biggest struggle was with new recipes, my conflicts more of the philosophical variety. Then my ex-husband came into my life and I was introduced to a new way to see the world. He enjoyed disagreeing, over whether to eat Mexican food or Chinese, which movie to

rent, or in which museum to spend a Saturday afternoon. It wasn't disagreeing with me that fueled him, it was tension, a charged environment.

I like peace. I like harmony. A friend once told me that when she entertained our small group of friends she knew that everything would go well if I was there. "You have a way of keeping everything nice," she said. Although it is true that my role in my own family is to keep everyone happy, and that there are some people who would argue that all women have that role, I wanted a marriage that ran smoothly. My ex-husband, on the other hand, seemed to enjoy conflict over matters both large and small.

Was it really important to eat burritos instead of fried dumplings? I would ask myself, and forego my craving for margaritas and nachos.

And so on our quiet night together, I scowled over food I didn't really like or want to eat. The marriage wasn't even running smoothly as a result of my giving in all the time. In fact, there was always a new point to debate, a new compromise.

After too many such compromises—not that movie, only science fiction from the midfifties, no museum except the Metropolitan—it did become important where I ate dinner and what movie I watched and which museum I visited. It became so important that a good part of my days was spent negotiating, bickering, angry. Giving up an evening of Mexican food became grounds for war. Then, at night, I would lie in bed wondering what kind of person I had become who fought over eating burritos. When I finally slept, I dreamed, again, that I had died.

———

I BELIEVE in love.

I believe in shaky knees, sweaty palms, a pounding heart.

I believe in love at first sight. I've had it, twice, and they have been my biggest, truest loves.

I believe that being in love, that being loved is, as Elizabeth Cady Stanton said back in 1860, "the open sesame to every soul."

I believe in marriage.

My parents have been married for forty-three years. They still hold hands when they go for a walk. They still kiss each other good night. Their story goes that on the night they met my father asked my mother to marry him. It took three dates for her to say yes. I grew up believing in the power of a love like that. I grew up wanting it. I still do.

I have heard that in Persian the verb "to love" means "to have a friend." Therefore "I love you" means "I have you as a friend." My ex-husband and I began as friends. We drank wine together and played Trivial Pursuit on opposite teams. I liked him. But my knees never shook when he walked in the door. My palms stayed dry. Well, I told myself, passionate, crazy love has gotten you nowhere but brokenhearted. This, I decided, was mature love. It was sensible. We split everything fifty-fifty. The price of a gallon of milk. A tank of gas for a car trip. Household chores.

On my wedding night, I watched a Mets game, then washed the floor of the apartment we were moving out of. He cleaned the bathroom. The wreath of flowers with long ivory ribbons that I thought looked romantic and medieval was tossed into a trash can on Broadway when

we went out to get more boxes for packing. Although a part of me was aching that night for some schoolgirl scenario, another part felt grown-up, practical.

In St. Martin, on our honeymoon, he took scuba lessons and I developed claustrophobia. It manifested itself in the hotel swimming pool, when I dropped to the bottom of the deep end wearing weights and a mask. I thought I was suffocating. The thing I loved the most—water—became frightening. I could not go back in without starting to hyperventilate. I sat by the pool, waded in the ocean, but did not swim.

We argued because I thought it would be fun to rent a Jeep and explore the island. "I'll rent anything but a Jeep," he declared. We argued because he would not buy drinks at the poolside bar and instead insisted on walking two-and-a-half blocks to an indoor bar where drinks, though cheaper, could not be taken outside. I sat alone, drinking frozen rum drinks by the pool while he drank inside.

My silk honeymoon chemise was worn once. "Gee," he said, "that makes your legs look weird."

When I called home from St. Martin, I wanted to tell my mother that maybe I had made a mistake. That maybe I was wrong after all, and the less sensible kind of love was the kind I wanted. But I had only been married for three days. So instead I told her how I had won big at the casino, that the weather was great, and that I flunked scuba lessons in the hotel swimming pool. To this day, I am still claustrophobic.

WHEN I was in high school I read an article about love in a women's magazine that advised women to look

hard at their new boyfriend's faults rather than at his attributes. Those, the magazine said, would dominate someday. So when friends asked me how come I didn't notice, or care about, the facets of my ex-husband's personality that helped to destroy the marriage, I can only shrug. They were all there from the evening we met. His love for conflict, his need for routine. If you saw them then, someone asked me, why did you get married?

Once I had a roommate who tended toward spells of depression—she wouldn't shower, she overate, she stayed in her robe and watched television all day. I grew to dislike her, to worry every time I walked in the door about what I would find there. When we went our separate ways, we became good friends again. It is so easy to tolerate the quirks and shortcomings of our friends. When my ex-husband and I were friends, I would hang up the phone when he became bellicose, bow out of an evening that didn't include what I wanted to do. I could say that I had a great friend who was a curmudgeon. I could even admire his eccentricities. But when those eccentricities followed me around all day, they were not as endearing.

As writers, we both worked at home, but my ex-husband couldn't work if there was noise—the banging of pans, my laughter on the telephone, the hum of the TV. How could someone who likes music playing in the background, who cooks to cure writer's block, who loves to hear a friend's voice long distance coexist with someone who is bothered by footsteps in the hall outside? When he and I were friends and went away skiing for a weekend, I found it funny to sit in a room with the door closed wearing a headset to watch *Regis and Kathie Lee* so he

could work in total quiet. It was a story that my friends and I laughed about. But when it's your life, it isn't as funny.

One of my greatest pleasures is a lazy Sunday morning in bed with the *New York Times*, "All Things Considered," lots of coffee, and the person I love. But my married Sundays were spent alone in bed, my cats on my stomach. "I get too antsy," my ex-husband used to say. If he felt like working on a Sunday morning, he made a no-noise rule. And so, one summer morning, in yet another room alone with the door closed and headphones on, something settled in me. I wanted my life back. I wanted music. I wanted to laugh freely. I wanted to walk through rooms with open doors.

I remembered once being told by someone that he loved me, but wasn't in love with me. Aren't they the same? I had cried. The boy, older, in college, shook his head wisely. Later, I used it myself. I'm sorry, I told someone, I love you, but I'm not in love with you. They're the same thing! he'd insisted. But of course they're not at all the same. I loved my ex-husband. I admired him. I respected him. He made me laugh. But sitting alone that day, I remembered how it felt to be in love. What I was feeling then, what I had always felt, was something different.

Once I decided that, my dreams about being dead stopped. Instead, I dreamed that I lifted from my bed and, with greater and greater speed, began to fly around my apartment. The sensation was wonderful, zooming above my desk, my stove, heading for the window that opened onto the street. Trying to get to that window, I knocked

into the brick wall of the living room. The next morning I woke up with bruises on my elbows and knees, convinced I needed to fly away.

For me, the question that most haunts me is not why did you get divorced, but why did you get married? I was thirty, the age when it begins to feel like spinsterdom is around the corner. I was ready to settle down, to make a life with someone. At the start of a new career as a writer, I wanted to plunge into my life, as if all that came before was a warm-up for something more. Somewhere inside me, a voice was screaming: "Let's go!"

But, too, there was the urge to be sensible. After all, I had done nothing in my life to date that was by the book. I had graduated with honors from college and went to work as a flight attendant. I had left everything and everyone I knew behind and moved alone to New York City to become a writer. I had dated men who made me quiver, with passion and longing and love. They were not the men my cousins or friends brought home and married. They were not employed by solid corporations. They did not drive solid automobiles. But I was in love with them. And somehow I always ended up brokenhearted.

Here was a man who fit my qualifications (a writer!) and my family's (a well-published writer!). Even though he didn't have to, he worked nine to five. He was, I thought, a grown-up. And so was I, because I was marrying for companionship and not passion. Soon after my wedding, I began to write a series of short stories about unhappy women who married men for all the wrong reasons and leave them for others with zing. In the early stories, the husbands triumphed, but the more I sat alone in

a room with the door closed and earphones on, the more my heroines escaped.

I USED TO harbor some 1970s notion about divorcées. Crowded singles bars. Bad Chablis. Sweaty men wearing too much gold. Women in spandex. There was something sleazy and shameful about it, I thought. But by the time I was ready to do it, that image had faded. I only wanted my old, pre-marriage life back. In many ways, I was uncertain about exactly what that had been. But I remembered how at night I used to sleep well. How being alone felt fine because there was no one down the hall not talking to me, keeping me away. In *The Female Eunuch*, Germaine Greer wrote that "loneliness is never more cruel than when it is felt in close propinquity with someone who has ceased to communicate." That was the loneliness I had begun to feel, the kind that hurt.

Instead of a singles bar of desperate people, I imagined my divorced self happily alone, my music shouting, my phone ringing, eating burritos until I couldn't eat them anymore. I imagined breathing easily again, staying up late, lounging in bed on Sunday mornings. When you live alone, doing these solitary things takes on a different meaning. You are capable, independent, content. But when your husband is in another room, that room's door also closed, those things done alone only make you lonely.

A FRIEND came to visit the other night. She was obviously distraught, puffy-eyed, with the corners of her mouth turned down.

"My husband wants a divorce," she said.

She told me what was going on, how he had changed and they had grown apart. The truth was that a divorce would make her unhappy; she loved him.

But then, past the tears and pain, she whispered, "I don't want to be divorced. To have an ex-husband. A first husband."

And even though I myself was divorced, had an ex-husband, I agreed. "It feels weird," I said.

"But so many people are," my friend said, nodding. "So many are divorced. And they're fine. Why, some have several exes."

"I'm one of those people," I said. "I'm divorced."

I remember my grandmother, disgusted, whispering about someone, "She's divorced."

We were Catholic. Italian. We did not get divorced.

My parents stayed married. So did my friends' parents. My aunts and uncles. What I imagined, what I believed to be true, was that I too would get married and stay that way.

For months before my wedding, I began to have stomach problems. My fiancé went away for a month and I felt happy to be alone. My stomach problems stopped.

"PMJ," a friend told me. "Pre-marital jitters."

But were they? Or was my body trying to talk my mind out of something? I had dinner with an old boyfriend, someone I had loved passionately. My knees still trembled when he walked into the restaurant. I made up games for myself. If this old boyfriend showed up at the wedding like Benjamin did at Elaine's in *The Graduate*, it would be proof that passion wins over logic. If he showed up, I

would run off with him while Simon and Garfunkel sang in the background.

My wedding day was beautiful. Clear, not too hot. It was the wedding I had always dreamed of—outdoors, large striped tents, a bevy of bridesmaids in lace. My old love stayed away, my silly fantasy of him playing Benjamin to my Elaine forgotten. I look at those pictures now, study them for clues. There I am, smiling, dancing, head thrown back in laughter. Was I really happy that day? Did I believe the "until death do us part"?

W H E N I got married, I took with me an old oak table and four antique chairs. I had had those chairs for almost ten years. They had survived nine moves, countless parties, the weight of hundreds of people. But when I got married, they began to fall apart. A loose leg, a cracked spindle, a weak seat. Until, one by one, they all broke. For a while, as each one broke, I moved in an old college director's chair to replace it. But then my husband inherited a large dining-room table that dwarfed the director's chairs, and we moved to a bigger apartment, and it seemed like it was time to buy new chairs for the dining room.

Of course, we couldn't agree on what the chairs should be.

Months passed.

We asked neighbors to bring their own chairs when they came for dinner.

For parties, I set up a buffet.

After much arguing, the style was agreed upon at last. We had been, by this time, chairless for over a year.

As I've said, we split everything fifty-fifty. My husband

decided, arbitrarily, that he would spend no more than thirty dollars per chair.

In the past, when he made decisions like that, I simply went out and bought what we needed myself—wineglasses, linen napkins, candlesticks. But this was now at the end of our marriage. Counseling had failed. We both knew it was over. So I didn't go out and buy our chairs. I had invested too much alone already.

I H A V E S E E N the pain of divorce.

Custody battles. Bad financial settlements. Children caught in the middle, taken away, turned against a parent.

I cannot say what other people should do. I cannot say that divorce is good. I cannot say that it is right.

I can only say that my divorce saved me. I weigh ten pounds more and feel hundreds of pounds lighter.

For me, the divorce was not difficult. I had been living in loneliness for years by the time my marriage ended, so that being alone felt uplifting, free. Still, I do not want to get divorced again, though I want to re-marry. Instead, I want to get married right this time—for love and passion and shaky knees. And I want it to last.

L A S T W E E K my ex-husband called me for advice about an apartment he was considering.

"The street is noisy," he said. "It gets heavy truck traffic."

"Forget about it," I told him.

"It'll drive me crazy when I'm working, right?" he said.

"You couldn't even stand the sound of laughter," I reminded him.

It wasn't until later that I thought about how, over our years together, he heard less and less laughter from me. At the end, there was none at all. I had robbed him, too, with my unhappiness, my bad moods, my frustration.

I laugh a lot these days.

When a friend commented that it was weird how my ex-husband and I called each other for advice, I laughed about his funny quirks, how the sound of trucks would send him straight to Bellevue. It struck me as endearing, his need for absolute quiet. Back before we were husband and wife, I found that lovable; I find it so again now.

"But you're divorced," this friend reminded me. "You're not supposed to be such good friends."

But that is just what we are. Good friends. Since our divorce, he has shared holidays with my family, played with my new baby, had drinks with my boyfriend. He has moved into Manhattan, the city he refused to live in when we were married, the city I love. He rents a beach house now with friends. For some reason, these things do not bother me. He has found other sources for conflict, I suppose, and I have found my old life, my old self again. Apart, we are happy. Apart, we can say "I love you" as the Persians meant it—"I have you as a friend." It's a wonderful divorce.

AN

HISTORICAL

ROMANCE

BY *Susan Spano*

$\mathcal{I}$ AM a very lucky woman. I have never been caught in the middle of a bloody revolution, gone hungry, suffered serious illness, or seen someone I love die. They say the loss of one's child is the worst, which may partly explain why I remain childless, and in general travel light through life. I fear loss, and have probably impoverished myself by avoiding possessions that could be snatched away. The worst thing that ever happened to me was my divorce, which took away my marriage, and something I loved even more—my husband.

"My life closed twice before it closed," Emily Dickinson wrote, despite the fact that she lived an apparently ruffleless life, filled with flowers, recipes, and letters from loved ones. No one knows exactly what happened to her on those two occasions, but if her father only scolded her or her kitten ran away, what does it matter? She knew

loss, because she described it perfectly—and I've known it too.

Still, oddly, I do not regret putting on the drop-waisted, pearl-colored gown my mother wore when she married my father just after World War II and making my own vows one overcast spring morning in a small Protestant church on Cape Cod some forty years later. Nor do I even regret loving the man with whom I made those vows. We stayed married for six years, and it's been four since we divorced. Four springs have come and gone with their lilac mementos of my wedding, and Easter Sundays to remind me of the desperate time when things flew apart. What I do regret now is the way I loved him—beyond measure and reason, through a romantic veil that I have only now begun to part.

Don't get me wrong. When I fell in love (such an interesting phrase—did I lose my footing or get pushed from some higher, firmer place?) I was not a green girl, eager to put my quirky mind, pining body, and excellent liberal education to use as some man's perfect mate. I came up after the feminist revolution among sophisticated people; my mother worked all through her married life and would have made a bang-up career woman had three children not come along. She and my father wanted most of all that I should get ahead, do well, achieve. And I was a good daughter, so I tried hard.

You see how lucky I was? No one stopped me from reading the Brontës, Austen, and Tolstoy at just about the time I got a training bra, mascara, and black patent leather heels for my confirmation. No one knew what a hash I'd make of novels like *Pride and Prejudice,* how I'd come to view even dashed, hopeless love as beautiful and fail to

discriminate between Emma Bovary and the heroines of the historical romances I also devoured, sitting in the deep wing chair in my parents' bedroom with a stack of graham crackers by my side. They of the deep cleavages and life-transforming loves. In college I learned how the great heroines diverged from the paperback ones, but it was too late; I knew that love was complicated, self-referential, not the be-all and end-all, but I felt something different. I was like a crisp-looking chocolate with a soft fruity heart.

Now I have a dear friend with a daughter that tender, poignant age who reads the same books I read, leading me to worry. Of course, I do not blame all my romantic turmoils on the syllabus of my youth, and would not ban the great books I misconstrued from households where young women live. In fact, a certain eroticism that can enrich a girl's life rises from a simple-minded reading of the "greats," whispering of the strange, wild realm of sex in the desert of fumbling adolescence. And my friend's daughter—who, after attending my wedding, asked her parents for a bride doll—was old enough to know that something had gone very wrong with my picture-perfect marriage when my husband stopped appearing at my side. Doubtless in this day and age, she also has friends with divorced parents and has glimpsed the limitations of love. So maybe she already understands the decidedly unromantic lessons of *Madame Bovary.* Maybe she's even harboring a tough, useful little kernel of cynicism deep inside. Maybe all childen who have felt at first hand or observed divorce will grow up a little more levelheaded about love than I was.

Certainly divorce can have disastrous effects on children, and I count myself lucky again to have parents still

married after fifty years. But would a kiss from Mr. Rochester have seemed quite so earth-moving had I suspected that romance is a pattern woven in lies? What else—besides his goldenness—would I have noticed when, as a college sophomore, I saw for the first time the boy who became my husband? For, of course, I loved him at first sight.

by
SUSAN
SPANO

NOW YOU KNOW me, at least as well as I know myself—and certainly better than I knew myself when I was my husband's wife, living on a tree-lined street of brownstones in a dicey part of Brooklyn. Around the corner was a restaurant run by Panamanians where we drank *café con leche,* a fish store where the mussels were occasionally off, and a Laundromat where I did our clothes even when it was really his turn. That I managed more than my fair share of the housework didn't bother me though; I was more fastidious, and he was so busy—an actor of considerable accomplishments, even if most of his starring roles were out of town. Nor did I mind our frequent, long separations because I loved his career in the theater, had my own writing and editing work to do, was by nature a solitary soul, and got to visit him for opening nights in interesting places, always wearing fancy new clothes. When he returned after a show had closed, we were tentative, relearning first how to cook together, then how to talk and be together, as well. The old sexual heat between us had cooled—I assumed that's what happened in marriage—replaced with an intense physical sweetness, and he was always telling me he loved me.

At least, that's how I remember it. He was usually cast as a romantic leading man, and was adept at the role; but

in real life he was my very own tall blond lead—I never doubted that. I'm now shocked by how willing to make sacrifices I was (perhaps because female self-sacrifice somehow seemed a necessary adjunct to romantic love), and think that our sex life was a kind of penury. But I can also recall lying in bed with him in the late afternoon, touching his brow, imagining that rays glinted from it, as if from some rare, burnished coin. I should be embarrassed to tell it, but I'm not. Maybe to regret you must love like that, I don't know. Maybe I simply still don't want to let that dreaming girl in her parents' wing chair go.

ONE RAINY March day just after he'd returned from the road, he was in the bedroom lifting weights and preparing for a difficult audition.

I was in the kitchen foraging for lunch.

He came to me and announced that he wasn't going to the audition, which amazed me though I didn't press him for a reason, just let him slip back into the bedroom to think. I stood there while the canned tomato soup bubbled on the stove, realizing something was happening—something big and bad, but I didn't know what. Then, as if directed by a voice outside myself, I followed him, stopping at the edge of the bed where he sat, his shoulders slumped, head down, and asked ever-so-slightly playfully, "Is another shoe going to drop?" But he said nothing, so I left.

He did not reappear for an hour, though I knew he'd used the phone. At last he came into the living room, standing before me this time, and said, "I've been seeing other women."

That is how my life once closed, though it went ach-ingly slow; I pushed hard against the shutting door and he couldn't clear himself away from it so easily either. I'm not sure what he was feeling, though I spent far too much energy trying to figure it out, to my own detriment. Now I've claimed this story as my own; I am its protagonist. I live with myself now, not him. I take care of myself—from my own laundry to my soul.

But I did not take care of myself then. I turned my face directly to the ugliness beneath the calm surface of our lives, sifting through it relentlessly, demanding facts in or-der to correctly reinterpret the past I'd lived through so ignorantly. He provided them like a shamed schoolboy pulling stolen marbles out of his pocket. I learned in a series of lacerating quizzes that he'd had affairs with many of the actresses in his plays, though he'd tidily ended the relationships before coming home; he'd loved just one of them four years ago and might have told me so had she felt the same way about him; I knew them all, because he'd introduced us, even sought my opinion of their acting skills (as if they had to meet my high standards before he'd take them to bed); he used to call me early every night, so that I wouldn't call him later and wonder where he was. During that awful time, I'd wake every morning at three with another question lying beside my head on the pil-low—nightmare monsters that wanted to be fed; some-times I wake to them still.

Betrayal was something completely new to me. It took its power from the fact that the person I loved most had found the worst way to hurt me. "At least I told you," he once said—he was staying temporarily with a male friend and we'd met at a restaurant in the Village (a safe zone) to

talk. *Yes,* I thought, *you are like an abuser who feels better for taking his wife to the emergency ward after beating her up.* I saw what he'd done as abuse for a time, and even attended a meeting for the "co-dependent spouses of alcoholics," since there were no groups for the co-dependent spouses of cheaters. Like some tired old cliché, I riffled through his desk drawers when he was away, checking his old calendars for salient dates and amassing phone numbers, fantasizing about divorce-court dramas and surprise phone calls to his lovers. *Hi, just wanted to tell you I know. Ever hear of sisterhood, you bitch?* And I once even incited him to threaten violence. We'd just come from another futile couples therapy session during which I'd listened to him try to articulate his confusion: He didn't know why he'd slept around, whether we should split up, if he loved me—indeed, what love was. I was very close to ending it and had already met with a lawyer; but I wanted more clarity before I made the decision to divorce, and to be a full player in the drama, if or when the final curtain dropped.

We were on the steep flight of steps that led up to our apartment when I accused him of lying about the latest in his string of women, who clearly loved him since she'd urged him to tell me the truth. And he'd told me, which had to mean that he loved her too, wanted to be with her, not me. Why couldn't he just say so and let me off the hook, show enough courage to be cruel but kind? I stumbled; he reached out to steady me and I knocked him away; he pushed me into the living room, with an arm raised.

"I'm not lying anymore. I *don't* love her," he said.

"Go ahead and hit me," I replied.

And then he started to cry.

I'd forgotten this until just now. I don't know what it means—that he either loved me in his way or didn't love me at all.

Between such episodes, when we both aired ugly parts of ourselves we never knew we had, I spent most of my time loathing myself. My friends queried me gently: *Weren't you a little suspicious? He was an actor, after all. Are you sure you didn't know? How was the sex between you?* (All I can say—then and now—is that I didn't know, and that the sex seemed good enough for me). So, on top of the betrayal, I got to feel ashamed. I got to hate myself, when the rage of Medea would have served me better; but I was ever a stranger to rage.

Easter was coming on during the worst of it, when people in the most wonderful hats lined up outside evangelical churches in Brooklyn storefronts with neon crosses. The cherry blossoms in the Botanical Garden were in bud, and I took to running for hours and miles, pounding out my pain in a season too beautiful for words, a place too ugly and lovely all at once. In the midst of everything I must admit a certain joy and frisson of excitement. *Great people can change their lives at will,* I thought. *I'm not great, but I can let change come, try to embrace it. What will happen to me? What will I become?*

My family and friends and all the green of spring sympathized with me, but my favorite stroke came from a woman on the street in Brooklyn, with three children in

tow. I was running and crying at the same time, and when I passed her she called out, "It's a man. You cryin' cuz of a man." I slowed until she drew a Bible out of her bag, then ran on.

I DID NOT find what I needed in therapy, although I tried dutifully. I could talk until the cows came home, articulating things that were true, for the moment at least. My husband could not talk at all. So there was no real communication. Our brief stint in couples therapy was a stop-gap measure, a way of asserting: *We are trying to work this out*. But I wonder. Possibly he just wanted to be rid of me as compassionately as he knew how, by putting me in the hands of a professional caregiver. I should have heard him when he said that he did not know if he loved me. It's just that he'd said he loved me so many times before. The dark had come so suddenly. I could still close my eyes and imagine day.

So, in an assertively cheerful office with Kleenex boxes strategically placed, we embarked upon what we took to calling "the process," leading where I did not know. But if we cut away the tangled emotional undergrowth, it seemed to me faintly possible that a better, new marriage awaited us; he would have to understand what he had done to me and why, then ask for forgiveness in a deeply felt way; I would have to see if I could forgive him. I started reading self-help books and thinking about psychology for the first time, which led me to a new vision of marriage as a beautiful, intricate machine—like an heirloom ormolu clock—that must be constantly worked on to keep it going, with the help of a therapist. I did not particularly like the idea of admitting a paid third party

into our marriage for the long haul, but the allure of the reconceived marriage was strong; it seemed a worthy substitute for romantic love, which had so let me down. At any rate, I was willing to try.

Of course, part of "the process" required that we both ask why our marriage had gone wrong, or more precisely, what each of us had done that had allowed my husband to take lovers. I approached the question with typical earnestness and self-involvement—for I tended always to turn it back on myself: *What had I done wrong? Had I in some way encouraged him to play around?* Friends noticed this tendency, and perceived it as unhealthy self-blame; given the situation, it seemed obvious to them that my husband was the miscreant, not me. Even my father—my family's Buddha—advised me to forget "the process." "Whatever the hell that is," he said. "Cut him loose right away."

But I knew a few things my father and friends didn't, or at least suspected things I only figured out later. My husband loved me—or once had—else why all the anguish? We'd *both* undervalued the importance of sex in marriage by letting it change and then languish; we should have worked to make it remain a central part of our lives, and he shouldn't have solved the problem in his own way. My penchant for being alone—which has turned out to be a great treasure to me now—had permitted him to seek the society of others. And surely most significant, by casting him in the role of the romantic leading man who'd brought me into his golden aureole by marrying me, I'd failed to see who he really was, weaknesses and all. Frankly, I'd failed to see anything beside myself and my own crippling romantic dream.

These are all good things to know, but I learned them by myself, without the help of a therapist. During sessions with her, she returned constantly to one question: *Why did he tell you about the affair now?* I realized what she was driving at, of course—that he'd done so now because he wanted out. But I couldn't reach that conclusion yet. When I even let myself contemplate it I grew angry at last. He'd told me the truth and sworn never to lie again— great. He was engaged in "the process"—swell. But if what he already knew or was finding out therein was that he wanted a divorce, then he had to say so; I wanted to hear the words from him.

W O M E N are more emotional than men. I hate to generalize, but in my experience this has proven so often the case that I take it for an axiom. What is more, being emotional fills a particular need in many women, filled by many men in a different way. Men do—they play sports, prefer seeing a movie to talking, trek in Patagonia, or at least imagine such adventures; women talk, ruminate, feel. But for me, feeling is itself an adventure, a journey through fearful, turmoiled places, an odyssey or hegira. Along the feeling way, there are tight, dangerous passages where one must decide whether to take a side path down into the valley or carry on. Feeling as far into a crisis as one can requires, like adventure, equal measures of courage and stupidity. I am happy and healthy enough now to be able to look back at the endgame of my marriage with a mixture of pride and amusement. How far along the feeling way I went. However, I would not want to undertake that particular emotional adventure again.

After a month of intensive therapy, my husband rejoined the cast of the play he'd been acting in before he told me about his affairs, though this time the production was booked at a theater in California, a continent away. I could have challenged him not to go, but didn't want my marriage to hang on this particular, relatively mundane issue; he could have given up the play, but wasn't compelled to—a sign I couldn't read at the time, even if it now seems as electric as any in Times Square. Then too, the distance might help, I thought, though the fact that his most recent lover was also in the cast certainly would not. Still, he swore he'd broken off with her and didn't intend to recommence the affair.

She felt differently, and pursued him—on the apparent assumption that it was now morally permissible to do so. But he held fast, even reading me the notes she wrote to him; everything between us was to be open and honest now, so we could see what was left of our relationship. We had marathon telephone conversations full of tears and recriminations, babble and stony silence, kind and hard words. His former lover occasionally tempted him, he admitted, but was chiefly an irritation. He was fully in "the process" now, in a way he hadn't been before.

The truth is that he was in his "process" and I was in mine, the two bound to intersect only one more time. Meanwhile, back in Brooklyn, I was also coming to life; frozen for so many years, the "soul's sap quivered," to paraphrase T. S. Eliot. Doubtless, the poet could not have anticipated that someday his words would be taken to include a newborn interest in sexy lingerie, maniacal exercise, exploratory forays into singles bars, and the relentless

search for willing listeners to tell my story to. I confessed the ugly truth to almost everyone I knew, and even made new friends so that I could tell them too. Revenge partly motivated me, since bruiting my husband's sins seemed a reasonable if inadequate way of getting back at him. But I also experienced the satisfaction of letting others into my life (formerly my husband's sole domain), and of their reciprocation—which came, I'm sure, simply because I'd at last dared to show them how far from perfect my life was. These friends—most of them female, because women make such good friends—are with me now, at the other end of the phone whenever I need them, as they were then.

One day several weeks after he'd left town, my husband had a fantasy that he shared with me about the two of us living in a woodframe cottage in Vermont, with cross-country skis leaning in the corner, spicy smells emanating from the kitchen, a dog by the hearth, and a baby in a highchair. He was very confused. Nonetheless, the vision had a staggering effect on me; I could take or leave Vermont, but the baby clinched it. Of course, I failed to recognize this as simply the postscript to a historical romance, the happily-ever-aftering of a leading lady and man. The moment seemed ripe to get together again, so I bought a ticket to California.

Later I decided that the airlines played a significant part in the termination of my marriage. If I'd sprung for the nine-hundred-dollar ticket that would have gotten me to California immediately, maybe we'd have caught the wave of my husband's feeling. Instead, while I waited for two weeks to leave in order to fly on the cheap, the wave broke.

Of course, I didn't know that when I finally arrived, sidewinded by the balminess and palm trees. I only knew that the reunion wasn't one of the most heightened moments of my life. At the airport we hugged like two logs that had fallen on each other in the forest. He looked strange to me, and not entirely attractive, with his hair oddly combed. But gradually it fell back into its accustomed blond disarray, and I started to know him again. He was the man I'd loved for more than a decade, beginning before he had hair on his chest. He *was* love to me. Never an abstract. Always him.

We argued again when we arrived at the apartment where he was staying, about I can't remember what and it doesn't matter—except that in so doing we fell back into the roles of wronged wife and shamed-but-angry-errant husband. Then he told me about a book he'd just found at a secondhand shop in the neighborhood. Now this strikes me as a ridiculous California cliché—next stop EST, then transcendence. But I was so achingly vulnerable that I listened.

"I recognize myself in it," he said. "It's about becoming a fully sexual being." He smiled sheepishly. "It's called *The Way of the Lover.* Here, I'll read you some of it."

We were sitting at opposite ends of a couch. I felt at once jet-lagged and adrenaline-charged. He began reading a passage about bad relationships, couples who stay together out of fear or guilt. Though tears started dribbling out of my eyes, he ignored them, perhaps because he'd seen me cry so many times before. But on some level I noted his unresponsiveness and filed it away. It was a new development.

It was *the* development. I stayed for two more days, slowly realizing that he wasn't even acting as if he loved me anymore. While there, I cheered at the film *Thelma and Louise*, considered the overtures of a handsome bicyclist I met in a park, saw my husband's play, if only to count the ways the actress who had been his lover was beggared in comparison to me, and felt the sun on my breasts at a nude beach north of town. I suppose, it was my turn to be a California cliché.

The end came with no fanfare, over dinner in a Mexican restaurant. He had a few days off, and the keys to a friend's condo in the mountains. But why he was contemplating taking me there I did not know; I could feel nothing from him; he had finally stopped lying—even on a thespic level.

And so I calmly said (again as if directed by some voice outside myself), "This isn't really working, is it? Don't you think I should go home and file for divorce?"

He cried and wanted to know how I could be so strong. He had no idea how strong I was, though I was beginning to see the full extent of his weakness. I'd been his victim, yet was also forced to be our judge. For some time I thought making me say the words was the worst, most immoral thing he'd done. But he didn't make me say them; I know that now. I'd reached the decision myself, in my own harrowing way.

B U T T H E R E *is* a moral point here. I hesitate to even suggest it, remembering how the eyes of many of my wise, loving friends glaze over at the very mention of *morality*. *Adultery* has much the same effect. But bear with me,

postmoralist thinkers, as I cut to the chase and finally consider the question of right and wrong. For, you see, I tried to work this out through psychology, which helped, but only so far.

For a time, I simply thought that breaking one's marriage vows was wrong, but then therapy helped me realize that marriage has always been and must still be elastic, that it can be refined and even fortified by troubles. Beyond that, I knew something about infidelity myself, having once cheated on a boyfriend. So I was not lily white.

Later, my dear friend with the teenage daughter put a new spin on things for me, though. She loved my husband, partly because simply by marrying him I had told her that she should. And when he betrayed me she wrote him a letter, because she felt betrayed too. In it she said: "It is a fundamental and absolute violence to willfully withhold from anyone the information she would need to make clear and rational choices about the substance and direction of her life. I am so thrown myself when I think of you—how can there suddenly be no you as I thought I knew and valued you—that I can't begin to imagine what it must be like inside Susan's head sometimes."

For a while I rested there, thinking that it is simply immoral to lie—and so hanged my husband. But I have moved on, and am likely to again, incessantly beating back. Now I can understand how my husband got drawn into a lie he was too weak to contain. I don't, however, believe that he didn't know he was hurting me—indeed, I even think he was occasionally blithe about it. This strikes me now as the true heart of the matter. Now I believe that it is immoral to be cruel. No matter how weak

you are, willful cruelty is immoral. There are no excuses. Everyone must, to that extent, be strong.

I SAW MY HUSBAND just two more times after that—once to divide the contents of our apartment and again entirely by chance. I did go back to Brooklyn, file for divorce, and flee, living for a year in the country, because a farmhouse in the northwest corner of Connecticut was offered to me. Can you imagine such luck? Such good friends?

If you have never been in New England in the summer, you cannot know what a Gilead it is, what true therapy there is in long walks beside the Housatonic River with an old dog, a telephone, books of poetry, peonies beside the fence, beets from the garden, and scotch on the rocks. Scotch is a New England thing—regardless, it was a drug I needed.

I convalesced slowly, time after time resisting the urge to call my soon-to-be ex-husband (generally when I'd had one more nip than was truly therapeutic). Before we'd parted, he told me that one of the reasons he hadn't been able to make the decision to divorce was his fear that he'd never see me again, that I would blot him out of my life. This, after all, is what I told him I would do, partly to punish him, and partly because I knew that friendship between us was impossible. I didn't care for him as a friend, I loved him. Now I had to stop loving him; seeing him would only make that harder. I knew many divorced couples who'd actually divorced in a friendly manner or become friends after splitting up; that they could do so amazed me, and seemed a mark of wisdom and maturity.

Maybe, someday, I could be that wise and mature, I thought. But I doubted it, because in my utter withdrawal from my ex-husband something else was going on. I'd thereby given the divorce meaning, made it one of my touchstones.

Toward the end of that first summer I went into Manhattan for the day. Since filing for divorce, I'd taken to tinting my hair and had found a stylist near my ex-therapist's office. I was on the subway heading there, sitting with my nose in a book. The Number One train stopped at Seventy-second Street and the doors opened, then closed. For several minutes nothing happened, so I looked up to see what was wrong.

He was sitting directly across from me, watching me. I felt my face turn red. The doors opened and closed again, as they sometimes do. I stood up.

And I suppose because he didn't know what else to do, he giggled nervously. I could have spat blood at him and damned fate for putting him on that train at that particular moment—I don't know which I hated more.

The doors opened once again. I walked off before they reclosed and the train finally clattered on.

MY FRIENDS look at my life since the end of my marriage and say I've got to be careful, because I'm going to have a hard time opening up to a man, if and when the right one comes along. Perhaps they're right. Perhaps I'm far from healed. I do sometimes still see a tall blond in the street and think briefly that it's my ex-husband. I do sometimes say vile things about him. And I do still have a hard time in the spring.

But I am surer now than ever before that I walked the right road toward my divorce, and that I have nearly let the love I felt for my ex-husband go. However, I don't want to see him again—ever. This is the stamp I put on my divorce, the meaning. I'm no longer afraid that I'd fall for him again if I did (believe me, what I felt on the subway wasn't love). I just don't want him to look into my face and giggle. I want my absence from his life to stand for something—that he was weak and cruel once, and that it was wrong.

By the same token, I don't want to let myself forget that I romanticized him, and in so doing made any true marriage between us impossible. I will always be drawn to romantic love but have learned that outside paperback novels, it's corrosive. Part sex, part makeup and lights, part need. Something to be wary of, to get beyond. In another year or so, I'm going to give my friend's daughter Virginia Woolf and hope that *A Room of One's Own* can still have meaning in her post-feminist world—as it must, for a sexist society cannot be transformed until women's hearts are.

These I take to be the lessons of my divorce, not of my marriage. I wonder if I ever really was married in the truest sense, and now take the much-adjusted ormolu clock model of matrimony to be the best. It is given to some couples to learn and grow in wedlock. "The faults of married people continually spur up each of them, hour by hour, to do better and to meet and love upon a higher ground," Robert Louis Stevenson wrote.

It was given to me to learn and grow in divorce.

A FAILED DIVORCE

BY *Alix Kates Shulman*

$\mathcal{W}$HY ARE terminated marriages called "failed," as though endurance were all? Perhaps a marriage, however brief, ought to be counted a success if it achieves the purpose for which it was undertaken—whether sexual heaven, freedom from parental rule, financial benefit, legitimization of children, companionship, citizenship. By this measure, some of the most successful marriages I know (including my first one) have been short. Of course, a marriage can also bring unexpected dire consequences: miserable sex, bondage, financial dependence or ruin, wretched children, boredom, terror. Such outcomes, to my mind, would damn a marriage as failed even (or particularly) if it should last unto death.

Similarly, a divorce can accomplish various ends and perhaps ought also to be counted a failure or success in light of the consequences. So a divorce that redeemed a

decent marriage before it failed or gave a proper burial to a putrefying one might be regarded as successful, while one that tormented the parties long after the final papers were signed might well be deemed a failure. Of my own two divorces, one was successful, one failed. The successful one was short, snappy, and to the point; the other one was drawn out, bitter, and messy—in these respects resembling the marriages they ended.

WHAT I EXPECTED

In the world of suburban Cleveland, Ohio, where I grew up in the 1930s and 1940s, any marriage that lasted less than forever was judged a failure and any divorce a disgrace. Divorce was so unacceptable that my friend Lydia announced that her father had died at Pearl Harbor rather than admit (as my mother later told me) that her parents had been divorced. In contrast, when the father of Cecily, another classmate, really did die (of heart failure), his daughter easily, if tearfully, acknowledged the truth. Not so Harriet, who moved from New York to Cleveland in junior high with her divorced mother. Sophisticated, and attractive enough to model for a local department store, Harriet's mother was presumed to be turning tricks whenever she had a date, a charge that rubbed off on innocent Harriet to ruin her social life. Where I grew up, divorced plus pretty equaled slut.

No doubt Harriet's mother had another view. In the larger world, where there were more possibilities than vamp or victim, it wasn't divorce per se that mattered, but who left whom and with how many children. In Hollywood movies of the time, divorcées were as often gay,

glamorous, and independent as they were pathetic, pitiful, and defeated. Rita Hayworth, Liz Taylor, Eddie Cantor, and Artie Shaw were renowned for the number of times they married and divorced—and proud of it. On the other hand, in books, abandoned women sometimes killed themselves.

The incidence of divorce in the United States which, like that of marriage, had been gradually increasing since the turn of the century, blipped upward abruptly just after World War II: all those forty-eight-hour-pass romances with uniformed heroes that couldn't survive the disappointment of civvies; the fatal strain of separation; international hanky-panky. (This, despite the fact that in most states, to obtain a divorce you had to prove adultery, abandonment, or some sordid crime—unless you took off half a year of your life to establish residence in Reno, or flew to another country if you could afford it.) But whatever the statistics, in white middle-class Cleveland Heights, divorce remained a scandal. The only thing worse, we believed, was never to marry at all—like "Aunt" Esther, the sister-in-law of my uncle Harry, a sad, skinny Gal Friday with her hair in a bun who sat quietly at our family gatherings, as embarrassing as a sixth finger. So much worse, in fact, that years later a friend confessed to me that she'd invented a husband for herself and kept in her wallet a false chronology of her life that could accommodate a husband and a divorce. Divorce was a clear admission of failure, but not to marry was catastrophe.

I shared these views but also had glimmerings of others. My mother, who in the 1930s worked as a designer of history projects for the WPA, had several divorced friends, all more interesting than the married moms. While

155

~

by
ALIX
KATES
SHULMAN

squarely centered in the striving suburban middle class, my mother became involved through her work with Cleveland's bohemian set: artists, intellectuals, musicians, and dancers who divorced as unselfconsciously as they undressed. Of her two best friends (in turn, mothers of two of my best friends, until third grade), one, a modern dancer whose artist husband died young, kept on marrying and divorcing and remarrying until she reached her fifth husband, and the other, a fellow historian at the WPA and wife of a celebrated violinist, divorced her husband when their daughter was eight and moved to the capital where, in the wartime boom, she developed a successful import-export business and remained confidently single. My mother's boss, a deep-voiced woman named Mary ("Lefty") Warner, with a powerful stride, broad smile, cropped brown hair she wore slicked straight back in a ducktail, and the kindest eyes I've ever seen, shared a house with her vivacious long-haired lover, Andrea Garrison, and Andrea's two teenage children, Danny and Ellen, all handsome, rangy redheads. That Andrea and Lefty were lovers seemed less remarkable to me than that Andrea was divorced, rendering her children pitifully fatherless. The spirited parties at their house, where my parents were the token straights, were—and remain—high points of my childhood: Andrea in flowing chiffon, Lefty in tailored slacks and shirt; animated debates, witty chatter, music, forbidden jokes, booze. Except for my four doting aunts, Lefty was quite my favorite grown-up. I am still grateful for her flattering attentions to me, as if I were an adult, and her patient expectation that I learn to strip all the way down to the white bone the delicious spare ribs she barbecued to a perfect crisp in their fireplace. But the

Garrisons, despite their flaming hair, are to this day a cipher to me. I cannot recall them without the embarrassment I always felt seeing Danny and Ellen fatherless, stripped of their birthright by divorce. That was the image that remained after my mother left her job and they vanished from our lives.

WHAT I SAW

Happily, my parents were as permanently coupled as a pair of gulls. (They are still married, at eighty-seven and ninety-three.) Alone of seven siblings (five sisters, two brothers), my mother maintained a neat nuclear family all her life, though not quite as neat as it appeared: When her brother's wife died in childbirth, my parents adopted the baby and promptly created me, so that a brother eleven months my senior was waiting to greet me when I arrived. In the early years, his father (my uncle), who lived in Pennsylvania and whom we called Papadear, paid us annual visits—until he remarried and stopped coming. One of my mother's sisters ran off to Chicago to live with a married man; one was falsely accused of murdering her husband who blew out his brains; one left her husband behind to travel solo around the world on a tramp steamer; and one, local radio's "Singing Lady," also died in childbirth, giving me a second brother for a few years, until his father remarried and took him back. I remember the wrenching day my uncle came to take away my baby brother, still see the once jolly, plump six-year-old stretch out his dimpled arms and wail for my mother, who stood weeping beside me until long after the black coupe had disappeared over Bradford Hill. From that day on I knew

the suffering of orphans, the havoc of a broken family, whether by death or divorce, which as far as I could see came to much the same thing. Soon my little brother became just another cousin, thin and sad. Of all seven siblings in my mother's family, only three had children and only one, my mother, was actually able to raise them. Still, as a child in love with both my parents, I unquestioningly assumed the inevitability, superiority, and necessity of the nuclear family. The families of both my parents were touched repeatedly by death and devastation—but never by divorce, which in some ways seemed worse, because unknown.

And yet, when I left Cleveland for New York at twenty, part of what I fled was that neat, predictable suburban sentence of coupledom, by which one's life seemed permanently settled at twenty-two. Having enjoyed in college a secret affair with a married professor my father's age, a father of five, I was already somewhat cynical about marriage. Not that I would eschew it myself—this was 1953, after all, and I was a woman. But with such counterexamples before me as my mother's glamorous friends and my wayward aunts, I determined to marry only on my own terms. Which meant that divorce, however unacceptable to the children of Cleveland Heights, must be my secret failsafe, my emergency exit. As necessary to a decent life as the possibility of abortion.

(Recently, I discovered in my parents' attic a folder of my freshman themes, from forty years ago. One is on the Salem witch trials; another, entitled "The Great Illusion," presents the following thesis: "Because of our modern American way of life, mate selection must result from intelligent analysis, rather than from romantic love, if suc-

cessful marriages are to ensue." Evidently, as a college freshman I was already leery of the consequences of losing one's heart, already practical about marriage.)

WHAT I DID

In New York, resenting the confines of dorm life (back when all dorms were single-sex, and curfews for women were strictly enforced), I married a fellow grad student before a year was out. I married partly for the privileges of adulthood, which meant freedom from external control, both parental and *in loco parentis,* partly for the fun of it, and partly to get the damned thing over with. Certainly not in order to settle down. Though I changed my name to my husband's and took a job to support us, it felt less like marriage than going steady—plus cohabitation and sanctioned sex. No wonder that five years later, at the age of twenty-five, I took five days of vacation time to fly to Ciudad Juárez, Mexico, and file papers for the first divorce in my family. When I untied the satin ribbon to read the document, the grounds, printed with a flourish on the crisp parchment paper, were specified as *"incompatible de temperamento"*—incompatibility of temperament, which, considering that the only grounds for divorce in New York was adultery, sounded rather frivolous. However, to my father, an upright lawyer, it was important that I avoid the scandal of a New York divorce (even though by then I had already begun to live with my next husband, who was awaiting *his* first divorce), and I was happy to oblige: I'd never been to Mexico.

That divorce seemed to me little more than a useful piece of paper, like the marriage that had led to it:

practical, even necessary, but slightly absurd. (Why should a paper determine one's living arrangements?) Once it was final, I never saw my ex-husband again, nor did we speak until, on the eve of his second marriage, he phoned to ask if I'd be willing to submit to an Orthodox Jewish divorce to satisfy his new wife's family. Apparently each jurisdiction required its own particular form of hocus-pocus; but whether the magic words appeared in English, Spanish, or Aramaic, sanctified by a judge, *abogado,* or *rebbe* made no difference to me, as long as they left me free. Again, I gladly obliged.

SURPRISE

My second marriage, to a man who became the father of my children, was another matter entirely. This was far more serious than going steady. Although I entered into it in the same carefree spirit as I had my first, dashing down to City Hall on my lunch hour and returning to work in the afternoon, once I quit my job to have children, nothing else about this marriage was remotely like the other. Living in a Manhattan apartment beyond my means with two babies, no income, and a philandering husband, I suddenly found myself as vulnerable and dependent as any traditional suburban housewife. No longer could I think of marriage as a lark, a pleasure, or a convenience; now it was the structure and lifeline of my children's lives. The debate about marriage has long been confounded by the fact that for some marriage is a prison and divorce a relief, while for others, particularly women with young children, marriage is a protection and divorce (given the virtual impossibility of enforcing child support) an impover-

ishment; and although the various reforms of marriage laws throughout this century have frequently operated to privilege the married, the institution has had such a complex history that what feels oppressive to one woman feels like security to another, depending not only on the class, occupation, and relative power of the people involved but on their personal relations, ambitions, and feelings. Once I had children, divorce, which I had always held in reserve to bail me out, turned from failsafe to threat; if my marriage came to an end, my children could be left fatherless, penniless, and bereft, fulfilling the worst anxieties of my childhood. The mother of my school friend Harriet suddenly flashed before me, a perilous shooting star.

When I realized the seriousness of my situation, I scrambled to alleviate my dependence and strengthen my position. I searched for freelance work I could do at home, took a sweet lover of my own, and, discovering a newly reborn feminism, embraced the movement that, with its dazzling ideas and expanding numbers, enabled me both to understand and to fight my predicament.

This is not the place to detail the profound influence of feminist ideas on my perception of marriage, motherhood, and divorce—ideas that transformed me from an anxious, homebound observer into an active shaper of my own life. But as part of my transformation, a decade into my second marriage, I drew up a marriage agreement by which my husband and I committed ourselves to equal responsibility for child care and housework. In 1969 when I wrote the agreement, the idea of equality in marriage was so outrageous that the piece appeared in many magazines including *New York, Ms., Redbook,* and *Life,* which gave it a six-page spread, and was attacked by Norman

Mailer, S. I. Hayakawa, and Russell Baker, among others. But, like the world that rests on the back of a turtle, at bottom, our agreement, for all the hoopla surrounding it, rested on nothing more substantial than our own floating goodwill. When that failed, we separated.

THE TRIAL

Our children were nine and eleven when my husband, claiming to be off for a two-week vacation, disappeared out West, leaving no forwarding address. At first I was relieved to be free of the constant tension and basked in the unexpected calm. But when the weeks stretched into months, with only an occasional call from a distant pay phone, and the children, as in my worst childhood fears, grew despondent and withdrawn, I became increasingly frantic. I had imagined a civilized divorce, with my husband ensconced somewhere across town, participating equally in child care, or at least seeing the children on alternate weekends. But he had something else in mind. Vacillating between remaining indefinitely in California with his lover and returning to us in New York, he made it clear that unless I took him back (or moved us all to California) the children might hardly ever see him.

Though I longed to be free of that husband, I was afraid to sacrifice our children, who were bewildered and betrayed by his disappearance and sinking daily before my eyes. I remember the exact moment I was stricken with a grim understanding of the stakes. The children, badly in need of cheering, had perked up visibly when I promised to take them one Sunday to the Bronx Zoo for the members' opening of an elaborate new birdhouse. Arranging

our weekend outings had long been their father's province, but, determined to be mother and father at once, I packed us a picnic lunch, and off we set. My forced smiles turned hopeful when, emerging into the dazzling light from a gloomy hour-long subway ride, the children dashed up the stairs before me, carrying my sagging spirits with them. Which only made it harder when, fifteen minutes later, milling around the birdhouse entrance with a large crowd of animated families all waiting to get inside, I saw how lost and sad my children seemed. Suddenly I knew what it meant for a family to be broken. Broken, damaged, and—the word circled like a buzzard over their heads—*fatherless,* that most potent dread of my youth. Seeing my unhappy children watching the scores of happy ones sitting atop their fathers' shoulders or clasping each of their parents' hands, and remembering my own anguish as my baby brother was wrenched from my mother's arms, I feared it wouldn't be long before my childhood terrors smothered my adult desires.

If I'd known how resilient children of divorce can sometimes be or that divorced parents would be commonplace in the next generation, I might have held out. But I was a creature of my generation, not the next, and felt acutely my children's present suffering and looming catastrophe. I tried to be strong for them, but as the months went by, seeing them slide steadily into the pit of depression I slid down after them. Finally, the pain became unbearable, and less than a year after it started I gave up in defeat and summoned their father back.

When he returned, at first we were flooded with false expectations and blissful relief; our sex was never more passionate. But before long the rejoicing fizzled into

resignation, and we reverted to what we were: a family of conflicts, crises, holidays, birthdays, and secrets. Without children we would certainly have divorced then, parting graciously and dividing our property neatly in half, as my first husband and I had done. Instead, until the children were grown, we arranged to spend as little time as possible together and still remain in a nominal marriage that was really divorce by other means.

WHAT I LEARNED

A decade later, when our arrangement finally disintegrated after twenty-five years of marriage (volatile years in which, fortunately, a lot more than mere marriage was going on in our lives), enough bitterness had collected that my second divorce was the customary nasty mess, the opposite of my first one. It dragged on for years instead of weeks, produced intransigence instead of compromise, exacted heartache and malice in place of regret, and cost half a fortune instead of the price of a trip to Mexico. By then our children, for whose sake we'd stayed tied, had gone off to college, but neither their age nor their absence protected them from the usual anguish and grief.

Now another decade has passed since our final papers were signed, and each of us has another mate. Still, my ex-husband can barely speak to me without an edge in his voice—which probably means our divorce is not yet final. How much longer will it take? A witty woman I know says that when lovers break up, getting over it takes about as long again as the pair were in love. But when children are involved, I wonder if the breakup of parents may not instead take about as long to get over as the age of the

children when the breach occurred. Ours were four and six when my husband began wandering, nine and eleven when we first split up, nineteen and twenty-one when we filed for divorce. That means we may still have some time to go before all the acrimony has been dissipated and our accounts are fully settled (though, judging by how dispassionately I am able now to reflect on divorce, I suspect it is nearing closure). It may also mean—as our children have begun to suggest—that we could have divorced much sooner, that in the end it's unclear which is worse, a failed marriage or a failed divorce.

DIVORCE
AS A SPECTATOR
SPORT

BY *Francine Prose*

SOME TIME ago, a close friend arrived almost an hour late to a dinner party. She explained that while dressing to go out, she'd had the television on for company. And when an announcer promised an update on Roseanne and Tom Arnold's raucous ongoing marital breakup, my friend found herself sinking into her chair, quite unable to move until she'd heard what unscripted disruptive drama took place that day on the *Roseanne* set.

My friend is a poet and literary critic, known for her caustic wit, her low tolerance for banality, for sloppy thinking and sentimentality. But no one at the dinner table expressed the faintest surprise that this bright star of High Culture should have been pinned to her chair by a chance to metaphorically get down and mud wrestle with the Arnolds.

A brief silence fell on the dinner guests as we each tried to imagine what new and thrillingly tasteless celebrity psychodrama had caused our friend to come too late for the soup and nearly miss the main course. Then softly, almost reverentially, someone asked, "What happened with Tom and Roseanne?"

Divorce has always been a subject of passionate public and private interest. One can't help feeling that the cows in the fields and the seals on the rock turn their heads and take notice when the bull (or the bull seal) exchanges one mate for another. Curiosity about divorce is as old as divorce itself, which, as we know, the Old Testament and then the Koran made so blissfully easy (for men). The response to Henry VIII's divorce resulted in nothing less than the radical redesign of European history. When Dickens left the mother of his small army of children for a pretty young actress, readers on at least two continents reeled from the horror and shock, and though the divorces of Colette and Isak Dinesen may have generated less outrage, they were still the talk of Paris and colonial Kenya.

But for as long as the Church—and then Victorian social mores—had a tight repressive hold on popular culture and moral imagination, divorce was still mostly whispered about, tinged with secrecy and scandal. But now the stops are out, so to speak. Divorce is front-page news, and never has our hunger for the gritty facts been so insatiable and exquisite. In France, we hear, there is a new magazine called—what else?—*Divorce*. Demanding every intimate detail, we exhort our reporters and cameras to follow the warring couple, interrogate and eavesdrop, to bring us

167

by
FRANCINE
PROSE

complete and unsparing reports from the bedrooms and the courtrooms.

Consider, for example, how Woody Allen's break with Mia Farrow generated more interest and discussion than most political campaigns. Everyone had an opinion, and debates became so heated that they often degenerated into personal attacks, into each sex accusing the other of the same bad attitudes and blind spots that are invariably recycled as live ammunition in each new flare-up of gender war.

As celebrity divorce grows increasingly more lurid and contentious, marital mishap has become a sort of spectator sport at which we can avidly follow the play-by-play. Centuries after the Romans abandoned their Colosseum, gruesome public divorce is what we have to take the place of bloodthirsty gladiatorial combat. And what's interesting to consider is what this curiosity means: What does our fascination with divorce say about us as a society, about our individual lives, our moral judgment, our marriages, our feminist sympathies, our hopes and fears, our integrity, our loyalties to ourselves, our spouses, our friends?

THERE'S ALMOST no point stating the obvious: that our society no longer respects or values personal privacy, that everything is seen as commerce, available information, every tiny fact accessible, the public's right to know. To want to keep one's own counsel and protect certain aspects of our lives from exposure is to risk being seen as neurotically withholding, or as being "in denial." Public figures who insist (often futilely) on their privacy are often described as "reclusive."

Meanwhile, confession is exalted not only as a therapeutic tool, an essential step toward recovery, but is assigned much the same value that used to be reserved for charity and good works. (One thinks of the celebrities wildly applauded and congratulated for bravely coming forward with accounts of personal crises that encourage fellow-sufferers to confront—and one hopes, solve—similar problems.)

And yet it seems to me that our voracious hunger to know about divorce far exceeds the parameters of what we've come to feel entitled to read in the newspaper or watch on tabloid TV. It's far more complex than the question of changing media attitudes, of the ways that the old rules have been reformulated by the gossip or self-help industries. It may well be that our desire to know about divorce—to watch it, as if it were indeed a spectator sport—is as innate as reflex or instinct, and as deep as our most profound feelings about love, sex, and death.

TO THINK ABOUT the meaning of our curiosity about divorce is to examine the nature of curiosity itself. The fact that we want so badly to know, and that certain privileged information seems so titillating and delicious, is a sign of how profoundly it touches on our deepest hopes and fears. Trivial subjects are never taboo. But the great mysteries often are—in particular, the endlessly fascinating and (despite the new climate of "openness") still mysterious subjects of sex and death.

Partly what intrigues us about divorce is its intimations of secrets concerning sex and death, or at least the death of love. Divorce represents the dark side of the mating instinct—an instinct about which we will never lose

our inquisitiveness and interest. Even in highly civilized, amicable separations, we intuit that the fact of divorce hints at some serious discord, misunderstanding or cruelty, sexual boredom or fatigue. It may be that couples do split up over the question of who does the laundry and dishes, but the helping professions are quick to remind us that something more important is usually at stake.

Perhaps that's the reason why nothing whets our appetite quite so much as the dissolution of those marriages that had seemed, on the surface, perfect. The unpleasant secrets, we feel, were more hidden, more closely guarded, buried deeper and therefore more valuable and more satisfying to exhume.

What we most yearn to know about divorce is who did what to whom (or stopped doing what to whom), who fell in love with someone else, who got violent, abused this or that substance, or in some way proved so difficult or impossible to live with that whatever passion or affinity had drawn the couple together began to seem like a big mistake, a costly *folie à deux*.

Years ago, the reasons (or the stated reasons) for divorce were relatively simple and straightforward: A man had tired of his wife and perhaps found someone new—or learned that his wife had dared to look at, possibly even found, someone new. But now that women have the legal and social option of initiating divorce, the possible reasons for ending a marriage have multiplied and our speculative interest has also grown to match the endless variant imaginary scenarios that divorce brings to mind.

Our hunger to know the facts of divorce is connected to our drive to understand love—and the opposite sex. Often, as I hear my friends talking about the breakup of

people we know or of stars we've never met, I'm reminded of how, as young girls, we got together and jabbered fervidly in search of some clue to the puzzle of why people fall in love—and, by implication, the riddle of how to make boys fall in love with us.

What we're asking when we ask about divorce is how people fall out of love. And if, as girls, we searched for answers about what boys really wanted, what we're asking, as adults, is what men and women *don't* want—what causes them to take a stand, to draw the line, to divorce.

The questions we pose, the information we seek from accounts of private or public divorce, are strikingly like the things we ask about death, the ways in which we read obituaries. How and why did it happen? What was it like? Was it accidental or inevitable? Who, if anyone, was at fault?

And what we're really asking is not strictly about the deceased or the divorcing couple. If we're honest, we're obliged to admit that our real (or at least partial) subject is ourselves. We may be seeking reassurance that the dead and the divorced were not like us—that they did reckless things that we would never do, smoked or drank, forgot to exercise, had unsafe sex, cheated on their spouses—so that the tragic thing that happened to them cannot possibly happen to us.

Alternately, we may realize that they are very much like us, and that what has befallen them is certainly (in the case of death) or possibly (with divorce) in our own futures (or already in our pasts). In which case, what we're asking is: What exactly was it like? How protracted was it? How painful? Was it like *my* divorce, like what happened to me? How did they get through it, and recover—or not?

Obviously, the questions we ask and the way in which we ask them have much to do with our own domestic situations (whether we're married, divorced, or single), with the health of our romantic relationships, and with our basic feelings about the institution of marriage. I've noticed, for example, that a number of my gay male friends are often more enthralled, disappointed, and horrified than I am by the details of divorce; quite a few seem to hold a sweetly romanticized vision of heterosexual marriage, a view mostly unavailable to straight men and women who have, through bitter experience, exchanged that idyllic notion for a healthy cynicism which allows them to be continually surprised (as I am) when a marriage works out.

Those who have already been divorced may find in the news of high- or low-profile divorce a reassuring sense of solidarity and camaraderie. Especially for the newly divorced, whose memories are still fresh and often wounding, each new public breakup may serve as a mirror for their own experience, a glass in which they can see yet another couple joining the legions of those who have been through it. Meanwhile the much-divorced and the determinedly single may see each divorce as confirmation of the statistically demonstrable fact that marriage is a lousy idea, hopelessly doomed from the start, with a history of disaster going all the way back to the Garden of Eden. Men and women, such cynics say, were not created, biologically or psychologically, to live together for very long in anything remotely resembling monogamous harmony.

I CAN REMEMBER intervals in my life when I found myself living with a man whom I had ceased to love and no longer wanted to live with, but whom—because

of my own laziness, inertia, and lack of sufficiently powerful motivation—I was unable to leave. In some cases, it
took me a very long time to realize or admit to myself that
I wanted to be on my own.

Perhaps what should have tipped me off was the puz-
zling fact that whenever I heard that friends (or even celebrities) were splitting up, I was suffused with vague
inchoate yearning and with something like the jealousy I
imagine prisoners experience on learning that one of their
jailmates has made a successful escape. I followed accounts
of divorce almost as if I were trying to comprehend a set
of how-to instructions: Who announced he or she was
leaving? What exactly was said? How much commotion
ensued? How long did it take before they were—sepa-
rately—happy again?

Conversely, there were times when, in the throes of an
unhappy love affair or just after a romance had ended, I
was drawn to stories of divorce much as the newly diag-
nosed collect optimistic anecdotes about intrepid long-
term survivors of life-threatening illnesses. At such times,
many of the greatest heroines of literature and history
(again, Isak Dinesen and Colette) were reduced in my
own damaged mind and heart to exemplars of women
who had endured rocky marriages, painful divorces—and
not only survived, but prevailed.

As I write this, at this point in my life, my situation
seems quite different. My husband and I have been together happily (knock on wood) for almost twenty years.
And though I know that there are many divorced men
and women who once beguiled themselves with the same
naive fantasies, my bet is that it will be death (and not
divorce) that will finally divide us.

Now when I hear accounts of divorce, I feel much the same sinking dread with which I react to news of untimely illness and death. I've become one of those who watch spectator divorce for reassurance that my husband and I are not at all like that warring couple: that there's not a chance we're making Roseanne and Tom Arnold's mistakes.

Not long ago, we visited with a friend in the midst of a divorce as seemingly lacking in rancor as divorce can conceivably be. Normally a sympathetic, soft-spoken man whom friends call in tears when their old dogs must be put to sleep or when their pipes have frozen and burst in the dead of winter, my husband began asking our friend a series of questions so personal and pointed, so oddly harsh and so intent on assigning guilt and blame that the tension in the room mounted dismayingly until at last our friend laughed and wisely said, "Come on, would you relax? It's not going to happen to you!" And I have to admit that it pleased me to hear that my husband was so threatened and upset by the idea that a couple—not unlike ourselves—could have decided to call it quits.

What makes it all the more complicated—especially when it's friends who are divorcing—is when our response to the separation moves beyond the realm of personal prayer (Please don't let this happen to us) and into the realm of moral or quasi-moral judgment. In such cases we're quick (often too quick) to decide who the guilty party is and who has been grievously wronged. We recreate, in ourselves, miniature Family Courts and get to play judge and juror.

This is often what makes celebrity divorce so much like an athletic event, a football game, a tennis match, or

prizefight. We choose our favorite players and cheer them on, often quite rabidly, championing their cause against those fools who are deluded or stupid enough to root for the opposite side.

Once again, personal projection comes into play and may interfere with the higher principles of strict jurisprudence. Consequently, it comes as less than a shock that our sympathies in these cases so often seem gender-determined.

Surely there are many men who secretly suspected that those who failed to see, say, Woody Allen's point of view were mostly women whose instinctively clear understanding of passion, love, and sex had been permanently clouded by a murky fog of life-denying feminism. But the truth is that many women know from harsh experience (or at least from a friend's harsh experience) what it's like to see a man wake up one day and suddenly realize that he himself will magically cease to age if he sleeps with a younger woman.

When a couple breaks up, the men in their circle of friends may express considerable shock that the wife could have given up such a wonderful, thoughtful guy, while the women may be equally amazed that the wife could have patiently endured the bragging egomaniacal bully for as long as she did. And certainly the media are not unaware of this tendency to choose sides. Editors and producers know that the gender conflict simmering away beneath the deceptively placid surface of our daily lives will boil over reliably in response to well-publicized divorces; the sex war is what gives such stories their heat, their currency, and the staying power that keeps them on our front pages and TV screens long after the quarrelsome couple

itself grows bored with its own complaints and accusations.

Again, it's more complicated when the divorcing couple are friends—that is, when we've long believed that both members of the couple are friends we value and cherish equally. It's well known that despite our most heartfelt resolve, we are frequently forced to choose sides. In such cases, our harmless little game of domestic court judge-and-jury takes on graver consequences: a friendship or, in many instances, two friendships are at stake.

What's disturbing is how frequently our sense of morality, justice, and fair play is subordinated to other, more shallow (or perhaps just more visceral) concerns. Though we may know beyond any doubt that the husband or wife was the innocent—or the guilty—party, we still may be chagrined to discover that we are drawn to stay friends with the one who amuses us more, the one whom we find more interesting: the one we simply like better, regardless of his or her sins against the aggrieved spouse.

It's happened to me more often than I'd choose to admit, and it's always painful—but in a way, a welcome reminder that I'm less high-minded and fair than I might wish to imagine. But isn't this also a part of what it means to be human? We're complicated, unruly, and susceptible when our hearts overrule our brains, when our instincts win out against what we call our "better instincts."

Perhaps that's something to consider when we sink into our chairs and watch Tom Arnold inform the cameras how much he still loves Roseanne, or Woody Allen tell a barrage of flashbulbs that he never molested his children. It's theater, it's show biz: Mad Max on the information superhighway. It's gladiatorial combat—but real blood's

being spilled, even if Roseanne and Tom are inventing the whole thing for publicity and will reconcile in time for tomorrow's *Entertainment Tonight*.

Someone is almost always in pain just beneath the endlessly fascinating surface of public divorce. And yet for many reasons, some good, some bad—but all equally basic to our human nature and therefore comprehensible—we can't stop ourselves from watching the combatants flail away, each of us a Roman emperor or empress, smiling or frowning, applauding or hissing, turning our thumbs up or down.

by
FRANCINE
PROSE

IN THE
COUNTRY OF DIVORCE

Confessions of a Soon-To-Be-Divorcée

BY *Daphne Merkin*

1. THE LAY OF THE LAND

Who could know it would be this way—that you enter
the country of divorce at your own peril and leave it a
changed person? (If and when you leave: Be prepared to
stay awhile; bring plenty of clean underwear and reading
matter; but most of all, bring lots of cash.) Who could
know, given the fact that divorce rolls so trippingly off the
tip of the cultural tongue these days—everyone's doing
it, at least one out of two couples—that you'd think it
would be easy, or at least not all that hard.

Well, think again. The breakup of a marriage, Ameri-
can-style—especially if there's a child involved—is more
in the spirit of war than you'd believe possible of a negoti-
ation involving two people who once slept side by side.
Amiable instances are rumored to exist, although I have

personally yet to encounter one. It's a rough sport, this divorcing game, and the financial bloodletting is not the worst of it. I realize that each person's experience is unique, but what I've discovered these past three long— *very* long—years is that a process that began in dire seriousness gradually took on, somewhere into the second year when my exhusband-to-be and I sat for hours in a shabby courtroom with peeling walls while our lawyers chatted and the judge listened to other cases, an atmosphere of the surreal. What was I doing here, in a near-empty room dominated by an American flag and a feeling of grim supplication? (Most divorces don't get as far as a courtroom, but once they do you're placing your fate in the hands of what you better hope will be justice.) And how would I ever get out?

In our beginnings are our ends, only in some of our cases the beginnings never get off the ground. I got married in a sea of doubts, a thicket of anxieties—pick whichever metaphor of turmoil you prefer, and it would apply—and although I suppose for some reluctant brides the institution of matrimony in itself exerts a certain calming influence, in my case I remained a reluctant bride from first to last. I say none of this happily, but it seems to me that it's important to tell the truth about one's own circumstances if one is to shed any light at all. My marriage had its besetting problems, yet I've come to think that what distinguishes a marriage which lasts from one that doesn't isn't how good or bad the union in question is but how tolerable the partners find it to be. We all know of atrocious marriages that continue to drip, Jackson Pollock–like, across the canvas of life until the death of one of the spouses, and of wobbly but not inherently

hopeless ones that topple over before you can say Raoul Felder.

What I'm trying to suggest is that there's some sort of psychic bartering that goes on within most enduring marriages—he's a bore at dinner parties, but he pays for the clothes and the shrink, or she's a bitch most of the time and still hasn't learned how to cook, but she looks great on his arm—that doesn't get articulated in public, because it's not in anyone's interest to do so. The great Marxist theoreticians notwithstanding, most cultures are profoundly conservative in nature. And marriage, however it gets reconfigured from time to time, is indubitably part of the proven way of doing things: It works, more or less; besides which, no one's figured out a better way of ensuring that the male of the human species sits down to breakfast with the female on an ongoing basis.

This, at any rate, is how I've come to see it, over in the muddy marshes of Divorce Country where I've gotten bogged down: Marriage is a complex, partial satisfaction of myriad needs—sexual, romantic, and economic. The institution varies so radically from one couple to the next as to lack all criterion of the "normative." There are those spouses who function with an almost claustrophobic quality of togetherness; others who prefer to live in different cities. But somewhere along the way, no matter what a particular marriage looks like from the outside in, the two people involved have to feel comfortable with how their respective sides of the equation tally. Contrary to advice-column wisdom, which has it that the small conflicts are what eventually do a marriage in, it is my belief that the big conflicts—clashing notions of intimacy, say, rather than tension over putting caps on toothpaste tubes—are what

land two people in real trouble. I, for instance, married a man who left me feeling lonely not because he wasn't home but because he *was*. I found myself circling him nervously, my troth plighted to this alien presence plopped down in the middle of first my one-bedroom and then our three-bedroom apartment, until the day came when I stuffed two suitcases full of courage and ran for the hills. I felt like one of the von Trapp family at the end of *The Sound of Music*, scrambling over the mountains that linked neutral Switzerland to Nazi Austria; I didn't know if I'd survive the journey, but I knew staying where I was would doom me to a worse fate than the one which lay ahead.

181

by

DAPHNE

MERKIN

2. CROSSING THE BORDER

I am lying in bed at two, three in the morning. My one-and-a-half-year-old daughter is asleep in her crib in her room with its lovingly chosen toys and stenciled border of pastel-colored ducklings. I have watched TV, read a sprinkling of magazines, and still I cannot fall asleep due to the anxiety that clutches at my chest. I begin making lists in my head, dividing categories into subcategories— an activity that has often soothed me in the past: How many divorced women do I know? Divorced women with children? Divorced women without children? Divorced women who have remarried? Failed to remarry? How long do you have to have been married before you get divorced for it to look like you've given it the old college try and aren't a complete failure? (If I stretch things, and include the months my husband refused to move out of the apartment and slept on a chaise longue in the living

room, it just makes the three-year mark. Which means I've been getting divorced as long as I've been married.) I look up at the ceiling and start enumerating my virtues as a marital partner for the benefit of the Great Judge in the sky: long legs, good hair, intelligence, wit, empathy, and erratic kindness. He shakes his head at me, and in my heart of hearts I know he recognizes that I am an inadequate person. Why else would I be getting a divorce?

3. TRAVEL TIPS
FOR FIRST-TIME VISITORS

Divorce is a country that doesn't recognize the high road; once you enter it, be prepared to put aside any mainland principles about decency and fairness. I'm on my second lawyer—third, if you count the lawyer I went to for several meetings before I decided she would prove too expensive. The next lawyer I saw was a partner in a less prominent firm; he was a softhearted, perennially distracted sort who I think I chose because he made me feel less guilty about standing up for myself. (My guilt had much to do with the fact that it was I who initiated divorce proceedings; the fact that my husband immediately retaliated by suing for sole custody of our daughter should have gone a long way toward assuaging that guilt, but strangely did not.) I had been told that this lawyer was "good for women"—and he did, indeed, seem to harbor little animus against either sex. But he also seemed to expend minimal energy on my behalf, and as the months went by and my phone calls went unreturned and my husband continued to live in our apartment *even though I had already filed*

for divorce, loudly finding fault with my every move as a mother (his specialty was to emit a mirthless chuckle whenever I spoke up against his rigid ideas about child rearing, as if to suggest that I was the last person to have any say in these matters), I realized I would have to make a change.

The lawyer I have retained since then is a smart, scrappy woman in practice for herself. My relationship with her has been tempestuous; it has survived any number of confrontations, ranging from her criticism regarding the tone of the message on my answering machine ("too flaky") to my criticism regarding her style of giving me instructions ("authoritarian"). My lawyer is involved in the feminist end of law, which initially alarmed as much as it attracted me: I wanted to make sure she understood that I was not getting my divorce on behalf of the women's movement and was not interested in taking a rhetorical — if right-minded — position that would endanger my chances.

Truth be told, there is nothing like a divorce to make a Madonna out of a Tammy Wynette. Nothing like a divorce, that is, to make even the most accommodating and least politicized female sit up and take note of the fact that the judicial system is run primarily by men who tend on the whole to favor women who stay home and busy themselves with *kinder* and *küche* — and to regard with punitive suspicion (however unconscious) those women who want it every which way, the career and the children and the divorce. In this regard, the more vociferous and unyielding claims of the women's movement (which include the devaluation of motherhood and the insistence on a theo-

183

~

by
DAPHNE
MERKIN

retical egalitarianism at home) have done an inadvertent disservice to divorcing professional women who also happen to be passionate mothers. It's a strange phenomenon, hard to understand until you're caught in the middle of it, but all the tradition-bound attitudes that men were left to struggle with in the last three decades while women were busy taking great strides forward to a new tomorrow seem to coalesce over the issue of child custody. "In the fifties," observes a psychiatrist I know, "you could shoot up heroin and you'd still get the child because you were the mother." These days fathers who want to be the custodial parent tend to be given the benefit of the doubt (up to 40 percent petition for custody, the majority of whom win), and the burden of proof has been shifted onto mothers, especially if they work outside the home.

4. LEARNING THE LANGUAGE

A question: Why is the vocabulary of divorce so woefully underdeveloped? I can understand how long ago in the dark ages of divorce, when unmarried women were still referred to as spinsters and the dubious concept of "quality time" hadn't yet been developed, the need for a more fluid terminology was scant: Divorce, when and if it happened, took place expeditiously, with the children generally assumed to remain with the mother. But now that divorce has become a thing of custody suits which stretch on for years, of forensic psychiatrists who painstakingly conduct interviews and pay house visits as though one or other of the parties dabbled in serial murder, of legal counsel that gets paid astronomic fees by the hour

and remains in one's employ longer than most housekeepers, I surely can't be the first person to find herself at a descriptive loss. Who is my daughter's father to me now that we are no longer married but not yet divorced? I'm talking semantics, never mind the more existential stuff: Is he, linguistically speaking, my *ex-husband-to-be*, which sounds like a mangled form of the future perfect, or should I refer to him as my *estranged husband*, which sounds even clumsier, as though he's been swallowed by a whale?

5. GOING NATIVE

Sex seems so far away, an island that's floated farther and farther off since I've been living alone. In the beginning of my divorce I didn't think about sex much, lost as I was in feelings that precluded erotic pleasure, feelings that had to do with ancient conflicts about the "wrongness" or "rightness" of my very being. Perhaps I wasn't lovable (even though it was I who wanted out); perhaps I didn't know how to love. How to explain this abiding sense of shame, this lingering feeling that it was all my own fault? I might remark that I find it curious that over the last three years not one person among my wide circle of friends has asked me how it feels to live alone—physically alone—after living with a man. It is as if my sexual feelings have become taboo, a link to the banished privileges of the connubial bed. . . .

These days, I find myself going into bookstores and furtively looking at the section that carries titles on divorce and child custody, hoping not to be spotted. After I

buy the books they lie, unread, on my night table as I escape into the romantic world of late-night movies; it seems I am not willing to become part of the divorced population on so official a level. When I'm not avoiding the subject altogether, I keep trying to figure out the reasons for my unease. True, there is the fact that I come from an Orthodox Jewish background where divorce is relatively infrequent, and all five of my siblings are married to their original spouses. But I gave up being Orthodox years ago and I now move in a world where divorce is rife. So how to explain it?

Ah, here we come upon the gap—crevasse, actually—between the statistical reality which is bruited about in magazines and the reality which is felt by one nonstatistical adult female within the context of her daily life. To wit: Divorce may not have the stigma it once had, but it is still cause for anxiety. Marriage, as one of my restlessly married friends says, is a "cover," a form of social armor: You can go to parties and announce "this is my husband" and the world will smile upon you as one of their suitably partnered own. The divorced woman suggests, by her very presence, a threat to the status quo; she carries with her the subliminal risk of her own instability, her lack of conviction about so important a decision as who she should marry. Worse yet, there is the dark aura of her singleness, and the accompanying specter of emotional neediness. Worst of all, she intimates at the possibility that the marriages around her are themselves as likely to fall apart as not. Present yourself as a married woman and you are free to indulge in "safe flirting"; present yourself as a divorced woman and you are perceived as a potentially dangerous predator.

6. HEART OF DARKNESS

It is the end of May, a weekend afternoon on the cusp of summer, breezy and shining, not yet oppressively hot. I am sitting on the benches facing Manhattan's East River, with a Walkman and a book. On the promenade behind me people amble, run, ride bikes, and parade by in a joyous celebration of family life—arms entwined, offspring perched on shoulders or gurgling in strollers. Everyone's a pair, everyone's been married for years, even the young-looking couples have an air of longstanding domestic contentment. Or so it seems to me, sitting by myself even though I am the mother of a four-and-a-half-year-old daughter, even though ten months before my daughter was born I got married in my parents' living room to a man I had known for six years. I am a woman in the middle of a divorce that seems to have gone on forever, and today my daughter is with her father, leaving me to my own devices.

I lean down to pick up a page of a local, residential newspaper that has landed near my bench. An advertisement in bold type catches my eye: It turns out to be for a group that meets weekly to discuss the anxieties and difficulties of people going through divorce. This could be taken for a sign from above, except that I am uncomfortable with the notion of divorce, painful as it is, being converted into yet another arm of the endlessly proliferating support-group industry. Then, too, I find it impossible to imagine discussing my concerns with complete strangers: Is there an amorous future after divorce? Will there ever be a second husband? How am I to define myself now that I'm no longer that solemn creature known as A Wife—

now that I've blown off the man I vowed to honor, cherish, and respect until death did us part? I recognize, of course, that I have other parts left to play—as writer, friend, mother, daughter, sister, aunt—but they all seem to pale next to this lapsed one: Once I was married, the wife of X; now I am not.

7. DREAMING OF ELSEWHERE

Not long ago I bought a video called "Divorce Can Happen to the Nicest People," since to this day I find it unbearably sad to discuss with my daughter why her parents no longer live together. Oh, I've trotted out all the *Good Housekeeping* seal-of-approval phrases and explained that no, I didn't think we'd all be one family again, and yes, Daddy and I both loved her the same as we always had even though we couldn't get along with each other. But there is something in me that rebels against the whole tinny enterprise of justifying inchoate adult behavior to a little girl grappling with abstract concepts like love and constancy and sorrow. So on a recent Saturday night the two of us cuddled up in my bed to watch the video. There was nothing precisely wrong with the film except that it failed to hold our attention. The most interesting thing about it for me was that the screenplay was by Peter Mayle—who went on to write the phenomenally successful books about going to live in Provence with his family. The video wasn't half over before Zoë had fallen asleep next to me, her mouth slightly open, her arms askew. I leaned over to give her a kiss, and then I lay in the dark, wondering whether Peter Mayle had written about divorce from personal experience, whether my own life

might change dramatically for the better after my divorce became final, and whether I would create a new family with the man I loved and go on to write best-sellers . . . and the horrendous particulars of my first marriage—the bickering and taunting and twisting of intimate details into weapons—would fade away. . . .

8. LETTER FROM ABROAD

by
DAPHNE
MERKIN

When I think about my divorce I keep coming back to the opening sentence of L. P. Hartley's *The Go-Between,* one of those gently cadenced British novels that is eerily familiar with the bleaker aspects of human behavior: "The past is a foreign country: They do things differently there." If you paraphrase the quote, it could apply just as well to the permanent present tense in which the breakup of marriages takes place: *Divorce is a foreign country: They do things differently there.* If I've learned anything from my sojourn in this strange land, it's that I'm made of tougher stuff than I once thought I was. You're born alone, you die alone, and you get divorced alone. It's taken me a while to wrap my mind around that obdurate fact, but now that I've finally adjusted to the chilly landscape I'm looking forward to making my way back one of these days to friendlier climes. Beyond the horizon of divorce shimmers the vista of Life-after-Divorce. I'm sure it's a terrain filled with potholes and roadblocks all its own, but from where I'm standing it looks like nothing less than paradise.

ABOUT
THE CONTRIBUTORS

D I A N A H U M E G E O R G E is a professor of English at Penn State at Erie, The Behrend College. She is also a poet, essayist, and critic whose books include *Blake and Freud, Oedipus Anne: The Poetry of Anne Sexton,* and *The Resurrection of the Body.* She edited *Sexton: Selected Criticism,* and, with Diane Wood Middlebrook, *The Selected Poems of Anne Sexton.* Her poetry, essays, interviews, and reviews have appeared in numerous periodicals, and in the *Best American Essays.* Her book of feminist travel essays, *The Lonely Other: A Woman Watching America,* is forthcoming.

E L L E N G I L C H R I S T is author of twelve books of fiction, poetry, and essays. Her latest book is *The Age of Miracles.*

ANN HOOD is the author of six novels, including *The Properties of Water, Places to Stay the Night,* and *Somewhere Off the Coast of Maine.* Her essays, reviews, and short stories have appeared in many magazines and newspapers, including the *New York Times,* the *Washington Post, Redbook, Glamour, Seventeen, Self,* and *Story.* She is a contributing editor at *Parenting* magazine and lives in Providence, Rhode Island.

PENNY KAGANOFF is a senior editor at Simon & Schuster. Formerly, she was editor-in-chief of *Kirkus Reviews,* a book review editor at *Publishers Weekly,* a columnist for the *New York Daily News,* and a judge for the National Book Critics Circle Awards. Her essays and criticism have appeared in a number of newspapers and magazines. She lives in Brooklyn, New York.

PERRI KLASS is the author of two novels, *Other Women's Children* and *Recombinations,* a collection of short stories, *I Am Having an Adventure,* and two volumes of nonfiction, *A Not Entirely Benign Procedure: Four Years as a Medical Student* and *Baby Doctor: A Pediatrician's Training.* Her short fiction has received five O. Henry Awards. She is a pediatrician in Boston, and is on the faculty of the Boston University School of Medicine.

DAPHNE MERKIN is the author of a novel, *Enchantment.* She is a judge for the National Book Critics Circle Awards and is on the editorial board of *Partisan Review.* She has contributed essays to the *New Yorker,* the

New York Times, Esquire, Mirabella, and other periodicals. Her second novel, *The Discovery of Sex,* and a collection of essays, *Fear and Trembling & Life Notes,* are forthcoming from Simon & Schuster. She lives in New York City with her daughter, Zoë.

MARY MORRIS is the author of two collections of short stories, two travel memoirs, and three novels, the most recent of which is *A Mother's Love.* She has also co-edited the travel anthology, *Maiden Voyages.* Her numerous short stories and travel essays have appeared in the *Paris Review,* the *New York Times,* and *Vogue.* The recipient of a Guggenheim Fellowship and the Rome Prize in Literature, she teaches writing at Sarah Lawrence College and lives in Brooklyn.

ANN PATCHETT is the author of two novels, *The Patron Saint of Liars* and *Taft.* She graduated from Sarah Lawrence College and the Iowa Writer's Workshop, served as a fellow at the Mary Ingraham Bunting Institute at Radcliffe College, and is the recipient of a Guggenheim Fellowship. Currently, she lives in Nashville, Tennessee.

FRANCINE PROSE is the author of nine novels, including *Bigfoot Dreams, Primitive People,* and *Hunters and Gatherers,* as well as two story collections: *Women and Children First* and *The Peaceable Kingdom.* Her stories and essays have appeared in *Best American Stories,* the *New Yorker, The Atlantic, Condé Nast Traveler, Antaeus, The Yale Review,* and the *New York Times Book Review.* She lives in upstate New York.

ANNE ROIPHE is the author of the novels *Up the Sandbox, Torch Song, Lovingkindness,* and *If You Knew Me,* and the nonfiction books *Generation without Memory* and *A Season for Healing: Reflections on the Holocaust.* She is a columnist for the *New York Observer* and a contributor to the *Jerusalem Report.*

JANE SHAPIRO's first novel, *After Moondog,* was a finalist for a *Los Angeles Times* Book Prize. Her story, "Poltergeists," which originally appeared in the *New Yorker,* is included in *The Best American Short Stories 1993.* Her short fiction and journalism have been published in the *New Yorker,* the *New York Times,* the *Village Voice, Mirabella,* and many others. She has taught fiction writing at Rutgers University and lives in Princeton.

CAROL SHIELDS has written two books of short stories and seven novels, most recently *The Stone Diaries,* which won the Pulitzer Prize, the National Book Critics Circle Award, and the Canadian Governor-General's Award. She grew up in Oak Park, Illinois, and now lives in Winnipeg, Canada, where she teaches at the University of Manitoba.

ALIX KATES SHULMAN is a political activist, feminist, teacher, and writer whose novels include *Memoirs of an Ex-Prom Queen, Burning Questions, On the Stroll,* and *In Every Woman's Life.* . . . Her essays have appeared in the *Nation, Atlantic Monthly,* and the *New York Times Book Review.* Her newest book is the memoir, *Drinking the Rain.* Ms. Shulman has taught at the University of Hawaii, Yale, and New York University, has been

a visiting artist at the American Academy in Rome, and has received NEA and DeWitt Wallace/Reader's Digest fellowships. She divides her time between New York City and an island off the coast of Maine.

SUSAN SPANO is a graduate of Mount Holyoke College and a former fiction editor for *Redbook*. Her articles have appeared in the *New York Times Book Review, New York Newsday,* and *New Woman.* As the author of The Frugal Traveler column in the *New York Times Travel Section,* she travels widely and frequently. Her home is Manhattan's West Village.